R

The Park Family

Lauren

The Awakening

The Park Family

Lauren

The Awakening

Lisanne Valente

This is a work of fiction from the imaginative mind of Lisanne Valente. Whilst the businesses, locations, and organizations named are real, their inclusion is used purely fictionally.

However, my sincere thanks go to those businesses who took the time to contact me and were delighted to give permission to name them in the book.

Matador
9 Priory Business Park
Kibworth Beauchamp
Leicestershire LE8 0RX, UK
Tel: (+44) 116 279 2299
Fax: (+44) 116 279 2277
Email: books@troubador.co.uk
Web: www.troubador.co.uk/matador

ISBN 978 1783062 614

British Library Cataloguing in Publication Data.
A catalogue record for this book is available from the British Library.

Typeset in Minion Pro by Troubador Publishing Ltd

Matador is an imprint of Troubador Publishing Ltd

This book is dedicated to my nieces

Lauren
Valerie
and
Mairi

Three of the brightest stars

Chapter One

The Heavens

Ambriel, the angel of communications, was worried! He rarely fretted, his organisational skills were almost as accomplished as those of an archangel, but he had discovered an anomaly in the registration of a family of Mistdreamers. Somehow, the earthly plane had been manipulated, and the Chisholm family had been omitted from the register.

In a time when knowledge was power, the heavens required all known Mistdreamers to be registered. These mystical humans and their descendants, had been given a gift from Archangel Omniel. He granted them the ability to cross into the heavens through their subconscious and to remain unseen by all but a few chosen angels. Ambriel, the Keeper of Communications, and Paschar, who guarded the veil between the two worlds and taught the Mistdreamers to identify reality from illusion, were but two of the chosen angels.

Omniel's Mistdreamers reported any unusual activities they may encounter. He hoped this would thwart another angel war and believed, with prior knowledge of revolt, troublemakers would be dealt with, and then the two worlds could be prevented from dissolving into anarchy and chaos, thus preventing untold death.

The stars realigned monthly, and the time was shortly approaching when the veil between mortal and the immortal worlds would open. Ambriel needed to ensure the impossible didn't happen. The Mistdreamers had to remain on their realm.

He knew, somehow, that Forcas, the Angel of Invisibility, was involved and that pandemonium would shortly erupt, not only in the heavens, but earth would be deluged by the immortals in all forms.

"Have you found him" he asked Paschar, the Angel of Vision, who was bemused by Ambriel's impatience.

"Not to be funny, Ambriel, but he's the Angel of Invisibility, it's difficult to see him when he does that thing he does."

Ambriel rolled his eyes "Now is not the time for humour, Paschar," he admonished as a deep-set panic began curling around his immortal heart. "You are the guardian that keeps both our worlds separate, how can you not be worried?"

Paschar watched his friend and frowned. Ambriel was a peaceful angel, always a calming influence on others, but now, he watched in disbelief as his friend rubbed his handsome face anxiously. "What's going on, Ambriel? This is more than not being able to find Forcas, you know he roams between Heaven and Hell. What is it you believe he's done?"

Ambriel sighed and touched Paschar's arm. "I cannot say, yet, I must speak with Omniel before I declare my concerns, he's the one in charge of 'oneness'.

Paschar's eyes widened, he had never heard Ambriel use a tone other than gentle; to hear sarcasm dripping from his every word was concerning. "Now you have me worried, Ambriel. What's wrong with you, what have you done?"

Ambriel stared into his friend's eyes, and fear shone like a beacon from his own. "I think I enabled a family of unregistered Mistdreamers access to Heaven," he replied anxiously.

Paschar shook his head and smiled. "That can't have happened, I would have been aware of anybody crossing between worlds…"

They turned to each other and said together, "Forcas!"

Paschar grabbed Ambriel's arm and started striding toward the heavenly gate. "We must hurry, the stars have moved early this month, and the veil is already down between our worlds. We have to get to Omniel."

When Lauren Chisholm was four years old, she announced that she no longer wanted to play with 'ordinary' people as she now had a much better and more favourite friend; one who was shiny, spoke in a voice that sounded like singing, and that he was the most "gorgeoustist person in all the worlds".

Her statement so freaked out her parents, they thought about taking her to a psychiatrist, in the hopes that Lauren would forget all about her "favouritemost friend in the worlds". But they knew who she was talking about. What is important, they knew *what* she was talking about. Their only course of action was to repeatedly tell Lauren that she was very good with her imagination and that some things were pretend and most definitely…*not real.*

They knew this course of action was wrong, but they were unsure of how else to help her face the reality of earth. Lauren was an earthbound human, and to fantasise about a world she would not be allowed to enter, was just not acceptable to them.

Cathy Chisholm thought long and hard about what she must tell her daughter, and on reflection, although it pained her greatly, she knew it was the safest way for Lauren to face reality.

Callum Chisholm, on the other hand, thought the best

course of action was to take their daughter to a hypnotist and erase any memories of "her favouritemost friend in the worlds", but he was aware that, perhaps, he was too overprotective of both his girls, and if Cathy thought her way was right, then he would go along her path and let her take the lead in instructing their daughter. However, should this path not work out, he had already put into place an alternate future for all of them.

And so, the painstaking repetition of the words, "It's just make believe, Lauren", were instilled into their child.

Lauren could see, even at the age of four, her parents were concerned for her. She knew they loved her because every night, as they tucked her into bed, they would tell her it was make believe, and they always told her how much they loved their little princess.

When they left the room, she was told, "You know I'm real, Lauren, never forget you're my princess, too".

She would then roll onto her side, make room on her small bed, and wait until he sat down by her feet. She knew he wouldn't move from her, and he would remain in his straight-backed, upright position throughout the night, watching over and protecting her. She would smile at him, then fall fast asleep, the colours of the rainbow taking her beyond reality and into her happy dreams.

Lauren checked her bedroom again and shivered. Her family had moved from Florida to Edinburgh ten years previously, and she still couldn't get used to the cold. She always loved the heat of Florida, the ability to wear a T-shirt, even in winter, was something she still remembered. Sometimes, she even wore a pullover in Edinburgh's summer.

Though she did love the city. It was more beautiful than Orlando. The history was seeped into the very streets in which she walked. The only similarity between the two cities would be the rain. It rained every day in Edinburgh, or so she thought, and it seemed to rain every day in Orlando. The difference in Orlando was, the rain stopped and the sun shone. Edinburgh, it just rained.

She smiled to herself and gazed out the window. She gazed upon Arthur's Seat to the east and then to Edinburgh Castle and sighed. She didn't care about the cold or the rain here, it was home, and she loved the place.

Her father, having decided upon returning to work in the head office of the family business, which was based in Edinburgh, had jumped at the chance at going home. He was born in Edinburgh and had longed, for sometime, to return and show the city off to his American wife and daughter. He promised a new beginning for the three of them…and it was.

The upheaval hadn't been that difficult. They left most of their furniture and brought only clothes and some favourite items her parents had bought over the years. Even saying goodbye to friends hadn't been too traumatic. She'd always been a bit of a loner, and most of her friends were just acquaintances. Children her parents engineered friendships with and, for their sake, she let them believe were good friends.

They weren't.

The only real down side to moving was saying goodbye to her grandparents. Although she didn't see them as often as she would have liked because they lived in Biloxi, Mississippi, they were still her family.

Visits to see them, were mostly done during the holidays, and the usual monthly trip was always made fun by her mom and dad's singing as they drove on the I-10 route to Tallahassee then onward, heading toward Mobile. The moment they passed through Alabama, her mom would start belting out "Sweet Home Alabama" with her dad trying to harmonise, dreadfully; neither of them sang in tune.

The trips were worth it just to sit on the swing on her grandparents porch, have a slice of her Grandma Mary-Pat's sweet potato pie, or to walk hand in hand with her Grandpa Tony, along the seafront.

Usually, when they arrived, it was to find her grandparents waiting on the porch for them, waving and welcoming. Callum parked the car and helped Cathy out. She ran straight into her dad's arms and sobbed.

"Now hear this, Cathy. This is an adventure, for all of you." He waved to Lauren and Callum. "None of these tears."

Cathy wiped her tears away but couldn't help her eyes from watering again. "I know, Dad, it's just that I'm going to miss you and Mom so much. You're going to miss out on seeing Lauren graduate. Meeting her first boyfriend."

Lauren grunted and rolled her eyes. "Mom, why do you always say that? Why do you always talk about my boyfriend. I hate boys, you know that!"

Grandma Mary-Pat stepped forward and held Lauren in her arms. "They're awful, smelly things, aren't they, Lauren? Your grandpa was one of them a long time ago, though, and he's not so smelly now, is he?"

Lauren glanced from her grandma to her grandpa. "He smells of sugar and the sea breeze, he's not smelly, Grandma," she said as she giggled and thought her grandma daft. Her grandpa chuckled and stuck his tongue out at Mary-Pat, who just shrugged her shoulders and smiled back.

"Well, one day, Lauren, like your mom says, you'll have someone who you think smells just right, maybe he'll even smell nicer than your grandpa!"

“Not likely,” Grandpa said. “He’ll probably smell like an angel.”

Cathy, Callum, and Mary-Pat went very still, and fear crawled through Cathy’s blood. “Dad, why did you say that?”

Tony was shocked and worried. “I haven’t a clue, I really don’t, it was like, something made me say it.”

Mary-Pat took Cathy’s hand and led her into the house. “All of you come on in, we’ve lots to speak about before you leave. Come on, let’s not stand out here on the porch discussing smelly boys. Let me get you all settled into your rooms, and then we can have a bit of supper.” Mary-Pat’s eyes peeked at Callum, and she shook her head. “I’ve got all your rooms ready. Are you okay to stay in your old room, Lauren?”

Lauren smiled easily at her grandma. “Yup, of course, Grandma, it’s home.”

They all walked into the house, silently, Callum watching the road over his shoulder, searching, trying to visualise something he didn’t want to see. The Spanish Oak sitting in the middle of the lawn swayed to an invisible wind.

Hurricane Katrina left a permanent mark on Biloxi, many houses still not having been replaced. Water Street was slowly being rebuilt, and her grandparents’ house, in a different form, was standing again. However, so much was taken in the hurricane, all the photos her grandma used to have around the home had been lost.

In their place, however, her Grandma Mary-Pat, decorated with her own works of art. Then, as before, the house was full of colour; vibrant colours everywhere, making it a home and not a house. And when Lauren slept in the room her grandma always kept for her, tucked under the new comforter, her dreams were colourful and happy.

They stayed with her grandparents for a week before leaving

for Edinburgh. Her mom had cried for three days after saying goodbye, not knowing if, or when, she'd see her parents again. Her grandpa's words when she left were instilled in her mind: "Lauren, follow your heart, listen to your head. Trust your own gut, and remember your adventure is just beginning. Don't feel sad about us, we've had many adventures, your grandma and I, our biggest adventure is ahead of us, but hopefully, not for sometime yet. Enjoy life, love hard, but live harder. Remember there are others, just like you, so you are not alone."

She sighed, remembering, and then thought about the new friends she had made in Edinburgh and how she had surprised herself by becoming close to other people. She always found it difficult to forge relationships, but here, she learned that the Scottish humour struck a chord with her and that the people were similar to herself. When they wanted friends, they were there. When they wanted to be alone, they were alone.

So far, though, just as she'd told her mom, she wasn't involved, nor did she have a boyfriend. Yes, her 'friends', some of them anyway, were boys. An involvement with one of her boy friends became what she considered to be a serious relationship, and unfortunately, she had entrusted him with her heart. Sadly, she realised her feelings were not reciprocated, and when she discovered her wrongly placed trust, it cost her dearly. Her first attempt in learning about love ended with a broken heart, a broken arm, and a distrust of certain types of men. She was glad to say, she was happily single, with no special boy, and that's the way she wanted it.

She closed the charming, lilac and pink striped curtains to block out the winter rain and turned on her purple bedside lamp. For a moment, she thought something moved in the corner. *Ugh, not another mouse*, she thought; she hated the small beasts. When she glanced at the corner of the room, there was nothing to be seen, so she put the movement down to her imagination.

She loved her bedroom, the colours were all soft hues of purple, her favourite colour. The only thing that wasn't purple was her carpet and fitted wardrobes.*Funny,* she thought, *I love purple, but don't have any clothes that are purple.*

"That's because it's your dream colour, Lauren," a voice whispered.

Lauren jumped, backed toward the door, and carefully examined her room. Again, she was unable to see anything other than her furniture.

"Look at your bed, Lauren."

Lauren knew she should be afraid but was mainly alarmed that she couldn't see whatever it was that was speaking to her. "Who are you?"

"Don't you remember me, Princess?"

Lauren closed her eyes and could feel a gentle push at her mind.

Forcas watched as Lauren began to shimmer, knowing she was unaware of her ability. She frowned, as she attempted to reach further into her mind, to see him better.

Blanketing himself in invisibility, he laughed silently at his jest; he enjoyed watching as people searched for the impossible.

"I thought you were my imagination?" Lauren opened her eyes to see Forcas. He was the same handsome man of her dreams. He was tall, well over 6 feet, and his dark brown, wavy hair hung freely to the middle of his back, and it begged for Lauren to run her hands through it. He wore no shoes, so his feet…wow, they were huge, and his naked legs showed off their powerful muscles. She took her time working up his body, taking in every inch of him. When she reached his hips, she turned an attractive shade of pink and then realised all he was wearing was a towel, tightly wrapped around his hips. His lovely, naked torso could have been photo shopped with its perfect washboard stomach. Her mouth watered as she stared at his massive chest and bulging biceps. Eventually, when, at last, her eyes rested on his face, she drank in the sight of his powerful jaw with designer stubble, his straight nose, and arched eyebrows. His almond-shaped eyes, the colour of the sea in Barbados, were framed by long, black eyelashes. *They were blue, no, not blue, green. Nope, not green,* Lauren thought.

She gazed deeply into his eyes and stared, mesmerised, as they swirled in fascinating hues, changing from blue to green. She could almost believe she was watching the tide ebbing and flowing, and she became completely hypnotised by them. Lauren's leisurely assessment took her eyes slowly to his mouth, and she knew she was lost. His lips could only be described as sinful. A wide mouth, that spread easily into a smile, showing off straight, white, Colgate advert, teeth. His lips were perfect. He was perfect.

She peered directly into Forcas's eyes, stunning him back to reality. "You can see me?" he asked, quite shocked by this turn of events.

"Of course, I can, you're sitting on the end of my bed, you always sit at the end of my bed."

Forcas grinned, bemused by her guile. "So, little princess, you've been pretending all these years to be deaf to my voice and blind to my presence?"

Lauren laughed, the sound sending magical waves of light through his body.

"Of course, I ignored you. My sanity was more important than your ego! How would you feel if you were told daily, the man at the bottom of your bed is just your imagination!"

Forcas nodded. "You are wiser than most."

Lauren was taken aback by that. "What do you mean by most? Can others do as I do, can others see you? Do you stay with others as well?"

"Ah, Princess," he said, cutting off any more questions, "at last, so many questions. Maybe I should do as you, and be deaf for a few years to your voice, what do you think?"

"Then I would follow you and find out, from the others, and get all the answers I need! I've had enough, always having questions, never having answers. The only answers are: 'It's just your imagination, Lauren.' I know they're lying, by the way! And then you turn up with your, with your wee towel, and bait me into this!" Lauren frowned and sat down on the small chair in her bedroom and immediately jumped up, squealing as she grabbed her behind. "Ouch, ouch, ouch! Oh My God! I forgot about the bloody straighteners, I forgot I'd put them on. Now I'm going to have a burnt bum…again!" she wailed.

Forcas waved away her moaning, and, with a sleight of his hand, stared deeply into her eyes, searching for answers. He was taken aback when her eyes closed, shutting out any further investigation for him.

"Open your beautiful brown eyes, Princess, let me see into the depths of beyond."

Lauren folded her hands across her chest, she was desperately trying to be brave, but her resolution was slowly crumbling. All she wanted to do was stamp her foot and cry, but she resisted the temptation. She was in the presence of the most handsome man she had ever known, and although only twenty, she believed herself to be more mature than some of her peers. The thought of stamping her foot would definitely go against her credibility. Instead, she closed her eyes tighter. *Now that's really mature,* she thought.

Forcas touched her arm, his movement so quick, she didn't have time to think, and, shocked, she opened her eyes. "How, how, did you do that?" she stammered.

"That's it, my princess, your eyes are open, you shouldn't close them to me," he purred.

Lauren could feel his touch on her arm and wanted to melt into him. His touch sent shivers through her body. As she raised her face to look at him, she sighed, put her head to one side, and lifted her hand to touch his face. "What are you? Are you my guardian angel?"

She was so stunned when he threw his head back and roared with laughter. "Your guardian angel?" He laughed louder.

Lauren was puzzled and a little scared by his reaction and pulled away from him.

"I always thought you were here to protect me, was I wrong?" She backed away further, then remembered the pain in her buttock. "Ouch, why do I always forget? Bollocks!"

"I see your vocabulary has grown since moving to Edinburgh. Tell me, do you know every form of offensive wording, or are you limited to the male parts of the anatomy?"

Lauren was in pain and needed some cream, again, and his sarcasm was doing nothing to help her temper. She knew she must get a handle on it or she would blow up in his face. She still didn't know who or what he was!

"Bugger off!" she shouted and marched out her bedroom and slammed the door. "Stop calling me princess," she shouted from outside her room. "I'm not your princess, or anybody else's friggin' princess! How's that for 'offensive wording'? And, no, I'm not just limited to the male anatomy, here's one from the female anatomy –Tit!"

Forcas blinked rapidly and shook his head in disbelief. It

wasn't often he was caught off-guard, but Lauren managed, in the space of five minutes, to twice catch him unexpectedly.

He stared at the door she had just slammed and, had Lauren seen, she would have run all the way to Hell to escape him, smiled. "Ah, but you are a princess, Lauren. You just don't know it yet, but I'll give you time."

As usual, she was hungry and wanted something to eat, so Lauren stomped her way down the carpeted spiral staircase, holding on tightly to the oak banister, in case she fell, which wasn't unusual; her other hand was placed gently onto her scalded bottom. She glanced through the wrought iron balustrade, to see if she'd remembered to close the front door, and was glad to see she had at least remembered to do that. Lately, all she seemed to do was forget things, the only time her mind worked as it should was when she was asleep.

The house was a stone built Edinburgh terraced home, in the Braids. It was a deceptively large house, the ceilings reaching twenty feet. Her mom constantly grumbled about the cost of heating the ceiling, which always made Lauren wonder why her mom would want to heat the ceiling.

The stairway and entrance hall were painted in a soft terra-cotta, and family photos hung everywhere. She wasn't sure what her mom would do if ever she lost these photos? Perhaps she would discover a hidden talent like Grandma Mary-Pat and start painting, maybe even open a studio, but she somehow doubted that would ever happen.

Grandma Mary-Pat had sent one of her works of art, and it hung in pride of place in the entrance hall. It was the first thing to be seen when the door was opened. Grandma Mary-Pat had painted a small boy being cradled in his mom's arms as they sat underneath a Spanish oak. The Biloxi lighthouse stood proudly in the background. The scarf on the mother's head was bright yellow, with small, terra-cotta daisies, and her son was wearing bright blue shorts together with a sunburst yellow T-shirt. The colours were as vibrant as her grandma. The whole image was one of hope.

However, that hope was lost on Lauren as she moodily jumped the last two stairs and turned right, entering the kitchen.

The galley kitchen was long and narrow, with numerous cupboards on each side. At the end were French windows that led into the small backyard. On the left, as you walked in, a silver "American" style fridge stood, making it easy for Lauren to nibble anything that might be within.

She opened the fridge and surveyed the Tupperware tubs situated in different areas. She knew her mom was a bit of a neat freak and that each shelf held different food types. Sometimes, just to annoy her mom, she'd put the vegetables beside the bread foods and wait until her mom opened the fridge to discover the change. "Who's been in the fridge? Why can't you realise that cross contamination can cause serious stomach complaints?" she'd yell.

On more than one occasion, she'd been with her dad when the war cry sounded. "You really have to learn, Lauren, that to piss her off means food doesn't come our way!"

Lauren picked up a large, blue container and removed the lid. Last night's leftover carbonara. *Perfect,* she thought, *loads of carbs, add some parmesan, make a coffee, and life will be normal.* She placed the tub into the microwave, hit the power button for two minutes, and waited.

And waited.

Her world stood still, all motion inside and outside the house stopped. She couldn't move anything but her eyes.

Suddenly, He was beside her, standing there, silently watching.

"Perhaps you shouldn't have angered me, Lauren?"

Lauren's eyes widened in fear, and, staring at him, she tried to move her lips, finding they too could move. She stammered, trying to formulate the right words.

The man standing before her wasn't the same as the one who, at one time, watched over her at periods throughout her childhood. Gone were the gentle eyes and kind mouth. In their place were eyes the colour of cold steel and lips that grimaced, instead of smiled.

"I, I, I didn't mean to anger you. You, well, you just annoyed me, and I needed to get away. I always need my own space when I feel like that."

He glowered and appeared even more threatening. His head moved from side to side, and he began to sniff around him. "What is that smell?"

Lauren tried to move, wanting to point to the microwave to show him the food warming in the oven. All she could do was move her eyes, to try to indicate what she meant. "I take it you're the one responsible for me being frozen like this?" she muttered.

"You are not frozen, the time continuum has been halted."

"Well, if you could undo the halting, I'd be able to show you the carbonara that's cooking in the oven. That's what the smell is."

Lauren thought it best not to irritate someone who could halt the time continuum, whatever that was, but he really annoyed her. He just stood, regarding her, in all his beautiful, scary glory, and he was really bugging her. She'd gone from scared to annoyed in two-seconds flat. Her raging emotions were so unusual…. She was considered to be a very stable person who rarely got annoyed and was happy most of the time, probably because her own company was all she sought, or needed. This man thing, or whatever he was, was infuriating.

"Lauren," his voice dripped ice, "I'd rather you didn't annoy me. It's not what I want."

That was it! She was going to blow her top, but before she got the opportunity to yell at him, she heard movement behind him. Keys were being placed in the front door, and it was opening.

"If you've stopped the time continuum, how come someone's coming in the house?"

Forcas turned quickly and moved toward the door, his body leaving a blur of colour in the frozen time.

"Lauren," her mom called. "Lauren, are you home, love?"

Forcas shielded himself in invisibility and watched Cathy enter the house. His surprise quickly turned to suspicion.

She scanned the space around her, moving slowly. "Lauren, come on, love, where are you? Please, tell me you're not in the kitchen. If you are, you'd better have put everything back as I like it."

Cathy glanced at Forcas and quickly turned away.

"Stop pretending you can't see me," he growled.

"Lauren, do you hear me?"

"Woman!" Forcas yelled. "How have you slipped through Ambriel's notice? Oh yes," he continued, "we, or should I say, some of us, have been aware for some time now, that you Chisholms have been fooling Ambriel. You are, how do I say this…people of interest to us."

Cathy's heart was hammering; how did he know this? She needed to reach Lauren, she had to see her daughter was safe.

This moment had been coming for so long, she and Callum could no longer delay the inevitable, believing their safe little world would not be discovered. But when everything around them stopped, her first instinct was to get home. Now she was facing the one Angel she always lived in dread of seeing again.

Using his power to cloak himself in an invisible shield, she knew it was he who was steering Lauren into the land where *Mistdreamers* went. The same place from which they, sometimes, never returned.

Just as she started to move, the front door flew open, and Callum came rushing in, taking her into his arms. "What the hell happened?" he asked, searching her scared face. "Where's Lauren, is she safe?"

Cathy motioned over his shoulder and bobbed her head in Forcas's direction.

"What, what is it?" He slowly turned his head and snapped it back when he caught a glimpse of Forcas.

Forcas was furious. "You too!" he screamed. "How has this happened? Is it all the Chisholms, or just the ones we have chosen to watch?" he asked slyly.

Callum glanced at Cathy, sharing their silent communication with one another.

Forcas began striding back and forth. "Let me get this right. You've both been aware of me, all these years, and yet you constantly tell her I'm in her imagination." He stopped striding and stared at them.

"Have you any idea what you put her through? Do you even *care* what you put her through? Do you care about the psychological damage you could have caused? Or did that not cross your minds?"

Callum turned and stared at him. "Do we care? Who the hell do you think you are coming into our house, holding our daughter prisoner in your time shift, and then you have the audacity to ask us, what we've put her through!!" Callum moved toward Forcas, pointing his finger at his chest. "What we did is called 'good parenting.' What you did is called…well, I don't know what it's called. Why couldn't you just have stayed away, why did you have to choose our daughter, couldn't you have chosen one of the others?"

"And how do you know of the others? Do you mean other Chisholms, or are there families of which we are unaware?" Forcas asked as he slowly moved Callum's finger from his chest.

Callum stared at Cathy, she lowered her eyes, and he realised his unfortunate mistake. "I'm only presuming others exist or—"

"Liar!" Forcas bellowed. "I ask you again, how do you know about the others?" He neared Callum and stood straighter, expanding his chest to its full width. Callum was six feet, two and a half inches, and Forcas towered above him. "This time, Callum Chisholm, tell me the truth, or when Lauren goes to the Quinque Caelos, it will be the last time you see her."

Callum hesitated, thinking quickly on his feet; he had to keep the secret, but what would happen to Lauren if he didn't tell the truth? Before he could say anything, Cathy took away the responsibility from him and uttered the words, "Because we're all family."

Forcas watched with doubting eyes. "Family? The Parks Mistdreamers are related to you? We know this, but how did you slip through Ambriel's register; how did he not know of this?"

"Do we have your word, you won't keep her in the land beyond?"

Forcas laughed. "Are you trying to bargain with me? Have you no sense, woman?"

Cathy was outraged. "Of course, I have sense, can't you see she's confused enough as it is? She needs to know which world is real. Lauren needs to know stability, that's what we've been trying to give her."

"And how do you know this world is real, can you see anything moving outside? How do you know my world isn't real? Tell me, woman, how have you done this?"

"It was really simple, actually," Callum interjected. "We used the name of our great grandmother."

"She was a Mistdreamer, I'm aware of her. Agnes Park, born 1800, taken to level four by Azrael."

Callum and Cathy both glanced at each other. "If you say so." Callum shrugged as he answered.

"Then she would be registered with Ambriel. All Mistdreamers have their names registered."

"Yes, she registered Agnes Park with Ambriel. What she omitted to do was register her maiden name, it wasn't important back then to include it. So the Park surnames are registered, yes, but Chisholm isn't a known, registered, Mistdreamer name."

Callum touched his brow and quickly added, "We didn't do anything wrong. We just wanted to have a 'normal' life and not do your spying!"

Forcas turned to Cathy. "That answers the Chisholm part, how did you slip through the net?"

Cathy bit her lower lip, aware she should share with him some information, and that it was best to stick as near to the truth as possible. "Basically, the same way, just a different surname…and I'm not giving you it!"

Forcas threw his head back and laughed. "Have you any idea the problems you've caused…?" Before either could answer, he added, "And do you know who they will blame?"

They stopped bickering when they heard Lauren shouting, "Would one of you, for the love of God, mind unfreezing me, PLEASE!"

Chapter Two

It has to be said that Dante, in his writings, nearly got it right. Almost. Heaven has five tiers. Heaven's levels are graded the fifth realm up to the first, the first being the Almighty ruler's. In order of importance, the second realm is where the archangel's are located. The third realm is for the saints. The fourth level is for those who have done holy acts and were virtuous on earth. The fifth level, is for the departed soul. All levels can eventually be accessed with all levels being perfect and harmonious, with love transcending.

Here's where Dante got it wrong, his writings of the Inferno declared that Hell was in nine tiers when it is the mirror opposite to Heaven's five tiers. The highest of the tiers being the fifth tier where, known by many names, The Emperor, The Black Lord, Beelzebub, Satan, or simply the Devil, exists. The fourth realm is the dominion of the kings of demons. The third realm is for nobles and presidents who are the rulers of legions of demons. The lower second, as it is known, is the territory for demons to exist, and the lowest level, the first, is for souls who, because of the way they chose to live their lives on the earthly plane, enter and remain, with no hope of exiting Hell, or moving up through the levels.

They exist in the abyss. The pit of darkness.

Demons can access all but the Fifth realm, and only if they have a valid reason. Mainly, they enjoy the First realm, where they get to torture new and old souls, revealing to them the true meaning of evil.

Beneath Hell's gate, and beyond the stairs that lead to Heaven, hidden in the stars, a warren of caves, appropriately called Cavernis Inferni, exist. Each cave is hidden from the other, and a shield of black magic seals the entrance to every one. No matter how hard an angel or demon tries, it is impossible to see inside a cave.

Some say each cave holds souls willing to do the devil's work and return to earth. Others state it is the educating centre for demons. A school, if you like, for learning the arts of demonic culture.

The only one able to see within the caves would be the almighty ruler, but even He has to be invited in. This would only happen if, by the slip of tongue, His name is spoken.

As this place is nearer Hell, those entering the caves guard their privacy carefully, and any utterance of His name happens once every ten millennia.

In one of the caves, a group of fallen angels have been meeting for one of those millennia. They are not completely fallen, and because of their works carried out on the mortal plane, the almighty ruler has allowed them access to the lower fifth level of Heaven.

The Black Lord, Satan, does not trust them because of their ability to gain entrance to Heaven and has limited their access to only the second realm of Hell.

Hell's caves, or Cavernis Inferni, held its advantages, Ramiel thought. For one, Paschar and Ambriel couldn't see him, therefore, they wouldn't be aware of the discussions being held between the group named Infidelibus. They, then, could plot, or simply discuss, whatever they thought was right, at the time.

Before the group joined forces, they were in groups of three, three being the subliminal number. The factions consisted of Xaphan, Adramelechk and Appoloin. Adramelechk was a Throne Angel,

therefore, his voice was directly connected with the Almighty ruler. When Xaphan descended into partial demonic status, his relationship with Adramelechk dissolved, and it could only be described, now, as friendly hatred.

Appoloin, the remaining factor, remained on friendly terms with both Xaphan and Adramelechk, but often found himself acting as go between, or peacemaker between the two. Whenever friction became evident, he did his best to try to prevent the inevitable full-blown battle. However, friction was inevitable whenever they were together

The secondary faction had been Forcas, Ramiel, and Kakabel. Forcas, now, was moving deeper into demonic status, and Ramiel was concerned that their friendship would have to be dissolved and, eventually, head down the same route as that of Adramelechk and Xaphan's friendship.

The last faction was Sammael, who chose not to align with just one angel, but with all. By doing so, he was alone.

Their dual status of 'fallen and heavenly' angels enabled them to walk the fine line between Heaven and Hell. However, as the Angel of Thunder, Ramiel despised the heat within the caves and wanted this meeting to end quickly, returning to his place in the Fifth realm of the heavens.

He examined the small group, noticing the growing discomfort each appeared to be experiencing.

Kakabel, the Angel of the Moon, sat with his head in his hands, fretting. Although his body had the appearance of a 'powerfully made' man, and his face was that of an innocent angel. He had blue eyes, fringed with long, dark lashes, and long, fair hair fell to the middle of his back in thick waves. At present, however, he had it tied in a tight queue. He was the angel of the constellations and stars and knew blame for the unusual change in the monthly shifts would be squarely landed on his shoulders.

Adramelechk, the Angel of Fire, was laughing at Ramiel's discomfort, and revelling in the heat! Ramiel could see through his act, the joking was to hide the fact he, also, was concerned. Adramelechk lounged on his back, his powerful arms behind his head. He wore a gold band on his head, indicating he was of a royal house. His thick black hair was wet and hung limply to his shoulders.

Appoloin, the Angel of Destruction, walked around checking his surroundings, glimpsing through the great gates intending to hopefully seize Satan and bind him before throwing him into the never-ending pit. By doing this, it was his belief he would, somehow, be reprieved from 'fallen' to 'heavenly' angel. The more rounds he walked, the more agitated he became. His long, powerful legs taking even strides, counting the number of strides it took for him to cover the whole area within the cave as they waited.

Sammael, as always, sat and watched. He rarely spoke, and when he did, he was listened to, but his eyes were dark with worry, and Ramiel was unable to read to what depths of concern Sammael held himself.

The other Angels thought Sammael believed himself to be superior to the rest. He had carried the soul of Moses to the heavens when he died.... Sammael was not in agreement with his brother angels. Carrying Moses had not stopped him from falling from grace.

The only other angel, besides Forcas, missing from the

group was Xaphan. He could no longer be regarded as an angel, his status to fallen was almost complete as he became part of the lower demon ranks.

Ramiel knew he would arrive at some point and have another inventive excuse for his tardiness.

The group, the Infidelibus, the 'nonbelievers', already distrusted Xaphan, now that it appeared he had joined the lower sections of Hell's demons. Always being late, and evasive when questioned, only encouraged more distrust. Ramiel knew this was a game Xaphan played, he had to consider whether now was the time to ask Xaphan to leave the Infidelibus. However, to ask him to leave could bring more problems. Perhaps it was an opportune time to be careful about what they discussed in his presence.

Ramiel understood why Xaphan had chosen to move over to the dark, to be neither one nor the other was more than difficult. Both sides of the divide not trusting any of them. It would be easy for him to join the ranks of Hell, of late, his darkness was slowly consuming him, another reason he wanted the meeting to end quickly.

He carefully examined the cave, the black walls glowed slightly red and orange in places, and resembled the coals of a fire just before they turned white. A fraction of the soft, orange light was escaping though the walls, casting shadows and illuminating each face in the room.

"Where is he?" Appoloin growled.

"By 'he', you mean?" Ramiel asked, knowing the answer.

"Why does he always arrive late, do they have not time implements in Hell? Could it be that, now he is a full-fledged demon, he believes he he can ignore our call?"

"Be careful what you say, Appoloin," Sammael whispered.

Kakabel jumped up. "What are you saying? Are we no longer

safe here, in the caves? Who could be listening? Who can listen? What have you heard?"

"Enough!" shouted Ramiel. "The time is not yet for questions, we must wait until we have heard from Forcas, and we must wait for Xaphan." A low growl echoed around the cave, coming from each one of the angels.

"I know, I know," Ramiel soothed. "I am aware of your distrust toward Xaphan, but we need him more than ever. He has the ear of the Kings, his demonic rule gives access to many regions within Hell."

"How can he help us, when he's chosen his side?" Kakabel was dumbfounded by Ramiel's continued support of Xaphan.

"If he continues to trust us, he can now bring us more information from the demon ranks. We will have more opportunity to know what is happening in Hell."

"I'm not sure I like where you're going with this," said Sammael. "You are using a demon to spy on demons, that's a dangerous thing to do to him. He was once our friend; last I knew, he still was our friend. Now you ask him to spy for us on the very ones who now have accepted him. Do you not think they will be aware of that? Satan is already displeased we use the caves, he will never trust us. You are putting Xaphan's very existence into danger."

"Ha!" shouted Appoloin. "What damage could he do, we're angels, we're not humans."

"He could be made human…" Sammael shuddered.

Ramiel winced at the thought. "Better to be 'fallen' than human. Who could withstand the pain they endure, only to suffer more when they pass to our side?"

"I've had enough, say what you want to say, Ramiel," Kakabel yelled. "I have other things more important to do than listen to more of your conspiracies."

Ramiel took a deep pause before responding, "Fair enough, let's begin, if Xaphan joins us then we can tell or withhold the information, as you all see fit."

Sammael groaned. "You're doing it again, Ramiel. You have to ensure he is aware of all the information, not just the crumbs you're willing to share."

"You'll all be aware of the change in the shift of stars this month?" Ramiel continued.

Kakabel visibly winced. "If this is all about blame, you can forget it, Ramiel. Whatever happened was little to do with me. Everything was set, as normal, for the monthly alignments, I did not carry out any extraordinary changes to the patterns of the stars."

Ramiel raised his hands. "No, no, Kakabel, I wasn't inferring anything of the kind. I was merely asking…never mind, stop being so touchy, this is not just about you, we are all involved in what's happening."

Kakabel flexed his gigantic wings, spreading them wide, his already tall, powerful frame now appearing, as he hoped, gigantic.

"You can put your wings away, we can all do the 'see how big I am' trick. In here," Ramiel waved his hands, indicating their surroundings, "it doesn't matter how big, how powerful, or how much magic you have. So sit down! You would think, after a millennia of meetings here, you would have learned that by now!"

Kakabel threw himself down on a boulder, and as he sat, his wing span hadn't completely reduced, and the tip of one of his wings touched the walls of the cave; the wall hissed, singeing one of his feathers. He quickly pulled the wings into his back, then folded them on top of one another. They melted into his strong shoulders and disappeared. All that remained was a small red mark, an indication that a burn had occurred.

"What news of Forcas?" asked Adramelechk.

"We know he has made contact with the girl, but are still not sure of her reaction, or indeed, if he has said anything about the plan."

"I think you put too many people in dangerous situations," Sammael stated again.

"And I think you don't ever put yourself in any one situation," Appoloin shouted. "It must feel good, sitting on your fence, not deciding which way to go and casting judgement all around. Why do you even bother with us?"

"I have obviously chosen, if I stand with you just now." Sammael was becoming distressed, he was sick and tired of the accusatory comments and glances. "What we are doing, just by being here, is dangerous, we threaten our entry to the heavens. The Emperor is already aware and angered by our meetings, but more importantly, we are imperilling the lives of humans and the eternal beings we call friends. We threaten the very cause we claim to be fighting."

Silence filled the cave like a shroud. They had all been thinking the same but were afraid to utter the words aloud, fearful that they might be true.

"What did I miss?" Xaphan stood looking at those he had once called friends. He had overheard Sammael and had not wanted to interrupt, he was one of the eternal beings that was in danger.

"Where have you been?" Ramiel asked. "Or should I not bother waiting for a response?"

"Depends on the response you want to hear, old friend. I have been…educating."

A shiver of disgust travelled through Ramiel's body. He watched Xaphan's eyes change from iridescent blue, to black, even the whites of his eyes turned black.

Xaphan's once glorious white wings opened, the four tiers

of feathers spread around in all their glory and were almost entirely black, some white streaks were still visible, but very limited. His six feet, six inch, muscular body glistened with sweat. He, unlike many demons, decided to remain in angel form and not choose that of a three-headed beast.

Ramiel hoped he still would get a chance to pull him into the light of angels, and with his rejection of choosing the beast's form, hope existed, but upon close examination of him now, he realised the opportunities to save him were sadly diminishing.

He stood in all his demonic splendour, the gold torques on his forearms glistening in the firelight. Angels all wore their hair long, sometimes reaching their waist, but now his dark brown hair was cut into his head, falling slightly over his ears. He had a slight crook at the bridge of his aquiline nose and a small scar indicating where it was once broken, but it didn't detract from his beauty, instead, it only made him look more handsome.

"I thought as much." Ramiel's lips went into a tight line, and his brow furrowed as he inhaled a sigh of displeasure. "Please, don't feel you need to educate us."

Xaphan swept his eyes around the room until they rested upon his old friend Adramelechk. "How do you find yourself, Adman?" he asked, using the nickname he had bestowed upon him, when their friendship had been like a boisterous melody.

Adramelechk turned to Appoloin, more than disturbed in hearing the name they had laughed about. "You may tell him I fare well."

"Tell him yourself," Appoloin growled, before stomping away.

"What news do you bring, Xaphan?" Ramiel wanted to be far from the caverns, and as quickly as possible.

"The Kings are worried. They believe a spy is within our fold."

Ramiel frowned. "A spy? Where? In the Kings' lair?"

"They're not sure, they believe it is coming from the caverns."

"That could be anyone, or anything. We have no need to worry. Do we?"

"The Emperor is aware of the spy and wants searches done of all the caverns. He believes the rebel is amongst us, it could be any one of us. What say you?" He turned to look at Adramelechk. "It could be you, Adman, the voice of G—"

All five angels turned and screamed in unison, "DON'T SAY IT!"

Xaphan's riotous laughter thundered inside the cave, the sound a deep, resonating blast. "Just testing," he chuckled.

"Surely he has no right to search the caverns?" asked Kakabel.

"Finding yourself a bit worried, are you, Klack?"

Kakabel moved quicker than light and pinned Xaphan to the cave wall. The smell of burning flesh filled the cave as the walls lit to a bright red and then hissed as the air became acrid.

"You will not accuse me again, of this or anything to do with spying."

Ramiel pondered the reaction of Kakabel; that was twice now he had overreacted to a simple statement. Distrust fed distrust, Ramiel knew it to be essential to discover the truth behind the words.

Xaphan pushed Kakabel from him and shook his wings, the noise in the cave became unbearable as his wings reverberated against each other. They had once made beautiful music, now the angels covered their ears, trying to escape the sound of souls screaming in torturous agony.

"Now that, is music to my ears," Xaphan declared.

"You are lost to us, are you not, Xaphan?" Sammael asked.

"I am here, am I not? How lost can I be?"

"You are aware of which I speak. You are lost to the Angel's light. Is there any hope for you?"

"By hope, I take it you mean, for me to rejoin the realms of the "harmonious, with love transcending" he sneered, "and be bored out of my eternal life? Not a hope, Sammael, go try to find another demon to save, this one's not going back into your *light*."

Adramelechk stepped forward. "You seem to have taken to this new life with ease. Perhaps too much ease, are we to believe you when you say you are with us?"

Xaphan narrowed his eyes and stared at Adramelechk, his pointed comment making its mark, but he refused, this time, to take any bait, too much was at stake for all. "You, brother angel, seem to know a lot more about the demon nature than you let on. Have you turned completely but are hiding behind your tainted white wings? Perhaps you cover them for a reason?"

Adramelechk spread his wings, the four tiers of white feathers tipped in black spanned and reached twelve feet in height. Large feathers nearly touched the ceiling, and before they could be singed, were pulled back. Before withdrawing into his shoulders, he shook them, each feather bouncing off each other, the quiet hum of a sweet melody flowed through his wings until they reached the tips, where the music stopped abruptly and turned to a scream.

"Do they look as though they are black, Xaphan? Are my wings the colour of evil?"

Xaphan was always impressed by Adramelechk, and this show of his angel status was for all in the room to attest to.

Appoloin moved between them. "What is wrong with you two? Why do you have to press each others' buttons, for the love of—"

"DON'T SAY IT!" they all shouted, including Xaphan.

"I wasn't going to say *it*, I was only…hell's teeth, it doesn't matter! Can we please get through the rest of this meeting without you two pulling your cocks out and measuring whose is bigger?"

The sniggering started with Kakabel, bouncing to Ramiel, then onward to Sammael until all six were chuckling like adolescent school boys.

"That word always makes me laugh," Kakabel spluttered through giggles. Another round of laughter erupted before their solemnity returned.

Ramiel turned to Xaphan. "This 'spy', who do they think, or what do the Kings think it is?"

Xaphan took a deep breath in. "They are unsure, but the feeling amongst demons and kings alike is that the spy is a Mistdreamer."

"Holy hell," Sammael whispered, "do they know which family?"

"That's the problem," Xaphan said hurriedly. "They can find no trace of who this Mistdreamer might be, it's as if they've never been registered and we all know which family that means."

Ramiel stood, shocked. "Then all our work for so long is wasted, our Mistdreamers are in terrible danger. You were right, Sammael, I shouldn't have put the humans in such danger, and for what?" He paused, worriedly turning the information around his mind. "Do we have any more information…? No." He answered his own question and continued as though talking to himself, "Forcas is still missing, we have no idea how or what he is up to."

"Then I suggest," Xaphan declared, "that more of you will have to descend to the earth's plane."

"Does that include you?" asked Admerelechk spitefully.

"Of course it does, so long as you take my place beside the Emperor, I'm sure I could arrange for the two of you to become better acquainted." He laughed wickedly, knowing his meaning was understood.

Ramiel shook his head. "We have spent enough time here, I believe no more is required to be said at this time. Thank you, Xaphan, and," he turned to everyone in the room, "my thanks to you all, we have to meet soon and work out the best way to ensure our Mistdreamers' safety. For now, we must go, before it is noticed we are missing."

He studied his friends and, sadly, wondered when next they would meet and how much further into the dark they would have wandered.

"Until next time. I will let you know, when the time is right. Somehow, I will arrange contact, but if any one of us discovers anything, or should urgent changes be necessary, I will leave notice for you in the usual place. Until then, stay safe, my friends." Ramiel raised his head upwardly, his wings spread, and his body dissolved into a myriad stars.

As all the remaining angels, apart from Xaphan, lifted their wings and raised their eyes upwardly, they spoke in unison to the departed angel, "Until then, Ramiel." Xaphan watched as his friends turned into dazzling strobes of multi-coloured lights, before they disappeared completely.

Chapter Three

Hiding deep in the recesses of the outer regions of the caverns, four demons and their leader waited. They watched as one of the Infidelibus exited the cave. Dark eyes watched with contempt as Xaphan strolled into the dark corridor. This was, indeed, a coup, one that would give him the greatest of pleasures reporting.

Xaphan turned to look in his direction. Quickly, he slithered deeper into the darkness, his body merging into the shadows. His demons transforming likewise. "Hurry, my pets," he hissed, his talons elongated. "Stay silent, keep hidden."

Xaphan shook his head and moved toward the shadows. It was as if he could sense something, someone, near, but stopped abruptly and raised his wings. His angelic light shone so brightly, the shadows were exposed for seconds.

"No matter, my pets, we are safe, he saw nothing, and we now have a good idea of all who attended. We can report to our King, we have witnessed traitorous dealings going on…."

He then turned to the leader of his demons. Rachauden, a demon of the first order and the only female of the assembled, was willing to do almost anything for him, her ambition having no boundaries. "Has the girl been able to see any more?"

Rachauden shook her head. "We have her watched at all

times, and she is beginning to break. She is not happy with the conditions and asks for her family; we are doing everything you ask of us."

"Excellent, excellent, keep me informed, I want to be watching when she breaks. We will continue the vigilance of her family, then decide when to take them. Once she knows they have been removed, she may be more susceptible to our demands."

"Do you wish us to go collect her humans now, master?" she asked

"No, I have a special reward awaiting them. Let me know when the woman is nearing breaking, my pets wish some time with her body, and they have been exemplary assistants." He patted one demon on the head, and his mouth turned into a sneer. "We will take them at her breaking point. I wish to be at their binding."

He threw his wings back, then pinned her with a malevolent look. "Mark my words, Rachauden, should you not make this happen, you will be placed in the first realm and treated just as the other souls."

The demons behind her began sniggering but promptly stopped when he glared at them before returning his attention to Rachauden. He was warming to the idea of all that could be done to her should she fail. He took a step toward her, and suddenly, raised his hand, pointing a withered, bony finger, with a five-inch talon, at her. The talon scratched her face, drawing a little blood. He glanced down at the blood, then, bringing it to his nose, inhaled its scent. His black eyes never leaving her face, she watched as he suckled the blood from his finger. His brows furrowed in anger. His spite and hatred aimed at her as his threat became more sinister. "You will remain in place until I declare you fit to leave." She could feel his breath against her cheek as he whispered, "And don't count on that being before the worlds collide."

He pulled his small, black wings behind him. "Make it happen," he shouted as he flew into the air.

Lauren shook from head to foot in rage. It had taken that thing twenty minutes to eventually decide to unfreeze her, and by that time, she was too angry to eat. So now, she was not only angry but even hungrier.

"Why didn't you tell him to do it earlier? I've been in the kitchen for twenty minutes, Mom," she whined.

"Well, actually," Forcas interrupted

"I'm not talking to you," she stamped her foot and yelled.

"Oops, now you've done it," Callum laughed.

Lauren glared at her father. "How could you let him leave me like that for so long?"

"Well, it's only been two minutes, Lauren…" Forcas smiled.

"You know it's not, just because the time has passed by in two minutes. OOOH!" she shrieked. "He's impossible, who the hell is he?"

"Let me introduce myself," said Forcas. "I am Duke Forcas, president of the third realm, Leader of thirty-six legions. I am also known by the names, Foras, Forrias. I am a leader in the speciality of teaching mathematics—"

"Stop!" Lauren yelled.

"But I have not finished with my introduction," he complained.

"Lauren!" her mom whispered urgently, "Hush, and listen to what Forcas has to say."

"Thank you, Cathy." Forcas grinned. "As I was saying," he

pulled an eyebrow down, trying to remember how far into the introduction he had reached when Lauren frustratingly interrupted his thoughts.

"Yabba, yabba yabba, duke of something, teacher of maths…"

Her parents rolled their eyes, this was not going well. Lauren needed to listen to Forcas, and they were astonished at the patience he was showing her. Lauren was beyond exasperation at the concern they were giving him. That concern should have been for her!

"Go ahead, Forcas, she's always a little testy when she hasn't eaten."

"And whose fault is it that I haven't eaten?" Lauren whirled on her father. "His!" she pointed at Forcas. "The Duke of the Underworld!"

Forcas sneered, "Not *the* Duke, just one of them, but it's excellent to know you are aware of where I'm from. Mayhap you should let your parents…and me, into that little secret, hmm?"

Lauren's eyes roamed around the lounge, avoiding any eye contact with her parents as they sat together on the big, comfy, red, three-seater sofa, which, she noticed, had been moved again, by her clean-freaky mom, and now was placed in front of the large bay window. On either side, were small tables with massive, ornate Chinese table lamps, that were turned on and illuminated the room with soft, warm light. Another two-seater settee was on the wall opposite the doorway.

Forcas stood to her right in front of a large fireplace. The mantelpiece held more family photos and a large Westminster chime clock, together with an assortment of china ornaments her mother had bought, or was given. She warmed her hands on the blazing fire. Forcas raised a shoulder in inquiry to her parents, who were sitting on the other side of the room, when Lauren turned as though to leave.

She stopped beside an oak cabinet that held Edinburgh crystal her mother lovingly displayed and put one hand on the handle to the entrance door to her left, contemplating whether she would walk out of the room.

Lauren loved this room, especially in the summer; whenever the sun shone through the window, the crystal glasses would bounce refracted light all over the cream-coloured walls, making thousands of rainbows.

Tonight, however, the curtains were drawn, keeping the darkness at bay, any light was coming from the lamps and the fire.

Forcas cleared his throat. "As I was saying, I am the teacher of mathematics and Logic. I am an expert in ethics and the virtues of herbs and precious stones."

Forcas watched in disbelief as Lauren raised her hand, covering a yawn that escaped. "Am I boring you, Lauren?"

"Well, really, y—"

"LAUREN!" both her parents warned.

Lauren muttered under her breath.

"What say you?" asked Forcas.

"That's another thing," she grumbled, "who speaks that way any more?"

"As it happens," he glowered at her, "I happen to speak like so! I am beginning to lose my patience, Lauren, and that's something you don't want to have to witness." He added the last matter-of-factly.

"Then why don't we just get down to the basics?" she asked. "Just tell me who you are, why you're here, and when you'll LEAVE!"

Cathy and Callum stared questioningly at each other. Cathy

shrugged her shoulders and shook her head. What was wrong with her daughter? She was never this rude. Callum glanced at Lauren and smiled. Recognising the signs before his wife did.

Attraction.

And his daughter was terrified of it.

"Unfortunately, for me, Lauren, I won't be leaving for a very long time, so you better get used to having me here." Lauren was about to complain, her hands flying into the air. "Don't!" he shouted. "Enough, you will listen to me."

Lauren was so taken aback by his raised voice, she stepped backwards and straight into the cabinet, which then began wobbling. "Oh, crap," were the last words she said before the cabinet began to fall on top of her.

A light appeared around Forcas, and he moved so quickly, a vapor trail followed him. One second he was standing before the fire, and the next, he was holding back the cabinet with one hand as he wrapped his free arm tightly around her small waist.

"How do you do that?" She blushed, then added, "Thank you, that could have been a bit sore if it had landed on me."

"Tell me, are you always this clumsy?"

She put her hands on her hips. "That's it," her lips went into a tight line. "I don't have to put up with this. Have you got a split personality or something? One minute you're oh-so-sweet, the next, you're a pain in the ass!"

Callum went to her and pulled her into his arms. "Lauren, enough of this, come sit with your mom and me, and we'll listen to Forcas and what he has to…together." He tugged her away and placed her between Cathy and himself on the settee.

"I do not mean to be offensive, Lauren, I am just concerned that perhaps more is going on than you simply tripping, burning, and falling."

He turned to Callum, who worriedly nodded. "This has

been happening increasingly around her, she was never clumsy before, and suddenly, the house seems to be falling around her."

"That's as I suspected," Forcas agreed. "Lauren, I am the Angel of Invisibility, and I am here to guide you through your transition into Mistdreamer. We have little time to develop all your skills, as it has taken some time to find you." He frowned at Cathy. "But the time we have, has to be used advantageously."

"You are an, an, an angel," Lauren stammered, then, puzzled, she added, "but I thought you were in charge of legions, is that legions of demons or angels?"

Forcas sighed, knowing what to expect next but continuing with his explanation, "I am what you would call a 'fallen angel'. I still have access to the lower realms of the heavens, but I also gain access to the realms in Hell."

He waited to see her reaction, waiting to see the disgust in her eyes at the realisation he was, as he told her, not the guardian angel she believed him to be. He dreaded to see the disappointment that would be in her lovely brown eyes and was astounded when she simply shrugged. "Guess we can't all be good all the time, can we?"

Perhaps, it was relief. Perhaps, it was the unexpected. Whatever it was, Forcas had not expected this reaction from her.

He could feel something strange happening to his body, his stomach felt very peculiar, as though there was something about to explode inside of him. It felt like a bubble, a huge bubble that kept growing larger and larger before it moved to his chest. Then it was moving into his throat.

Forcas watched his body, expecting to see a viper come forth, but his eyes opened wider when he glanced at Lauren, just before the bubble exploded into the air. His laughter filled the room, causing smiles from the three Chisholms sitting on the settee watching him.

He snorted and chuckled, completely taking himself by surprise.

This time, when he gazed at Lauren, his smile was soft and genuine. A change had come about, for him. He enjoyed that feeling of unexpectedness, he was enjoying being surprised regularly, and hoped this delight would continue; he was intrigued by the possibility that she was able to surprise him. It was new, and it was for this he constantly found himself searching, long before he had fallen. . .

He was enjoying being with Lauren.

Callum regarded Forcas with the eyes of a father whose daughter was about to go on a first date…and glared. Forcas shrugged, not recognising the parental glower, thinking only that it was simply discomfort in his being within the household. As far as he was concerned, there was not much he could do to change the situation. He had to be here. He must be the one to teach Lauren, to guide her through the Mistdreamer paths.

In actuality, this was an assignment he had dreaded, when, twenty years prior, he was informed of his duty, but now, he was eagerly anticipating whatever time they would have in sharing the unexpected.

He was happy. He could not remember the last time he'd said, *at this moment, I am happy.*

Lauren peeked at her dad, then Forcas and wondered what was passing between them. She glanced at her mom, raising her eyes in question.

"Don't ask me, kid, it's a man, macho thing, I think."

"Dad," she thumped her dad's arm, "stop it, he's an angel, for the love of heaven!"

Forcas leered and laughed again. "Aye," he said, his voice sounding just like her father's beautiful Scottish brogue, declaring with pure devilment, "but a fallen one, hen. That means I get to have a wee bit of fun."

Callum stood up. "Not with my daughter, you don't! I'll ask you to keep your mitts to yerself!"

Lauren wanted the settee to open up and swallow her. She thought her face couldn't turn any redder....she was wrong.

Forcas watched Callum, unsure of what to expect next. He knew he was pushing his fatherly buttons.

Callum was furious, he raised his fists and moved toward Forcas, whose humour fled as quickly as it had arrived. "Do you really think you should, Callum?"

Callum's breathing was becoming laboured, his heart was pounding, the fury he felt made the blood rush to his head. Logical thinking was flying out the window as he watched the massive angel standing before him.

This angel was leering at his daughter, his baby. The blood rushing through him pounded in his ears, shutting out Cathy's words.

"Callum!" she shrieked. "What the hell's wrong with you?"

"Did you not see the way he was looking at our baby? He was ogling at her, I tell you."

That was when Lauren realised she could go even redder and turned a beautiful shade of crimson!

Cathy was stunned, then she saw how embarrassed Lauren was, so she grabbed Callum's arm. "Will you give it a rest, you're being ridiculous."

"But look at him, he must be at least a thousand years old; he's too old for her, I tell you."

Lauren crawled into a ball on the settee and wished and wished for it to open. "Oh, please, Dad, please, stop, when will you realise I passed childhood years ago?" she moaned.

"Actually," Forcas said, rather pleased with himself, "I am

two and a half trillion years old, in angel terms but here, on this plane, I'm only twenty-six. Is twenty-six too old for your daughter?"

Lauren stood up, covered her face with her hands, and moved to the door. Forcas touched her arm as she moved to pass. Her body began to tremble at his touch, hot tingles igniting a chain of passionate energy through her. His touch made her want to melt into him. To touch him. To kiss him.

She peered into his beguiling eyes, her embarrassment complete. Not only did her dad act like a caveman, but she was also mortified at experiencing the unexpected responses of her body. She pleaded silently with Forcas to let her leave. He nodded and stood aside.

"I apologise, Callum, I have no right to rile you in such a way. I was just enjoying a fleeting moment of pleasure and was carried away on a whim."

Callum was shocked at receiving an apology, he'd fully expected a duel to have to be carried out in order he save his daughter's innocence. *Did angels duel or merely zap anyone in their way,* he thought?

"I see you are a little perplexed, Callum. Truly, we cannot be at loggerheads, not now. She is approaching her twenty-first year, is she not?"

Cathy nodded. "Yes, next month. The family, maybe a few friends as well, are getting together, and we will have a small party, to celebrate."

"Then that is an excellent time for me to be introduced to the other Mistdreamers who have avoided the register of Ambriel."

Callum stood still, unsure of what to say. Cathy held his hand and smiled reassuringly at him. "Of course, Forcas, some will be attending, but obviously, not everyone will manage to come. Some members of the family live a distance away and won't manage the journey."

"Then, we should make it happen," Forcas said with authority.

"I wish that were possible, but because of the distance they must travel, we didn't invite those family members who live far away. They understand this and do not take offence, it is practical not omission, and Lauren just wanted a small 'get together' with her close family and friends. She wanted my parents to come as well, but her grandpa is unwell and won't be able to make the long journey." *Phew,* she thought.

Forcas narrowed his eyes. "You are avoiding the truth, Cathy. Beware, by doing so, you could be endangering your daughter even more. It is imperative you understand changes are happening, movements in the heavens and hells that will affect her time as a Mistdreamer."

Cathy was acutely aware of the omissions she made in her statement, but she had, as usual, stuck, as closely to the truth, as was possible. To waiver from the 'almost' truth, could lead many a person into confusion. So it was best to stick, as near as possible to it as one could.

"I trust that before her twenty-first moon, you will have the truth for me?"

"I don't know what you mean," Cathy snapped and moved toward the exit Forcas was blocking; he grabbed her arm, stopping her from leaving.

"Get your hands off my wife," growled Callum.

"My, my, first your daughter and then your wife. You protect your women by glaring and shouting, but the most important part of protection is to avoid danger. Both of you," he nodded at Cathy then at Callum, "are lying to me, both of you are causing your daughter to be put into a position she will find exceedingly difficult to understand or even handle." He pointed at Callum, and a shock of electricity shot from his finger, the blast hitting Callum squarely in the chest. Stunned, Callum fell backward onto the settee. Cathy screamed and ran toward him. Just as she began to move, Forcas formed a figure of eight with his other hand, one finger pointing at Cathy. She fell to the floor and lay in the foetal position.

"No…neither of you say any more of your lying utterances. I am displeased, but I will forage and find the truth. You will wish, when I find the truth, you had told me all beforehand. In the end, it will ultimately be me, not you, that protects Lauren. Make no doubt of that, Callum, husband of Catherine, son of Henry and Fay Chisholm, direct descendent of Agnes Park and the original chosen Mistdreamers."

Forcas drew an invisible line, his fingers pointing at them once more, and removed whatever compulsion he had placed upon them. He turned and opened the door, then left the room and went in search of Lauren.

Callum and Cathy stared at the open door he exited.

"Crap," said Callum, "we are in such deep shit!"

Chapter Four

The Scottish branch of the Park family has origins in the northwest of Scotland and can be traced as far back as the twelfth century. They were a proud and defiant family, fiercely defending their right to the throne of Scotland and as a sept of Clan MacDonald were entitled to wear the MacDonald crest and tartan.

One of the forebears marrying into the Park family was a Bailliol. Although female, she was a direct descendent of King David of Scotland, and in the thirteenth century a Balliol would become king….for a short while.

The Parks' became more powerful through hard work and well-informed choices. Their decisions to buy land and use only family to work the land worked in their favour. Their choice of grain was barley, which they used to make their own brand of whisky. All the while they were making a name for themselves, they maintained their allegiance to the MacDonald as their clan chief and as a sept of his clan, remained under his protection.

However, as the Parks' power increased, they became a clan in their own right, and as the ban on wearing tartan was lifted, with the blessing of the MacDonald, they proudly wore their own tartan of bold green and blue, highlighted with lines of bright red.

The Park family were not wont to stay in one place and travelled across the width and breadth of many lands until they found an area that would be of benefit to their clan. Once they found a place that had the feel of somewhere they could call 'home', they would purchase land and plant more barley. The required outbuildings, needed to hold the fermenting golden liquid, would be the first buildings erected. Once they were in place, the hard work of propagating and cultivating the barley would begin. Once that was started, they knew they were home, and they settled in.

Some travelled to Ireland, as this was a place thought to be as magical as Scotland, and the ones who moved to this part of the country, managed to hide their identity quickly.

But most of the Parks remained in Scotland. They chose to move around the different regions within the country, setting up new communities and choosing the appropriate grain to grow in the fertile soil but one that would give a quick return on their investment.

The Highlands became home to a few, and those few, as it happened, would appropriate land quickly. Then the planting of barley would begin, and a future of very profitable endeavours in the making of whisky would be put into action!

Edinburgh was another place that became home to some. At the time, land was plentiful, so they cannily purchased several acres in the Morningside area, and instead of planting barley, chose to become dairy farmers. The region was awash with taverns and hostelries that provided succour for many travellers, and as such, were in great need of the produce the Parks could supply.

The Parks throughout Scotland continued to have a good working relationship, and the name grew extensively, their profits always put into the family businesses in order for further growth and profit.

Whenever they built their homes, the family crest was immediately embedded into the stonework of the buildings. The crest itself was a helmet and visor sitting atop a red shield. In the shield three stag are triangulated on a gold background. One of which is positioned above a red and white chequered band. The helmet is adorned by a bright comb of red feathers. A stag stands above the feathers, watching. Waiting for something or searching the land.

A bold signal to anyone that this was a clan that would defend their land, while watching for new opportunities at the same time as protecting their family, whilst also ensuring they would be stronger and better in the future.

The Heavens concluded these Parks were the right humans to become the premier Mistdreamers. In their wisdom, the Heavens, therefore, decided this would not be the only gift to be bestowed upon the original Parks, or Parcs/Parke/Parkes, depending upon which century the scribes were writing the name. They also resolved to grant them the additional gifts of leadership, invention, imagination, and many of them were presented with differing forms of artistic qualities.

Some became writers, others chose to follow in dance, in future generations, a great number became actors. Then, in the twentieth century and beyond, some developed their artistic talent in another direction and became wonderful animators.

For every gift granted, there is a specialist angel assigned to the recipient to ensure that gift is developed to its maximum potential. The angel ensures this talent is passed to future generations, thus enabling the heavenly gifts to flourish and grow, as is designed by the heavens.

However, the original Park families not only maximised their potential, they learned quickly how to enhance the amazing gifts they were given. They became the teachers to their children, encouraging them to develop their skills, making certain the future generations used them properly and to their best advantage.

The specialist angels who were assigned to the original families, watched them for a few centuries and were not only delighted in their progress, they were astonished and deeply proud of the Parks' usage of their gifts. They were satisfied that future emerging generations were being taught to their full extent, how to get the most out of their capabilities.

The gift of leadership was used to its best advantage in this regard, teaching and encouraging those with gifts how to develop their skills and capitalise upon their abilities and how, where possible, to increase their gift capacity. Then, when the time was right, the knowledge they learned, would be passed on to a new generation of Parks.

And so, a certain amount of apathy grew within the angels who were watching over the Parks. Their mission was to, first, present the family with the gifts from the heavens and to watch over the family, guaranteeing they were applied properly and to their best advantage. Furthermore, to secure the gifts were correctly passed to new generations. These had not only effectively been employed but were carried out beyond their expectations.

The angels trusted the Parks with the gifts and began giving them less supervision, believing they were more than capable of managing them. The leader of the Angels suggested to the other angels that they give the Parks more freedom and then, on occasion, check to see the gifts were being utilised properly and that they were continuing to educate new generations on how best to use their gifts.

It just so happened, the leader of the specialist angel group was Forcas, the Angel of Invisibility! One of the many titles he held was also that of the Angel of Leadership. He watched the earlier Parks nurture, educate, learn, and improve upon all the gifts they had received. It was he who thought it a waste of his, and that of the other angels', time to continue scrutinising the humans who, he believed, surpassed even the angels' knowledge of these gifts, and that they were, therefore, more than capable of handling whatever the future might hold.

The other specialist angels responsible in the realisation of the Park family's potential, consisted of: Ramiel, Xaphan, and Kakabel, who all, together with their Angelic designations, also held the titles Angels of Imagination, Invention, and the Arts.

Ambriel registered the four specialist angels and observed them. He completed the relevant documentation on receipt of the reports given, and when all were in agreement with Forcas's judgement in backing off from the continued supervision of the Parks, he also voiced his concern and was more than a little worried about the occasional checking in on them.

He wondered what Forcas meant by occasional, and the response given was 'whenever necessary'. He put his trust in the angels, deeming them to be the professionals, and tried to keep his apprehension to a minimum; he was, ultimately, outvoted on the subject of constant supervision.

When, in the mid-nineteenth century, Agnes and Archie Park registered their children Ramsay, Alexander, and Graeme, they had become aware of a shift in the regulation of supervision that they had been receiving and chose, at that point, to omit Agnes's maiden name of Chisholm with Ambriel's *Register of Mistdreamers*. The next two hundred years of Park marriages occurred with a certain regularity. Each male child married at a designated age, and then their children were born with, and at, specific regularity.

The Register was always informed when a female child was

born, it was also informed of Park marriages, but as the early twentieth century arrived, the register of Park names was slowly dying from the Mistdreamers in the Edinburgh region.

The female Park children were now marrying into other Mistdreamer families, and their children were registered under the father's surname, diluting the Park name even further.

Agnes and Archie decided, upon their marriage in 1835, they would pass down the knowledge of the gifts but no longer wanted to be part of the Angels' agenda. And so the Chisholm plan was put into action.

Agnes registered her sons as Parks and her grandsons, who were born from 1870 through to 1880, as Chisholms. The plan then, was for the Chisholm men to marry at age thirty, wait five years before their first child was born, and any consequent children would be born at five year intervals.

And so the plan was working all the way to, and including, 1955 when Callum Chisholm was born. The plan continued with the birth of his brother Alexander five years later, and according to the plan, in 1965 the baby, Graeme, named after is great-great grandfather, was born.

The three brothers' Chisholm grew into striking men. They were tall, all of them reaching more than six feet. They were well-proportioned, with long legs, large chests, and wide shoulders. Although not musclebound, their arms and legs were powerful, and they chose to keep themselves fit. Although unaware of their good looks, they attracted attention wherever they ventured. They often acted like little lads as they larked around with each other, but this kept them close to one another and laid the foundations for their friendship.

Graeme, the youngest, was the tallest, at six foot three. His wavy, sandy-coloured hair fell to his shoulders, slight curly bangs fell on his forehead above straight eyebrows. His heavily fringed, sparkling blue eyes, always filled with mischief, were his strongest asset, and the Chisholm aquiline nose and large mouth made him look more like an Adonis than he cared to believe.

Alexander, the smallest at six foot one, like Graeme, wore his black hair long but preferred to tie it back with a leather thong. Straight black eyebrows sat above hazel eyes fringed with black eyelashes, his aquiline nose a little bent after being broken when he fell off his bike as a small child. Of the three, it was Alexander who retained the strongest Scottish brogue.

Callum, at six feet, two and a half inches, wore his dark brown hair short, just below his ears. His brown eyes were like molten pots of chocolate, and like the other brothers, he was fortunate to have thick eyelashes and straight eyebrows. His wide, sensual mouth always wore a ready smile, but his charm was in his ability to listen and understand beyond the words he heard.

The resemblance, when the brothers were together, could be recognised instantaneously, yet apart, they were very individual.

They all attended Heriot Watt University, where, during the four years of further education, they experienced fun, drank, made new friends, and met some girls. They were delighted with the outcome of actually passing their degrees and, if they were honest with themselves, it came as a bit of a surprise, as none of them thought they expended a great deal of energy into studying. Then when they left university, they decided to go into business together.

Callum and his brothers bought a small, inauspicious shop in Grove Street, Central Edinburgh and set up a business, where they put to good use their knowledge of business, computing studies, and criminology.

They painted the business name CAGE LTD in bold black letters on a red banner above the shop front. The shop door was situated in between two six foot by six foot windows, which contained words, painted in bold, yet discreet, black letters, displaying the company motto. *We will free you...The Truth is our business.*

Inside the shop, Callum's desk faced the door as one entered, the other two desks were at angles to his and opposite each other. They all sat on ergonomic chairs, and an array of chairs were available for any customers. Each table held the best of all technical equipment, which was kept regularly up-to-date by Graeme. The newest software was always bought or downloaded. The best tracking equipment was available to all three of them should they have a specific job which entailed using such technology. There was one more small table, which was placed behind Callum's desk; it held a coffee machine and cups, together with essentials. Above this table, on the wall, hung five TV screens, each screen displaying differing areas in Edinburgh. Data was displayed on each screen, in the lower righthand corner, that of the date, time, and the region in Edinburgh.

Their detective agency was set up to be a low-key affair, but the business was situated near the hub of police activity, the Lothian and Borders central premises which were in Torphichen Street, just a mere five minute walk from their shop. They built a good relationship with most of the police who, in turn, passed some business to them, but all in all, they continued to have a regular flow of customers.

Within five years, the business was in need of diversification and expansion. New modes of operation were being introduced in the US, and the brothers felt it was time one of them dipped their toes into the US market. Callum was the one chosen to see what opportunities might be available to them in the US, and after much negotiation, in 1985, he moved to America.

The branch CAGE inc. was set up; originally the expectation was to begin their American venture in California, but Callum quickly learned there was an excess of similar enterprises, so he headed south to Orlando, where he registered the American division, and after advertising for staff, he carefully scanned resumes and quickly hired two retired policemen who he believed would be more than capable of handling the work that came their way.

He was able to leave them to carry out the assignments that began pouring in and found himself travelling to all areas in the US to determine the potential resources and funding of new projects. His contacts were mainly with the CIA and the FBI, both of which were an unknown quantity to the Edinburgh setup.

His associates were rarely in the office, and Callum decided it best to employ someone who could take care of all the enquiries and run the business when he was not in town, therefore, he advertised in the Orlando Sentinel for a capable office manager/administrator.

One of the first resumes he checked out was that of Cathy Graeme. His senses told him not to look any further, but his professionalism knew he was required to interview at least four applicants. He chose four that would definitely not fit the bill he required.

When the tall, slim woman walked into his office at 3:45, her dark eyes looking nervously around, she put her head to one side, and when she saw Callum, smiled nervously. Her smile lit up her face, and she took his breath away. Her stunning looks floored him. The attraction he felt to the beautiful woman was instantaneous. Her long black hair fell softly to her shoulders, gently accentuating her slim, oval face. Her high cheekbones and straight nose only drew him in more to the brown, almost black of her eyes. Her lips were wide, and when she shyly smiled, her white teeth would bite her lower lip. Her feminine gentility moved him in such a way that all he wanted to do was claim her.

He knew she had to be his.

Callum wondered how he managed to stumble through the interview, not recalling anything he asked. When the interview was over, he offered her the job.

Callum fell in love with her at first sight, and two months later, at age thirty, he married his Cathy.

The Edinburgh office was also in dire need of some decent administrative assistance, and so Alexander interviewed a few candidates. Like his brother, his senses drew him to one specific resume. After a short interview, that was unnecessary as far as Alexander was concerned, he employed Linda Alexander. They had both laughed themselves senseless because of the confusion their names caused, but had fallen hard for each other. Then, ignoring the plan, they were married in 1985.

When Graeme announced he had eloped with his childhood sweetheart, appropriately named, Angela, the world in Mistdreamer land began to shift. He also married in 1985.

Five years later, three girls were born, one to each brother Chisholm. Each girl born in the same month. Lauren was the first girl, born to Callum and Cathy Chisholm. Alexander and Linda Chisholm were blessed with their beautiful daughter, Valerie, a week later. Then the cherry on top came two weeks after Lauren's birth, when Mairi was born to Graeme and Angela.

There should have been rejoicing and heavenly choirs, but Linda died shortly after the birth of their beautiful daughter, leaving Alexander distraught. Unable to cope with the birth of his daughter and death of his wife, he threw himself into his work, often working on dangerous assignments with the police, assisting them whenever needed. He employed nannies to take care of his daughter, finding himself incapable of touching her or looking at her without being reminded of Linda. His sadness turned to anger and embitterment, which he wore like a voluminous cape around him, all too evident for everyone to see.

Callum and Graeme tried desperately to pull Alexander from the depths he had fallen into, but to no avail. He continued to wallow in his sadness and bitterness. He became an unreasonable human being, made even more disagreeable in the company of his brothers and their families. It appeared to Alexander that all around him had happiness, and he alone was chosen for punishment. He rejected his daughter.

And then Angela disappeared.

She left no note. She just got up one morning, left her tiny daughter with a neighbour, and was never seen again.

The neighbours frantically called Graeme at midday, asking when his wife would return for their child. Graeme rushed to the house and collected Mairi. His neighbours' were worried for him and the baby, but their fear lay more with the unexpected disappearance of Angela.

She had not given any indication of postpartum depression and had appeared to be perfectly content with the baby. She was, truly, an incredible mother, with patience beyond Graeme's means or control.

Alexander was the first to appear on Graeme's doorstep when he heard the news of Angela's disappearance, promising he would do all he could to find her. It took the pain of his brother for Alexander to realise what was happening to himself.

Before he began his search for Angela, he returned to his house, no longer a home without Linda, he believed. He acknowledged the new nanny before going to the crib, where he gently picked his tiny daughter up and pulled her to his chest. He breathed in the milky smell that was tinged with peaches, and…baby.

His body began to shake, but he held on tightly to Valerie, as though the tiny being was the strength he needed. His tears fell like an April shower in Edinburgh. The nanny, concerned the baby would become agitated, tried to remove her from her father's arms, and in her desperate attempts, Valerie became distressed. Alexander's tears stopped as he watched his baby daughter sob into the bosom of this stranger.

He smiled kindly at the woman, an unspoken understanding passing between both, and with a slight nod of her head, she smiled and handed the babe back to her father. The moment Valerie lay in her father's arms, she stopped sobbing and snuggled into his large, strong chest.

And the bond, although later than it should have been, was, at last, forged between daughter and father. A bond that would last a lifetime and beyond.

Ambriel was concerned because the Parks' name had all but been eliminated from his Register. He still kept tabs on the descendants of the original family, even though their names were no longer Park. They were from the original chosen Mistdreamers and, therefore, still required the 'occasional supervision', and as Mistdreamers, their children had to be registered.

When he examined the register, his concern turned to worry. Running his finger down the list of Parks, he could find no male Parks being born within the last two hundred earthly years, in the Scotland region.

That's when he realised, something was very wrong…and his worries turned to fear.

The Parks had simply ceased to be…

He checked and double-checked his entries carefully, just to be sure, until he found the point of change, and that's when Ambriel started to pay attention and began to panic.

For nearly two hundred years, Mistdreamers had gone unchecked and unsupervised, and the heavens had no knowledge if any Park Mistdreamers existed. According to his records, they didn't exist, but it was simply not logical, and if Ambriel was anything, he was logical. The male descendents had not simply died out, something, or someone, had caused the system to be distorted.

Then Ambriel saw her…

There was no mistaking the captivating girl walking around the heavens, she was a Mistdreamer, and he had no idea who she was…and then, as quickly as she appeared, she disappeared.

Chapter Five

Lauren checked herself again in the mirror and was quite happy with what she saw. Her shoulder length, brown hair was tied up on top of her head and held by an emerald hair comb. Soft tendrils fell around her heart shaped, oval face. Her high cheekbones wore a light dusting of soft pink blusher, and the long, black eyelashes that fringed her sparkling, hazel eyes appeared longer, with the benefit of mascara. Her button nose, normally covered with a smattering of freckles, was powdered, but the lustre of youth still shone through the powder.

"You'll not be wearing that, surely." Forcas's deep voice broke through her thoughts, as she glanced over her shoulder trying to get a glimpse of what her backside looked like in the long, green dress she was wearing.

"Please, Forcas, could we perhaps keep the pleasant, calm atmosphere going just for a little bit longer? Especially tonight, it's my birthday party, don't ruin it for me."

It had been four weeks since she had learned that Forcas was an angel, and the atmosphere in the Chisholm household, although tense, was manageable. Lauren's parents avoided Forcas at all costs but were resigned to the fact their daughter could spend time with him and, therefore, didn't make too much fuss when they saw them.

Not that they did anything more than talk. Lauren had decided she actually liked Forcas, which came as a surprise. Yes, he could be a bit uptight at times, but she guessed that was the whole angel 'thing'. After their initial meeting, she thought he was fun to be around. He put her at her ease, which was quite the opposite to the way he made her parents react. Her father's scowls were always done behind Forcas's back and made Lauren giggle.

Forcas had explained that a change would be coming her way after her twenty-first birthday. The dreams she had been experiencing, since she was a small child, would soon make sense. Lauren wasn't too sure of this, to her, they were simply dreams. Yes, they were coated in mystical, beautiful colours, but they never really amounted to much more than colours and beautiful music. But Forcas had said that would change, and he would be with her when they altered, to ensure that she would be led in the direction that was ultimately predestined for her.

He had promised to help her make sense of past dreams and help her recall the content. She found this absurd because all she dreamt about were colours, lots of colours.

In the four weeks of learning that had passed, he had done his best to instil the wisdom and understanding of different stones. On numerous occasions, she was left helpless with giggles when he had assumed the role of 'magnificent angel', and had tried to make her understand that he was "the omnipotent being in all matters relating to magic and stones".

His perception of himself had changed with Lauren's help. He had no idea he was 'autocratic', a word she often threw at him when he was trying to embed some knowledge into her. He merely thought he was right, in fact, he was well aware of how right he was, but Lauren did not appreciate him enforcing her to understand this. Whenever he stormed at her that he was right…he knew the lesson would shortly be over as he watched Lauren cross her arms over her chest, tap her foot, and scowl at him until he gave in and would admit, "I am mostly right, perhaps not always, but in the matters of stones and magic, listen to my words!"

For four weeks, he had encouraged her to open her senses and acknowledge her life was but a speck in the ocean of time. That the worlds she was aware of, were not the only ones in existence.

He would hold her hands and ask her to close her eyes and imagine herself wandering across the different universes of which he spoke. The moment he touched her hands, her body would be set aflame with a passion she had never known before. A connection would be made for an instant, and then Forcas would abruptly cut the connection and remove his hands.

For four weeks, he had taught, she had listened.

He had touched, and she thought her body was set on fire as his appeared to turn to ice. She had tried to do as he asked but could never accomplish it all because of his disconnection.

Tonight was her party, and she intended to have fun. Forget all the training and teaching for a few hours and enjoy herself with family and friends. Maybe get a little drunk, laugh, and dance until the small hours.

Forcas was not going to spoil the evening by being a total dickhead. A very cute dickhead. But a dickhead, nonetheless.

"I don't mean to put a damp cloth on your evening, but you can see all the way down to your backside in that cloth on your body!" he moaned.

"It's a dress, Forcas, a party dress, for my party night, and it's supposed to be 'daring' and it's dampener, not damp cloth."

"As you humans say, 'whatever'. The dress is obscene, not daring."

"Oh, go fly a fig. I don't care. I'm wearing it, if you don't like it then go away. Anyway, look at you! Do you intend to wear anything but a towel around your bits tonight? Surely, you've got something more appropriate for a night out. Or am I going to be lucky and you can stay behind and wait for us coming home?" Lauren wiggled her eyebrows suggestively, all the while grinning at Forcas's stunned expression.

"I will be attending the party," he said somberly, then turned and marched out the room.

Lauren stared at the door for a few seconds after he had walked out before she returned to complete her makeup. "What should it be tonight, which lipstick? The 'Passionate Pink' or the 'Scrumptious Scarlet'...mmm." Lauren scrutinised her face in the mirror and smiled knowingly. "It'll be the 'Scrumptious Scarlet' tonight, I think," she said as she coated her lips, her lower lip pouting as she applied the vibrant colour. *I have plans for someone's heavenly body. Even if he doesn't want mine,* she thought sadly.

Forcas stood outside Lauren's room, not sure he understood why he was feeling so angry. He knew all about the seven deadly sins, he just never had the energy to experience them, they took so much time away from existence, and he was always amazed when another soul popped into Hell because he or she, had lost control because of one of them. Yet here he was, and he knew the emotion going through him was jealousy, but of what? Lauren? He wasn't jealous at all, not of her precisely, but what about those who would be looking at her tempting little body tonight?

"Where the hell did that come from? Tempting? We're talking about Lauren...Oh dear, man, she's got me talking to myself now!" He marched off in search of Callum. The plaid he was going to wear, was the original Park tartan, but he'd seen how others used the kilt in this century and was aware his might not be the right one for the occasion.

By the time he walked into Callum's room, interrupting him as he kissed Cathy, he was wearing the full kilt outfit, and he was in a foul mood.

"Excuse me!" Callum roared.

"Excuse you for what, did you do something wrong?"

"I meant you, you ignoramus. Don't just barge into our room – knock."

Forcas raised an eyebrow and nodded. "Apologies, I had forgotten your gentle sensibilities."

"It's not mine you should be thinking of, it's Cathy's. Come on, man, use your head. It's just not acceptable, and it's kinda rude as well."

Forcas breathed patiently. "I have apologised, and I will not do so again."

Callum shook his head and let out the breath he wasn't aware he had been holding, taking in the dark frown Forcas was wearing. "Okay, what's up this time?"

"Have you seen the dress she intends to wear?"

Cathy put her arm on Callum's chest and gazed up into his beautiful brown eyes. "Let me," she said quietly. "You finish off getting ready." Then she turned and saw Forcas in his outfit for the first time "Wow, you look…amazing, but a little too Mel Gibson, *Braveheart*. Have you considered wearing the kilt of this century?"

Forcas lifted his hands and pointed at her. As he moved, Callum placed himself before the offending digit and his wife.

"What?" asked Forcas. "Oh, you thought I was going to…" he shook his finger, "no, not tonight, and you wouldn't have time to stop it, anyway. I was just going to point out that the reason I came in here was to ask should I be less 'Mel Gibson'?

You have answered, thank you, please, return to whatever it was you were doing."

Then he turned and left the room, leaving Callum and Cathy looking at each other, astonished.

By the time he opened Lauren's door, he was donning the Park kilt of the twenty-first century.

When Lauren got her first glance at Forcas wearing the kilt, she was glad she was sitting down. The man, or angel, could put Adonis to shame. He even wore that constant glower in a sexy, vampy way tonight. "Oh my, Forcas, you look fabulous," she said breathlessly. "You're wearing the Park Tartan."

She drank in the sight of him greedily. The blue and green tartan somehow accentuated his exotic blue eyes. He wore his hair loose around his shoulders, and the cream, Jacobean shirt blended perfectly against his olive skin. "You will be the centre of attention, I don't know if I like that, when it's supposed to be my night. Well, me and my cousins', anyway." She licked her lips. "Wait until my cousins get a sight of you, they'll all want a shot of you. You'll be dancing all night."

Somehow, although she loved her cousins like the sisters she never had, the thought of them even touching him, didn't fill her with delight. *Valerie, with her sexy body and charm, could quite easily get Forcas into her arms. And Mairi, the tall, willowy blonde, who was destined to be the best actress ever, why would he look at me again after seeing either of them?* Lauren thought.

"I think it is you who looks, not fabulous, Lauren...You are stunning. And I don't think I'm happy with other people looking at you. This is all very new to me, and I will have to learn how to control my temper around anyone who nears you this evening."

Lauren caught her breath and smiled shyly, her eyes shining brightly, the threat of tears near, at his words. "I do think you have just paid me a compliment, in a Forcas, round the back door kind of way."

Forcas held his arm out for her. "Come, Lauren, let us go to this party and get back home again." Lauren walked forward and placed her hand on his arm, and as she turned, she caught sight of both of them in the mirror.

Forcas stood nearly a foot taller than her diminutive height, even with her wearing three-inch heels. Her emerald green, sequined dress with the bodice cut to hug her breasts, blended to perfection with the green of his Park tartan. The dress hugged her slight frame as though it were another skin, drawing attention to her hourglass figure. Her round, upright breasts, small waist and hips all were emphasised by the beautiful, shimmering material.

At her knees, the dress flared out before it fell to the floor, encircling her feet. She carried a small, clutch bag, which matched her gold *Laboutin* shoes.

As she watched them in the mirror, a fleeting thought crossed her mind: *Who are those beautiful people.* She snapped out of her dream and laughed nervously, "I know I shouldn't say so, but we look very good, don't you think?"

Forcas was too busy studying Lauren, his thoughts turbulent and worrying. Emotions he had never felt before were tumbling through his mind, causing utter chaos to his subconscious. His humanly reactions were incomprehensible to him, and they were driving him to distraction. So when Lauren asked, he didn't respond immediately because his mind was totally preoccupied with his own inner turmoil. Until she tugged at his arm, pulling him towards the door, he had been lost in his own frantic world. Her smile faded with the misinterpretation of his lack of response, but she was determined nothing would spoil this evening.

Forcas shook his head, acknowledging Lauren. "Sorry, what did you say?" "Nothing, it's not important, we'd better start heading downstairs or Dad will be up to see if you've interfered with his daughter." Lauren laughed lightly, her nerves getting the better of her again.

"Your father need not worry, I would not harm you, Lauren…this 'interfering', I take it you are talking about sex?"

Lauren blushed to the bottom of her toes. Pulling her arm from his, she marched to the bedroom door. "Stay, go, suit yourself, Forcas, I'm leaving." Quick as a flash, Forcas held the door closed. "I have offended you, Lauren, and that was not my intent. Humanly endeavours and responses are clouding my judgement at the moment. You look, so…so…very beautiful, I am extremely confused, and that cannot be tolerated. I am here to guide you, not to make your life difficult."

Lauren let out a sigh and then smiled. She hadn't realised how tense she was, neither had she been aware of how much she had wanted Forcas's approval.

"You think I look okay?" she barely mumbled.

"You look much better than simply *okay*, Lauren, you are stunning, you take my breath away."

Lauren lowered one eyebrow. "Erm, I think that's enough, Forcas, you can overdo the praise a wee bit. I'm glad I look okay, there's no need to be sarcastic."

"I was merely letting you know how lovely you look. I was not being sarcastic. You will be the belle of tonight's ball."

Lauren gave Forcas a steady look before laughing, "You haven't met my cousins yet, have you? Hold that praise until you meet Valerie and Mairi!"

"I am sure they will not come up to your standard."

Lauren chuckled. "You really have to give it a rest, Forcas, and try and remember you're in the twenty-first century, not some mediaeval time. Nobody talks like that anymore." She ogled him up and down. "Try to relax, chill your body out a bit, stop looking so stuffy; you're very handsome, but a bit stuffy! You'll never get a click tonight with that air of superiority!"

Forcas was completely baffled. "Click? What on earth is a click?" He snapped his fingers. "Why would I want to do this?" He narrowed his eyes and watched as Lauren held her stomach with one hand and covered her mouth with the other, trying to stop the spluttering.

"You are teasing me, are you not?" He was trying so hard to remain rational, but she was playing with his mind. "I like the 'very handsome', and I know I am superior, but this *stuffy* and *click* are words not usually known. I am presuming again, you are referring to sex, or the prelude to the act?"

That was it, Lauren couldn't contain her laughter anymore and fell to the floor howling, tears streaming down her face. Callum had heard the crash and barged into the room.

"What the hell is going on, we've been waiting for you two downstairs for ten minutes. What did you do this time, Forcas?"

"Dad, Dad, don't worry," Lauren managed to spit out in between hiccuping laughter.

"I keep telling you, Callum," interrupted Forcas, "your daughter will remain safe in my company."

"Oh, I know that now," said Callum. "I'm beginning to think it's you I should be afear't for!" He turned to his daughter and helped her from the floor. "I think you need to stop piddling around with Forcas and get downstairs. This might not be the quiet party you wanted, but there are many relatives waiting for us at the Balmoral hotel, so get your little ass into gear and get downstairs and tell your mother to stop worrying, that her hair is amazing and that she looks superb! Move it, girl!" Callum smacked her bottom gently before adding, "And by the way, you look absolutely gorgeous. I don't think I have ever seen you look more beautiful. You were right to go with the green dress, it" Callum paused, withdrew a hanky from his sporran, and dabbed his eyes, "well, Lauren, you're all grown up, lassie. My wee one is a woman now."

"Oh, Dad, you're going to make me cry, don't." Lauren bit her lower lip, trying desperately not to cry.

"I can't help it, Lauren, you are the most beautiful girl. Look at yourself in the mirror." Callum took Lauren's arm and led her to the mirror. Forcas watched as her father touched her cheek then pointed to her in the mirror.

"Look at you, your hair, your eyes, all of you. You're perfect, wee one, simply perfect."

Forcas smiled as he watched Lauren look at herself then turn to her dad. "I love you, Dad, thank you for being my dad."

"Being your dad was the easy part, letting you go is the hard part."

Forcas shuddered, a sudden cold chill grew within his body as an evil force began to encompass the room, and he growled from behind them.

Callum turned to look at him "What? What is it, Forcas?"

"Did you no' feel that," he asked.

Callum was assuredly worried. "What? I didn't feel anything, what's the matter?"

"Perhaps it's nothing, but I must investigate quickly, there was a, how is it you say, a movement, a change in the worlds. It could be with Lauren reaching her twenty-first years, the tumblers of the universe have begun to shift. I must check this out."

Lauren was close to either crying or losing her temper, she wasn't sure which. Her dad had just said the most beautiful things to her, she was excited about her evening, and now, as usual, Forcas was throwing a bucket of ice all over her good humour.

"You had to do it, Forcas, didn't you?" she said angrily, as a force around her compelled her to say bitter words.

"What would that be?" he replied, just as coolly.

"You just couldn't have me enjoy the evening without you making it all about angels. All about the universes. Could you not give me one goddam evening to enjoy with my family before going on and bloody on about Mistdreamers?"

Callum glanced from one to the other, then back to his daughter. He had seen the look on her face a few times as she was growing up and knew when her temper got the better of her. It was never a pretty sight, and the consequences were always unpleasant.

"Lauren, you are the one going to spoil the evening if you don't calm down, not Forcas. Let's go downstairs and see your mom, she can't wait to see you in the dress. Now, come on." He turned to Forcas, who now stood with his hands on his hips, his expression dark and furious. Callum decided it was better he remove Lauren before the pair ended up exploding. "Come, Lauren," he urged, and when she didn't move, "Enough of this, we have guests waiting. Move!" he all but shouted.

Lauren turned from glaring at Forcas to her dad. "Sorry, Dad, what did you say?" She shook her head uncertainly. "What's going on?" she said, just as her body became as rigid as steel and she began to fall.

Forcas moved like light and caught her before she even hit the floor. "What's happening, Forcas?" Callum asked.

"She is being consumed, we must act fast before the energy takes her. Her first visit mustn't be to Hell, she must meet with Ambriel before she meets The Kings."

"Well, the first thing she should do is get to her party! For the love of God, Forcas, can you not help her?"

Forcas lifted her and carried her to the bed, where he sat and cradled Lauren in his arms. Gently, he blew on her face; the breath leaving his body to cover her face was a mixture of air and light. "Lauren, come back, you are not ready yet, come back to earth and me," he whispered.

Lauren's body began to soften, the rigidity melting as Forcas's words began to penetrate. Slowly, she opened her eyes to look into the stormy sea of Forcas's worried gaze. "Come back, Lauren, come back to me..."

Lauren lifted her hand and brushed it against the side of Forcas's face. "I'm here, what happened?" she stammered.

Callum harrumphed. "You fainted, it must be all the excitement of the party." Forcas dragged his attention from Lauren and turned deadly eyes to Callum, silently daring him to refute his lie that hung in the air.

"Let's get moving, Lauren, we really must rush, the car's waiting for us outside." Callum had organised a limousine to take them to the Balmoral, hoping it would add something even more special to Lauren's evening. Now he wasn't even sure they should be leaving the house. It was obvious from Forcas's demeanour that he was more than a little anxious about Lauren's faint.

"Your father is right, let us go to your party and have fun." Lauren stared directly into Forcas's eyes. She didn't want to see the lie blaring out from them, and sadly considered letting him know she was aware of it, but she began shifting toward her father, removing herself from his lap. Forcas grabbed her around her waist to hold her steady, the simple touch sending shivers throughout his body, which, in turn, was reacting in the most ridiculous of humanly ways. "I'm fine now, Forcas, you can let go of me."

Lauren wondered at his response to her movement and thought to herself that it was almost possible Forcas felt something more for her than she had originally believed. She was quite prepared to say that what she felt of his body beneath her, was most definitely more than the affection a teacher should have for his pupil.

She leapt from his lap, totally confused, and began spluttering. "Right …okay…let's go, Dad, erm, are you coming… I mean are you? Oh, it doesn't matter, I'm fine, let's go."

Callum raised a quizzical eyebrow at her, then at Forcas, who simply shrugged nonchalantly. "It is time," he said. "Let us meet the Park masses. I am so looking forward to being introduced to them all." Callum groaned and turned toward the door. "Is there a problem, Callum? Is there something you are omitting to tell me of this evening?"

Callum stopped suddenly and again turned to look at Forcas. "I don't know how many times we have to tell you this, but nothing is wrong, and nothing is being held from you. Now, if you don't mind, Cathy will be worrying, needlessly. Let's get out of here."

Lauren was surprised by the conversation between them and was about to ask what was going on, when her father took her arm and led her gently out the bedroom.

"That's right, Callum, son of Fay, get out quickly before I see what you really are hiding from me." Forcas checked the room, positive the evil that had enveloped it prior to Lauren passing over had now evaporated. Forcas had felt this evil before, and he knew time was moving faster than he would have liked. Lauren had to pass into Mistdreaming quickly.

Chapter Six

"Well, holy hell, if that doesn't take the biscuit! Our Lauren's gone and gotten herself a boyfriend." Mairi whistled as she watched Lauren and Forcas walk past, arm in arm. Lauren glared at them as she passed. Then she peeped over her shoulder towards her cousins, stuck out her tongue, wrinkled her nose, and wiggled her eyebrows. "Then she goes and does that!" Mairi chuckled.

"Holy cow, what a boyfriend, did you see his ass, Mairi?" asked Valerie "What is it the Americans say? "You could bounce a dime off it", or something like that. Geezo, the man is ripped!"

"Just look at her, she's all ladylike, holding his arm, and then makes that face." The two girls laughed out loud and knew any minute, Lauren would be over to talk to them.

Lauren let go of Forcas's arm. "Excuse me for a minute while I talk with my cousins." Forcas moved to go with her. "Please, give me a moment, this will be girl talk, and I don't want you listening in."

"Girl talk?" he asked. "Can this girl talk not be repeated to me, are there more secrets you are not sharing?" he asked, frustratedly.

"What are you going on about?" she said. "You're being ridiculous, go talk to my mom and dad, I'm sure you can go all weird with them." Lauren turned and walked to her cousins.

They had arrived minutes earlier, and Callum had ushered the four of them from the car, into the Balmoral's huge reception area. Lauren had glanced up at the beautiful ceiling. She then stared all around her, drinking in the atmosphere, loving the feel of the old building. Outside, it had hardly changed, and although the hotel had undergone an amazing refurbishment, it still kept many of the original features from its days as the North British Hotel. The revolving door was not electric, and the interior was brighter due to the upgraded lighting. Glass panelled doors opened into one of the bars, bringing a more modern aspect. On the whole, it remained the same.

The bar still had its rich walnut surround, but instead of it being all wood, it now was adorned in a soft mink suede fabric. The carpeting was lush and patterned in a tartan designed by Kinloch Anderson, the tartan makers. This royal blue and red tartan was designed specifically for the opening of the newly refurbished North British, when it changed it's name to The Balmoral. The giant staircase that stood predominantly in the middle of the reception area was still the grand stairs people loved to walk down, especially when they were dressed for a night out. Now the new mechanics of elevators were installed, allowing weary travellers some respite from a multitude of stairs.

As they had entered the hotel, the first people she saw were Mairi and Valerie. They could hardly be missed, they were so glamorous. Mairi was dressed, as usual, to perfection in a long, blue silk, halter neck evening gown, designed by Vera Wang. The colour matched her astounding, ice blue eyes. The collar of the dress was studded with tiny diamante. When she turned, Lauren could see her bare back sparkled with iridescent powder.

She wore her hair like Lauren, on top of her head in a soft French twist, and had pinned it with a beautiful, antique sapphire clasp. Mairi held her tall, lithesome body elegantly.

Men literally bumped into each other when they saw her. And she was totally unaware of the commotion she caused wherever she went, which only made her more appealing.

Valerie stood beside Mairi wearing a strapless, dark red velvet evening gown designed by Stella McCartney. The dress was spectacular. Cut low above her breasts, it showed off her exquisitely curvaceous body to absolute perfection. She was an inch or so taller than Lauren, and the soft flow of her dress gently outlined her amazingly sensual body, highlighting her small waist and tight backside.

Her auburn hair fell freely down to the middle of her back. It was softly arranged around her face, tiny tendrils curling around her forehead and at the sides of her face, emphasising her beautiful, almond-shaped blue eyes. Around her neck, she wore a diamond and ruby choker, accentuating her creamy skin.

Valerie's laughter echoed around the reception area, and as she laughed, heads turned. People desperately tried to find the source of the heavenly sound. When she spoke, people listened, some didn't hear anything she said as they were so entranced by the angelic sound and it only made her laugh more. She had lost count of the times she had heard, "Excuse me?" or "Sorry, what did you say?".

Lauren's smile beamed across her face as she neared them. The three of them huddled and cuddled each other, screeching as they bounced up and down. Their laughter echoing off the walls, causing all in the hotel to smile. The love and affection they had for each other was openly displayed, and their joy became addictive. Others wanted to join in and happily turned to whoever was with them. The atmosphere soared from cheerful to euphoric.

"Did you forget to tell us something?" Mairi asked innocently, when they eventually calmed down.

"Like what?" Lauren wasn't sure she wanted to answer, or how to answer.

"Eh, the Godlike candy that was on your arm when you came in the door," Valerie said as she shamefully ogled Forcas up and down seductively. "I mean, look at that, he is so ripped. Where did you meet him, and does he have any friends?"

"Valerie! For God's sake, you're a teacher! If your kids knew what a slapper you were, you'd never get a job anywhere!" Lauren almost shouted.

"Eh, excuse me, when did you become the teacher police? And my kids would never know I was a 'slapper' and, by the way, I'm not."

Lauren had the good grace to look down, ashamed. "I'm sorry, you know I didn't mean you were a real slapper, just a… God, you know what I meant," she exclaimed.

"Wow!" Mairi said when she glanced at Lauren.

"What? What is it? Have I got something on my nose, is there a big plook appearing on my chin? What?" she squealed.

"Well, wouldn't you know it," Mairi and Valerie said together, "you've fallen in love."

Lauren felt as if she had received a blow to her stomach. It was so utterly ridiculous, the mere thought of loving Forcas just wasn't possible. They hadn't shared anything other than his knowledge. Oh, she knew she had feelings for him, but love? No, not that she was aware of. "No, I'm not, not really. I do like him, though, but I know love is a two way street, and I can't go falling for someone again that just doesn't feel the same about me."

"Aw, Lauren," Valerie put an arm around her. "Not all guys are jackasses like that creep Dylan you went out with."

Valerie nodded at Mairi, who added, "Come on, Lauren, you know she's right. Dylan was an idiot, he's the loser. It was three years ago, time to get over it."

"I am over him, really. I know it was a 'learning curve', I just wish I hadn't had to experience it. He was kinda nasty, especially at the end."

Valerie began to fiddle with her hair, a sure sign she was becoming a little anxious, and Lauren smiled at her. "Why are we talking about that loser? It's our twenty-first birthdays, and you two look fucking amazing!" The three of them broke into enthusiastic laughter again.

"Look at you, Lauren," said Mairi seriously, "you're stunning, your eyes, they're sparkling, seriously, you're so beautiful. Wow, your dress! Turn around, let me get a look at the whole thing." Lauren spun slowly, her dress shimmering and twinkling as though she wore a million stars.

"I think," Valerie said, "we are all gorgeous, and tonight we are going to have some fun. Look at us, simply the best."

"Cue for a song," said Lauren.

"Please, please, don't sing," Mairi said as she started to cover her ears. Lauren laughed again and promised to only sing when there was music, and Valerie promised likewise. They all knew that when they did sing, people had a tendency to go to sleep.

"I intend on imbibing a few champagnes tonight," Valerie said, chuckling. "What about you two?"

Mairi and Lauren both nodded in agreement. "I intend to dance until my feet bleed," said Mairi.

Lauren scrunched up her face. "I'm not so sure about the bleeding feet, but yeah, I intend to dance until my legs are wobbly and, of course, lots of imbibing," she said with a grin. Lauren glimpsed around to see Forcas watching her intently. "But I know what I really want to do."

Valerie and Mairi gazed in the direction Lauren was staring. "Oh, yeah," said Valerie, "are you going to tell us about him, or are you too scared?"

Lauren sucked on her lower lip. “I don’t know how to explain him, I don’t know if what I say is breaking some kind of commandment,” she said worriedly.

“Then just spill it,” Mairi said.

“He’s an angel,” she blurted out.

“You got that right,” Valerie agreed.

“No,” said Lauren, “I mean, he really is an angel.”

Mairi and Valerie both stared at her, then turned to look at Forcas. “Seriously?” they said together, in disbelief.

Lauren glanced down at her dress and removed an invisible fleck. “Seriously. He’s here to help with me passing into Mistdreamer status.”

“Are they real? The Mistdreamers, I mean. I thought all that was cabookie talk from Grandma. Remember how she used to tell those stories to us about Heaven and the scary demons from Hell?” All three nodded.

“Cant say I was ever enthralled hearing about the demons, specially as a little kid, but like you, Mairi, I thought she was making it up,” Valerie admitted.

“Well,” said Lauren, “it turns out, she was telling the truth, not stories. Did neither of you have a ‘special’ friend only you could see when you were little?”

“I had a great imagination, Dad said, I always spoke to nothing, hence the actress occupation,” admitted Mairi.

“What about you, Valerie, did you have a ‘friend’ just for you?”

Valerie pulled her eyebrows down, touched her lip with one of her manicured nails, and thought back. “I just had my dollies, stuffed animals, and bears that I lined up and taught. I cant really remember anyone else.”

Mairi and Valerie were stunned. “Are you saying we’re Mistdreamers, as well?”

Lauren lowered her eyes, embarrassed, and shrugged her shoulders. "I don't know, I suppose you could be."

"Then how come we haven't met an angel?" Mairi asked.

"Yes, how come nothing has come to us?" Valerie wondered.

"I think I can answer that," Forcas's deep voice sounded behind them.

"For heaven's sake, Forcas, I asked you to give me some time with my cousins, stop creeping up on people."

"Lauren, I think your cousins asked a question that you have no answer to, is that not right?"

Valerie nudged Mairi, and both girls gazed up at Forcas, then nodded. "Yes, how come we don't have an angel?" they asked.

"Shhh, keep your voices down," Lauren whispered.

"Why? Nobody can hear us, they're all frozen," Mairi said matter-of-factly, stunned at the realisation of what was going on.

Valerie peered around at everyone standing still. "Oh, this is just not happening, not tonight. I want to get drunk, dance, maybe kiss a few people, not this. Not frozen people."

Mairi watched as everyone stood unmoving, and laughed. "Choose one now, Val, and go kiss him!" Both girls started to snigger and seriously focussed their attention around at the men in the room.

"Please, tell me you aren't listening to her." Lauren was shocked.

"Well, why the hell not?" Valerie asked. "It's my birthday, and I'll do what I want to." Before Forcas could speak, the girls grabbed imaginary microphones and started singing, "It's my birthday, and I'll snog who I want to." They bumped into each other, then lost their balance and fell against each other in a heap of laughter and frothy material.

"Anyway," Lauren said, trying to get back to some kind of normality as she attempted to stand up, "Forcas, please, unfreeze them, it's our birthday…" "Hold on…hold on," the girls said, "how come we didn't get an angel? Are we Mistdreamers, too?"

"Delighted to answer, ladies," Forcas said as he stepped forward. "The reason you didn't get your allotted angel is because we knew nothing about you. You can thank your uncles and fathers for that. Yes, you are also Mistdreamers, and now a crash course will be necessary for both of you, and I don't think there will be enough time. I have barely covered the essentials with Lauren, and she now is in her twenty-first year."

Valerie sniffed. "I think we can worry about that after tonight."

"Yes, let it go tonight, Forcas," Lauren grumbled. "You can teach them tomorrow, enough with the pink stone, red stone, blue stone. Let us have our birthday party and please, unfreeze my bloody guests!"

"I don't think you understand the urgency in this matter, Lauren," Forcas exploded. "There is danger for all of you if you do not fulfil your Mistdreamer potential."

Valerie hooked her arm into Lauren's, who hooked her arm into Mairi's, and the three of them turned away from Forcas. "Well, hell, honey angel," Mairi said truculently, "if you've frozen everyone, then it's a free bar, and we are going to drink it dry of champagne. So suit yourself, angel, join us or piss off!"

Forcas began to raise his arm to stop them, but stopped halfway and watched as the three giggling ladies swanned towards the bar, their three bottoms wrapped tightly in velvet, silk, and shimmering green materials. They laughed and hugged each other, and Forcas thought he had never seen anything quite so eminently gratifying in quite a few millennia. They were right, although time was of the essence, a few hours of pleasure could harm nobody.

He walked to the bar, where the cousins sat on bar stools, and placed four flute glasses before them. He opened a bottle of champagne, then poured. He handed one full glass to each of the girls. "Then, young Mairi," he handed her the glass, "young Valerie," he handed her a glass, "and, of course, the beautiful Lauren," he said as he handed a glass to her, "I would rather join you," he said as he raised his glass to drink, "than piss off. I think the evening would, on the whole, be much more pleasurable being with you, than not."

Lauren sighed, "He can be quite the debonair angel when he wants to be, ladies. Let him stay."

Valerie nodded her head after she had finished her glass of champagne and raised it for another one. "Okay, he can stay, but he has to unfreeze the people."

Mairi lifted her glass, waiting for a refill as well. "Totally agree with you, unfreeze the people."

And with a sleight of hand, so deftly done that none even noticed him moving, all around was once again in motion. "That is such a handy trick, can you teach me that, too?" Valerie asked. "It would be great in the classroom when all the kids are just screaming at me." She hiccuped and handed Forcas her empty glass. "Time for another, I think," she whispered.

"I concur," yelled Mairi as she handed him her glass.

Forcas raised the bottle to Lauren in query. "Lauren, do you want to partake again?"

Mairi put her hand over her heart, pretending to swoon. "Did you hear that? If I were texting, there would be three letters O-M-G! How amazing do you talk? 'Partake', geez Louise, you have to teach me that, keep your freezing butt people trick, teach me how you make love with words!"

Lauren began to fidget, both her cousins were flirting outrageously with Forcas, and he loved being the centre of their attention. She had known this would happen, they were bright, shining lights to her dull shadow. She didn't resent them in the least, she just wished she could be as bright and beautiful as them. "Lauren?" Forcas said again as he lifted the bottle.

"Yes, I think I will," she said and handed her glass to him.

"May I make a toast then, ladies?"

All of them had just finished their third glass when he spoke, and they nodded collectively. "Just a wee bit more," Valerie said and leaned forward.

"Thass a good idea," Mairi said.

"How else you gonna give a toast if we've got none champers," slurred Lauren.

Forcas refilled their glass and raised his, to toast them. "To the beautiful Chisholm ladies. May your birthdays be all you had hoped for. May your dreams be realized, and may your wishes be granted."

They clinked their glasses together and all said, "Cheers, Forcas, thank you."

"Uh-oh," said Mairi, "look out, here comes trouble."

They all twirled around on their seats, just as the bartender asked Forcas to get out from behind the bar.

"Mom, Dad," Lauren said sweetly, "where've you been?"

Callum glared at Forcas. "She's drunk…already?" he asked in disbelief. "What have you been giving her? Angel dust?"

Forcas shook his head, the bubbles and alcohol from the champagne causing him to lose his balance slightly. "Ah, the renowned Chisholm sense of humour," he said as he slapped Callum on the back. "One day you'll have to remind me that I'm an angel with incredible powers. What say you?"

"Just look at the state of her." He glanced back at his nieces.

"Them as well, we've been here a total of five minutes….Did you do that time thing again, Forcas?"

Cathy hid her smile and tried desperately not to laugh, both at her husband's indignation and at the state her daughter and nieces were now in. "Callum, I'm going to find Alexander and Graeme, they can help with this." She kissed Callum on the cheek. "Try to keep cool and remember it's their birthdays—"

Before she had the chance to finish her sentence, the three ladies burst into song, belting out at the top of their voices, "And we can drink if we want to".

Cathy laughed and walked away in search of her brothers-in-law, leaving Callum to, hopefully, handle the situation with some kind of diplomacy, but she knew there was no chance of that!

Forcas smiled stupidly, trying hard to look innocent. "What time 'thing' would you be referring to? The interruption of the time continuum? Is that to which you are eluding?"

Mairi, Valerie, and Lauren simply fell of their seats and landed on the floor in a crumpled, undignified mess. Not even the angelic tinkling of Valerie's voice could bring anything but a scowl to Callum's face. "Not funny, Forcas. They have a whole evening ahead of them, and they can't even stand. Look at them!"

"Stop being a growler, Callum," Forcas grunted.

The three ladies started sniggering, covering their mouths with their hands, and when Forcas spoke, Lauren yelled aloud, "My dad's a growler."

Callum grabbed her arm and pulled her from the floor. "For the love of the almighty, Lauren!"

Forcas stepped forward and held Callum's arm. "Remove your hand from her body, or I will shnap, sorry, snap, you in two!"

Lauren was horrified and put her hands on Forcas's chest. "Iss okay, Forcash, iss my dad, remember? Relax, please."

Callum shook his head, stunned at the reaction from Forcas. He released his hold on Lauren and apologised, "I didn't mean to grab you, kiddo, it's just you're a wee bit tiddly, and we have about a hundred guests wanting to meet the three of you," he said as he raised his eyes to look at the dishevelled forms of Valerie and Mairi. "They're all going to wonder how the three of you can be so drunk in a matter of minutes."

Forcas leaned over to Valerie and Mairi, who were still on the ground holding each other up, and offered them an arm each, which they gladly grasped. With no effort whatsoever, he gently pulled them to their feet. Valerie began patting herself down, as did Mairi.

"Nah, we're still perfect, Mairi."

Mairi smiled, threw her head backwards and then onto her chest in an over exaggerated nod. "Aye, juss perfet."

"Oh, good Lord, your fathers are going to kill me," said Callum.

Mairi put her hand on Callum's arm. "Sno problem, Nuncle Clam, Val and me…" She started giggling, and Valerie tried to focus her eyes on her and then she started giggling, too. Callum rolled his eyes. "Diss you hear that, Nuncle Clam? Val and me, sounds like Val and me, diznt it?"

Valerie nodded. "S'ma name, Val and me." They both began laughing helplessly.

Forcas tucked Valerie and Mairi's arms into the crook of each of his. "We're ready," he announced. "Lead the way, Callum, we are going to dance this eve."

"Why me?" Callum whined. "Why could it not just be a simple but perfect evening. Why?"

"Becuz," Lauren said, poking her dad in the chest, "you

brought a nangel!" Lauren suddenly stood up straight, and turned sharply away from her father. "I want to dance," she said before moving away from their small group.

Lauren weaved toward the grand staircase, and Forcas, with Valerie and Mairi on each arm, followed her, taking the exact route she led. Two steps to the right, four to the left, one to the right, three to the left…

Callum shook his head and snickered quietly at the idiotic sight ahead of him. "It's their birthday, and they can drink if they want to," he sang softly as he tenderly watched the quartet eventually reach the staircase.

Callum was already on his way to join the group, when, seconds before he moved, he saw a figure emerging from below the staircase. He couldn't make out clearly who or what it was, as it was shrouded in a black mist, but it merged with those walking up the stairs. It had a shadow-like quality, but he knew there was more substance to it than merely air.

He could see the nefarious figure clearly tracking the girls wherever they went. It hid well, and it moved amongst the guests, secretly following them toward the room that they had hired for the evening.

He searched desperately for Cathy, he had to tell someone.

Forcas was right, they had endangered all the girls. Whoever was following the girls, whatever was following them, was definitely not here to wish them well and join in their birthday celebrations.

Chapter Seven

Rachaudan was hiding in the shadows, beneath the grand staircase of the Balmoral, and resentfully observed the drunken antics of Forcas and his female following. *It was typical of him,* she thought, *to have adoring beings hanging onto his every word.* Had she not been so concerned with her mission, she would have found his fan worshipping even more distasteful than usual.

As it was, she was unsure and frustrated at not being in complete control of certain elements of this mission. Too much had been left to trust, and she trusted nobody. She had no idea which woman to grab this evening because the information passed to her had simply been, "Take the birthday girl", yet all three, she was informed, were 'birthday girls'.

"Would the master be displeased if I took all three?" she wondered crossly. "Mayhap, this is his ultimate goal. Mayhap, he wishes to have control over all of these women?"

"In any event, they will not know what has hit them when I take them. The Dark Lord himself will be in awe of my capaciousness." She admired her own aptitude in assessing the problem. Her amazing strength and capability, to leap from world to world in mere moments, would make this course of action possible. However, she still mentally debated whether this was the right option.

If this was, indeed, the right choice to make, it might increase her credibility, perhaps even her position, with the master. However, a wrong decision would then leave her destroyed. Her power would be confiscated, and her wicked soul would then be in the master's hands to be manipulated at his will, and he was not known to be merciful.

She blamed the whole untenable situation she now found herself in, on the Mistdreaming "birthday girls" and, of course, that idiot, Forcas.

Rachauden's evil thoughts in his regard were limitless, causing an unprecedented fury to erupt within her body. The inner loathing reacting instantly, producing a sinister green mist to surround her. She could barely contain her hatred and spite as they threatened to overwhelm. Attempting, desperately, to regain control of her body and her temper, before the invisibility shield was compromised and people became aware of her presence.

She breathed deeply and evenly, marking each cautious footstep with a single intake of air as she carefully started moving forward, calmly following, then interweaving within the group ascending the stairs. She slunk behind them as they walked into a dimly lit room, where she remained, continuing to hide behind groups of revellers, all of whom were either holding or drinking glasses of champagne whilst talking loudly amongst themselves. They appeared to be completely unaware of the evil standing so close to them, totally lost in their own enjoyment.

Rachauden wanted to laugh until she cried. *Humans are stupid*, she thought. And careless. And ignorant. Thanks to their ignorance, she would be the victor. It was she who would bathe in the master's exaltation. She alone would be the one who would sit beside him on the throne he had chosen.

With a gleam in her eye, Rachauden watched as Forcas wrapped his arm around the small one in the green dress when he brought her to the dance floor.

She had spat venom upon seeing him enter the hotel. Again, her information was Forcas would not be seen in public, and therefore, she was aghast at the sight of him, strolling into the hotel with the Park family. She had not expected this in the least. *More misinformation from the master's source*, she thought. But no matter, in the end, the master would reign, and he would bleed these Mistdreamers until they were begging for peace. A peace she knew he would never grant. As a reward for her hard work, maybe the Master would grant her the gift of tormenting Forcas. She knew it was unlikely, his power was even greater than the Master but he, too, could be controlled, and the delight she would have to see him bend to her will, although merely a marvellous fantasy, was a thought that filled her with a contentment she knew was not allowed.

The master would deplete the Mistdreamers of their energy and leave them broken. The pain they would endure would leave them dried up and hunched over like withered old women. They would become a play thing for his demons, just as the one before them had now become. Rachauden was disgusted at the unpleasant thought, was this what the master planned for her should she fail?

She had watched the Mistdreamer being broken and had recognised the power within her that the master wanted for himself. To some degree, Rachauden was almost afraid of the energy contained in the Mistdreamer. The master was welcome to it, as far as she was concerned, and shuddered at the thought of anyone obtaining such energy. She believed it to be anathema to choose the absorption of such a force into one's own being.

Too much power eventually became redundant, and a Mistdreamer's energy had no bounds.

Eventually, the master got his wish. It had taken a long, delightfully slow process.

She broke.

To watch her now being used by the demons was pathetic. To be bound and chained in such a way was demeaning, even for a Mistdreamer.

Rachauden swore it was not going to happen to her. This was her chance, this was her mission, and she would not fail the master.

Callum grabbed Cathy's arm. "Where's Graeme and Alex" he all but screamed at her?

"What's wrong, Callum" she said, frightened chills suddenly permeating her body?

"I don't know, I'm sure I saw something follow the girls upstairs, we have to find my brothers. Where are they, Cath?"

"Whassup, bro?" Graeme said lightheartedly from behind Callum.

"Are you having a good time yet, big brother?" Alexander's deep, resounding Scottish brogue asked as he slapped Callum gently on the back.

Callum whirled around to look at them, his face etched with worry.

"What the hell happened?" Alexander asked.

"We've only been at the bar, here's your *Glenmorangie*," Graeme said as he handed Callum the glass of whisky. "You look as though you've just seen a ghost, what the hell happened?"

“Can you feel that? It’s as though time has been shifted, and I know Forcas wouldn’t do that, not tonight, not without a really good reason. It’s something happening to the girls, I think they’re in danger. I saw…hell, I don’t know what I saw, I just saw *something* follow them up the stairs into the room.”

“What time shift? What’re you talking about? What was it you think you saw, was it an angel? What…what did you see, Callum?”

Callum grabbed the arms of both his brothers. “Forcas has this time stopping thing he does, but it doesn’t feel like this! This is like…well, it’s as though time is slowing. Oh God, I don’t know, but if it wasn’t Forcas creating this time anomaly, then whatever followed the girls is slowing time for a reason. I don’t know what followed them. All I can tell you is it isn’t from this world, and it isn’t here to either help them or wish them a happy birthday. It’s evil, and nobody else saw it despite the fact it was standing beside some of our family and our friends as they were going up the stairs!”

Graeme and Alexander knew better than to question anything Callum had encountered. It wasn’t the first time Callum had ‘seen’ something. He had often warned them about approaching danger, or foretold an event prior to it happening. When Callum asked them to be careful, they knew to watch both ways and behind them before they made any moves On many occasions, this gift had helped in more than one of the cases they had worked.

The three brothers turned their attention to Cathy. “Go, all of you, go, I can’t run fast in these heels, I’ll follow you up. With luck, whatever you’ve seen, Callum, might not be there, but if it is, go save our girls if you can.” She then watched as the three six foot plus men ran and took the stairs two at a time. They ran as though the very devil was at their ankles.

Lauren walked into the Beauly room, on the second floor of the hotel, and let out a happy sigh. The room was simply spectacular. The massive Edwardian fireplace was aglow with smoke free fuel and was burning brightly. The ceilings were ensconced with elaborate period cornicing and two original chandeliers from the 1902 building had been kept, but upgraded from gas to electric lights. Their intricate brass filigree design sparkled with the reflection from the blazing fire and soft lighting.

Eight round tables with twelve chairs, adorned with white linen covers and red bows, were placed in a circle around the dance floor. Each table was covered in a thick, white linen cloth, and in the centre, a decoration of red roses encircling gold, green, and blue candles, which flickered gently. Every table groaned with an assortment of magnificent foods from the buffet. The options were vast, and with such a wide range of foods, even the discerning palate would be content that something was available to suit all. An abundant selection, ranging from Haggis parcels, King prawns in filo pastry, salmon kebabs, chicken goujons, soy sauce yakitori chicken skewers, mozzarella and vine tomato focaccia, to marinated beef with dill cream dip made for a decadent appearance. All the different foods, together with six bottles of champagne, and Lauren realised what a brilliant evening lay ahead!

In the middle of the dance floor, a small table stood on an elevated platform and held the birthday cake. A three-tiered chocolate cake, with white chocolate curls around the side of each tier. On the top tier there was a chocolate decoration moulded in the shape of an angel. A ribbon of the Park tartan was wound around the base of the cake, and three very large candles of red, blue, and green were joined in a triangular fashion and entwined with silver tinsel and placed in the top tier.

Lauren gazed lovingly around the room and thought it was perfect. Balloons, in the colours of the Park tartan, were strewn in various places. Matching coloured streamers hung from the ceiling. The three, twenty-foot, arched, French windows that led out to individual balconies, were framed with white fairy lights. The windows faced directly onto Edinburgh castle, which stood regally above her like a giant, silent sentinel.

Edinburgh Castle had guarded the city for twelve centuries and now, as Lauren gazed up, she watched, as the moon cast its enchanting light, silhouetting the majestic building against a purple sky. The high, grey stone walls stood proud and tall, and she marvelled at the magic and mystery it possessed and the myriad secrets it concealed.

Lauren was briefly aware of music filtering in around her senses. Recognising Van Morrison's "Brown Eyed Girl", her body swayed in time to the music. "Lauren, would you care to dance?" Forcas asked, as he put his arm around her.

Lauren was still lost in the magic of the castle, the magic of the room, and the magic of the night. Looking into Forcas's eyes, she smiled. "I would love to," she said, just as he took her hand and led her onto the dance floor. "I love this song," she murmured and placed her hand in his, entwining their fingers. Her other hand lay on his chest, directly above his heart.

Forcas pulled her closer into his body, one hand against the bare skin of her back. His thumb and forefinger ran gently down her spine, and she softly moaned at his touch. The sound sent lightning bolts through his body. He wanted to move away, he thought it was imperative he try. But he savoured the way her body melded into his, as if she had been made…just for him.

He lifted her hand to his lips and caught a lock of her hair between his fingers. He rubbed her hair between his fingers and was fascinated at how soft it felt. When he raised it to his lips, he inhaled her scent, a mixture of oranges and jasmine, a fragrance unique to her.

The music moved their bodies in a symbiotic rhythm as old as time. As one, they moved around the floor, oblivious to the many eyes watching them as they danced. It was as though they were alone, just the two of them. Lauren could feel the effects of the champagne begin to fade and was glad that her memory of this evening, everything, including her dance with Forcas, would not be wrapped in an alcoholic haze.

"You are very quiet, Lauren, are you not enjoying yourself? Is my dancing not acceptable? I watched how to do this from that TV programme. But I am glad you are not wearing the dresses some of those young ladies wear."

Lauren was puzzled. "What TV show? You aren't talking about *Strictly* are you?"

"Yes, I do believe that is the one. They spin their partners quite often. Would I be right in assuming you do not wish to spin?"

Lauren nearly cried out in horror. "Do not even think about spinning me," she croaked. "Are you saying you don't dance in Heaven?"

"There is not time for such frivolity, not now…."

"Wow, I can't wait to get there, it sounds a bundle of laughs, what do you do all day? Pray?"

Forcas turned a quizzical eye on her. "Why would we pray? We are in Heaven."

Quick as a flash, Lauren answered, "Ah, but you're not there, are you? 'Cause you're a 'fallen angel', that means you abide in Hell?"

Forcas stopped dancing and removed his hands from her body. "What? What did I say wrong?" Lauren asked, suddenly bereft at no longer having his arms around her. She had felt safe, secure in his arms, the world had consisted of just the two of them when he held her. "Well, tell me, Forcas, what did I do wrong, this time? You're not upset about me saying the FA thing are you?"

"Lauren," Forcas began, "listen…I hear no music, it has stopped. Pray tell, what is the FA thing?"

"Fallen Angel, get it, FA?" she said, shrugging her shoulders.

"Why would I be upset at you stating the truth? I am a fallen…sorry, FA. I am accepting of this fact. I spend my time between Hell's upper level, but also Heaven's lower levels. It is an agreeable existence."

"Then why do you need me and the other Mistdreamers?"

"Lauren, I do not believe standing on a dance floor, at your party, is the most appropriate place to be discussing this. Perhaps when I was teaching you, then would have been a more suitable time to raise such questions." Taking her by the hand, Forcas ushered her to the table at which her cousins sat. They were in the throes of emptying another bottle of champagne.

"Why the soor puss, Lauren?" asked Valerie, whilst attempting to open another bottle. Forcas grabbed it before she dropped it; he pushed the cork easily, and it flew into the air. Someone gasped as it flew into them, but they could not see who it was.

"Shorry," yelled Mairi holding her glass to Forcas for a refill. "Yessssss, Lauren whas the problem?"

Lauren laughed at Mairi's dishevelled appearance. It was so unlike her; normally the figure of perfection, she now was slouched over the table, one arm holding her head, whilst the other was flailing around with a glass in her hand.

Valerie nodded toward the corner of the room. "Have you

seen all the presents over there? I hope they don't want us to open them all tonight, I'll never remember who gave us what. I won't even be able to read the cards in the first place!"

Mairi started to giggle, but hiccuped. "I saw, hic, you dancing, Lauren, hic, with an Angel.'"

Valerie dived at Mairi and grabbed her by the shoulders. "Oh no, Lauren, she's gonna barf!"

"Am not," she said, swallowing the rising bile.

"Are too."

Lauren rolled her eyes, this was the story of her life with her cousins, they always, one, two, or all three of them would find themselves quarrelling. It usually ended badly, with them all getting into trouble from their parents. "Will you two shut up," Lauren whispered. "I can hear our dads coming up the stairs, and I don't intend getting into trouble on our party night because you two can't hold your champagne."

Mairi and Valerie stopped bickering and stared at Lauren, then, together, they said, "Ooooh".

"Well, get you," Valerie added, "sorting us out big style." She laughed. "How can you 'hear' our dads?"

Lauren thought for a moment about that and wasn't sure of the answer. "I can just hear them, that's all, and they're running." Her eyes sparkled. "Maybe it's our presents."

Mairi attempted to stand but fell down onto the chair again. "Presents? Yup? I want mine, where's my dad?"

"Shut up, Mairi," Valerie hissed, "you're doing it again, wheesht!"

Mairi put a hand over her mouth.

"I told you," Valerie grumbled, "you're going to throw up, aren't you?"

Mairi's big blue eyes turned to Valerie, her hand tightened across her mouth, and she nodded.

"Where's the nearest loo?" Valerie asked Lauren.

Lauren pointed to the door. "Out there and turn right, do you want a hand?" "Eh, duh! I'm not taking her by myself, look at the state. I can't believe she's my cousin, we've had the same amount to drink, you've been dancing, we've been drinking, and she's nearly under the table!"

Lauren and Valerie each put an arm under Mairi to haul her out of the chair, when Forcas gently moved them both to the side. "Let me, ladies," he said and bent down and lifted Mairi into his arms as though she weighed nothing. "Point me in the right direction, and make sure nobody else is in the ladies' room. I wouldn't want to offend anyone by walking in carrying a beautiful maiden." He winked at Mairi. Lauren groaned, Valerie sighed, and Mairi's eyes widened as her hand tightened across her mouth. "Huuway, Forcash," she said from behind her hand.

"Excuse me?" he asked.

"I think you'd better run with her, if you can," Lauren said. "She's about to vomit."

Forcas moved so quickly, nobody saw him as he shot through the crowd holding Mairi safely in his arms. He willed her stomach to stop rolling, and when he reached the rest rooms, threw open the door and carefully placed Mairi in front of a toilet. He then held her head with one hand as he gently rubbed her stomach with the other. His index finger pressed upon her stomach, and waves of heat flooded her body.

Mairi took a deep breath and began to rise. "I'm fine, Forcas, what did you do?"

"Just a little angel magic. I think you should be well for the rest of the evening. Shall we return to the throng?" Forcas held his arm out for her.

"I think I'll walk on my own two feet, if you don't mind. I get the feeling Lauren won't appreciate me holding on to you."

"And what makes you believe that? She is simply my charge, I am teaching and preparing her for the Mistdreamer life that awaits her, should she choose to go in that direction."

"Are you saying we have a choice when it comes to this Mistdreamer stuff?"

"You have no choice in being a *Mistdreamer*, you simply are *Mistdreamers*. What you decide to do with that ability and power is up to you. I don't believe many *Mistdreamers* have chosen to ignore their gifts."

Mairi considered this as they walked back to the party room. She waved to Valerie and Lauren and smiled when she saw them. Lauren marched quickly over to her. "Are you okay, did you blow?"

Mairi took her hand and laughed. "Actually, I didn't. In fact, your angel boy here did some magic trick to my tum, and that stopped the vomitus rollius!"

Lauren smiled at Forcas and was about to speak to Valerie when her father and uncles came rushing into the room. "Where is it?" Callum shouted. Forcas was immediately on alert.

"Of what do you speak, Callum?"

"Something is here, something followed the girls up the stairs, hiding all the way, making sure that nobody could witness it. I think it mucked around with time....Not the way you do, Forcas, but I'm certain time slowed for us!"

Forcas studied the whole room, looking carefully into the shadows in the corner. "I feel nothing, there appears to be no malignancy here at the moment."

"I'm telling you, I saw it creeping up behind them!" he exclaimed.

"Callum, I do not doubt you witnessed something, it is perhaps the same evil that attempted to enter your home earlier this evening. Did you per happenstance manage to garner some idea of what this may be, or perhaps even glimpse a likeness?"

"All I could see was a black veil covering its body, it could have been male or female. It was very slender and moved swiftly, and it was able to hide itself in the shadows."

Forcas closed his eyes and considered all that Callum said. "I am not totally certain, but it could be a demon who is able to make itself invisible. As far as I know, there are only a handful of demons who can do both invisibility and time shifting." Holding his hands up to deflect their anguish, he added, "But there is no presence here at the moment, I can assure you. I have a suspicion of who it may be. She is a demon of the first rank. I will have to check, but will ascertain if it is she. Should it be her…this does not bode well. I will discover who this is, but I think you should try to relax and enjoy this celebration you are giving all the girls, there is little you can do at present." He gathered in the appearance of the two men with Callum. "Am I to understand you two are the brothers of Callum?" he asked. "Did either of you witness this being?" Graeme was first to move forward, "Aye, you have that right, I'm Graeme, this is Alexander but, no, we didn't see it. If you're doubting ma brother's word, I'd think again if I were you." Forcas raised a quizzical eyebrow and was beginning to lift his arm when Lauren approached.

"What's going on, Dad?" Lauren asked. Although the question was directed to Callum, her eyes never left Forcas.

He answered, not giving Callum the opportunity to speak. "I am of the opinion that there is a problem. I will research before we expand upon it and only then, will give you any more detail, Lauren. Why don't you, for the time being, enjoy this evening? You truly have a multitude of work to do from tomorrow." He gently stroked her head, a slight pressure was placed against her brow, and Lauren's anxiety eased.

Cathy joined the group and took Callum's arm. "Lauren,

tonight, have fun." She turned to the brothers. "Do you three not have something you want to share with the girls?"

Alexander smiled sheepishly and flicked a strand of his long hair behind his ear. "That's right, I believe it might be time for birthday presents."

Valerie was the one who let the girls down by squealing, she then covered her mouth. "I'm sorry, Mairi, Lauren, I can't help it. I LOVE birthday presents."

Alexander kissed the top of her head. "Then, my little love, you aren't going to wait any longer." He signalled for the music to be turned down. That's when Lauren realised what was going to happen and groaned in embarrassment. "They're going to speachify," she said to her cousins.

"Oh no," Valerie and Mairi said in unison.

Callum stood beside the cake in the middle of the dance floor and signalled for his brothers, Cathy, Lauren, Valerie, and Mairi to join him and was handed a microphone. He quickly glanced around the room, checking for the being he had witnessed following the girls, but could not see it. He smiled at the guests, kissed Lauren, and began speaking into the mic. "Twenty-one years ago, we three brothers were blessed with our daughters. It has not been plain sailing to get to this point. We have suffered terrible sadness and indescribable loss." Callum drew in a breath, emotion overcoming him as he remembered the pain his brothers had endured. Alexander and Graeme both touched his arm in unspoken acknowledgement, before he continued. "Yet," he contemplated his brothers and smiled, "we have survived, all of us, and the love for our girls is eternal, it has no bounds."

Forcas cleared his throat, and Callum grinned at him. "We know our girls have many adventures to face yet, and we know they will be courageous in their endeavours. They will be brave when in danger. They will shed light in darkness and will bring calm in troubled waters, but until then, we would like to hand over their birthday gifts. Each gift comes, not from us, your parents, but with love and admiration, from the whole Park family. Everyone here, girls," Callum waved his hand around the room, "wish you a happy birthday."

Callum lifted a large box and handed it to Lauren. " May life's journeys always be remembered."

Alexander lifted a smaller box and handed it to Valerie. "May home be a reminder of your heart's desires."

Graeme stepped forward to Mairi with a small box. "May you find your journeys lead to life's answers."

As the girls began to unwrap their gifts, their family and friends began clapping, whistling, and cheering.

Mairi was first to open her present and, carefully watching her dad, she narrowed her eyes in query as she held up a set of car keys attached to a Swarovski, crystal-encrusted, Mini Cooper key ring. "Dad?"

"Well, you couldn't start your new acting career and not be able to get from one place to another. It's a Mini Cooper S," he said excitedly, then, taking in her puzzled expression, added, "It has lots of buttons, I'm sure you'll have fun driving it." Mairi stared at the key ring, still unsure of the exact nature of her present. Not daring to expect it to be anything more than the beautiful keyring she held. "Dad," Mairi's lower lip began to quiver and her eyes filled with tears, "it's beautiful, I've never had a key ring so lovely."

"Mairi, will you stop acting blonde!" Her dad laughed. "You've got a new Mini Cooper car, not just the key ring, muppet."

The tears she had so desperately tried to hold back began to fall. "I didn't want to believe it, I didn't think you'd buy me something like that." Sobs racked her body as she threw herself into her dad's arms, crying against his strong chest.

Graeme stroked his daughter's hair and held her tightly. "Happy birthday, my angel, I would have bought you something flashier, but don't want you to bring too much attention to yourself on this acting job you've got. You're already getting the wrong sort of attention, and I'm not going to be with you in Liverpool when you go on the stage every night."

"What do you mean 'the wrong type of attention'?" She sniffed as she pulled away from him.

"Look at you," he smiled indulgently, "you're beautiful."

Alexander stepped forward. "Eh, before you start bubblin' all over his shirt again, lass, let's get the other presents out." He pulled his niece into his arms, "Happy birthday, bonny lass."

"Thank you, Uncle Alex." She moved to Callum. "And you too, Uncle Call, Aunty Cath," she sniffed.

"Lord, she's gonna start more waterworks," Valerie moaned but smiled, knowing she wasn't going to wear as well as Mairi when her time came.

"Come on then, Valerie, it's your time now," her dad coaxed. Valerie carefully unwrapped the small parcel, knowing it was her father who had wrapped it. For years, he had wrapped her presents identically, with a huge gap on one edge for her finger to slip under and rip at the paper.

The paper fell to the floor, and Valerie stared at the four-inch square, blue velvet box. "Well, open it, girl," her dad urged.

"I'm scared, no, not scared, a bit apprehensive."

"Then open it, and your anxieties can be put to rest."

Valerie slowly lifted the tight lid and glanced down upon a Chubb key, on a Swarovski crystal-encrusted tiny house, on a keyring chain.

She turned inquisitively at her dad. "What's this, Dad? Don't get me wrong, I love the key ring, but what's the key?"

Alexander took the key from her and turned it over. "Look at the address: Number 4, apartment 1G, Heriot Row, it's yours, my girl. Deposit and a year of no mortgage payments, so you can, at last, put some of your teacher's salary into the bank and maybe save some money!"

Valerie was stunned, she kept staring at the shiny, red jewels on the little house as they winked beneath the lights of the room, almost hypnotising her as they danced and sparkled. "Sorry, Dad," she said and shook her head, "did you say Heriot Row, but I don't live there."

Graeme slapped Alexander on the back. "I think she's got Mairi's illness, she's caught the 'blonde' bug."

"You do live there now, or whenever you choose to move in," Alex said, nodding at her, hoping that an understanding of her actual present, was at last becoming clear.

Valerie stepped back and glanced at Lauren, then Mairi. "But, but, but."

Alexander started to worry. "Have I done the wrong thing, girl? I didn't think you were happy in that place you're at just now, I thought you wanted your own space. It's not too fancy, mind, just a small garden apartment. They said "Two bedrooms" but I don't know anyone that could sleep in the wee room. It's big enough, though, for a desk and computer," he prattled nervously and smiled sadly. He had always tried to understand Valerie, but perhaps she had needed the help of a woman this time, perhaps he wasn't the right person to have decided the gift she would like. So many doubts flooded his mind.

Valerie watched as her dad became despondent and launched herself into his massive frame, throwing her arms around his strong neck. "I love you, Dad, I love you," she sobbed. "Thank you, how can I ever pay you back for everything you've done for me, everything you gave up for me?"

Alexander began to relax and breathed in the sweet scent of his girl, the peaches fragrance she wore took him back to when she was a baby. He held her until her sobs died, then he gently placed her on the floor. "You owe me nothing, sweet girl, you have given me everything I have ever wished for…well, maybe not everything, there is that woman you work with…" he said with a wicked smile.

"Eww, Dad, that's just horrible." Valerie punched his arm, and laughed through her hiccupping sobs.

"And what did that dirty little mind of yours work out that I meant? I honestly worry about your perverted thoughts sometimes." He shrugged through his laughter, at his brothers. "What did I do wrong, lads?"

"Well, you two geniuses seem to have ruined the night by getting your daughters to cry, let's see if it's three for three, shall we?" Callum asked. "Okay, Lauren, I've got the tissues ready, start unwrapping."

Lauren glanced warily at her mom and dad and ripped open the large box and gazed down with disbelief at a Hassleblad camera. Her mouth fell open as she tipped and turned the beautiful machine in every direction. Her eyes wide with amazement, she gazed over at her parents. "You got me a Hassy?Are you serious?" she squeaked, really squeaked. "My own Hassy?"

"I take it you like it, kid?" Callum asked, his smile splitting his face in two. "You're now entitled to join the elite Hassleblad family and get all their secrets to helping you start that photography career you keep telling us you want to begin."

"But, Dad, it's an h4d-60, it has APL processing, medium format…"

Lauren was about to launch into the specifications of the camera when her mom put a stop to the technical data lecture. "Lauren!" she laughed. "Do you like your birthday present?"

Lauren's eyes narrowed quizzically. "MOM, DAD," she screamed and ran at them with her arms wide open. "It's too much, I can't believe you bought me a Hassy. Are you sure? OH MY GOD, I've got a Hassy!"

Lauren stopped suddenly, just before reaching her parents, and as though oblivious to the onlooking crowd, began to spin in circles with one arm flailing around as the other held onto her camera. When she became dizzy, she froze mid spin and carefully tied the camera around her neck.

That was when she joined her cousins, and burst into tears.

A loud cheer echoed throughout the room, members of her family stomped and clapped, then a spontaneous round of "Happy birthday to you" rang loud and true in her ears. The sound to many may have been like a herd of elephants honking, but to Lauren, it was heavenly.

"Well, Princess, are you happy?" Callum asked. "Did we do good, because you have certainly done us proud, my lovely girl?" Callum touched her face gently, then, with one finger, tilted her chin to see into her eyes. Lauren, too overcome with emotion, simply blinked. "Then what about blowing out the candles and let's have some cake, you know how the Parks can be when chocolate is just sitting around not being eaten." Callum screwed his face up in horror. "We don't want another scene like the last one," he paused, "that was awful, how embarrassing having to call the police to get your Great Aunty Claire away from the chocolate fountain!"

Lauren started laughing, her whole body shaking with delight. "Stop it, Dad, you're horrible, that's just not true. However, I'd hate to have to drag Mairi or Valerie away. Look at them, you'd think they'd never seen a chocolate cake before!"

"That does it!" Callum walked back to the table with the cake. "Ladies, it's time to make a wish, and have some cake. All you Parks remain on your seats…a slice will be brought to you."

Lauren giggled when the guests groaned.

Lauren, Valerie, and Mairi held hands and formed a circle around the small table. Callum, Alexander, and Graeme stood behind them, placing their hands on each daughter's shoulders.

Each girl had their own candle to extinguish. Cath lit one candle after the other, then turned to their guests, she nodded to them, and again, "Happy birthday" was sung. Lauren, Mairi, and Valerie watched each other and smiled a secret smile then, in unity, blew out the individual candles. Plumes of blue, green, and red smoke rose above the cake and danced exotically beneath the lights, sensually intertwining, before dissipating into nothingness.

An eerie silence filled the room, then one person stood, raising his glass to the heavens, and shouted, then another, and another. Lauren watched everyone joining in, as one clan, with a common goal, their shouts sounded more like a battle cry and were deafening. "Sinn coisich comhla ri aingeal," they roared.

Forcas watched the girls happily cram chocolate cake into their mouths, then he scanned the room, regarding their families circumspectly. They were aware of his presence, they knew what he was, and he was astonished to watch them retreating, all carefully guarding themselves against his inspection, and rapidly blending into the background.

To avoid any further investigation by him, they raised a hasty toast in the girls' honour. However, they were not quite quick enough for their collective cry to not have been understood by him. The double meaning all too prevalent, especially now. Their words echoing in his head as he moved his eyes, from one girl to the other, until his eyes found Lauren's, and she smiled at him, her eyes lighting up as he smiled in return.

Yes, he thought, *we walk with the Angels.*

Chapter Eight

"Would you care to dance with me, again, Lauren, or do you think your family would object?" Forcas asked. At the same time, he took Lauren by the hand, then he led her onto the dance floor, without giving her time or the opportunity to respond.

"I guess you've answered for me," she said, as his arm hugged her waist. "Careful of my camera!" Lauren gently moved it so that it hung down her back, the ties now placed at her throat.

"This camera, it is important to you?" he said, as he glided her towards a set of open windows leading to a balcony.

"I've always loved taking photographs, I've even done a couple of courses at college, my arts degree had modules in photography, but so far, I've not been able to really use it. Don't get me wrong, I get the occasional photographic assignment, but I want to be where the action is, right there, where things are happening." Lauren stopped and smiled wistfully. "Where are you taking me?"

"I will take you on a journey you will never forget, if you allow, but for now, I thought you might like to take in some air and look at the stars. I know I would like to see the Castle again, it's been a few centuries since I've seen it."

Lauren was surprised. "A few centuries? You've been here before, then, I mean to Edinburgh?"

"I have been here many times, just not for long periods. I arrived in the twelfth century as they were building the chapel in honour of your good Queen Margaret. When I came here in the ninth century, the Castle was merely stones, but a beginning was there, and when I came six million years ago, it was to witness your very own volcano erupt and then die."

"Holy hell, Forcas, you're as old as time," she exclaimed.

"Well, actually, Father Time is a lot older than me, but I am nearly the age he has reached, yes, so I think that makes me very old, doesn't it?"

Lauren saw the flicker of amusement cross his eyes. "You're teasing me, aren't you?" she asked, not sure if he was playing her false.

"And here we are," he said as he stepped onto the balcony and stared up at the Castle. "It is a magnificent piece of human work, guided, of course, by angels, or it would never have been built correctly."

Lauren shook her head and chuckled, doubting his word now. "If Angels were guiding them, why did it take five centuries, and probably more, to complete? I think you're joking with me, Forcas."

"I, perhaps, am teasing you, Lauren, it seems an appropriate night for some of that, do you not agree?"

Lauren glanced at the sky, the stars sprinkled across the dark blue canvas of the night. The Castle, towering above like a shadow against the night sky.

Forcas drank in the beauty that surrounded him and pulled Lauren into his arms. "I know not what you do to me, Lauren. I am unsure of this body, it reacts in a most unusual way whenever you are near me. I want to touch you, hold you against me, and feel your warmth penetrate my skin. I want to…" Forcas took Lauren's face in his hands, she closed her eyes in anticipation of the moment. He desperately fought his need to lower his face to hers but, eventually, could take no more. Admitting defeat, he brushed his lips against hers. He merely intended to simply taste her, but his lips seemed to have a mind of their own, and the gentle touch changed as his lips crushed against hers.

Stunned by the immense sensation he was experiencing, he suddenly pulled away from her, leaving her feeling bereft without the warmth of his body touching her. She kept her eyes closed, the heat of their kiss still on her lips, and tried to regain some control. She consciously tried to focus, positive that the world had tipped on its axis. He watched her, mesmerised, her lips still pouting and tingling from their kiss.

Forcas could stand it no more and roughly pulled her into his arms, then covered her mouth, grinding his lips upon her own welcoming lips. Her lips were soft and pliant, melding into his. As he tasted her sweetness, it reminded him of some forbidden fruit; he let his tongue delve into her mouth, brushing against her teeth, and the pleasure sent a tremor of desire throughout his body, pushing him to take more. He went further, taking possession of her sweet mouth, and she gave herself over to the mindless hunger that was building inside. He continued to move his lips upon hers, they were punishing, becoming more insistent, changing into a dance of burning promise with his tongue's probing exploration moving from gentle teasing to a luxuriant, frantic probing.

The soft teasing she returned sent his passion to run wild. He could not get enough of her, but knew he must temper his burning desire, and so he slowed the kiss, keeping her within the circle of his arms.

Lauren was lost, she had never been kissed quite so thoroughly in her life. He hadn't just kissed her, but had ravished her mouth. She kept her eyes closed, not wanting the moment to pass. She longed to remain in his embrace. "Forcas," she whispered, leaning away from him, seductively meeting his gaze, totally entranced by his beautiful face. "Can you do that again, please?"

Forcas threw his head back and laughed. "I fear I may never tread the streets of Heaven again, for you are a small, but immensely tempting, morsel of flesh!"

Lauren tried to move away from him, but his arms tightened around her. "I didn't say no, did I, Lauren? I just cannot believe how I am so easily tempted by you. I told you I have visited your earth on many occasions, in many different centuries, but I cannot understand why this body should act so peculiarly on this journey. Never before has my body reacted so strangely. It grows when it should remain still and sends bolts of desperate need throughout."

Lauren blushed. "Are you saying, erm, are you saying you are…well, that you have an erection?"

"An erection, that's it, I am like a pole! This is ridiculous, what is it you do to me that makes this body go like a pole?"

"Are you telling me you don't have sex in Heaven…or Hell?"

"We copulate, but not in the way your bodies join. We find your whole execution of the act, well, we find it simply…messy. We join quite satisfactorily, in both of the worlds, with a lot more sophistication."

Lauren tried desperately to contain her laughter, but deep inside, she was so proud of herself for being able to make an angel lose control. "I have no idea what it is I do to you—" She didn't get the opportunity to finish as Forcas again covered her lips with his.

His lips still covering hers, he spoke against her teeth, "You are like ambrosia, I need more of you." Groaning in surrender, his lips began to move, his tongue tasting her, and once again, her mouth was being crushed deliciously and thoroughly.

Holding her, he moved them steadily, so that she was backed against the balcony wall. He pulled her into his arms, and she gazed up, excitedly anticipating his next sensual move. He carefully adjusted the camera so that it no longer stuck into her lower back and shifted it, letting it hang to her side. He pushed a leg between her thighs, but the tight-fitting garment gave no leeway. He silently cursed but would not be deterred, placing a finger on the silky material at the juncture in her thighs. Running it seductively down her leg to her knee, the material loosened. He pushed his thigh forward, gaining better purchase as he grabbed her hips and pulled her towards his hardness. Lauren moaned, as she felt his body's desire against her stomach, her hands rested on his neck. Dreamily, she stroked him, her small hands sending shivers through his taut body, her fingers curled through his hair.

Her desire was reaching fever pitch, closing her eyes when the kiss changed and became even more demanding. He pushed her head backward, exposing her neck to him, and desperately, he placed ardent lips to the curve of her neck. Sucking softly, nibbling gently, he continued to kiss and taste her, working his way up the side of her neck until he reached the soft, sensual hollow, just below her ear. Her surrender almost complete, Lauren thought she had to be asleep, this was just as she had fantasised in her dreams. His kisses were setting her body aflame, and she could no longer contain her desire as her body began trembling.

Forcas was relishing the heat of the moment, his body's reaction to her, soft tremors sending a wave of tumultuous pleasure through him. Lost to his own fervent desire and to the new sensations he was experiencing, he was only aware of Lauren quivering in satisfaction against him.

She began to shimmer, her body glowing with an incandescent light. As he continued to nip and taste her, the intensity of her emotions began to have an unusual effect on her body, there was a subtle, but very definite transformation occurring.

Forcas felt the shift in her senses, and his tight hold on Lauren loosened as her body began disappearing beneath his hands. Alarmed, he quickly pulled away from her, just in time to watch her body gradually disintegrate into countless, tiny, sparkling particles. She desperately tried to open her eyes, panic crossing her face as she lashed out with hands turning into a ghostly transparency. Lauren frantically tried to grab on to him, but she was aware of not being able to hold him, and terror enveloped her.

"LAUREN, WAKE UP…COME BACK!" Forcas screamed in horror, "NO!!"

Then, just like that, Lauren was gone.

Chapter Nine

"Aaaaaagggggghhhhhhh!" Lauren's screams echoed in her head as she managed, at last, to open her eyes. Quaking inside with terror at what was happening to her, and shaking with fear, she glanced quickly at her surroundings.

Expecting to see, well, she was unsure of what she expected to see, however, what she definitely didn't expect to see, was… her house…with the door open. In fact, every door in the street was open, and the houses…they were all…clean.

Not that any house in Riselaw Road was dirty, they were lovely granite built houses, homes typical of areas in and around Edinburgh. They certainly were not made of a sandy-coloured stone that appeared to radiate a soft shine.

She observed everything around her, speculating that it was The Braids, Edinburgh.

And yet it wasn't.

And she had been here before.

The road's were not covered in black tar with the necessary, white road markings separating the carriageways and the, 'can't stop here, ever' double yellow kerbside lines were nowhere to be seen. Instead, the roads appeared to be made of a pale grey stone, and there were no road markings at all.

The gardens to each house she recognised as being mostly,

the same. Lovely Scots fir trees were planted in some, however, the grass seemed to be more luscious. The flowers in every garden exhibited magnificent riots of glorious colour, and surrounding her was a dazzling display of joy. She marveled at the explosions of bright, exciting hues, colours of blue that were more brilliant than a summer's day sky. Reds, oranges, violets, yellows, purples, all of which, were more vividly fascinating and exotically sensational than Lauren had ever seen in the street before.

Lauren knew they had not been there prior to the party.

Lauren was more than a little confused and a little scared. *No,* she thought, *I'm not a little scared, I'm terrified.*

She pinched herself, hoping to wake up, positive that she was in a dream. It had to be a dream because she knew this place from her dreams. As she nipped herself repeatedly, nothing changed.

Lauren wondered why it wasn't raining, or snowing, where was the wind? Why wasn't it freezing?

Lauren faced westwardly and raised her eyes to the skies, where there should be a blanket of stars, she stood below a blue sky and a warm, inviting sun. Turning to the South, the Pentland hills were in the distance, and at this time of year, they would normally have a light dusting of snow, instead, they carried the colours of summer and autumn heathers.

Above the hills, another sun shone down upon them.

Lauren then turned to face the East. From her bedroom window, she was able to view Arthur's Seat but on ground level, although the Braids was one of the highest points in Edinburgh, the sight was blocked by Edinburgh's skyline of houses. Yet today, she could see the dead volcano standing in all its green finery.

Above it, another sun shone down upon the sleeping lion.

At this time of year, and at this time of night…there shouldn't be one sun in the sky!

She reflected calmly, there wasn't one sun in the sky. No… there were three!

Lauren tried to regain some composure, believing it would be easier to ignore the impossible; by doing that, she might even be able to regain back some of the sanity she knew had definitely been lost when she fell asleep. She was asleep, wasn't she? *I'm not in Kansas anymore. I think this is real, I think I've been here before, but when? It all feels too real to be a dream, everything around me, the suns, the street, even the flowers, they are all so very familiar.*

Different strains of music were sounding from her neighbours' homes. Louis Armstrong could be clearly heard singing "Georgia" in Mr. and Mrs. Tennant's house. While across the street in Jimmy and Jessie Sullivan's home she could hear Pavarotti's incredible voice belting out "Nessun Dorma".

In the house at the end of her street, where the lovely Janet Ruby and Toni Marie lived, she could definitely hear Elvis. She was positive it was not a recorded version of one of his songs, but the King himself.

Above his velvet crooning of "Blue Suede Shoes" she could hear Toni and Janet's voices singing along. Another voice she recognised was someone clearly having fun with the girls, and Lauren knew this was the brother of one of her close friends. She could positively identify Simon Fisher's voice ringing out, "Uh huh, well, uh huh, ooh, Blue Suede shoes." Toni and Janet laughed hysterically, and she imagined Simon falling onto them, his body a shuddering mess of delight.

"Can you believe she called herself Moomy?" Toni yelled.

Simon's giggle could be heard echoing around the street. "Well, my Hazel's no better, have you seen her twitter name?"

Lauren heard more laughter, then a silent pause shortly before Janet asked,"What's a twitter?"

Lauren gave up listening when their riotous merriment overshadowed Elvis trying to sing.

She gave up trying to think logically.

She knew this was not Edinburgh, because her lovely friend Simon…was dead.

And yet she knew it was him, knew without a shadow of a doubt it was Simon, she would recognise his laughter and his sweet voice, anywhere.

A tear fell to her cheek, she could hear Simon…and he was happy.

Lauren continued to panic.

I have lost my mind, she thought and nipped her upper arm again, *because I can hear Donna Summer singing "Ooh, love to love you, baby"*.

She was alone, frightened, and confused. She was also singing along to Donna Summer!

Forcas was nowhere to be seen, the party had disappeared. Her parents, cousins, all the guests, where had they all gone?

No cars were in the street, and she heard more vibrant musical notes being sung from inside her home. *That's the Bee Gees*, she thought. *I know that song, Mom and Dad play that all the time. What's it called?* Her mind raced through the volumes of songs her parents played. *That's the one, "You win again". I think.*

Slowly, she opened the gate and walked along the path toward the house. Listening to the singing, wondering why her parents had left their ipod on, but the music sounded as though she was standing at a concert. The tones and melody were so realistic.

Walking into the house, she opened the living room door

and gasped, a terror gripping her heart. Sitting on her settee, three of the Gibb brothers were playing their guitars and singing another of their famous songs.

"Excuse me," she managed to stammer, "can you tell me how you got into my house, and what you're doing here?"

The Gibbs laughed as one of them, she thought it was Andy, sang a dud note, but nonetheless, they continued to play.

"I said excuse me," her voice raised above their notes.

"Did you hear that, Robin?" the Andy one asked.

"Yeah, bad acoustics in this place, let's go next door. We can jam with Elvis, if he's there."

"Man, I hope he is, it's a real bummer always missing out on playing with him. Spose, though, we could always find Roy and jam with him. Now we're talking a real legend."

"Are you seriously trying to tell me that you don't think Elvis is a legend?" The 'Andy' brother was horrified. "Of course not, he's defo a legend, but we just never get to jam enough with Elvis, if we hurry we might catch him. Think I can hear the last notes of 'Blue Hawaii' being sung."

The three brothers' Gibb stood lifting their guitars; they proceeded to walk straight past Lauren and out of her house.

"What the hell is going on here? Where the hell am I? Wait just now, did he say "jam with Elvis?" OH MY GOD, I'm DEAD! I knew it was the *real* Elvis singing with Simon. Great! Simon will be as chuffed to bits, but I'm dead too, and nobody's speaking to me."

Lauren slumped onto the settee, she was desperately trying to be brave, but the whole frightening experience was making her very weepy. That, together with a mixture of anger, resentment, and terror, and she was baking a massive emotional cake in her brain.

"Hello, Lauren," a soft, feminine voice said beside her.

"Oh, bloody hell!" Lauren jumped. "What a fright you gave me, I was lost in my own thoughts…wait a minute." Lauren paused, she was still scared, but she couldn't hide her curiosity, that outweighed her fear. "Who are you? Do you know where I am, I know this," she indicated the room, "looks like my house, but it's not really. Can you tell me where am I? Did I die? What's going on?"

"Hello, Lauren," she said again. "How are you?"

Lauren tipped her head sideways and raised an ironic eyebrow.

"Oh, I see, it's getting a bit much just now for you, isn't it? You don't have to answer that question, then." The lady smiled indulgently. "You seem a bit perturbed, would you like to walk with me a while and get yourself calm?"

"You know, lady," Lauren spoke slowly, hoping the woman wasn't addle brained and would understand the trauma she was experiencing, "I'm sure you're a very pleasant person, so don't take this the wrong way, but I am not in Edinburgh, or Scotland or my universe." She pulled her eyebrows down and pursed her lips. "I don't believe so, anyway. I don't know you, I don't know what's going on, and one thing's for sure, I certainly don't really think I want to walk in a fake Edinburgh with anyone." Lauren exhaled loudly. "You could be a mass murderer, for all I know!"

"Lauren, let me assure you, I am most certainly not a mass murderer, I am—"

Lauren interrupted, "And whose word do I have on that? Yours? I don't think so, *missy van hissy*. You appear out of fresh air, in my house, wearing nothing but a flimsy, white dress. You look very kind, but you are here, wherever here is. You're likely as dead as Elvis next door!"

The woman began to smile. "Oh yes, and smiling won't help!

I don't think I want to hear and see dead people, who, by the way, totally ignore me when I talk to them, and no, I don't think I want to 'get myself calm'!"

"Well, perhaps if you sat a while, we could talk and get to know one another?" She smiled again, a worried look crossing her beautiful eyes. "Come, Lauren, sit with me. I am not sure how long you have been here, do you know?"

"Well, I was sitting until you just appeared, frightening the life out of me. Now there's a stupid statement, *the life out of me*, I'm dead, so how can I have any life in me?" Lauren's bottom lip began to quiver, she had done so well to keep a grip of herself, but she could feel the torrent of emotion begin to overtake her senses. Deciding she had to sit before she fell, she moved to the settee and touched it carefully. The first time she sat on it, she was positive it had moved into her.

Cautiously, but in her own unladylike manner, Lauren sat down with a thump, expecting to hear the groan of old age the sofa usually made as she sat, and looking around to move the uncomfortable cushions her mom insisted on littering upon the settee, she was pleasantly surprised when the cushions puffed up around her; she felt as though she were sitting on a cloud. Lauren was noticing subtle differences within the room, when the cushions moved into her sides, forming a wall of feathery protection around her. "What the…what is going on with this settee, it normally creaks, and the cushions….it's as though they're alive! Oh my God!" Lauren jumped up quickly and fell into the woman's arms. "Please, tell me this isn't like one of those awful scary movies, when the house becomes alive and eats the people in it."

The woman chuckled, really chuckled, at Lauren's horror. "Oh, I'm so sorry, Lauren, I am not laughing at you, it's just funny to think of anything here, eating us." Then she guffawed!

"Well, holy hell, aren't you just having a great time at my expense?" Lauren said snottily.

"It appears that way, but it's not true. Please come, Lauren, let us walk outside. Isn't it lovely hearing music all around?"

"Actually, I prefer to hear it coming, either from a stage at Murrayfield, or out of my ipod, I'm not too over the moon at being able to stand beside Elvis and the Bee Gees!"

She pondered this statement for a moment. "Do you know why you're here, Lauren, or how long you have been here?"

"I've only been here for about half an hour, I think, not much longer, and no, one minute I'm on the balcony of the Balmoral hotel, kiss…em, being with someone. The earth moved in amazing ways and *poof*, I'm here in the land of the dead! So no, I have no idea, other than Forcas was teaching me about my Mistdreamer role recently."

"Have you not spoken more with Forcas about the expectations of you in your Mistdreamer role?" the woman asked.

"You know Forcas…who are you?" Lauren was surprised and suspicious, but then again, she wondered if this was another angel.

The woman let out a sigh. "I'm Linda, and I'm here to find out what you've discovered."

"L,L,Linda," Lauren stammered, "do I know you?" Lauren's voice wavered as she spoke, she already knew what the answer was going to be and didn't want to hear it.

"On the earthly plane, I would have been your aunt."

"B, b, but you're…you're dead! Oh, God, I knew it, I'm dead!!" Lauren threw herself on the settee and started sobbing. The settee began to cuddle into her, and this time, she wasn't afraid and, she took pleasure in the comfort it shared. "I know I sound pathetic, I know it's stupid…but I don't want to be dead,

I was having a good life." She turned angry, tearful eyes to Linda. "I was having a GREAT party!"

Linda sat beside here and cradled Lauren in her arms, stroking her hair gently. "Hush now, Lauren, of course you're not dead, if you were dead the Gibbs would have seen you. Do you think spirits, that is what you call those in this world isn't it, are rude? They can't see you because you still live on the earthly plane."

"Then how can you see me? You died twenty-one years ago."

"I did, Lauren, but…but that's a story for someone else… and for another day. What you are is a Mistdreamer, you know this, people who have crossed into this world will not be aware of you, and only a few chosen Angels will be able to see you," she said worriedly. "Mistdreamers who have moved into this plane will also recognise your aptitude but will leave you in peace to carry out your assignment, but you must be careful." Linda scanned cautiously around her, not wanting to say much more. "We are aware there is a traitor amongst either the Mistdreamers or the angels, but we have yet to discover who it is." Linda sighed before continuing, "Forcas was supposed to warn you and instruct you, where is he, did he tell you anything? This would all have been so much easier for you if he had tutored you correctly."

"Hold on a minute there, Linda," Lauren managed to squeak. "Assignment? What assignment, what are you talking about?"

"Oh, for the love of the almighty!" Linda exploded. "Has Forcas told you anything? Has he instructed you at all, or even given you an idea of what you are expected to do while you are here?"

"I only learned about being a Mistdreamer a few weeks ago, and since then, Forcas has been teaching me about quite a number of things." Lauren rolled her eyes upwardly. "Especially stones; Lord, it's so boring!"

"Lauren! Have you been paying attention to his instruction? He is a master in the discipline of the usage of precious stones, together with innumerable other assets he will guide you in."

"I know, I know, ethics, the virtues of herbs, and logic."

Linda smiled to herself. "I know it may have been a little tedious..."

"A LITTLE tedious, have you sat in the same room as that supercilious git when he's 'pronouncing the good and evil' between a sapphire and a ruby?" Lauren mimicked Forcas and trembled, with the memory of his kiss that popped into her mind.

Linda laughed. "I have, indeed, listened to Forcas teach." She was more than a little surprised at Lauren's attitude towards Forcas. "What is it about Forcas that sets you on edge? Why do you think he manages to get under your skin?"

Lauren turned a very pretty shade of red and stammered, "I, well, I don't want to listen to him talking about stones..."

"Ah, I understand." Linda nodded. "You have feelings for him?"

"I'm not sure about 'feelings', but I certainly want to explore his...." Lauren held her lips tightly together, afraid of what else she would blurt out. She had not intended to speak of Forcas in such a way, but Linda had drawn out a response from her easily. It was as if she weaved a spell around her, and Lauren was shocked at what she had nearly said.

"What are you?" Lauren asked, horrified by her loose tongue.

"I am a Guardian." Lauren opened her mouth to speak. "Before you ask, I am not a Guardian Angel, I am a Guardian of Mistdreamers, on the heavenly plane. I watch over the newly born who come here, and I guide them to Ambriel."

"Do you mean babies, or do you mean new Mistdreamers like myself?"

"I mean the newborns, you would call them babies. You have been a Mistdreamer for many years, Lauren. You have information that needs to be collected in order that our settled lives and the happiness in all the worlds continue to exist. Ambriel is the Angel of Communication, he registers the Mistdreamers and guides them from human understanding to acknowledge their transition into this world, aligning an appropriate angel guide to assist them on their new travels.... Normally, Mistdreamers would report to him any findings they discover on their assignments, and then he notifies Omniel. He does the best he can to assist wherever possible and, I add, normally, it would be he you would report to with any information you may have discovered."

"You keep saying 'normally', why is this different for me?"

"Because Ambriel has not registered you or your cousins in his Mistdreamer book. He has no knowledge of you."

"Forcas told us this." Lauren added, "Well, he actually was a bit cross with Mom and Dad, then he froze us...anyway, this Ambriel, the Angel of Communications, isn't too good on that part, is he? He seems to not have been 'communicating' too well with us Parks, has he?"

"That's as we wished, Lauren, we wanted the three of you to have a normal existence on earth, and I now believe we were a little hasty in making that decision. Nobody was to know what would happen if you went unregistered."

"What would happen? What are you talking about? This Ambriel, is he aware of us now? Does he even know I'm here?"

"I am most definitely aware of your presence in this world, Lauren." Lauren jumped at the sound of a deep voice coming from behind her.

"I have seen you on more than one occasion. The last time you 'popped in' was when I searched the register to see who you were, to investigate who you reported to, and when I could find no trace of you, I had to take matters further. Yet, I have not informed Omniel, but Paschar has been watching Forcas in the hope he informs you of the happenings on this plane. I take it that is why you have begun this assignment? Forcas has given you the details now?" Lauren was stunned, he had just appeared behind her, and then he had proceeded to inform her of people she had never heard about, assignments she had no knowledge of, and Forcas was being watched....She tried desperately to make sense of all his words, but was in complete shock.

Linda lowered her head, in deference to the senior angel.

Lauren watched Linda, noticing her bowing to him. "I don't know you from Adam, I don't know where I am. I've just met my 'dead' Aunty Linda, and now you're telling me you're Ambriel! Paschar, who's he, and Omniel?" Lauren was beginning to lose her temper, the fear and uncertainty was beginning to manifest through her anger. "Let me say this real slowly for you...WHO...ARE... YOU?"

Ambriel's long, dark, curly hair framed his face and fluttered in a soft breeze, billowing to reveal his handsome face. Lauren gasped when the Angel tugged on his strong, unshaven face, his startling blue eyes wide with astonishment. A grin spread across his ridiculously handsome face, revealing straight, perfect, white teeth. "Let me introduce myself to you properly, Lauren." He stepped toward her, holding his hand out. "I am Ambriel, the Angel of Communications, it is I who has made an egregious mistake that has allowed a family of Mistdreamers to go unprotected, or", he paused, "let me amend that statement, I *believed* they were unprotected." He continued, "I have had no knowledge of certain elements within the Park family, your branch, specifically, I should say is, until recent times, a family I have not known about, and, therefore, I was unable to register them. Because of this, I believe you now might be in danger." He lifted a hand, stopping her from speaking. "No, Lauren, please listen."

"Park family? But we're Chisholms, and what do you mean we're in danger?" Lauren said worriedly. "How are we in danger? We didn't even know we were Mistdreamers until Forcas told us a few weeks ago."

"So Forcas has met with you? Has he explained everything about the expectations we have of our Mistdreamers? Did he also manage to tell you what your assignment was this time? Who you were going to meet, and who will assist you?"

"This time? What are you talking about, this time, I haven't been here before!"

Ambriel fixed resolute eyes on Linda. "Have you managed to give her any information?"

"I was telling her some facts just before you arrived, but I was unsure of how much you wanted her to know. It must be said though, I don't really know very much either, do you want me to be aware of everything?"

Ambriel shook his head. "No, Linda, you have carried out what is expected of you, there is no point in putting you at risk as well. I have sent two now to protect both Valerie and Mairi, I only hope we are not too late."

Linda's eyes widened with panic when she heard Valerie's name, but she trusted Ambriel would put in place the appropriate action to ensure her daughter's safety.

A loud boom sounded outside the house, and Lauren jumped in surprise. "What on earth was that? Don't tell me you have thunderstorms here....By the way...where is here?"

Ambriel turned to Linda. "I believe that was Azrael, he is

bringing with him…" looking to Lauren, he lowered his eyes. "He will have an important soul with him. I would like you to go meet him as he enters, Linda."

Lauren's curiosity was tweaked, and she dearly wanted to know what was happening but assumed, with Ambriel issuing orders to her, that this was part of the care she gave to new Mistdreamers. "Is it a baby coming here, a new Mistdreamer, that you will have to take care of, Linda?"

Ambriel answered. "Not this time, Lauren, no, but someone who is a special…visitor, and a friend that Linda will speak with. Eventually, when Linda has resolved the situation, I am sure you will want to meet. In good time," he clasped his hands together and sighed, "but first, I would like the opportunity to speak with you, give me the chance to find out more of you and your cousins, would you?" His beautiful eyes pleaded with her to understand.

"I, sort of suppose so, but you are going to have to tell me what's going on and where I am. I take it this is Heaven, it must be if Donna Summer and the Bee Gees are here." She smiled a sad smile.

"Yes, it is one of the levels of Heaven as would be described in your world. Now, Linda, if you wouldn't mind seeing to our visitor, Lauren and I will have some time together, privately." Linda nodded once, and looking upwardly, she crossed her arms over her chest and dissolved into millions of tiny, bright stars.

"That is SO cool," Lauren said, impressed.

"As you cross dimensions, your transastralation is even brighter than Linda's."

"You mean, I do the millions of stars thing and then disappear?"

"Well, Lauren, I am fairly sure you do, or you wouldn't have reached this part of our universe, what do you think?"

"I think I am asleep, that I, perhaps, took drugs, and I'm having the most hallucinatory dream of all time, that's what I think!"

"And I think you are just a little afraid. That, perhaps, you are remembering another time?"

Lauren worried her lower lip with her teeth, she had already come to that conclusion and had attempted to convince herself that she was, indeed, imagining the memories that had begun flooding her senses. She wanted to be safe again, on earth, dancing, eating cake, laughing with her cousins. "Oh my God, my family, what will they be thinking?" She turned sad, worried eyes to Ambriel. "You have to let them know where I am, you have to help them!" she all but shouted at him.

"Tell me, Lauren, were you with Forcas shortly before you came here?" His innocent question was asked with just a bit too much smugness, Lauren thought.

"And if I was?" she dodged answering.

"Well, what I am going to ask is perhaps a little personal, I do not mean to be rude," he hastened to add, "and I am doing my best not to use the word 'but'...but what were you discussing with Forcas, just before you arrived here?"

"Well, you're the angel, why don't you tell ME what I was discussing?" she retorted. *Two can play this game*, she thought.

"But, Lauren, I am merely an angel, not the Almighty. We do have certain gifts, true, but we are not omnipotent. There is but one with the knowledge of all, and he uses his power selflessly, believing every being has the right to privacy...and to make their own mistakes?" He smiled as he added, "And what game would we two be playing?"

Lauren's hand flew to her mouth in shock. "You can read my mind?" Horrified, she tried, desperately, to eliminate any residual thoughts of Forcas, that may be lurking dangerously, in her mind! "Not fair, Ambriel, not fair at all!" she whined. "Are you going to tell me who this Azrael is, then?" she changed the subject, not wishing to discuss what had happened between Forcas and herself.

"Ah, Lauren, you are misdirecting me, I see where you are going. All right, Azrael is one of our four Angels of Death. He brings souls into this level."

Lauren caught her lip with her teeth, again. "Are you saying someone has just died, and this someone, I know?"

"Let us go back to the previous conversation, Lauren, and not worry overmuch about Azrael's work, what say you? Now, where were we?" Ambriel lifted his fingers and counted off one at a time, starting with his pinky. "You were with Forcas." He moved to his ring finger. Lauren was fascinated with his hands, his long, straight fingers, those of his right hand, each one bore a tattoo the whole length of the outer side of the finger, in what looked like a Celtic design. "You were alone with Forcas." He touched his middle finger. "Had you partaken in some alcohol?"

As he moved to his index finger, Lauren held his hand, indicating he should stop. "We were on the balcony of the hotel."

Ambriel was unsure he understood. "Hotel?"

"It's mine and my cousins' birthdays, we were celebrating in a hotel in Edinburgh. We had just opened our presents."

Lauren screamed, taking Ambriel by complete shock. He grabbed her. "What is wrong, Lauren, are you all right?"

Lauren held her neck and, still screaming, found the little bow she had made. Her hands went to her back, and she pulled forward her new camera. "My Hassy, it's here with me. How could I forget my Hassy?" She paused, looking upwards incredulously. "Oh, yes, that's right, there was the small reason of meeting the Bee Gees, hearing my friend and Elvis and, oh yes, being in a different Edinburgh. Do you get it, Ambriel? I have a camera in HEAVEN!"

Ambriel shook his head. "And this camera, what will you do with it?"

"Oh, dear Lord, what do you lot do up here? You don't have sex, you don't party and dance, and you don't know what cameras are, good grief, it must be a hell of an existence. Perpetually being good and doing nothing whatsoever. Don't you ever get bored with doing nothing?"

"Hell is an existence, but a totally different one from the one we experience, yes. Please, go back to the start of that sentence, Lauren."

Lauren turned a lovely shade of pink, almost the same shade as one of the flowers in the gardens outside her house. "Erm, which part of the sentence, I don't think I can remember all of it." She tried again to turn the conversation, "But don't you like my Hassy? It was a birthday gift from my mom and dad."

"It won't work this time, Lauren," Ambriel said seriously. "What did you mean by 'we don't have sex'?" He stared at Lauren, sudden realisation taking hold of him. "Please, tell me you and Forcas have not copulated?"

The pink blush Lauren had worn, was now a lovely shade of crimson.

"No," she said, turning away from Ambriel. She sat down on the settee, luxuriating in the safety the chair was providing. "We did not copulate. I hate that word, can't you say "sex"? It's not such a nasty word!"

"I trust you didn't have sex either," he bellowed.

"For goodness sake, keep your shirt on, Ambriel, we just kissed."

Ambriel sighed. "Oh, then, that's fine." He raised his eyebrows sardonically. "You merely kissed an angel. A fallen angel. An angel sent to keep you safe." With each sentence, Ambriel's voice grew louder until he was nearly shouting at Lauren. She knew she should be terrified of him, but instead, all she could think was, *I wonder when he'll turn into stars and puff into the air.*

Mid-rant Ambriel stopped and glared at her. "Puff into the air! I don't 'puff' anywhere!" he said solemnly.

"That is just so wrong," Lauren exclaimed, "you shouldn't be reading my thoughts!"

Ambriel had the decency to look contrite. "My apologies, Lauren, you are quite right. You should know, however, I can only 'read' a mind for short periods of time. Now, where were we?" He put his long index finger to his chin and looked to the ceiling. Right at that moment, Lauren could visualise the Angel, he looked just like a Da Vinci interpretation of one, minus the wings. At that thought, Ambriel let loose his wings.

Lauren had never seen anything so beautiful in all her life. As his wings stretched out from his shoulder blades, they almost reached the ceiling of the room. They were whiter than virgin snow. She had never heard any sound so sweet; as the feathers tickled each other, they tinkled and chimed like a billion crystal bells.

"You did it again, didn't you?" she laughed. "I'm sure that's a sin isn't it, pride?'

"I did listen, yes, but it's not pride. I wanted you to see for yourself, how an angel looks. This is our form, not the human body that Forcas has taken. He has wings also, has he shown them to you?"

"No," she shook her head, "he has never done anything to jeopardise himself, or me."

"You, of course, mean…apart from kissing you?" he was starting to become aggravated, again.

"Yes, apart from kissing me, and I believe that to have been the heat of the moment, perhaps the romance of the night and the beauty of Edinburgh all rolled into one. I doubt there was anything special in that kiss for him." *But there was for me,* she thought. Then gasped as she glanced to Ambriel. If he heard her thoughts, he said nothing; she prayed he hadn't been listening.

Ambriel began to withdraw his wings, their music warming the room as he folded them into his back. "I did not show you my wings to cause fear, just to let you see we are different."

"I don't think you needed to show me your wings to know that, though I'm grateful you did, mind you, as they're quite sensational. But I kinda figured out when I was a little girl that you were, well, that Forcas was, 'different.'"

Ambriel waited to hear what else Lauren knew. "Were you afraid of Forcas when he visited you?"

"Never, I was delighted he was there, I had to listen for years to my parents tell me he wasn't real, but he spoke to me and… and…"

"…and, Lauren?"

"I'm not sure."

"Come now, Lauren, you've gone this far, come, tell me what else Forcas did."

Lauren turned sharply at his words. "Are you trying to *blame* Forcas for something? You appear to be thinking he is the cause of some great problem in my life. Well, you couldn't be further from the truth. Had he not been in my life, I would never have had such happy thoughts, happy experiences, happy dreams… oh." She shook her head, memories flooding back, memories she had long since hidden, or deliberately forgotten, she was unsure which.

Lauren watched Ambriel's face change, gone was the worry and tenseness she had witnessed, in it's place, he smiled.

"I know you," she at last said. "I remember you, but you can't know me because I was invisible when I came here."

"When you came here," Ambriel gently prodded.

"Yes, when, I came here in my dreams."

"Lauren, do you remember what you did, or who you visited when you came here?"

"I'm not sure…I am remembering, but I need some time to think, I need to get my thoughts together and make sense of what I can see, of what I can feel, it's all jumbled up, like a jigsaw, you know the end result is there, but you have to put all the pieces together." She looked, with sadness tinged with hope, at Ambriel. "Do you understand what I'm talking about?"

"Lauren, I know exactly what you're talking about, and I have just the person who can help you decipher all these jumbled up thoughts."

Ambriel called out to the sky, speaking in a language unknown to man, and as ancient as time.

"Lauren, let me introduce you to Ramiel, the Angel of Thunder. He can interpret visions and assist you in understanding what is happening."

"Hello, Princess, it's been a long time. Welcome back."

Lauren looked up into the laughing, ice blue eyes of, her "favouritemost friend in the whole worlds", Ramiel, and knew she was definitely in Heaven.

Chapter Ten

"Wah-my-ell, wait for me, I've only got ditto legs, I can't bink dike you, pees vait."

Ramiel stopped and turned to watch the little girl, on her chubby legs, running towards him. Opening his arms, she ran straight into him with total trust. "Well, my princess, where have you come from?"

"I wuv you, Wah-my-ell," she said, putting her head onto his shoulder. *He smelled like toffee,* she thought and she loved that almost as much as she loved Ramiel.

"You have to go back, Princess, you're too little to be here."

Lauren's eyes filled with moisture, and one big tear fell onto his chest.

"Don't cry, my precious girl, you'll come back, you know you will."

"I know, Wah-my-ell, I de-mem-ba, but I'm a much bigga gel now, I'm a veh-way ka-wevah gel too, I nee-way out of dia-pas." Turning, she looked down at her padded bottom, which was sitting comfortably on Ramiel's arm; she nodded her head, her mass of soft brown curls bouncing madly, in all directions, as she enthusiastically bobbed her head. "See, nee-way there."

"You are the cleverest girl, Lauren, but you know what? I

think you should come back later, when you're just a little bit bigger. What do you say?"

Lauren pouted her lips. "You said dat de dast time, and I vaited and vaited and den I got bigga, and now I nee-way am fwee." She held up her chubby little hand and folded down two fingers, holding the folded fingers tightly, should they dare to pop back up.

"Lauren, do you remember the last time?" he asked. *It surely wasn't possible,* he thought.

"Of cose, I do, you snuggled me, dike dis." Lauren's eyes widened, and she shook her head from side to side. "But I was too ditto to move, and I was all wapped up in my blankie and you tissed my head and tissed my fingas. I was just a babee."

"Do you remember that, my lovely princess?"

Lauren's childish giggle sent a rush of love through his being, and he pulled her tighter into his arms, not wanting to let her go.

"Well, Lauren, it wasn't that long ago, and the next time you come, you won't be hurried away. Just wait, and you'll be back soon. You've got other friends, don't you?"

"I got Faw-cas, he sits on my bed, but mommy says he's not real…but he weally, weally is, Wah-my-el, coz he talls me his pah-win-sess too."

"And you are, my precious, you are our princess."

Lauren woke up with a start and sat straight up in bed. She reached out and turned the bedside lamp on but couldn't stop shivering. Her mind was playing tricks with her, dreaming was not supposed to be so realistic, yet she knew it was real, this wasn't a fantasy.

"Are you all right, Princess?"

Lauren was startled from her thoughts hearing the deep voice. Grabbing the covers on her bed, she pulled them up to her chin and stared at the chair in the corner of her bedroom, and the man sitting watching her worriedly.

"How did I get here? What happened?"

"I think this has been a day much too overwhelming for you, I'm aware of what happened between you and Forcas. Before I brought you here, Ambriel gave me some information. I believe he is going in search of our invisible friend, as we speak." Ramiel's lips turned up at the edges into a half smile, half leer. "That *incident,* together with finding yourself here, then you had a rush of memories, and I'm afraid…well, simply put, you fainted."

"Oh, God," Lauren moaned, "I acted like a right girl, didn't I?"

Ramiel laughed out loud. "If by that you mean, it all became a bit too much to handle, then yes, I'll accept that. In any of these circumstances, however, I believe any person, girl or boy, would have been more than overcome. If, though, you mean the sight of me made you pass out, then I think I'll have to work out why I make people faint." He wrinkled his nose and shrugged his shoulders. "I'm not that bad to look at, I don't have three heads. Well, not yet anyway."

"You're Ramiel, I know you, I remember." Lauren paused. "I'm not sure if I remember or if I'm just remembering dreams, I'm so confused."

"Hush, Princess, stop fretting, that's what I'm here for, to help you work out what happened in the past, and hopefully, we can find out who or what you might have seen. Please," he said gently, "let me help you. Tell me, did you have a dream just now?"

"Was it a dream, Ramiel, or was it a memory?"

Ramiel sat on the bed and gently touched her knee. "Why don't you tell me what happened, and we can work it out, together, what say you?"

Lauren held still, her head spinning, so many thoughts flooding her mind. Suddenly, she dropped the covers and threw herself into Ramiel's arms. "It's you," she cried. "I remember you, you were my friend, my best friend."

Ramiel stroked her hair, he cared deeply for her, loved her and protected her to his best ability. He had kept her safe and knew when she discovered the extent of what he had done, she would be unhappy, but for now, she had found him again. He swallowed and struggled with his composure but knew he was losing the battle when Lauren began to sob into his chest.

"Come, Lauren, why don't we take a walk, we can talk and enjoy each other's company. You can get me up-to-date with Forcas and what he's been up to, and then we can see about your assignments and what you remember, what say you?"

"I'm not sure I want to go out there again, it's strange seeing Edinburgh that isn't real. Why make Heaven like Edinburgh?"

"Well, why not? Do you never wonder when some people claim to have seen a spirit if, in actuality, they have. That somewhere, the veils that separate life from the beyond have opened a fraction, allowing some, with ability, the opportunity to witness what is beyond?"

"That doesn't really answer the question, why Edinburgh?"

"It is simple, you live in Edinburgh, should the veil open and you saw, Orlando, perhaps, you would not recognise anyone or the place you were viewing. This would be the same for someone in Paris, the veil would open and allow them to see into the Paris of the other world."

"Oh, that makes some sense, I suppose, I just thought there would be streets of gold, houses like diamonds, angelic, heavenly choirs, rivers of…well, you get the picture I assumed was heaven, I didn't expect it to be the Braids but without tarmac."

"Lauren," he persisted, "you are only on the fifth level of Heaven. There are four more tiers to this world, and, of course, it is the same in the kingdom of Hell. Five tiers, in reverse order to Heaven."

"I guess that sort of knocks it on the head for atheists and agnostics, it must blow their minds when they die and discover our earthly plane isn't the end."

Ramiel laughed. "How I've missed these discussions, you always had such a curious mind, always pushing boundaries."

Lauren's mouth fell open. "We've had discussions, you and I?"

Ramiel grimaced as he stood up and stepped away from the bed. "Perhaps, we will talk about this later. I don't want to rush you with too much information, but yes, we have had many discussions, and I have always enjoyed your wit and intellect. I look forward to showing you the answers to the questions you seek." He laughed again and added, "And as for the atheists, they find themselves happy to continue in the same vein as they had on earth. They would never be happy to know there is an almighty ruler, or something greater than humanity. And agnostics are just delighted to no longer be sitting on a fence."

Ramiel shook his head and chuckled as he walked to the bedroom door. "You know, you don't have to get out of bed and dress, why don't you try…now, what was it you used to call it?" He thought for a moment. "Oh, yes, '*blink*', why don't you think of yourself, clothed, downstairs standing beside me and '*blink*'. Then you will see what happens." He opened the door and started to leave when he turned to see her close her eyes. "I shall see you in a few seconds, Princess."

Lauren watched him leave, closing the door behind him. She felt happy, yes, there were other emotions running fast and hard through her head, ones that she would deal with, when she was with Ramiel, but for the moment, she was content. She had her friend back, and yes, she remembered him.

Now what was I to do, she thought. *'Blink', think of him downstairs, no jammies on, dressed and standing beside him and blink.*

Lauren pictured Ramiel standing at the front door, then she imagined herself removing her pink polka dot jammies and dressing in her light green, sleeveless, cotton dress, the one with the tiny yellow buttons on the bodice, then she imagined slipping on her white, canvas sandals and a lemon cardigan. *Now blink*, she thought. Lauren closed her eyes quickly, holding them shut for three seconds. When she opened them, she expected to see Ramiel, but was disappointed to see her wardrobe door wide open.

Looking down at herself, she saw she was still wearing her pyjama trousers, and now, she was also wearing a lemon cardigan. *Well, I almost did it, maybe a little push is what I need.* Lauren closed her eyes and let her mind work, colours swirled and circled around her as though she were in the centre of a spinning top. She nearly laughed aloud with the excitement she felt. She wanted to lift her arms and spin until she was sick with pleasure. Instead, she opened her eyes and found herself looking into Ramiel's handsome face. His smile was so wide, she giggled at his obvious surprise.

"You *blinked,*" he said.

"I *blinked,*" she replied and couldn't hide the wonder she was experiencing. "It was like magic, I couldn't do it the first time, but when I concentrated, I got caught up in the moment and watched as everything flew around me." She laughed joyfully. "It was so much fun." She grabbed Ramiel's hand. "I'm sorry to have taken so long, I was just enjoying it so much, it made me feel lightheaded."

"Are you happy, Lauren?" he asked softly.

"For the first time since I arrived here, yes, honestly." She stretched up and kissed him on the cheek. "You always make me feel happy, you always knew how to cheer me up."

Ramiel cleared his throat and opened the door. "Let's walk, Lauren," he said as he held his arm for her.

Lauren considered closing the door, but reckoned there wasn't much point, she didn't believe there would be many thieves in Heaven, and besides, her neighbours all had their doors wide open. Taking Ramiel's arm, she took her first steps out of her house since meeting Linda. It seemed like an eternity ago. "How long have I been here, Ramiel?"

"In earth time or in the other world time?"

Ramiel opened the gate and frowned as he saw the door to the house open. "You didn't want to lock your door?"

Lauren laughed. "I was just thinking that there is no point, how many thieves are likely to be in Heaven?"

Ramiel's concerned look surprised Lauren. "What is it? What are you going to tell me? Is this what Linda was talking about, the traitor you have amongst you?"

Ramiel nodded. "Yes, Linda is right, there is someone, or something, amongst us who is causing havoc, not only with this world but also with the one you have come from, and you are the key, Lauren, you are the one who can help us discover who it might be."

Lauren stopped in the middle of the street, waiting for Ramiel to close the gate, when she pushed past him and ran to the door of the house. Slamming it shut, she nodded and then returned to his side. "I haven't a clue how I'm going to get back in, as I don't have a key, but there's no point in taking chances, is there?" Grabbing his arm, she tugged, and they began walking east, Arthur's Seat looking very welcoming to her at that moment. "Come on, Ramiel, there's no point in dallying, we better get started on whatever it is we've to discover together."

Lauren could hear music coming from the houses as she walked along the street, a countless number of people long passed, and those not so long gone, rang loud and true from behind the walls of her neighbours' homes.

She heard the beautiful sounds from musicians she had once enjoyed listening to, often in the comfort of her bedroom. Certain melodies had been part of her youth, they had woven a musical tapestry for her throughout the years of her growing into adulthood.

On occasion, when hearing of the death of a musician, whose work was included in her tapestry, she often felt she had lost a good friend and was saddened by their departure. It was strange feeling such loss, especially when she didn't know the artist personally, but somehow, their music was part of the woman she became and, therefore, held a special meaning to her, and as such, she believed, on some level, she did know them.

But here, these gifted artists were alive, and their music was as rich and meaningful as it had always been.

"You know what I find peculiar, Ramiel?"

"Tell me, what would that be?" he asked, waiting to see what interesting response would be returned.

"Everyone is inside, and on such a beautiful day. The suns, now isn't that really odd, three suns are shining down upon us, yet nobody is walking here but us. And another thing, where are all the angels?"

Ramiel chuckled. "Lauren, they're not really inside. Some might be, but take a closer look around you. Really open your mind."

Lauren took another step, enjoying the warmth, taking

pleasure from being in Ramiel's company. She glanced at him, it was difficult not ogling him. He was as sinfully handsome as Forcas, his stunning blue eyes twinkled with amusement, and she blushed, readying herself to lower her eyes from her searching gaze of him, but not before she had the opportunity to look at his wide shoulders and broad chest. He wore a white V-necked T-shirt, that showed off his six pack, chest, and small waist. Curly blond hairs spilled over the top of the tee. His black trousers covered small hips, but the material was stretched tightly across his powerful thighs and calf muscles. His biceps, although bulged, were toned and were lightly kissed with a natural, golden tan.

His honey blond hair was shorter than Forcas's but was still long enough to reach his shoulders, and fell in soft waves. His jaw was strong and unshaven, his angular chin and high cheekbones only accentuated his slim face.

Lauren was aware he was watching her, and an unspoken question hung in the air. He was her friend, she remembered him, and she loved him because he was her friend, and as handsome as he was, he was not Forcas. *He is definitely drop-dead gorgeous*, she thought and laughed.

"If you've finished your inspection of me." Lauren gasped, caught out in her perusal, and turned from him. "Don't be like that, Princess, I have to speak with truth, however uncomfortable it makes you feel." He added with a smile, "And I must admit admiring how you have turned out, as well, but me, I always looked like this." He sensually caressed his hands over his body, giving her the opportunity to openly enjoy what she saw.

"It does not, however, make my ego any bigger to hear you laugh after espying myself. What was it you found so comical? Do I have a big bottom, or is there another feature of me you find amusing?" He smiled in bemusement.

Lauren was horrified. “I was not laughing at you, I was laughing at my feelings, if truth be told.”

“Princess, what feelings would they be, please remain open and honest with me, because by doing that we can venture into the puzzles inside your mind.”

“Well,” she said cautiously, “I was thinking how very handsome you are.”

Ramiel could not hide the eager smile that erupted across his face. “You think I’m handsome? I am in your debt.” He moved to her and held her hand, bringing it to his lips. Gazing deep into her hazel eyes, if she hadn’t been so acutely aware of him, she might have missed the trace of sadness that crossed his eyes.

“But what are you also not telling me, sweet Lauren?”

Her lips wavered, and she caught her lower lip in worry. “I was also thinking,” she eventually said, “that I love you.”

Ramiel frowned and pulled back from her. “This is true, you speak the truth to me?”

“I believe I have always loved you…as a friend, Ramiel. I was remembering how very important you are to me.”

“Come on, Lauren, waste no more time, tell me your thoughts. I will not be offended, it is enough that you love me, as I have you for a long time.”

Lauren rushed ahead with her next words, not wanting to hear any more of Ramiel’s declaration. “But I was thinking you weren’t Forcas.”

Ramiel sighed in relief. “This is good to hear. You feel you have bonded with him? You are aware of the differences that might hold you apart, I presume. Ambriel will definitely have ensured you would know them,” he said ironically.

“As I said to him, I am aware he is an angel, I have feelings for Forcas, yes, but they have not been explored, I just know that

I love being in his company. He annoys me to here and back, but he makes me laugh. He makes me feel whole…"

"…and you have fallen in love with our dark angel, have you not?"

"I don't know, Ramiel, you may be right, I am not sure, and for the time being, I think I have too much to consider before contemplating the depth of my feelings for him, don't you agree?"

Ramiel was unsure, but bowed his head in agreement. "It may well be you are correct at the moment, I am unsure of human love, but you are here to fulfil your Mistdreamer destiny, and I am here to ensure that happens and to make sure you are safe in the pursuit of your fatalistic journey." He glanced around him. "There is something here with us, I need you to concentrate and '*blink*', we must go."

Lauren stepped into his arms. "Concentrate, Lauren, we must move to Arthur's Seat, think of us there, NOW!" Lauren let her mind spin, and the colours revolve around her, yellows, purples, reds, and oranges moved as one, encircling her mind; drawing Ramiel into her thoughts, she blinked.

And when she opened her eyes, she and Ramiel were standing 823 feet above Edinburgh, right at the very top of Arthur's Seat. *Or the twin version of the hill,* she thought.

"Are you about to tell me there was evil beside us? Evil in Heaven?"

Ramiel shook his head. "I never said anything about evil being near." He winked. "Just to move quickly!" He laughed aloud, and Lauren crossed her arms over her chest and tapped her foot.

"You're playing with me, aren't you, Ramiel? Not nice, Mr. Angel, not nice at all!"

"Ah, my apologies, sweet Lauren. I did not feel like sharing you with anyone at that particular moment. And Kakabel can be a little distracting when he is seen."

"Kakabel? I take it, another angel? Why was I not able to see him, I thought as a Mistdreamer I was able to see angels?"

"You are quite right, yes, you can see all angels. Kakabel, who, by the way, is the Angel of the Moon, and has a tendency to, erm, distract those who see him."

"You mean he's another gorgeous angel, don't you?"

"I am very certain his looks outshine most angels, yes."

"So are you going to explain why I couldn't see him?"

"Sorry, I was getting around to explaining that, he was not yet in your presence. I could merely sense he was close, he had not as yet appeared, and I decided to get us away before your wits were taken away from you, making you unable to retain any information I want to instill within you."

Lauren grunted her disapproval. "I, Mr. Angel," she poked her finger into his chest, "am not a simpleton, and it doesn't matter how much he can 'outshine' angels, he would not have distracted me from what I need to learn, in order for me to get this supposed assignment over and done with and let me get back to my life."

Ramiel looked embarrassed. "My apologies again, Lauren, I should not have presumed to know your actions. Shall we go back, or shall we enjoy this moment and look beyond the Firth of Forth?" He pointed to his right.

Lauren gazed at her city, she was always amazed at how Edinburgh transformed under sunlight. It was a magnificent city, but with the sun shining, it was sensational.

"Let us sit, Lauren, and rest for a while, the day is perfect, is it not?" Ramiel held her hand and gently pulled her onto the warm grass. She sat for a few moments, waiting for him to give some kind of sign to show in which direction he intended leading the conversation. When he kept silent, she stretched out on the grass. With her head leaning on her arm, she turned on her side, so that she could have a good view of the city and beyond.

Aware that Ramiel remained silent beside her, she closed her eyes. Although there was a need for expediency, she did not see the harm in resting for a moment.

Purple mist surrounded her, the sun had disappeared, and she felt ice forming on the ground. She looked down, surprised to see she was no longer lying in the grass, but standing in a cave. The mist pulled at her senses, encouraging her to move. It flowed around her, touching her hair, her face, it felt like silk as it softly fluttered about her, stroking her arms, bonding with her. Vaporous fingers nudged her back, pushing her forward, urging her to give herself over and trust the coloured fog. It was promising safety and knowledge .

She allowed the mist to lead her forward, it encouraged her to properly witness her surroundings. She studied the walls, dark, cold, wet, coal-like stone, with irregular shapes, that had no sign of life, no light.

Had the mist not been near, she would have screamed in panic, but its reassuring presence calmed her. She moved with the mist when an opening came into sight, and it led her out into a dark corridor, lit with fire torches. The corridor was straight and long; with limited visibility, she could make out the shapes of doorways at equidistant points on both sides.

Walking stealthily, shivering quietly, from the cold and her own fear, she was unsure of what lay ahead. She stopped when the first scream tore into her body. Pain gripped her, and her legs folded; she hit the stone ground. Her breath left her body, and she grabbed her chest in abject terror. Her legs could not move; they felt as though a thousand needles were jabbing into them over and over again.

The mist covered her legs, and, withdrawing the pain, it forced her to stand.

The next scream made her blood freeze and her back go into spasms. It was a woman, and she was being tortured. Whatever pain was being inflicted upon her, Lauren was experiencing.

The screams were coming from the farthest away room, awareness that this was where the mist was going to lead her made her throw an arm out. She had to steady herself, her terror was coming in waves, and she stretched out her hand in order to lean against the cold, hard wall for support. The mist enclosed around her hand, preventing her from making contact, as she discovered the walls were burning hot coals.

When she stepped forward, one of the doors opened, and Lauren was stunned by the figure that emerged. A creature entered the corridor. Perhaps seven feet tall, with a grey, lizard-like body and tail, which appeared to be covered in scales. The beast wore a green, buttoned waistcoat, which Lauren thought was quite remarkable. She glanced up, and was shocked to see it had a human head with wild, long, shaggy, brown hair.

Its lips were stretched over silver, dagger-like teeth, his wide nose had flared nostrils, and eyes that burned a fiery red were searching all along the corridor, until they finally rested upon her.

She was petrified. The mist entered her mouth, taking away her breath and her ability to scream. Instead, she stood silently watching, waiting to see what fate would befall her.

The beast slowly turned from her, stalking in the other direction. Creepily, it advanced to the opposite end of the corridor, where it entered the room from which she had heard the agonising screams. When the door opened, the woman's suffering shattered Lauren's mind, and her quaking body fell in uncontrollable torment.

"Lauren, you are safe." She heard Ramiel's voice emerging through the mist. "Lauren, do you hear me?"

Lauren nodded her head, unable to speak, unable to breath.

"Where are you, Lauren?"

She opened her mouth, but nothing came forth. The mist encircled her, comforting her.

"Where are you, Lauren?"

"I'm, I'm in a corridor, there are caves everywhere, someone is screaming, she's being tortured. They're hurting her, I have to help her," she whispered.

"Lauren," she could hear the agitation in Ramiel's voice, "Lauren, you can't help her. You must be careful, you are too little to help her."

Lauren screwed her face up. "Little, what are you talking about? I'm twenty-one."

"Lauren," Ramiel begged, "look to yourself, look at your feet and hands, do it quickly," he urged, "do as I say."

Lauren lifted her hands and began examining them. She turned them palm upwards, then to the back of her hands, then palm upwards again. "What on earth is going on here?" she asked.

"Tell me, Lauren, how big are your hands?"

"They're tiny! They're the size of a five-year-old's hands, maybe a six-year-old, at the most," she laughed.

"Study all around you, Lauren, take mental notes of what you can see, and try to explain everything. The minutest of details could help, but be cautious."

"It's so cold here," she began, "and the monster has gone into the room where the woman is being hurt," she cried.

"The monster?" Ramiel asked. "Can you describe him?"

"He's huge, with a grey, lizard body and a human head, but he has red eyes." She shook with disgust at the memory.

"He is a demon minion of the first order," Ramiel said matter-of-factly. "They do not normally venture into the cavernis but are attached to Demon Kings."

A scream ripped through the caves, and Lauren hugged herself, grasping her stomach as agonising waves crushed into her belly. She held it tightly, in the hope she might retain the food she had eaten earlier. The pain moved from her stomach to her breasts. Something was twisting her skin, pulling it, grabbing. *No, not my skin, it's the woman in that room*, she thought.

"Lauren," Ramiel gently coaxed, "separate yourself from the torture, let us find out what is happening. Come, child. Do not be afraid, you will be safe." His voice surrounded her within the mist, it was as though he were a major element within the protective coloured fog that wrapped tightly around her.

Her mist, her Ramiel.

This magical mist encouraged her and gave her strength to, at least, try to glimpse inside the torture chamber.

Steadily, she put one foot in front of the other until she reached the chamber. Closing her eyes, unsure of what she would do next, but knowing she had to glimpse inside the room, she began to concentrate on what might be beyond the locked, heavy, steel door.

Her body began to shimmer as her thoughts focussed on the woman being tortured. Fear of what was happening to the woman, and her frustration at being unable to help, forced a deep reaction within her, causing her body to dissolve into tiny particles which then intermingled with the purple mist.

She floated in the mist, her body now free of its skeletal structure, and she inspected the door for an opening. Where the door met the cave wall, she manipulated her mist to drift through the slight opening. She was so absorbed in her action, she was surprised, when she eventually looked up, to find herself inside the cave.

She took her time assessing the room, it was not as dimly lit as the first cave she had found herself in, a fire torch hung on each of the walls. She stayed close to the floor, her mist hidden within the shadows, searching for the prisoner. The beast stood directly before her, blocking her vision, and she moved past him but could feel eyes watching her.

"She is here, I can sense her," a woman said.

From the corner opposite her, deep within the shadows, Lauren watched as a man slowly emerged. "I see nothing, where is she?"

Lauren stopped moving, trying to fuse her mist into the floor.

"She is here, I tell you!" the woman said, seconds before she let out a terrifying scream. Lauren floated upwardly, she had to find the cause of her pain. As she centred herself in the room, she noticed she was beside the Lizard beast, who was completely unaware of her. The man who had emerged from the shadows was desperately trying to see her, his eyes searching for her, but he, too, was oblivious to her presence.

Lauren gazed upon a four poster bed with a steel frame structure. Handcuffed to the bed, naked, with her legs splayed wide, was the woman she had heard screaming. Her long blonde hair was stuck, with sweat, to her face and head. Her blue eyes squinted as pain hit her again, and she screamed in agony as she threw her head back, slamming it into the wall.

The man stepped closer to the bed and grabbed her arm with his hand, his fingernails elongated into talons that bit into her skin, causing her to yell. Only this time, it sounded as if she was enjoying the pain he inflicted upon her.

"Again," she said hoarsely, "do it again, it helps."

Lauren was so confused. She floated nearer to get a better view.

"I see you." She froze when she heard the sinister whisper. "Mama, I can see my cousin."

Lauren slowly turned her head, her eyes searching for the person who had spoken, and for the first time since entering the room, became conscious of the small child standing to the right of the tortured woman.

"She's there, Papa, do you see her?"

"I see nothing, my young prince....Angela, do you see your niece?"

Chapter Eleven

"Where is she?" Callum grabbed Forcas by the collar and pushed him against the balcony wall. "Where the hell is my daughter?"

"Do you really believe, Callum, you should be manhandling me?" Forcas raised an eyebrow and stared into the frightened, worried eyes of Callum and chose not to react. Forcas wanted to kill and knew Callum Chisholm should not be the recipient of his dark thoughts.

Callum withdrew his hands from Forcas's jacket and ran his hands through his disheveled hair. "Forcas," his voice broke as he tried to form the correct words, "where is she, what happened to her?" Callum's ire increased. "What were you doing with her out here on the balcony?"

"What we were doing out here, together, is none of your business," he replied warily, but added, "I promise, I will find her, I know not where she is, but I have an idea of who may be able to help. Callum, do not lose hope, she will be safe, of that I'm certain."

"How can you be so certain when you don't know where she is?" he shouted.

"I witnessed her transastralising into another dimension."

"She has gone into Mistdreaming form, hasn't she? It's what Cathy and I have been trying for years to prevent."

"Why would you want to prevent the natural progress of her humanity?"

"Because it's time you Angels sorted out your own problems and stopped putting us into your petty fights."

Forcas stood tall, pulling his shoulders back, making his appearance even larger. "Our petty fights, as you so kindly put it, Callum, are often caused by humans. They are ended by us, but if they are not, then the whole of humanity is at risk of being exterminated." Forcas pressed his forefinger into Callum's chest. "You are well aware of this. You know of other civilisations that have been destroyed, simply because communication did not reach us in time. Perhaps, you should take some responsibility for the actions of your forefathers when they decided to wipe you from Ambriel's list. Perhaps, there would still be certain civilisations in existence if you had done your jobs as Mistdreamers instead of backing away from the true fight."

Callum was incensed. "The 'true' fight? What gives you the right to believe your disagreements are our responsibility? That whenever one of your angels falls off the wagon–so to speak–then it is our problem, and we, as Mistdreamers, are the ones who must discover the problem, then to cap it all, we have to report our findings, thus placing ourselves in even more danger."

Callum drew a breath, desperately attempting to cool his temper down. "Don't shake your head at me, you know it's true, you know you put us in mortal danger every time we do your spying for you, then our very existence is at risk when we have to report our findings. And it's simply because you lot won't talk to one another!"

"Do not dare to think you know what is right, Callum Chisholm. Your interpretation of a Mistdreamer's role in the protection of civilisations throughout the universes, makes them sound inconsequential, the risks taken by the first generations of Mistdreamers petty and immaterial.

Forcas was fuming, he ignored Callum's brothers, who now had rushed onto the balcony, their faces clearly displaying fear and concern.

"What the hell is going on?" Alexander said. Forcas ignored him and continued with his tirade.

"You demean your own kind with your words, simply because you chose the coward's option of taking no stand at all. Do not think to group Lauren or Mairi or Valerie into yours and that of your brothers' category. Your daughters will be the light that shines even brighter amongst Mistdreamers and," he prodded Callum's chest harder, "you have known this since their births." He said to Graeme and Alexander, "You three have always known your daughters were special, and you decided to hide them. You three are the ones who have endangered your own daughters, not the angels sworn to keep them safe. Yet again, Callum Chisholm, you prefer to ignore the truth, you choose to deny your own responsibilities and offload them onto the past generations, who bravely carried out the job asked of them, instead of hiding and letting others do their job for them."

Callum's hand fisted at his side, a red mist enveloped him as his anger exploded within, and before anyone could stop him, he punched Forcas on the nose. Alexander and Graeme jumped on him before he threw a second blow.

Forcas was stunned, blood gushed from his nose, and it was painful, he had never felt pain on the earth realm before. He held the bridge of his nose tightly with one hand, scrambling with the other to find something that would staunch the flow.

Alexander handed him a clean, white, laundered handkerchief. "You deserved that, Forcas," he said as he pushed the hanky onto his nose, then, grabbing his hair, he pulled

Forcas's head back. "Hold your head back for a minute, and press the hanky against your nose, that'll help stem the blood flow."

Coming to his senses, Forcas held the blood-soaked cloth to his nose, but instead of holding his head back, Callum watched as he shook it from side to side. "My thanks, Alexander," he said, handing back the freshly laundered handkerchief.

"Callum," he declared, "I will forego any punishment of you for that action. I believe you are under considerable stress because Lauren is following her Mistdreamer role, and now she finds herself walking in the other dimension. But I warn you, Callum Chisholm," he threatened dangerously, "you will never raise a hand against me again, the consequences, should you attempt this action, will lead you to a dimension you have only heard about in your nightmares."

Forcas stepped toward Callum, then Alexander and Graeme, protectively, moved in front of him, but Forcas raised his hands, and an invisible rope lifted them from the ground, carrying them over the balcony, suspending them above Waverley Station's glass roof. Alexander and Graeme struggled to free themselves of the unseen rope and desperately tried to hold on to something that would save them from falling to their deaths as they were held high above the ground.

Callum started towards his brothers but was halted in his tracks. Forcas glared with anger at him. "Do I make myself clear, Callum? Do we understand each other?"

Callum's eyes roamed to his brothers as they hung in the air, then he returned his gaze to Forcas and abruptly nodded his head. "I understand, everything," he said angrily. "You make all the rules and we obey, you should have considered using dogs instead of humans. I'm sure they're more obedient and easier to train. But then again, you can't bully them by using their family in a dangerous game, can you?"

"Your words should be carefully chosen, Callum. You have pushed me to the edge, and I am most concerned that you are able to continue in your role as Mistdreamer, perhaps this is a consideration that must be acted upon. Then Lauren would no longer be your concern, at all."

Callum was clearly terrified, his brothers no longer struggled but were listening to the power game Forcas was forcing upon him. Their years of carefully protecting the girls, hoping the Mistdreamer status would pass them by and the cocoon they had woven around their lives would remain in place. Callum felt utter despair; it looked as though their world was falling apart.

"Give me back my brothers and stop threatening their lives, it is beneath you, Forcas."

Alexander and Graeme stood beside Callum, and Alexander scratched his head, as he turned to him and said, "What're you talking about, Callum? How was he threatening us?"

Forcas held his nose as blood poured from it, then he raised his eyebrows. "You think I was threatening your brothers? In what way did I threaten them?"

"You held them over the balcony with some invisible rope and were going to drop them onto Waverley Station!"

Graeme touched Callum's hand. "I think you need to sit down, Cal, the beer's gone to your head. We've been standing beside you all the time. Forcas hasn't moved, apart from holding the hanky to his nose to stop the blood."

"You should not have punched me, Callum," Forcas began but was stopped when Callum interrupted.

"This is when you threaten me and warn me you'll send me to another dimension, take away my Mistdreamer ability, and take Lauren away from me, is that right?"

"I know not what you talk about, but this is when I apologise for my ranting. I do not withdraw all of my words, but those calling you and your brothers cowardly, I do. It was wrong of me to say such things...Wait." Forcas shifted his head and looked up and around him. "Are you saying it was I, who threatened your brothers?"

Callum quickly added, "And threatened to take Lauren from me, should I not follow your orders."

Forcas was shaking his head. "Why would I say such things, Callum? You have no orders, I cannot take Lauren from you. I can, however, put you in a dimension you might not enjoy." He added with a cynical smile, "But why would I choose to do that? Because you punched me? Do you not think I have experienced worse than a simple punch on the nose?" Forcas pointed at the bridge of his nose. "I think you can see it has been broken before."

Forcas let go of his nose. "Pray tell me, Callum, when did I pronounce all these threats?"

Callum rubbed his face and touched his forehead. "Right after you stopped your nose bleeding..."

"As you can see, my nose continues to bleed, a matter that concerns me, as this is a new experience on this realm for me. Please, tell me how I managed to stop the flow then, of my own volition, started it again?"

Callum wasn't entirely sure; he was losing all sense of perspective, reality was crumbling around him, and his mind didn't appear to be grasping the true facts. What was real and what wasn't, everything was now confused.

"Are you being honest with me, Forcas?" he asked. "Are you saying you didn't threaten me, or hang my brothers over the balcony?"

Exasperated, Forcas stepped toward Callum and held his

arm. "I give you my vow, it was not I who did these things. You were having a vision, a cruel one placed in your mind to cause as much disruption as possible. What I would like to know is how you managed to pull yourself from this illusion. What did you say or do, that brought you back to reality?"

Callum looked around him to his brothers, who were now watching him closely, concerned for him. "I'm not sure if I am back from the illusion, maybe I am still there, and this is not reality. And if I am within the illusion, perhaps that is where Lauren is and I can find her here?"

Alexander stepped nearer Callum and pulled his nipples. "How's that for reality? Did you feel that?"

Callum bent over, holding on to his nipples. "Ouch, you don't have to do that so hard; you're a sadistic bastard, Alex!"

"And you were roaming onto the fields of La La Land, with your 'is this reality' speech. There was only one way to prove this is real, so I did it."

"I get the picture." Callum covered his nipples, afraid of another 'grip' from Alexander. "If this isn't an illusion, then what happened?" He looked to Forcas. "You say I was having a vision, but it was you that was threatening me in my vision. Why would I think that?"

"I don't believe it was simply an illusion, or vision, I think something, or someone, is playing around with you." Forcas said concernedly, "I cannot stress strongly enough, again, that you will all have to be very careful for the next few weeks, keep a vigilant eye on Mairi and Valerie. The worlds are changing, the veils between our worlds appear to be shifting, and now that Lauren has gone to Mistdreamer, it could be that she is the key to solving this puzzle."

"Have you an idea who is playing with Callum's nerves?" Alexander asked.

“Yes, I think I have a very good idea but need to contact a friend to confirm my belief. This vision, together with the ‘presence’ you witnessed this evening, are very worrying.” He looked at the brothers before continuing, “I must go and speak with my friend. I will do my best to keep you as informed as is allowed.”

“What the hell do you mean by that?” Callum asked. “You’ll keep us informed up to a point, is that what you’re saying? What about Lauren, will you keep us informed about her?”

“Callum, you must understand that some things are outwith your understanding, and it is not permitted to share everything we know. I will do my best, I promise,” he said, holding a hand up, preventing any of them from asking more questions. “I will find out what I can, I will search for Lauren, and I will keep her safe. If she is with Ambriel just now, then she is safe. I promise to do my best.”

Callum was slightly placated by Forcas’s reassurances, but his unease at not knowing Lauren’s whereabouts, or the situation she was in, was driving him to distraction. That, together with the vision he had experienced, had Callum struggling for breath. Holding his chest as pains shot through his body, he turned pained, frightened eyes to his brothers.

Gasping for breath, he could feel himself losing his life force, and his existence was being drawn from his world.

Forcas grabbed Callum’s arm, jerking him violently, attempting to help him regain control of his body. Black spots appeared in Callum’s vision, and his eyes rolled to the back of his head when more pain gripped his failing body. He was aware of how easy it would be to give up, let go of life, and free himself of the pain.

“Callum!” screamed Alexander. “Callum, don’t do this to us, come back,” he continued yelling. “Callum, think of us, you can’t leave us! We're not the whole without you, you must stay until this problem is sorted." Then turning to Forcas, he shouted, "For God's sake, Forcas, you're a bloody angel, can't you help him?"

Cathy ran onto the balcony in time to watch her husband fall into Graeme's arms. "What's happening? Oh my God," she screamed. "Callum!" Moving quickly, she held Callum's head to her chest, allowing Graeme to hold the rest of his dying body. With tearful, pleading eyes she looked to Forcas. "Please, Forcas, I beg you, for the sake of our family and for all Mistdreamers, please do something to help my husband, don't let him die," she sobbed. "Not tonight, please, God, not tonight!"

Forcas hesitated, shaking his head. "I am but an angel, Cathy, I do not have the right to give life."

"You must be able to do something," she cried. "Don't let him go, not tonight, on their birthdays. Not when, wait," she looked around her, "where's Lauren, where is she? She needs to be here with her dad." She looked at Alexander. "Alex, please, go get Lauren, she needs to be here."

Alexander moved toward Cathy and gently took her hand in his. "Cathy, she's gone."

Cathy let out a pathetic cry of anguish. "Gone? Gone where? She has to be here, go find her!"

"No, Cathy," Alexander interrupted, "she's gone to Mistdreamer."

"What?" she screamed, then angrily, she turned to Forcas. "DO something, you can't take my daughter and my husband on the same day, haven't we done enough for you?"

Alexander and Graeme let out slight groans. "What?" Cathy asked. "What's wrong with me saying that? Surely, you agree, am I the only one who thinks it's time we had a break from Angel problems?"

Alexander put his finger to her lips. "Hush, Cathy, enough

has been said tonight of these thoughts. Callum has already made it known, quite verbosely about how we feel. Let it rest for the moment, and let us concentrate on helping Callum." A brief sob wrenched from his chest. "Or, if we can't help him, we make some peace with him. We need to call for an ambulance, quickly, and get him to hospital, where he'll be comfortable."

Cathy dropped Callum's head into Graeme's lap and lunged at Forcas. "You did this, you took him from me, you give him back to me, give him back, now. Don't let him die, Forcas." Large tears streamed down Cathy's face as she held onto Forcas's shirt.

Forcas could stand it no longer, he removed her from holding onto him and placed Cathy into Alexander's waiting arms. "Take her," he grunted. Then he took Callum from Graeme's arms and cradled him on his lap. Lowering his head, he breathed into Callum's mouth.

His breath was tinged with blue as it moved from his body into Callum's. A breath as cold as ice. Callum's body became rigid in his arms, his eyes remaining closed.

Cathy watched, her grief becoming inconsolable, and Alexander held her close, his senses pouring through her, comforting her as best was possible. She jerked from his arms and threw herself at Callum, screaming at Forcas. "You've killed him, you killed him, how could you do this?" Slapping Forcas across the face, she looked to her brothers-in-law, and shaking her head morosely, she spun and ran from the balcony.

"I think twice in one night is enough for me to be hit. I will tell you both now that Callum is not dead, but he neither is alive, it will be his will that brings him back, or takes him to the next world."

Graeme put fingers to Callum's throat, desperately trying to find a pulse. "It's true!" he exclaimed. "He's alive, we'd better get him to hospital. Where's the bloody ambulance?"

"Take him home," Forcas said. "There will be no need of hospital, the medical profession would stab him and try to find out why he still lives. I am sure it would not help him to be disturbed in such a fashion, he would be best served in his own home, surrounded by that which is familiar to him. It could prove more beneficial, if he cares to recover."

"When will we know if he's coming back to us?" Alexander asked.

"That, I cannot tell, I have given him breath to allow survival on this plane, whether he chooses to evict that breath, only time will tell," Forcas said sadly. "Take him home, keep him safe, and I will go and find Lauren."

Graeme gently lifted his brother. "What will we say to the guests?" he asked Alexander.

"I'll handle that, just get him home, the car's waiting outside the hotel, still. Thank heavens, we decided on keeping the limousines all evening. Best get him there, and I'll let people know the party has to end early. They'll understand, and if they don't then they shouldn't have been invited in the first place."

"What about Cathy, what do you want to do about her? Do you want me to go look for her when I've put Callum in the car?"

"She's maybe already waiting in one of the cars for us? What do you think, Forcas?"

"I think I am the last person she would wish to see at the moment, and I would like to go in search of Lauren, but if it is your will, I will look for Cathy and put her mind at ease, as best I can?"

Alexander considered what he said and, thinking about all else that needed dealing with, he told Forcas it would be for the best if Cathy was found. "She's bound to be in a worse state, she thinks Callum's dead, and she's run through the hotel in tears. Best you try and find her before you go for Lauren, and meanwhile, Graeme will take Callum home, and I'll get rid of the guests."

Forcas and Alexander helped Graeme carry the rigid Callum into the Beauly room. They were surprised to see only Mairi and Valerie waiting. "Where did everyone go?" asked Alexander.

Valerie stepped towards her father. "When we saw Aunty Cathy coming from the balcony, in tears, they all began leaving. We didn't want to go until we knew you were safe," she said, holding Mairi's arm.

"Is everything okay, Dad?" asked Mairi.

"Your uncle was dying, and Forcas gave him some chance of life, we won't know for sometime whether or not he wants to live."

The girls were shocked, their hands flew to their mouths, and their eyes watered with unshed tears.

"How can we help?" asked Valerie.

"For now, get home, and when we have any news we'll let you know."

Forcas drew Alexander's attention. "What?" he growled. "What's wrong?"

"I think the girls should remain in your company, and you should all go back to Callum and Cathy's home. It would be better, for the time being, that they are with you. Perhaps by remaining at Callum's side, by talking to him, they might be of help?"

Alexander realized it was nothing to do with helping Callum, although it couldn't hurt, but was everything to do with keeping the girls safe. Until they knew what this unseen enemy was that threatened their lives, it would be for the best, he decided.

"Erm, right, Forcas. You have a point." Looking at the girls, he asked, "Is that okay with you two?"

Mairi was first to step forward. "Definitely. Uncle Cal's always been there for us, now it's time to give a little back to him."

Valerie looked around her and screwed her eyes up as she searched for something. "Where's Lauren?" she asked. "Don't you think she should be here with her dad?"

"Yes," said Mairi, "what about Aunty Cathy, what will we do about her, she's awfully upset, should we go and find her?"

"There's no need," Graeme answered. "Forcas is going to look for Cathy, and then he'll search for Lauren."

"And where is she?" Valerie asked again.

"She has gone into Mistdreamer," Forcas answered. "Now, if you will excuse me," he said, as the girls mouths fell open in amazement, "we have a lot to do before this evening ends." Then he muttered, "And not all of it is going to be pleasant, in fact, I doubt any of it will be pleasant."

Glancing at Alexander and Graeme, he bid them good luck. "I hope that Callum chooses to remain on this plane, he is still needed here, and with Lauren now in Mistdreamer, she will need his love and support when she does come back." He then added, "I will, as I said, do my best to locate her. I have the ability to find missing objects, as yet, a missing object has not been a human, but there is so much at stake. We need to all be prepared."

"Whoa there, angel boy," Valerie said, "what do you mean 'prepared'? What must we be prepared for? Is the world coming to an end? Coz if so, I have a lot more to do in this life than be prepared for angel problems!"

Forcas's eyes narrowed. "You most definitely are your father's daughter!" Looking at Alexander, he added, "Mayhap you should have taught your daughter her mother's values, or did you forget she was part of this woman?"

"For the love of God," Graeme shouted, "could we, perhaps, have this discussion at another time. As much as I want to help, Callum isn't light, and if we don't get moving, it won't be a heart attack that kills him, it'll be me dropping him on his skull!" Nodding to Alexander and then Valerie, he added, "And, personally, I don't want that on my conscience, do you?"

"Sorry, Uncle Graeme, I just wish angel boy would stop being so bloody cryptic and speak in English, but you're right, let's move!"

Mairi whispered into Forcas's ear, "She's a bossy bissum when she starts, must be the teacher in her. I've never been bossy in my life!"

Forcas laughed, the first time since Lauren had transastralised. "I somehow think your father may disagree with you. Let us move and get on with this evening, and thank you, Mairi."

"No need to thank me, bud, just find my cousin, that's thanks enough. We'll work on Uncle Callum. And," she added, "I'm not falling for that line of bullshit; you want us all together for another reason. Yes, I'm sure Uncle Callum has something to do with it, but staying together keeps us all safe, doesn't it?"

"Yes, Mairi, you are right. Until we know what the danger is that faces all of you, then I think it best to remain close to each other."

"Lucky it's the holiday season then, and school's closed," Valerie interjected. "Mairi, grab a couple of those bottles, if we're going to do this tonight, we're going to do it with flare!"

Mairi chuckled and picked up three bottles of champagne.

"Here, your ladyship," she said, handing the bottles to Valerie. "Let's go and save the world." She laughed and walked to Valerie, sliding her arm into hers. "First I have to go to the loo, I'll see you out at the car."

"You need to see someone about your bladder," Valerie said. "You're always peeing!"

"I would rather you did not separate," Forcas reminded them.

"Forcas, I'm going there." Mairi pointed to the restrooms, which were situated in a small corridor ten feet from where they stood. "I will be two minutes. You can wait here for me, or go there." She pointed to the cars waiting outside the hotel. "I somehow doubt from there to the cars I'll get into much trouble?"

"I will wait for you here and watch Valerie exit the hotel," he said, crossing his arms over his chest.

"I swear, if you stand there like that, waiting for me, Forcas, I will never come out of the toilets." Mairi tried to hide her embarrassment. "I will not be long, I swear, haven't you to go and find Lauren?"

"I have, but I must find Cathy also." Forcas edged away from them. "You will be safe, I see Alexander returning for you. Will you both remain together?"

"I'm going to the car, Forcas, so I'll be with my uncle. Dad will wait for Mairi. So I'll be taken care of, it's Lauren you need to concentrate on finding; don't worry about us." Looking at Mairi, she smiled nervously. "Mairi," she said, "hurry, please."

"I promise, big cuz, but let me go or there will be a puddle on the floor!"

Forcas watched Mairi run into the restrooms. "You can go now," Valerie said. "Go find our big cousin, keep her safe and bring her back to us, Forcas. We'll both be okay."

"If you are sure." Forcas nodded to Alexander. "I must go now, Alexander. Take care of these ladies, I will find Lauren."

"What about finding Cathy? Where's Mairi?" he asked Valerie.

"Two guesses to your second question. As to the first, we thought Forcas should go search for Lauren, we can look out for Cathy. I bet she's waiting at home, if she is, we'll see her when we get there. Maybe, when she ran out of the party room she went to the restrooms?" She shrugged her shoulders. "It's a possibility, and if she's there, Mairi will bring her to the car. Either way, we'll find her, and it gives Forcas more time to get Lauren to safety."

"Good thinking, Batman." Alexander smiled and tousled Valerie's hair, as he had done all through her life. Then he turned to Forcas. "Go find Lauren, Forcas, we'll deal with Cathy, she'll need her family."

Forcas looked around him, then, lowering his head, he closed his eyes, and, wrapping his arms around his body,he disappeared.

"That was cool, Dad."

"Come on, Valerie, let's get you to the car. I'll wait for Mairi and watch you leave the hotel to make sure you're safe, we have so much work to do tonight," he said sadly. "We have to get your uncle to fight for his life."

Chapter Twelve

Cathy sat in one of the stalls in the restrooms, her arms wrapped around her body, holding herself tightly, hoping to chase away the fear that gripped her heart. She had watched Callum die, he had left her! He had promised never to do that, and Lauren was gone as well; she had left her, too.

She was alone.

Another wave of desperation swept over her, and a deluge of tears flooded down her face. Sobs racked her body as she wailed in grief. She knew she was being ridiculously selfish. "But I'm alone," she silently screamed.

"Hello?" a female voice called.

Cathy ignored her, she was too upset, she wanted to be alone, she *needed* to be alone. Gripping her arms even tighter, she slumped against the cold, tiled wall. Her scorched, tearstained face cooled as she lay pressed against the wall. The terror of her situation grabbed her again, the senselessness of her predicament. The years of untold loneliness facing her were too much to bear. How could she exist without Callum? He was her life. Her one true love.

"Hello?" the voice called again. "Are you okay, in there?"

Cathy wanted to laugh, it was a ridiculous question. How could she be all right? Surely the woman heard her crying? If she did, then she must know the answer to her question already!

"I'm sorry, what a stupid question," she said. "Of course, you're not all right, I can hear you crying. I mean, is there anything I can do for you?"

Cathy let out a loud laugh, mixed with sobs; it sounded like a croaking frog.

"Oh dear, have you got a cold? Let me get you a glass of water and maybe a paracetemol. Would that help?" she continued with her kindness.

"No, I don't have a cold," Cathy sobbed. Did she hear a relieved sigh coming from outside her stall?

"I'm sorry again, I thought I heard you cough?"

Cathy waited, if she didn't speak again, the stranger would leave her alone. Surely, she realized she wanted privacy, not some stranger asking questions.

"I don't mean to be impertinent," she insisted, "but I saw you running from the room in tears, and I was just concerned for your welfare."

Cathy's heart was breaking, but there was something in the way she was speaking. Something unusual in her choice of words. She tried to work through her haze of sorrow to sort out what it was she was hearing, but all that she could feel was the death of her husband. All that engulfed her was the emptiness of her future.

"Let me help you. I have been through sorrow myself, perhaps there is something I could do to ease your suffering."

"Unless you know how to bring someone back from the dead, then there's nothing you can do," Cathy tearfully shouted.

"Oh," the woman sighed, "I am so sorry to hear of your loss, was it someone very dear to you?" She was encouraging Cathy.

Cathy wiped tears from her face, rolled down the toilet

tissue, and blew her nose. "He was my husband," she said as another flood of tears shook her body.

'Did he die recently?" she asked.

Cathy screamed, her torment grabbing her heart. "He died tonight. Tonight, on my daughter's birthday."

"Please," the voice coaxed, "let me help you, I'm sure there's something I could do to ease your pain."

"Ease my pain!" Cathy said. "Unless you know of an angel that can bring the dead back to life, then there's nothing you can do to help me!"

Silence.

Cathy wondered why there was no reply.

Grateful that the woman had left, also a little embarrassed by her outburst, she wept again, leaning against the wall. Alone with her pain to sort out what she should do.

First, I need to find Lauren, she thought, *no, first, I need to get out of here and find Callum.*

"I'm sorry that I know of no angel that can bring dead people back to life."

She had returned.

"You're back," Cathy said. "I thought you had left."

"No, I never left, I have been pondering your situation. There must be another way I can aid you. I have certain…gifts."

"Oh, please don't tell me you're a psychic and you're going to communicate with my dead husband."

"I would tell you no such thing. Although such people do exist, it is probably too soon to communicate with your husband. No, I meant I might be able to soothe your pain. That is the gift of which I speak."

*I just keep making an arse of myse*lf, Cathy thought. *Hell I'm allowed to, I've just lost my husband.*

"To be honest, I think it's a little too soon to be soothing my pain. It's something we have to endure, isn't it? Grief, I mean."

"Most definitely, you have to work through the pain, but when this has only just happened tonight, the pain will be very raw, and I would imagine it is like an open wound just now. All I propose to do, is close the wound, for a time, so that it doesn't fester."

"Medical metaphors for grief, that's all I need," Cathy groaned.

"I am sorry for that," the woman replied. "I know of no other way in which to explain how I can help. If you choose not to accept my help, I understand completely, but as one woman to another, and I am a woman who has experienced what you are going through, well, let me say, if I'd had the opportunity for my pain to have been alleviated, I would have jumped at the chance. I would have wanted anyone to take away some of the pain I endured. Even if it was just for a little while."

Forgetting her own sorrow for the moment, Cathy's heart reached out to the other woman, realizing that she had been in Cathy's shoes. Something inside her broke, she couldn't refuse the help of someone who knew what she was going through. Yet, she still wasn't feeling comfortable enough to leave the safety of the cubicle.

"What can you do to help?" Cathy asked curiously.

"I call it 'rejoining', it's a case of facing reality." She hesitated. "I know your reality is very new, but perhaps now is the best time to face it. Then, I would get you to reconnect with the original pain, by that reconnection, I know you will be relieved of the trauma you are now experiencing."

Cathy considered this. "So you want me to relive the moment he died in order to have no grief? Sounds a bit wacky to me, and you say this works?"

"Actually," said the woman, "I know it works, I have seen it on several occasions." She continued, "I believe it would make you feel much better, even if only for a short while, surely it would be worth it?"

Cautiously, unsure of the stranger, Cathy asked, "How come you're here tonight? I'm not that lucky to have this kind of help when I need it the most."

"It just so happens, there is a psychology convention going on tonight, and I am one of the speakers at this meeting. We were in the room next to your daughter's party. Let me say, the laughter we heard this evening made us all want to join you instead of listening to boring old speeches from me and others on the 'intrusion of grief on the stable mind'!"

Cathy found herself smiling. "It was a good party," she remembered, "and then…" Her breaths began to come in short pants.

"Then your husband died? I am so sorry for the loss you feel. If you would like my help, just say, if not, then I'm afraid I must rejoin my fellow practitioners."

"I don't want to feel this pain," Cathy sobbed, "but I know I have to go through it. I don't want to, but I have to find my daughter."

"Your daughter?" the woman asked. "I thought you said she was at her birthday party?"

"It's a long story; she was, then she wasn't, and now I have to find her and tell her that her father died."

Cathy rested for a moment. The woman was promising her no pain, and without this pain she could, perhaps, tell Lauren what had happened this evening. She could tell her without the awful, emotional tidal wave that would go with her announcement.

"I think you might be right. Give me a moment, I would like to get rid of this pain, just until I tell her about her father."

"Take all the time you need, I'll wait for you here."

Cathy mopped up her face again, then tidied her hair, patting it into place as she stood. With a heavy heart, she exhaled deeply and unlocked the door to the stall. "All right," she said, "how do we do this 'rejoining' you say is going to take away my pain?" She smiled through her tears.

"Oh, that is so simple, dear Cathy," the woman said as she stuck the knife into Cathy's belly. "You just go and see him again."

Rachauden looked down upon the bleeding and dying, stabbed body of Cathy Chisholm and smiled. "You'll be with him in…" She looked at the clock on the wall and counted ten-seconds. "You're there now."

Chapter Thirteen

"Lauren, Lauren, wake up!" Ramiel shouted.

Lauren opened her eyes and sat up, with a start. "Oh my God!" she exclaimed. "Was that a goddam dream or was that reality?"

Ramiel took a quelling breath to relax his very frayed nerves. "What did you see, can you remember?" he asked.

"Remember?" she shouted. "Hell, I was there!"

"You were in Hell?"

"No, I mean…never mind, it's just a saying, Ramiel. I wasn't sure if it was real or if it was a dream." She turned and looked directly into the beautiful blue eyes of Ramiel, and nearly melted, until she remembered what had happened.

"I spoke to you! You answered me! You put me there, didn't you? You knew it was going to be dangerous, how could you do that to me?"

Ramiel sighed, he had known this time would eventually come, and in some small way he was glad that, at last, she realized the truth about him, not that she was yet aware of all that he had put her through, but she was making her own surmises about the events she had experienced.

That he had *made* her experience.

"So many questions, maybe we should start with an easy one, what say you?"

"Did you know it was going to be dangerous?"

"That's not really a very easy question, could we start with a different question, please?"

"Was it real? How's that for easy?"

"Yes, it was real," he replied.

"Was I in danger?"

"It depends upon what you saw, or whom you saw?" he answered warily.

"I spoke with you, were you there with me?"

"I was there in a form, yes, but I am unable to see what you can, I can only be of minimal support, unfortunately." He had the good grace to look down, now feeling very guilty.

"Lauren, can you remember anything of your dream? Let me help you interpret what it is you saw, and we can work from there to the next step."

"By next step, I take it you mean the next time I was here, because I know now I've been here a few times, the only problem is, I don't remember anything about them."

"And that is why I am here for you, to help you remember what you experienced, and when we know what you saw we, the angels, will figure out the best way to handle the problems you have come across."

"Where do I begin?"

"Why don't you start at where you found yourself, was it in your home?"

"You know that's not right, I spoke with you, you answered!"

"You described a lizard-shaped man."

"That's right, and you told me he was a demon. I followed him to where the woman was being hurt." Lauren began to panic.

"You're safe, Lauren, you're no longer there, you are here, in Edinburgh, on Arthur's seat, with me."

"Only it's NOT the real Edinburgh, is it?"

Ramiel lowered a quizzical brow. "Not the 'real' Edinburgh? Of course, it is, look around you!"

Sure enough, when Lauren looked, people were milling all around, some struggling to climb the hill, others jogging easily. *She could quite easily slap those people*, she thought.

"Let us return to your Mistdreaming adventure, Lauren. Did you follow the beast?"

Lauren replayed the scene in her mind, and panic again arose within her. Ramiel rested a hand upon her chest, speaking, as he did this, with a strange language. Within seconds, Lauren was totally relaxed.

"You did a 'Forcas' magic trick didn't you?"

Ramiel laughed. "Forcas does magic tricks, does he? I can't wait to see my old friend and find out what he's been showing you!"

"I just call them magic. I know they're some kind of Angel spell, but to me, they're magic."

"Who is to disagree with you, Lauren? There are many worlds in this universe, I know of several who, should mortals be aware, would call them the land of the Fae."

"Are you telling me that fairies exist? Aw, come on, Ramiel," she laughed.

"Such a closed mind, and I was hoping for greatness from you. Why do you think there are no other beings besides yourselves? It shows great arrogance to assume you solely live in this universe, or that you think there is only *one* universe."

"Maybe so, but Faeries?" She leaned her head sideways and looked heavenward. "I used to dream about faeries, I loved playing with them…."

Ramiel smiled. "So you have met the Tuatha Dé Danann in Mistdreamer, have you?"

“Are you serious?” she asked happily. “Really?”

Ramiel’s enigmatic smile was answer enough. “That is not really what we should be concentrating on, maybe later when we have worked out our little problem, we could return to find out when you visited Tír na nÔg and what you have been told by the Tuatha Dé Danann!”

Lauren was totally intrigued, the thought of mystical beings, magical sprites, and who knew what else she may have met, filled her with wonderment. The joy of exploring new worlds was a dream come true.

“Lauren, can we get back to what you saw in the Cavernis, please?”

“Oh, right, well, you heard me talking about the lizard man?”

“Yes, I explained he is a demon of the first order, normally found on level two.”

“The woman was screaming, she was in such pain, they were torturing her.” Lauren breathed deeply, slowing her unsteady pulse. “I followed the beast into the room where she was screaming, and there was a man, hidden from me in the corner, but he wasn’t hurting the woman, he was encouraging her.”

“I’m lost,” Ramiel said, confused. “Encouraging to do what, what was it you saw?”

“I’m trying to recall,” she snapped. “You have to remember, what I was witness to was seen through the eyes of a child, so my understanding will be that of a child, surely?”

“That would be right, Lauren, and that is what I am here for, to assist you in understanding those events in Mistdreaming.”

Lauren looked at him and made a face. “I think there’s more to what you’re saying, I might have believed you a few years ago, but after tonight, you’re not just helping me understand. It’s like you’re doing a report on me!”

Ramiel's exhaled breath was so soft she barely heard it, but she knew she had hit the right chord. She was spying for him.

"I need to know more of what you saw, Lauren. Can you help?"

"Be more truthful in future, Ramiel, maybe you wouldn't have pissed off so many Mistdreamers if you'd only told us the truth!"

"The truth!" he exclaimed. "What truth would that be? Would that be the truth you want to believe in or the actuality of the situation we are going to find ourselves in if I don't interpret these dreams correctly?"

"Keep your shirt on, Ramiel, remember it was me who was in danger, not you!"

"I have no intention of taking my shirt off, Lauren."

"Oh Lord, you angels, do you understand sarcasm, have fun, I know you don't have sex, but for goodness sake. 'Keep your shirt on' is an idiom, a phrase!"

"Lauren, I understand sarcasm, it serves no purpose, as to the '*no sex*' we will go back to *that* point in the future, as well! Please, continue with your Mistdreaming sight."

Lauren screwed her face up and frowned, then closed her eyes, trying hard to focus on the memory of her Mistdream. "He stood in the corner of the room and was whispering to the woman on the bed."

"She was on a bed, not tied to the walls, or chained?"

Lauren gasped in exasperation, "If you keep interrupting, we're never going to get through this," she moaned. "Yes, she was on the bed, but, hold on," she said, recollecting the image. "Yes, her hands were handcuffed, I think handcuffed, or maybe tied, to the bed, and she was wriggling all around the bed, moaning in pain. Then the man, who was hiding, stepped forward and…"

"Yes, Lauren, he stepped forward and did what?"

"He lengthened a talon and cut her, he made her bleed, then he cut her again."

"Torture by knife, it's a common way of extrapolating information."

"No, you don't understand, Ramiel!" Lauren screeched. "She was *enjoying* the pain. She asked him to do it again, I don't think he wanted to, he hesitated and asked her if she was sure about wanting more before he cut her again. Then she laughed and begged for more."

"What? She was wanting pain? Did you see anything else?"

"When she was hurt, she started screaming that someone was there, that *I* was there and could he not see me, that's when…Oh my God!"

"What Lauren, that's when what? What happened?" Ramiel asked worriedly.

"That's when the little boy said he could see me."

Ramiel jumped up, fear coursing through his body. "Oh no, please tell me it isn't so." He began walking in circles. "The child could see you? He was aware of you?"

"The man asked if he could see his cousin, then asked the woman if she could see her niece. It was my Aunty Angela on the bed, and the boy was her son. The man called him his 'little prince'!"

Ramiel pulled Lauren to her feet. "We must go and find Ambriel, he must hear this immediately." She dropped her hands as he pulled away from her and stood. He began walking in circles, running his hands through his hair. "No, wait, maybe we should speak to someone else, before talking with Ambriel." He muttered as he walked and frantically pulled at his hair.

Lauren watched with disbelief, an angel panicking was quite an impressive sight, but perhaps not one that filled her with confidence. After all, he was the one who was supposed to be making sense of her experiences, and here he was rambling on about what should be done, as though he had no clue of what she had gone through!

"Erm, Ramiel, could you maybe share with me some of your thoughts? Maybe, tell me what's going on?"

Ramiel stopped his pacing and looked at her. "What's going on? Lauren, I am honestly not sure, I have a feeling of dread, and I am not sure who to trust with the information I have just received from you. I am trying to make sense of it, that is what I do, but I don't want to believe the conclusions I have come to; it would be too alarming to believe them."

"Alarming? Dread? What can't you understand? What did I see that has you so worried, Ramiel?"

"From what I can perceive, you witnessed a family, a child and his parents."

"Yes, that's what I thought, my concern is that one of the parents is my aunty, my cousin Mairi's mom, in fact." She turned startled eyes to Ramiel. "That can't be, surely, that can't be? She walked out on Mairi when she was only a little baby. Oh, dear God," she said, finally realizing the awful situation she had come upon. "Oh, please tell me it can't be true, Angela is alive and living in Hell and has a child?"

Ramiel dropped his head into his hands. "I think that is the case, I believe your conclusions match that of mine. I need to know, Lauren, did you get a chance to see what the man looked like?"

Lauren shook her head. "I was too engrossed with the woman on the bed, and when the little boy said he could see me, I panicked. I was so frightened, and then you were waking me, pulling me from the scene, so I didn't see anything other than the markings on his fingers and the fact his talons grew at will."

"Can you remember the markings, anything at all, Lauren?"

"I'm so sorry, Ramiel, no, nothing," she said despondently.

"Lauren, I have to ask you, I apologise in advance, but would you be able to go into Mistdreamer again?"

"I want to, for you, Ramiel, but I'm exhausted, and I don't know what good it would do you if I go there again and come back with even less information than I've given you this time." She pleaded with him, "Can I have a rest? Then, I promise to go back again."

"I am just grateful, Princess, that you are willing to venture there again after your last trip. You must have been very frightened then, you were only six years old." Taking her hand, they began to walk along the path leading them away from Arthur's Seat. "Let us return to your home, and we shall take you back to Mistdreamer later, and perhaps, get a better understanding of what has happened."

"Do you need to tell Ambriel the things I saw?"

"I do, but first I must speak with some friends and ask them if they can help in working out who you met. I don't want to lead you back to Mistdreaming without some indication of who it might be. At least we have an idea of one you might meet again… Angela." He frowned.

"And the little boy, I think you're forgetting him. Angela was aware of my presence but couldn't see me; her little boy, that's a different story, he could see me!"

"You have made a good point there, Lauren. Would you like to *blink* or are you happier taking in this lovely air and walking some time with me?"

"Walking sounds just fine, I need to clear my head. I have to try to work out for myself," she held a hand up to stop him speaking, "I need to, Ramiel, make sense of this, you have to understand, this is my family. I don't know the impact this might have on Mairi, she will be so hurt at this, she already believes her mother abandoned her. Thank heavens my mom is safe with my dad. I don't know what I'd do if it was different."

"Of that, I must agree with you, Lauren, but I doubt the heavens have much to do with your parents' safety." He smiled. "Let us walk, Princess. I think you are right, this lovely air will clear our heads and maybe prepare us for the next task."

Lauren worried her lip and held on to Ramiel's arm as they meandered down the hill. The breathtaking beauty of Edinburgh and the peacefulness of their present situation, together with having to concentrate where to place her feet as she walked, was silently seeping through her pores and relaxing her taught muscles. Looking at the centuries old buildings across the landscape, she knew if they could endure the Edinburgh weather, then it was possible for her to cope with more of Ramiel's requests.

Surely, it won't be as daunting as my last Mistdreaming walk, she thought.

"You are worried, Lauren?" Ramiel eventually asked.

"I can't say I'm not. I'm hoping I'll be as brave as the Edinburgh buildings and cope with whatever it is you are hoping I've seen."

"Edinburgh buildings, Lauren, are inanimate objects, and I believe they were built this way to withstand the bitter wind that can blow through the city. You, on the other hand, are a very precious person, and one we cannot afford to lose. That is why I must confer with friends before I ask you to go on another mission, I do not want to put your life in any more danger than it is now."

"You believe I'm in danger?"

"I think you have been in danger since you were born, when your parents decided to omit your names from Ambriel's list, yes. We have done our best in trying to protect you but I believe you and your Mistdreaming cousins have encountered an evil, one which we have been unaware, and by doing so, you are all in danger."

Ramiel took a few moments; he needed to say the next few words carefully. "I have always believed you, Mairi, and Valerie to be the 'chosen' Mistdreamers, and that your task would ultimately save our worlds. I did not dream your entirety would be put at risk. Your cousins will have to be placed with someone very capable, and they will have to be removed from the earth's plane to somewhere safe."

Lauren stopped walking and released herself from his arm. "What are you talking about? Move them where? Will I ever see them again?"

"I am just speculating, it is not imperative at the moment, and it will be dependent upon what we discover from your Mistdreaming, so let us not worry overmuch about it at the moment." He returned her arm through his and continued walking down the hill. "Come, Lauren, we must get you home. Perhaps, now is the time for us to *blink*? Yes?"

Before she had the opportunity to agree, Lauren found herself back in her bed, wearing her soft, fleecy jammies. Sighing with exhaustion, and delighted to be in a warm, safe place, she curled up under the fluffy duvet. She closed her eyes, wishing everything she had experienced was a dream, hoping all around her was unreal, but she knew better, and her mind would not allow reality to become illusion. Exhaustion eventually prevailed. No purple haze came to collect her, only a feeling of immense sadness washed over her, just before she fell into a deep slumber.

Ramiel watched Lauren as she slept, her thick, long, dark eyelashes resting above her cheekbones. She slept now as she had done in childhood, with one hand under her face, and the other fisted as though ready to strike, lying beside her on the pillow next to her face. She was beautiful. She was brave and strong.

She was his daughter.

"She can never know," Ambriel said from behind him.

Without turning, and continuing to look upon Lauren, he replied, "I am more aware of that fact than anybody and need no reminder of my duty."

"So long as you *do* remember!" Ambriel added.

Ramiel turned and moved towards Ambriel. "And what of your duty?"

"Need I remind you, this whole *situation* need not have happened had you done your job in the first instance!"

"Oh, I will admit we, as guardians of Mistdreamers, got it wrong. We should have been more watchful, but," Ramiel poked Ambriel in the chest, "whose idea was it, in the first place, to *use* humans in aiding our war?" Fury was erupting within Ramiel's chest. "Who was it that put them in this perilous state?"

Ambriel grabbed Ramiel's finger. "I am well aware of the situation the Mistdreamers are in, but the decision to have them support us was not a sole decision. The Council of Angels required assistance, we could not have managed to prevent the second war without their aid." Ambriel shook his head. "But we could not have predicted the recent turn of events." He emphasized, "*I* could not have predicted them. However, I might have been able to prevent the catastrophe, had I known of this family of Parks." Now Ambriel was poking Ramiel, "Whose decision was it to hide this family from me? Perhaps, if you had been more prudent in your observations, this whole mess could have been avoided."

"Who is blaming whom, for what?" a thunderous voice bellowed at them.

"Forcas, you have decided to make yourself seen. Maybe you could inform me of what has been happening in Lauren's life."

"I should kill you, Ambriel, you have endangered her family, all of them. You must have been aware of the veils of time opening. Why did you not protect them?"

"Are you seriously threatening me, Forcas? You, who should have remained in the lower planes? You, who have merged with demons and evil alike, yet here you deign to tell me – me – that I have erred in my job, when it is you and Ramiel who have been remiss in your duties!"

Ambriel waved his arm, and Forcas found himself inside a cage. "You, Forcas, you and your band of Infidelibus are the ones who have endangered these girls, not I. I have not known about them!"

Ramiel's eyes widened. "You are aware of the Infidelibus?"

"Of course, we are aware. Paschar and I have been watching the comings and goings of you all for a millenia."

"Omniel, is he, too, aware of us?"

Ambriel hesitated. "Of that I am not sure, if he knows, then it is not through any report I or Paschar have made to him. We chose to let your little band work together and hoped that you were working to assist the mortals. It does not appear to have been that way, or am I mistaken?"

Forcas rattled the bars of the cage. "Let me out, now, I have much to tell you."

Ambriel watched Forcas. "I think not, Forcas, when your temper cools might be when I release you, until then, you can remain behind those bars."

"Let me out, I say! I have to be with Lauren. I have to tell her what has happened."

"I think telling her about her father can wait," said Ambriel.

"Her father, I have taken care of that, it is her mother she must hear about."

"There is nothing written about her mother," Ramiel interrupted, "she is safe with Callum for as long as he lives. Their ring of safety was guaranteed by the Council."

"Yes…for as long as Callum lived," said Forcas.

"Oh, dear God," cried Ramiel, "was it he that Azrael brought over? If so, you must let Forcas return, Ambriel, he has to protect Cathy, or let me go, in his stead, to aid her."

Ambriel shook his head, first at Forcas, then at Ramiel. "You should never have 'helped' Cathy at all! That was never your place, we have already decided upon who will support her in the next months. She needs a strong angel to help her come to terms with her grief in losing Callum. He will make sure she is safe until we know what is happening."

"Do you know who the Council has decided upon?" Ramiel asked.

"One of your cohorts, Appoloin."

"Appoloin?" Ramiel held his breath, this was not the name he had expected to hear. "Why have you chosen him?"

"Not that I need to share with you our reasons, but in this instance, you may have some rights to understand our decision. We believe Appoloin is too close to the demonic world and hope by granting this mission to him, it might pull him to safety and away from the dark. You must agree, every being is entitled to second chances."

"Sometimes third and fourth," Forcas echoed out loud what Ramiel was thinking.

"I seem to recall you, Forcas, being given exactly the same opportunity we are bestowing upon Appoloin, and you, Ramiel, you also were given a chance to show the Council that you could perform the tasks given. One of them, was to show us that you could protect a human in your care." Glancing down at Lauren, he added, "Unfortunately, you went a little too far and created this beautiful person."

Forcas was stunned. "You, Ramiel, you fathered Lauren, does Callum know?"

Ramiel stared at his friend. "No, he does not, and neither should you have been told." Looking at Ambriel, he added, "What were you thinking? Or was it always your intention to tell Forcas, perhaps, you should just make a universal announcement and tell all. And, after telling me to remember *my* duties!"

"I cannot believe you would commit such an act of betrayal, Ramiel. How could you do this to Callum?" Forcas was still dumbfounded.

"Do not presume to pass judgement on me, or Cathy. She, too, is unaware of my involvement in the conception of Lauren, she believes it to be Callum, and that is the way it will remain."

"You took her without her knowledge, what the hell are you, have you been replaced by a Demon King?" Forcas shouted.

"Of course, I didn't," Ramiel screamed back. "Cathy was unable to conceive and was desperate for a child, I merely aided her conception."

Ambriel watched the two friends yell at each other, amazed by the passion they were inciting from one another. He could perhaps understand Ramiel's concern in the involvement of Lauren's birth, but Forcas's overreaction was stimulatingly interesting.

He smiled.

"What do you think is so funny, you idiot, get me out of this bloody cage!" Forcas yelled at Ambriel.

"You have found love, Forcas," Ambriel replied simply.

"Well, it had better not be with my daughter!" answered Ramiel.

"Where's your daughter?" asked Lauren.

All three angels groaned.

Resting his hand upon her eyes, Ramiel whispered, "Sleep, Lauren, hush, child, you will not remember."

Lauren's eyes closed, and she whispered, "I will not remember, must sleep."

"I think we should continue this conversation in another area, it will not be good for Lauren to learn of this just yet."

"Just yet?" Ambriel said. "You do mean *ever,* don't you, Ramiel?"

"Have you ever thought, Ambriel, that perhaps if we had been more honest with the mortals, and with Mistdreamers in particular, we may not have had the discontentment from them to begin with?"

"I have thought that for many years, yes, but that has nothing to do with the biology of procreation!"

"Would you, please, let me out of this cage?" Forcas yelled.

"Yell once more, and wake Lauren up again, and I'll send you, in the cage, all the way to the third sector of the universe!"

"You wouldn't dare," Forcas whispered.

"Would I not?" Ambriel hissed. "Just try it again, and let's see how fast you get back. Even with your ability to jump through space and time, it will take years to get here."

Ambriel lifted his arms, his hands facing upwards, elbows into his side as though in worship, then, with his eyes closed, he brought his hands together.

"The veil is closed," he said, "we can talk freely."

Ramiel cast his eyes around, they were in the second level of the heavens. Peace and harmony surrounded them, angelic choirs could be heard at a distance, and their presence could not be detected by any but the almighty.

They stood in a seventy-foot, circular room, which had a

thick marble floor. The walls appeared to be a blue sky with white, fluffy clouds, whereas the ceiling had the illusion of a dark night with millions of bright, tiny stars strewn across a black canvas brightly illuminating the room.

"What have you learned, Forcas?" Ambriel asked.

"I should strangle you for putting me in that cage. Why give us wings just to clip them at your whim?"

"I doubt *clipping your wings*, as you so graciously say, when you want to kill one of us, is done on a *whim*. You needed to regain control of your emotions, that was the only reason I curbed your freedom, no other."

"I am unsure of whom to trust, Ambriel, I know not that I can even trust you. I have been close with my Infidelibus brothers and would like to inform them of my findings before I come to you with my conclusions. I would like them to help analyse my understandings."

Ambriel nodded. "And you, Ramiel, what have you discovered?"

"Like my brother Forcas, I, too, wish to go to the Infidelibus and pray for their guidance in making sense of what I have been informed. We mean no disrespect to you, Ambriel," he added quickly. "We have, as you informed me, been together for a millenia. As a group, we have relied upon each other, not only for our lives, but with secrets that have gone no further than our small group. I would wish for their perspective before I make any formal assumptions that would be put to you."

Ambriel stroked his chin as though in deep thought. "You both trust those members of your Infidelibus group, that much?"

Both Ramiel and Forcas agreed without hesitation. "We were falsely under the misunderstanding that you were unaware of our group. It seems we have a lot more to discuss, when next we meet."

"Then I suggest you arrange to meet soon. Time has shifted, and the veils between all of our worlds are opening. We endanger more than simply mortals by having these veils open. You must speak with Kakabel, he will have some idea of why the constellations are realigning. He is, after all, the angel in charge of this."

"The last time we met, he was very defensive, he believes someone, or something, has managed to disrupt the veils without his knowledge," said Ramiel.

"Then we really have a more serious problem than was originally indicated." Ambriel continued, "I must have some form of report as soon as you have discussed within your group. I hope at some point we, as angels, will once again trust one another."

"That will only happen," said Forcas, "when we discover who the traitor is amongst us; until then, I will trust none other than my Infidelibus brothers."

"And what will you say, should one of those, whom you trust so dearly, be the traitor?" asked Ambriel.

"I will say nothing," Forcas said somberly. "I will kill him."

Chapter Fourteen

Appoloin waited in the main hallway of the Balmoral hotel, he had seen Forcas with the Chisholm brothers, as they carried the body of Callum from the hotel, before he went in search of Cathy. He was being entrusted by Ambriel to guard the woman and took this responsibility very seriously. It had been a thousand years since Ambriel or the Council of Angels had placed him on a mission, and he looked forward to proving himself, once more, to them.

He could smell something. He began sniffing the air around him, not able to define exactly the constituency of the smell. Sniffing again, he faced the direction from where he could ascertain the smell was emanating, and he began to move in that direction.

Just before he reached the area from where he could smell a pungent aroma, a door opened, and a smiling Rachauden, demon second class, of the first order, emerged.

"Well," said Appoloin, "who do we have here, and what, pray tell, has you looking like the proverbial cat who has eaten the canary? What are you so pleased about? Nothing good, I am fairly sure about that."

Rachauden cursed, she had been so excited and pleased with her kill, she had forgotten to conceal herself.

"It is none of your business what I am doing here, Appoloin, go find yourself another playmate. I am sure there is one waiting your company on the fifth level."

Appoloin grabbed his chest, as though struck with a sharp pain. "You wound me, Rachauden, does this mean I can no longer play with *you*? Have you ended our fun just when I was about to hear you scream my name?"

"I would never scream your name in anything other than disgust, don't fool yourself, you weren't that good!" she spat.

"Not good? Again, why do you insist on inflicting such pain on me?" He asked sarcastically, "Is it because there were so many others between your legs before me that you can evaluate my prowess so easily? No, wait," he laughed "there had been nobody between those legs before me, so I'm guessing there has been a few since?"

Rachauden threw her hand to his face, but he caught it easily before it made any contact. "Ah ah ah, Rachauden, showing your temper will not help your cause in aspiring to be the lead demon, will it?"

"You are an imbecile, Appoloin, you always were, nothing will change, but I will make you pay for what you have done to me."

"Done to you!" Appoloin was incensed, "Don't make me laugh, it was something we did together, to my deep regret and embarrassment."

Appoloin caught the drift of the pungent smell coming from behind the closed door Rachauden had exited. Narrowing his eyes, his demeanour changed as he grabbed her arm. "What have you done?" he yelled.

"I sorted out a problem. No," she added, "I ended a problem, and now we can get on with our plan."

"Your plan, what plan would that be, world domination, greed beyond greed? Or simply pain for the fun of it?"

Rachauden's eyes widened. "Pain for the fun of it, now there's a wonderful thought." She rubbed against his groin. "What about we practice together and see what comes," she giggled, "or not."

Appoloin pushed her away from him in disgust. Revolted that he had ever wanted to be with her and horrified that his body still responded to her insinuations.

"It won't work this time, Rachauden," he snarled, "get in there, and let's see what you have done."

Pushing the door wide, he pulled Rachauden with him as he entered the restrooms. As he stepped into the main restroom area, he looked down at what was causing his foot to stick to the floor and saw the bright red marks he had left underfoot.

"What the hell?" he said, baffled. Then his eyes followed the red snaking river as it spiralled towards a pool that gathered beneath the lifeless body belonging to Cathy.

He grabbed Rachauden around the throat. "What have you done? What have you done?" he screamed.

Rachauden let out a choked, ecstatic laugh.

Appoloin saw the red on the floor and Cathy's still body, and then the red consumed him. He held onto Rachauden's neck and squeezed it until her eyes began to bulge. The colour was draining from her face, and it changed to a mottled purple as she desperately gasped for breath. The more she choked, the harder he squeezed. Her hands flew to his face, clawing, scratching; her talons elongated, they sliced into his skin, leaving deep welts.

He ignored the gouging of his face, accepting the pain as punishment for being too late to save his charge. "You thought you could live, didn't you?"

Fear crossed Rachauden's face.

"You thought because you were a demon, you would not die,

but, you stupid bitch, you are in human form, on their plane. You *can* die." Appoloin lifted his head to an unseen moon, keeping his one hand tightly held around her neck, he pushed his other hand into her chest, ripping through layers of skin, sinew, muscle, and bone until he found her beating heart.

Clamping his hand around her heart, he pulled and crushed it from her chest, and held it before her dying eyes so she could see her own end.

He stared at her bulbous, unbelieving eyes as the light began to leave her body. "You *can* die and now you *will*."

Appoloin dropped her like the garbage she was onto the floor and lifted Cathy; he had to call upon Azrael. Tenderly cradling her against his massive chest, he settled the dead weight gently. He spun carefully around and stepped onto the lifeless form of Rachauden, a last defiant insult. Preparing to leave the room, he heard sniffling coming from the furthest away stall.

"Who's there?" he asked. "Come out and show yourself, or I will come in and get you."

"I'm sorry," Mairi sobbed, "please don't hurt me."

"Come out and let me see you." Appoloin cursed, he had not realized someone else had been in the restrooms.

Mairi cautiously opened the stall door and stepped out. "I, I, I didn't see her," she stammered, her petrified eyes unable to look away from the woman lying in his arms. "I was in too much of a hurry to get in and then leave." Lips quivering, she forced her horrified, blue eyes to look up at Appoloin. "And then I heard the door open and voices, yours, I think, and someone else."

"What was it you thought you heard?" he asked.

"At first, I thought it was a lover's quarrel, and I didn't want to leave the stall and interrupt and then, and then," she began sobbing.

"Go on, what did you hear?" Appoloin urged.

"I'm not saying," she screamed. "I just want to go home, I want my aunt, give me my aunt!" She began frantically pulling Cathy from his arms, but he tightened his hold around her body.

Appoloin froze. "Your aunt?" He watched as she grabbed at him furiously. Terror having taken control, hysteria now her elemental force. Her eyes glazed over, grief and sadness breaking through her fear and, exhausted, she crumpled to the floor. "You killed my aunty, how could you kill Aunty Cathy? What did she ever do to you?"

Appoloin was taken aback, first by her attack, and then her words struck home. "Wait just now, little one, you think I killed Catherine?"

"Didn't you, isn't that what I heard? You said she was a demon." Hysteria was again building inside of Mairi. "She wasn't a demon, how could you think that of her?"

"I am not sure you should see this," he said doubtfully, "it is not a pretty sight."

"And you think the bloodstained body of my aunt is? You are an evil pig!"

"That is not what I meant." He blew out an exasperated breath. "There is another body on the floor, and you are in too overwrought a condition to witness the state it is in." He remained before Mairi, blocking the sight of Rachauden from her. "But this thing on the floor is the one that murdered your aunt."

Mairi began to push Appoloin to the side, trying to get a glimpse of what lay on the floor, but he remained solidly in front of her. "Let me see," she insisted. "If you don't then I will not believe you, I'll always think it was you who killed her."

"Are you sure you will be able to cope, you are very traumatized just now?"

"Move!" she shouted.

"If you are certain," he said and slowly moved to let her see the corpse.

Blood was sprayed over the walls. Mairi's mind began to wander, her eyes flickering, her head began to spin, and she knew she was about to faint. "You killed her," she gasped. "She killed Cathy? Why?"

Appoloin watched the colour drain from Mairi's face, aware that she was seconds from passing out. "Azrael," he yelled, "Azrael, hear me now!"

"You called," drawled Azrael, the first angel of death. The tall, dark angel looked every bit as frightening as those on earth believed him, with his long, dark brown hair hanging in waves to just above his waist, and his black, brooding eyes, which were heavily fringed with thick eyelashes, always had a look of cynicism about them.

His high cheekbones and straight nose highlighted an angular, narrow face, and now, he had chosen to sport a small mustache and goatee, adding more mystery to his ridiculously handsome face. As with all angels of death, his wings were magnificent and always on display. The soft, black feathers would wrap around those he carried, keeping them secure and protected until they reached their destination.

Appoloin watched as Mairi fell onto the floor in a dead faint.

"Azrael," he said solemnly, "I hold in my arms our beloved sister, Catherine Chisholm. Please take her home. I would have journeyed with you, but I think I should tend to this little one first. I wish to make certain she is returned safely to her family."

Gently, he placed Cathy into Azrael's waiting arms. "This has surprised me," Azrael said, confused."I did not expect this one's death tonight, I had been informed of another to collect, but he appears to be still in this plane. This is sorrowful news." Azrael shook his head sadly. "Rest assured, Appoloin, I will care for her and make sure she awakens without fear, when she is home."

"I think more is going on this eve than we are aware," Azrael said as he glanced around to see Rachauden on the floor. "How will you dispose of that one?" he asked.

Appoloin shrugged. "She should become one with the surroundings she has died in, and will not reach either Heaven nor Hell as her death leaves her neither human nor demon. She is nothing but part of this building, until they destroy this place."

"As it should be, so shall it be." Azrael blew his breath all around Rachauden, and as it covered her body, she turned to sand.

"I wish you well. Take care of the little one, I do not wish to collect her before her time is due."

Azrael spread his wings and then wrapped them around both himself and Cathy, enclosing her in their warm splendour, shrouding and obliterating her from the death scenes.

"Safe journey, Cathy," Appoloin prayed, as Azrael lifted his head to a ceiling that was not made of bricks and mortar but was one that displayed all the worlds in the universes. Azrael cradled his precious cargo and flew high into the sky before rapidly disappearing as though a black hole had opened and sucked him inside.

Appoloin watched as the universes re-formed to become the ceiling of the restrooms in the Balmoral hotel, then, turning to face the door, he bent down and lifted Mairi into his arms, then exited the restrooms.

Alexander tapped his foot and looked again at his watch, wondering what could be causing Mairi to take so long in the restrooms. *I hope she's not being sick, she didn't drink too much tonight,* he thought, and just as the thought entered his mind, he saw a man-mountain exit the ladies' room, carrying a woman. *Another one with a wee bit too much to drink,* he laughed silently to himself, until he took a closer look.

"Would you like to tell me where you're going with my niece?" Alexander asked Appoloin.

"You can prove you are related to this girl?" Appoloin asked.

"I'm not sure how I can prove it, would my driver license do?" he said sarcastically. "In any event, I think you should hand her over to me. This should have been the best evening of her life, and now, I believe it has turned into the worst. Who are you, and what are you doing carrying Mairi?"

"Mairi?"

"Yes, Mairi Chisholm, my niece, now hand her over!"

Appoloin smiled sadly. "You are the brother of Graeme and Callum, this is so, is it not?"

Alexander narrowed his eyes and lowered an eyebrow in query. "You know that because…?"

Appoloin looked around him as people walked in and out of rooms; the noise from the bars below suddenly seemed very loud. "Perhaps here is not the best place for us to discuss this. Do you have somewhere else we can speak? There is much you need to be told."

"Em, buddy, I ain't going anywhere with you until, A – you tell me why you're holding my niece, and even more importantly, B – who are you?

"I am Appoloin, Angel of Destruction."

Alexander groaned, "Not another bloody angel!"

Appoloin was roughly the same height as Alexander, and his chest was as wide. Where Alexander was dark, Appoloin was blond.

"I saw Forcas with your brothers, exiting this building. You are a Mistdreamer, you should only be visiting with him on another plane, not on this one."

"I'm not visiting with any angels, he's been here for weeks, *visiting* with my brother Callum and his wife, Cathy. He's been teaching their daughter, Lauren, how to fulfil her Mistdreaming destiny. Something, I may add, that we did not want for any of our daughters!"

"Forcas? You say Forcas has made himself known to all of you?" Appoloin frowned then asked, "He found his charge then? Where is he?" *At last I can find out what Forcas has discovered.* A little help would be a definite bonus.

"He's gone in search of Lauren. If that's who his *charge* is, she disappeared from the balcony."

"I do not understand your words, and I must ask again if we could discuss this in another area. Your niece, although very beautiful, is beginning, strangely, to become heavy in my arms. This is an unusual occurrence for me, it could be your atmosphere, but I feel I must lay her down before I drop her!"

"Geez Louise, where do you guys learn to speak English? You're an angel not *Superman*." Then, looking at Mairi lying in his arms, he asked, "Can you carry her to the car?" Alexander watched Appoloin, as the question appeared to be misunderstood, he continued, "Oh, come on, they don't know about cars, up there?" He rolled his eyes upwardly.

Appoloin looked towards the ceiling. "Up there?" he asked, then laughed. "I'm sorry, I could not help my jest." Then he added sincerely, "Perhaps now is not the right time to find humour? Yes, I am aware of your modes of transportation."

"There's always time to bring a smile, we're just worried. Oh, Lord, forget it, come with me."

Appoloin walked carefully down the stairs, Mairi's head resting on his shoulder. Following Alexander to the opened doors of the hotel, he exited, walking out onto Princes Street. A chauffeur held the door of the limousine open for them, and

Alexander stepped inside first. Appoloin followed with Mairi, who remained unconscious, in his arms.

"Is she all right?" shouted Graeme as he attempted to move but couldn't because Callum lay stretched across one of the bench seats inside the luxurious car, his head resting on Graeme's knees. Valerie sat on a bench seat at right angles to Graeme's and beside Callum's head. She was gently stroking his forehead whilst softly talking to him. At Graeme's raised voice, she tore herself from her ministrations and shock grabbed her when she saw Appoloin carrying Mairi.

"Dad?" she cried.

"Hush, Valerie," he said, sliding along beside her and taking her in his arms. "Let's hear what has happened before we pass judgements. It's not time to mourn, yet. We have too much to do."

Appoloin held Mairi in his arms as he rested in the seat. "This is better," he said. "I feared I would drop her at one time." He watched as Mairi's eyelids began to flutter open. A slow, tender smile crossed her face as she gazed up into Appoloin's blue eyes, her hand lifted and gently caressed his cheek. "You're here, you came back again," she whispered.

Appoloin moved his head to the side, puzzled at her words.

"What's she talking about?" asked Graeme. "Who the hell are you?"

"Appoloin is my name," he said, not taking his eyes from Mairi.

"He's another angel," added Alexander.

"Great, we just get rid of one and another one appears, what's he the angel of? And what's he here for?" asked Graeme, his eyes never leaving his daughter's sleeping form.

"I was sent to watch over and give protection to my charge, but I arrived too late," he said sadly.

"Your charge, who would that be?" Alexander felt dread seep into him, and he wished the conversation was over, that it had never begun. He closed his eyes and watched colours swirl through his mind, gathering momentum to the inevitable vision that was coming. Unlike Callum, whose foresight led to avoidance of situations, Alexander could conjure up and visualize scenes or places, and in most cases, people.

He saw Cathy's face.

With deep sorrow, he looked upon the still form of his brother Callum, memories of years gone past and the pain he had experienced through loss echoed in his mind. "Did you know?" he asked Graeme.

"Did I know what? What did you see just now?" he asked tersely.

Appoloin interrupted. "Perhaps now is not the time, mayhap it would be right to discuss this when we have arrived at Callum's home and have him resting, safe from what we will be speaking about."

"Are you saying you don't want him to know, or is he already aware, wherever the hell he is just now?"

"I believe it would be more beneficial for Callum to rest through this, without the disturbance of us talking, that is all I am saying."

"Dad," Mairi cried, "Dad." She began to fret in Appoloin's arms.

"Give me my daughter!" yelled Graeme.

"Dad!" Mairi screamed.

Appoloin smiled down at Mairi, then placed two fingers over her eyes. "Hush now, child, sleep." Mairi's eyes blinked twice then closed, and her breathing became deep and restful.

"You bastard, what the hell did you do? Who the hell do you think you are?"

"I put her to sleep, that is all, she, like Callum, needs to rest. In her peaceful slumber, she will find some healing and I, as I previously said, am Appoloin, Angel of Destruction."

Graeme leapt from his seat, dropping Callum's head as he lunged for Appoloin's throat. Valerie grabbed her uncle's head, keeping it in place. "Angel of Destruction! What did you destroy, my girl? I didn't ask you to heal her, I asked what you did to her?"

"Is this the welcome Forcas received as well? Did he have to endure this hostility?" he asked angrily. "I," he stressed, "I, have done nothing to your daughter, she was in the wrong place at the wrong time, she witnessed that which should not be witnessed. That is it put simply for you to understand. Now I have given her some rest so she may heal and return to you as a more coherent person!"

Alexander lay his hand on Graeme's arm. "Let it be, Graeme," he said sadly. "I know how frustrated you are, but let it be till we get back to Callum's, then we can sit and discuss what's going on here. Hell," he continued, "this was supposed to be the happiest evening for all of us." He repeated his statement made earlier, in a state of shock at the dreadful turn of events, and he shook his head in grief. "Now look at us, look at Callum, he's neither dead nor is he alive. Lauren's disappeared to God knows where in Mistdreaming, and Cathy…"

Graeme sat back in the seat, once more holding Callum's head; he caught the slight waver in Alexander's voice. "Cathy," he asked bewildered, "have you seen Cathy? Oh, Lord, that can't be good."

Alexander put his head into his hands and wept, "Leave it, Graeme, I don't want to talk about it with Callum in between worlds."

The car stopped abruptly, and Valerie looked outside,

amazed that they had arrived so quickly at the Braids. She turned to Appoloin, who smiled in her direction, nodding his head in silent acknowledgement.

"We're here, Dad," she said. "How are we going to get them both into the house?"

"I'll take my daughter now," Graeme said, not waiting for any argument from Appoloin as he pulled Mairi into his arms.

Appoloin moved to Callum. "Let me carry your brother for you, Alexander. You and your daughter could prepare the room for him so that he may rest easily."

Valerie took her father's hand. "Come on, Dad, let's get things done, I think it's going to be a very long night."

Chapter Fifteen

Ramiel called the Infidlibus together in the usual fashion. He stood, waiting impatiently for the group, beside Forcas. Forcas strode back and forth across the cave in anticipation of seeing his friends again. When they eventually arrived, they crept, silently and cautiously, into the cavernis. Their wings held tightly anchored, they transastralised into the caves, not wanting a sound to radiate, ensuring nothing was alerted to their presence.

For once, Xaphan made a punctual appearance. To the surprise of those waiting, he arrived with Adramelechk, the two having forged a tumultuous alliance. Their past friendship now buried in a pit of hurt where forgiveness remained unattainable, they were putting in place the foundations to build a new partnership. Trust was the main issue in preventing a future friendship, in Adramelechk's eyes, but he wanted to ensure the safety of the Mistdreamers, and if it was a case of realigning himself with Xaphan, if that was the cost, then it was a small price to pay for those who had put themselves in jeopardy to keep angels safe.

"What news, Ramiel?" Xaphan asked.

"Let us wait until we have all gathered before proceeding," Ramiel answered.

"How are thee, Forcas, does thee fare well?"

"I am well, thank you, Xaphan. I see you remain in the old speech, do you not think it time to change it and come into a new century?"

"I have tried, old friend, but my natural speech creeps back into the language whenever I find myself in your company. Be grateful I am not speaking in Greek or Latin." Shaking his head with a smile, he added, "Those were difficult days, learning new and different languages was not the easiest time for me!"

"I think you jest," Forcas laughed. "You, with brains that can outwit all of us put together, found learning Greek hard?"

"There is a saying, is there not, 'It's all Greek to me', yes?" he asked. "Well, I think that saying is appropriate, especially for me, it is not an easy language and to have to top it off with Latin. Dear heaven, thank the almighty he bestowed more languages upon the worlds that I, at least, could master!"

Ramiel drew in a tired breath before speaking,"And here comes Kakabel, how fare thee, Angel of the Moon? Have you witnessed any more changes in your world?"

Kakabel shook his head, and, sullenly, he sat on a cold rock. "Why the need for such secrecy, Ramiel? It's bad enough we have to meet here, but surely the time for 'cloak and dagger' is passing? Can we not continue with our lives more freely yet? What news have the Mistdreamers brought for us to help our plight?"

"We still await Appoloin and Sammael, keep tight until they arrive, there is much to discuss."

"And I have much to do, so make haste, please."

Kakabel walked to the middle of the room, and the angels cautiously watched him. His bare chest glistened with sweat, while the hot embers within the cave reflected red against his powerful physique, and he, like the other angels in the room, had folded his wings carefully, anchoring them into his back. In their place, he displayed a black ink tattoo which swept up on either side of his broad back. The symbols of wings, painted in ancient aramaic text, were the same engravings that each angel bore.

To his left he wore a fine-looking broadsword, and it was held closely into his side with a beautifully engraved leather scabbard, the lower part being tied to his calf with a thick, leather strap. The silver hilt was engraved with what appeared to be a design of Celtic origin.

"Why do you stare at me? What did I state that has caused such a reaction? I am busy just now, I have much to do, I must hurry."

Xaphan stepped forward and grabbed his shoulders. Ramiel withdrew the sword from it's scabbard. "What is more important than the safety of our Mistdreaming charges, Kakabel?" asked Forcas.

Before Kakabel had the opportunity to answer, Sammael entered. "Why do you hold our brother? Let him go, he has done no one here any harm. What has he done to earn this treatment from you?"

"Welcome to you, Sammael," Xaphan said sarcastically. "Why do you enter a room and speak without first understanding what has happened prior to your arrival? Why should you care the reasons we feel obliged to restrain our fellow Infidlibus?"

"I care because he is one of us. We must trust one another. These are difficult times, we must depend on each other, not accuse!"

"Then why does he persist on telling us he has much to do, we must make plans to help the Mistdreamers," Xaphan shouted.

Ramiel handed the sword back to Kakabel. "I am sorry, brother, we are all anxious. You are right, of course, Sammael, we must trust one another. If we lose sight of that, I believe we will be lost."

"Lost from what?" Appoloin said as he appeared.

"Where have you been?" asked Forcas. "You were supposed to meet me in Edinburgh, I waited but had to leave. What delayed you?"

"Straight in there with the questions, Forcas. You still do not trust me, do you?"

"I trust nobody that is as close to Hell as you." Turning, he spoke to Xaphan, "That includes you, my brother."

"And you, who walks amongst the demons, we are supposed to trust you?" asked Kakabel.

"Enough!!" roared Ramiel. "We are not here to take bites out of one another, we are here because we are supposed to have faith in each other. What has happened to destroy this bond we have shared for so long?"

"The traitor," Xaphan said. "It is he that puts us at each other's throats, until he is found then we will continue in this light."

"Then we have lost even before the battle has been fought," Ramiel said sadly. "We have stood together in bitter rivalry and in friendship, yet always, we have remained as one, can we not try to combat this evil together? Can we not come together, once again, to destroy that which is threatening our Mistdreamers?"

"We are all present now, what has happened?" asked Sammael.

"Forcas has been assisting Lauren in developing her Mistdreaming potential and his success has been," he looked to Forcas and raised an eyebrow, "it has been, *interesting*, would you not say, Forcas?"

Forcas bristled at the insinuation. "I have developed her to a certain stage, yes."

"But she found herself on this plane rather suddenly, did she not? How did that come about?"

Forcas felt like a young mortal, he wanted to shuffle his feet and look anywhere but into the piercing stare Ramiel was throwing at him. If his blood ran hot, he knew his face would turn red; luckily for him, he had ice running through his angelic veins!

"The way she transastralised to this plane and the reason she did so at the point we had reached in her education is immaterial, the fact is, she is here. What we need to know is what you discovered with her."

"Aherm." Ramiel cleared his throat. "Yes, perhaps that is a discussion for a later stage, but mayhap you need to advise other 'educators' of what is suitable to teach and what the ground rules are when guiding Mistdreamers?"

"I was professional in all my teachings," Forcas protested. "I instructed her in the relevant practices of gemstones and what to expect in passing into Mistdreaming, throughout the time I was on the mortal plane." Forcas could feel embarrassment creep over him, it was incredible, he had never felt such a way in his life. "I resent the implication otherwise," he added.

"I think you're protesting a bit too much, Forcas," Xaphan said and laughed. "What did you do to sweet Lauren, she's a baby, isn't she?"

"She is twenty-one mortal years, hardly a baby, she is a young woman now."

Xaphan sniggered. "I have a fair idea of what you may have been *teaching* the young woman." Others began to titter, joining Xaphan's laughter, apart from Appoloin who looked as confused as Forcas looked irritated. Ramiel wished they would all stop acting like overgrown children, especially when their ribaldry was about his daughter!

Ramiel glanced at Appoloin and was surprised to see him not joining in the laughter. "Is there a problem, Appoloin, did you chance upon something while on the mortal plane?"

Appoloin shook his head as though trying to obliterate a thought. "Yes, I did meet with a problem. Is this why you have called the meeting? Do you know that of which I have done?" he asked, resolved to hear the worst. "I do not regret my action, but the mortals are in need of my assistance, and I must return as quickly as possible."

Kakabel grunted in disgust. "Appoloin claims to have to rush, and yet not one of you attack him. I have much to do and you disarm me. What is happening to us? Why is this mistrust aimed solely at me?"

"You have made a very valid point," Ramiel concluded. "I have called you all here," he began, "because of the discovery I made when venturing into Mistdreaming with Lauren."

"She has already encountered her first experience?" Forcas asked, shocked.

"She *encountered* her first experience when she was eighteen months old."

"What? Then why was I sent to aid her in crossing into this world if she has already accessed her abilities?" Forcas asked frustratedly.

"She *was* a baby, then, Forcas. She crossed into Mistdreaming again when she was six years old, that is when we decided to erase her memory of her experiences."

A loud gasp was heard from the angels. "*We* decided?" asked Forcas, "Who's we? You chose to keep this information from your brethren Infidelibus?" Forcas raised his body to its full height, his frame expanding threateningly. "You have been playing us false all this time, Ramiel. How do we know you are not the traitor amongst us?" he asked angrily.

"I must apologise to you, I can only reassure you that it truly is not me who has been betraying our secrets." He hung his head in shame. "I told Ambriel of Lauren's crossing, and he was suspicious when I claimed she was the child of one of the American Mistdreaming families. He had no record of this child, so I then had to tell him of her origin."

"And what origin would this be?" asked Sammael.

"It is a very personal one, only two are aware of this, and I am loathe to share, but if it will prove my innocence, I will tell you, though I would prefer to keep this to myself."

Xaphan was first to speak. "I think in this instance, Ramiel, you will have to share this secret with us. It is not the first one we have listened to, and it will not be the worst. But indeed, you have to convince us you are not the traitor. How could you keep something from us, yet share a confidence with Ambriel? We," he waved his hand around the room, encompassing the angels within the cave, "are at a loss as to why you would trust him, yet not us?"

"Ambriel was made aware of Lauren's origins because of her second crossing into Mistdreamer. I had to assure him that she was not a threat, that she was being taken care of and would not return, until the time was right." He looked to Forcas. "Until she had been *educated* and was ready to work on our behalf."

"So you decided to wipe a child's memory?" Sammael asked, horrified.

"We had to; had we not, she would never have returned, and she is too valuable to us to not help."

"Why?" asked Adramelechk. "What did she witness?"

Kakabel smiled cynically. "There you do your trick again, Ramiel, you steer the conversation in the direction to which you feel comfortable and away from the cause of our concern."

"Which is?" Ramiel stuttered.

"Which is, the origins of this girl Lauren."

"How will telling you this clear my name?" he said furiously.

"You said it yourself," Xaphan whispered. "Her origin is your salvation, it must be important, or, as Kakabel rightly pointed out, you wouldn't be avoiding the issue."

"Tell us," said Sammael, "trust your brothers; or do you trust nobody, as with Forcas?"

"I can't believe I have to do this," he shouted. "We have been together for eons."

"Stop it!" bellowed Forcas. "Tell them, trust them, Sammael is right."

"I promised this would not happen, I promised I would always keep her safe, this is not going to keep her safe!" Ramiel turned from his friends and raised a worried hand to his forehead, rubbing it furiously. "She's my daughter," he said at last. "Lauren is my child, not Callum's."

Forcas lay an arm in companionship around Ramiel's shoulders and looked around at the other angels, who were stunned in disbelief.

"Em, how?" asked Kakabel.

Ramiel spun around and glared at him, then the question penetrated. "You think I had sex with her? I did not," he said, outraged at the very thought. "She is not that kind of person, she is faithful and true to Callum."

"Sorry to interrupt," said Xaphan, "but she can't be that honest and true, if it's your child." He shrugged his shoulders.

"She is my child, she is of my seed."

"An IVF baby?" asked Kakabel.

"How do you know of such things?" Forcas asked, impressed.

"I read, Forcas, it's something you should learn. I go on the

Internet, the mortal plane has many interesting things we, here, could use."

"Pfft, I doubt that," said Xaphan.

"Angels," Sammael barked, "we are moving away from the subject, and the hour is late. Let us get on with this meet, discuss what we are here to discuss, and return to our positions, please!"

Kakabel ruffled his feathers. "He isn't attacked, either," he grumbled.

"You've made your point," Forcas yelled. "We're sorry, we should not have held you, get over it."

"So if she's not an IVF baby, how is she of your seed?" asked Kakabel, ignoring, but amazed by Forcas's venture into 21st century English.

"Are we going to go into the realm of human mating now? Because I find it quite distasteful. The ins and outs of how they perform, it's just a subject I'm a little uncomfortable with," said Sammael.

The other angels all nodded in agreement, embarrassed by having to discuss the act involved in Lauren's conception.

"Callum's seed was replaced with mine, that is all. Now, can we leave this matter and move to the reason we are here?"

"And there we have it," Xaphan exploded, "too much information!"

Shuffling his feet, irritated that his privacy had been exposed, Ramiel's patience was quickly ebbing. "Could we please get back to the reason we have congregated here!?" he yelled.

"Please!" grunted Xaphan. "What news of the Park family? Did you fare well with them, Forcas?"

"That I did; I met with Lauren, and as I said, have been instructing her on the merits of gems."

Xaphan rolled his eyes. "Poor girl, I'll bet she was bored senseless."

Forcas allowed a small smile to cross his face. "She did complain on many occasions about the "utter boredom of it all", yes, I do recall her mentioning that fact several times."

Xaphan laughed and slapped his friend's back. "She's young and will learn. What else has happened that we are unaware?"

Ramiel hushed them. "Do you hear that noise?" A scurrying sound could be heard from outside the cave.

"It will be demons attending to their own; let us continue," Xaphan urged. "What of you, Ramiel, what have you learned that may enlighten us?"

"I took Lauren into Mistdreaming so that I may assist in deciphering her experience. I discovered that, despite our attempts at discouraging her to Mistdream, she is able to cross here without the assistance of any angel presence."

"How long have you been aware of this?" asked Forcas.

"About three earthly hours!" Ramiel answered angrily. "I was aware her Mistdreaming was taking her to other planes, she has visited with the Tuatha Dé Danann, and I believe, they have encouraged her to visit regularly, of this we can be grateful. It would have been better for her to visit with the fae than encounter a Demon King."

He took a breath, steeling himself for what he had to tell them. "She witnessed one of the Demon Kings on her second Mistdream."

Forcas interrupted. "Do you know which one? If we can find out that information, then we can surely narrow down our list of traitors?"

"MY thoughts exactly," Ramiel said, "but she could only see some of the scribe markings on his forefinger and was unable to understand what they meant."

"A fat lot of good that is, then," Kakabel spouted.

Xaphan grabbed Kakabel around the throat. "Be careful

what you say about her, she is endangering herself for us. You have yet to prove to us you are *not* the traitor. You, who is in charge of the veils of time, the very veils that are coming apart under your watch!"

"Let go of him!" Sammael pulled at Xaphan's arm, wrenching Kakabel free from his grasp. "I think we have done enough finger pointing at each other this sorry eve. Maybe we should be listening to more of the evidence you have to put before us, Ramiel?"

"Agreement." Ramiel bowed his head in acknowledgement.

"If she has witnessed a Demon King, she is in certain danger, have you anyone guarding her at the moment?" asked Forcas.

"I have left Elemiah with her. His presence is reassuring, and he will alert me if anything occurs."

"Ha!" snorted Kakabel. "The Angel of Inward Journeys is a useless prat, he could no more fight his way out of a paper bag. How is he going to defend her should the enemy decide to find her?"

"You deride your fellow angel, yet you still have no answers regarding the veils? Elemiah, should she begin to dream or move into Mistdream, will be able to protect her. He is in her subconscious at the moment, guarding her."

"Well, let us hope she crosses water, as that's supposed to be his sole purpose, is it not? Care for those travelling."

"How little you appear to know of your brethren, and why would you deem that particular job to be inconsequential? He also retrieves insights from minds. Perhaps we should have him take a look inside your mind and see what it is you are hiding from us, what say you?" asked Ramiel.

"Let us move on," said Sammael. "What else did you discover on your journey with Lauren?"

"She was aware of a woman being tortured, and because she

was a little girl, found it difficult to understand what was, in actuality, happening."

"But you were able to assist, were you?" asked Xaphan.

"Up to a point, I, like all of you when in the mist, can see nothing, but only feel the emotions of our Mistdreaming charges. She was understandably frightened when she heard a woman screaming, but she is a brave girl, and with a little encouragement, she entered the room in which the torture was taking place."

"Do we know where that place is?" asked Forcas.

"Unfortunately, yes," Ramiel answered. "I believe it is here in the Cavernis."

"How was she able to enter? We are unable to access any caves when in use."

"That is one of the reasons these Mistdreamers are so important to us. It would appear they can gain access anywhere, all the realms of Hell and Heaven. Every plane we have encouraged humans to believe do not exist, these Mistdreamers *know* are real, and some, Lauren for instance, have indeed, found themselves in these lands. Lauren appears to be able to Mistdream whenever and wherever she chooses."

"Holy Hell!" exclaimed Forcas. "She is in danger, and so are her parents. We must get back to earth and put in place more protection for her family. Cathy must be found, she disappeared in a state of despair before I came here."

Appoloin cleared his throat. "I believe," he said sadly, "there will be no need to go in search of Cathy."

"You have found her already?" Forcas asked excitedly. "Great news, well done, now we can get Archangel Michael to put safety measures in place for her."

"You rush ahead, Forcas. Let us hear what Appoloin has to say to us. What is it you wish to share, Appoloin?" asked Ramiel. "What is it that troubles you?"

"You mean apart from the Mistdreamers we cannot prevent from gaining access to all the universes? You mean apart from that little problem?"

"You digress, Appoloin, what is the problem?"

"Cathy is dead, she was taken to the fourth level by Azrael."

Forcas grabbed Appoloin's arm. "You jest, you surely jest, she was safe on the earth plane, just distraught because of the status Callum is in."

"About that status," Appoloin started. "Azrael was confused when he came to collect Cathy, saying it was supposed to have been a man he was to take. Mayhap you need to explain yourself as well, Forcas."

Ramiel rolled his eyes. "What have you done this time, Forcas?? Your job was to assist Lauren in her understanding of Mistdreaming, help her cross into the other realm…"

"Yes, but I was not aware you had already assisted in that part of my 'job', mayhap you also need to share a few more of those secrets you have very carefully avoided telling us about."

"Don't avoid the subject, Forcas. Out with it, what did you do?"

Forcas ran his hand through his mussed up hair, the memory of the pain Cathy had experienced still very fresh in his mind. He had wanted to weep himself as the agony of loss had torn through her. So he had done what he thought necessary. "I breathed life into his body."

Forcas could almost feel the air being sucked out of the room with the angels' intake of breaths.

"But, but," Ramiel stammered, "you can't, you have given him our energy, you have given him *your* energy. You cannot survive without it, what have you done?"

"How could I not help, Ramiel? Tell me how I could stand and watch her heart break? Her daughter had just transasstralised into who knows where." He carefully omitted the mighty creator's name. "Then she witnessed her husband dying from a heart attack. I could not watch her go through so much pain. Unfortunately, she ran, not knowing Callum still lives… sort of, anyway."

"But that was not your decision to make, surely you know that?" Ramiel flustered. "What do you mean, "sort of"?"

"I am aware I should not have interfered, but if you had been there, you would have done exactly the same thing."

"I can assure you, that is not the truth, there are a sequence of events that have to take place, and perhaps Callum's death had to occur, then, at that moment." He stressed, "Maybe his death was an important factor in ensuring the safety of another, did you think of that? You should not have interfered!" Ramiel paced the floor, his mind trying to mentally compute the consequences of Forcas's actions.

"So you're saying you wouldn't have interfered?" asked Xaphan, frowning in disbelief.

"That is exactly what I'm saying," Ramiel barked.

"So giving your seed to Cathy was not interference," he said shortly.

"That was….that was,"

"That was, that was, what?" Xaphan mimicked.

"That was different."

The rest of the room snorted at his response.

"You hypocrite, you have the audacity to lecture Forcas on his acts." Looking to Forcas, Xaphan continued, "Foolish as they were, he did it with the best of intentions. What were your intentions, nay, your reasons, for impregnating a human with angel seed? That was done once before, and look what happened to him in the end!"

"Firstly, *she* was not impregnated by an angel," Ramiel said miserably, "and in the second place, I did not personally impregnate Cathy, Callum did that."

"Do not split hairs," Xaphan whispered, "you are as guilty as Forcas. You may not have personally taken part in the *dance of love,* but your seed did and look at the chaos it has caused!"

Ramiel sighed loudly then sat on the rock Kakabel had vacated earlier. Bending his arm, he leaned on his knee and buried his face into the palm of his hand. The angels watched quietly, knowing Ramiel was fighting inner turmoil as he contemplated Xaphan's words.

"I know you're right," he eventually said, raising his head slightly so that his chin now rested on his knuckles, "but I have to ask. Kakabel, how did you manage to sit here without burning your backside?" Jumping up from the stone, Ramiel grabbed his buttocks in feigned pain. Smiling to his friends, he continued, "As I said, you are right, Xaphan. I am a hypocrite; of course, I interfered. I should not have, and neither should you have, Forcas." Lifting his hand to stop Forcas speaking, he continued, "Nay, do not say anything, no matter how well meaning, it was interference. I think it's a sign that these humans have become a lot closer to us than simple Mistdreamers."

"You've only just worked that out? You, with a sleeping daughter in the fifth realm of the heavens?" asked Xaphan, a small smile on his handsome face.

Appoloin's face grew dark. "I have not completed all that has happened," he said morosely.

Forcas looked appalled. "You mean there is worse to tell us than Cathy dying?"

"I'm not sure if it's worse, but as Ramiel said, 'actions and consequences.'" He paused. "Perhaps my last action will have consequences, of that I am unsure. I know what I did was right, and I do not regret it. I know, positively, I would do it again if the same scenario arose, but I am beginning to think there is more at stake here than what I think should be done."

Ramiel clapped his hands together. "At last, someone realises we cannot just do anything we want. Holy dear, tell us what else has occurred and pray, do not hold anything back. Perhaps if there are consequences, we could delay some of the inevitability if we go through everything very carefully."

"Wait a moment," Sammael whispered, "do you hear anything?"

"What is it you hear?" asked Ramiel.

"It's as you said, a scuffling, but I do not know where it comes from. Is it the same noise you heard earlier, Ramiel?" Sammael raised his fingers to his lips. "Hush, listen, friends, do you hear anything?"

The room was as silent as the night. "I hear nothing," Xaphan eventually said.

"Nor I," Forcas, Kakabel, and Appoloin said together.

Confused and slightly ill at ease, Sammael began to grow restless. "I know I heard something, I feel it is time we draw our meeting to an end."

Ramiel nodded. "You could be right, but we must first go through some of the events. I am sure we are safe in here, I must explain about Lauren's Mistdreaming."

"But you have informed us already," said Forcas. "Perhaps you should not have erased her memory, it would be easier to retrieve her experiences had you given her that benefit."

"Now is not the time to go through that again, Forcas," Ramiel said guiltily. "What's done is done, I feel deep regret at the actions I perpetrated on my girl, but I believe what she met with has to be shared. Appoloin, you, too, must give us a detailed report before we decide which step to take next."

Kakabel stepped forward and touched Ramiel's arm. "Tell us, so we can get out of here, I, too, am feeling uncomfortable, something is amiss."

"Lauren witnessed, not the torture of a woman, but one lying handcuffed to a bed, asking to be given pain."

"Ah, a new soul entering the first realm," Xaphan said, logically.

"I do not believe so, why would a Demon King present himself to a new soul? It is not logical."

"It could have been a human worshipper of the master, you know how they believe they should be given pain as a treat for following him, very strange beings, I think," Xaphan concluded.

"There was a child in the room," Ramiel managed to say. "He could see Lauren and called her 'his cousin', and the woman on the bed was her aunt; although she has never met her, the king asked if she could see her niece."

"What?" The angels forgot their concerns about the discomfort in the room when they heard the information Ramiel was passing on.

"Her aunt?" asked Forcas. "Linda, the mother to Valerie?"

"No," replied Ramiel. "Angela, Mairi's mother."

"And now I have to tell you my information," Appoloin said worriedly. "It was not just Cathy who died this eve but Rachauden also."

Forcas and Xaphan said together, "The demon of the first order? What has she to do with any of this?"

Forcas held his breath. "I knew someone was at the party this evening."

"What are you talking about?" asked Ramiel.

"The girls' birthday celebration was held tonight, and Callum witnessed a demon following the girls to the party room, but I could sense and see nothing. I had sensed something earlier and then…" He stopped before exclaiming, "For the love of Amergin!"

"What?!" they all shouted.

"After Lauren transastralised, before Callum's heart attack, he had a vision of me threatening his brothers. The whole vision and concern for Lauren's disappearance, I believe, is what led to the heart attack. Rachauden has been taught by King Baal in the arts of disappearing and invisibility. She has been taught the art of illusion, creating a different scene for Callum would be simple. It could only last for a few seconds, but that would be long enough for her."

"And you say Rachauden was killed this eve as well, how do you know this, Appoloin?" Ramiel asked, a little afraid of what they would learn next.

"Because I killed her," he stated and breathed a sigh of disgust.

"You killed her!" Xaphan said in disbelief. "Why would you kill a demon?"

"She had murdered Cathy, she stood over her body laughing and told me she had ended the problem."

"Listen, now I hear that sound, do you?" Kakabel asked. They all listened, and they could hear sobbing, then they heard a sharp intake of breath. Then silence.

"What was that?" asked Sammael.

"I fear we have been found out. Our visit tonight has been spied upon," said Ramiel. "Perhaps all our visits have been watched, but whatever we said tonight has upset it."

"How could we not see it?" asked Forcas.

"It must be a Mistdreamer, one of their own," said Xaphan. "I knew they were disgruntled at having to help, but I didn't believe they would wish to cause harm to us."

"You are jumping the gun, again," said Ramiel. "Before we go making assumptions, let us look at all the facts, but not just now."

"Thank the heavens!" Kakabel yelled. "I really do have to get back, before you all pounce on me again and take my sword!"

"We must think carefully, and the next meet will have to be somewhere else, but we have to figure out who this might be. I, meanwhile, will go through more of Lauren's Mistdreaming. Forcas," he looked to his friend, "I believe you need to meet with one of your friends. Xaphan," he turned to him, "can you go with Forcas, a presence of two would be better when meeting with the Demon Kings, do you not agree?"

Both agreed and began to move, when Ramiel glanced over to Sammael and Appoloin. "Sammael, find out what you can about the child Lauren witnessed. Appoloin, get back to Mairi quickly, and Kakabel, find out who is tearing the veils of the universe!"

"On my way now, until we next meet," Kakabel said and disappeared.

"Let us go, my friends, I think we are near to finding out who this traitor is, but I have a bad feeling about this, one that makes me believe our Mistdreamers must be taken to safer realms."

"Until next time," Sammael said and disappeared.

Appoloin nodded and transastralised.

"Do you really believe we must move them?" asked Forcas.

"Without a doubt, but speak with your friends and then get the information to me. We can work out what must be done to save them." Ramiel glanced at Xaphan. "It is time to share what you have learned with Forcas."

"More secrets, damn it, Ramiel!"

"This was necessary," Xaphan interjected, "and only Ramiel

and I were party to my mission. Come, Forcas," he slapped his friend on the back, "let us make happy, as I, with a lighter heart, can share what I have learned in the deepest recesses of Hell's gates. Grateful, I am, to not have to return again."

Ramiel watched the two near demons disappear in friendly banter and waited until he was certain the silence enveloping him was the cavernis and not the entity that had intruded upon their meeting. Certain he sensed nothing, he raised his arms and spread his wings, and as Lauren would say, "blinked" his magnificent body sparkling like a million diamonds before he, too, disappeared.

Chapter Sixteen

"Who might you be?" Lauren asked sleepily, as she opened her eyes to see another incredibly handsome man sitting at the bottom of her bed.

"I, Princess, am Elemiah, at your service, my child," he said with a voice as soft and gentle as a warm summer breeze.

Lauren drank in the appearance of the angel. *Absolutely stunning*, she thought. *I wonder if there are any ugly angels.*

"It would depend on your definition of *ugly*". Elemiah said.

Lauren turned a lovely shade of pink. "It's so unfair when you angels do that, it's just rude, you know, listening in to someone else's thoughts. It's a bit like a psychic telling you she can see your future, then tells you it, when you haven't asked and don't want to know anyway!"

"You speak of prophets?" Elemiah asked, surprised. "I was unaware there were many left that could foretell. I know your father has the ability, but he is of a rare breed. Who are these 'psychic' prophets you speak about?"

"There're thousands of them, they've got psychic hotlines, you can write to them, have parties with them, they're everywhere. Some are better than others, it has to be said, though." She smiled when she noticed Elemiah was more confused.

"Let's pass on the psychic thing," she said, chuckling. "Which angel are you?"

"I am Elemiah," he said again.

"No, I mean which Angel are you an angel of? Like Forcas is the Angel of Destruction."

"No, that would be Appoloin," Elemiah interrupted.

"Sorry, I was kidding." Then she quickly added, "I forgot you angels don't 'do' sarcasm."

"Humour, you speak of humour…sadly, we need to be taught quite a lot about fun, I believe."

Lauren's eyes widened in surprise. "Wow, an angel who admits he doesn't know, see, or hear everything."

Elemiah let out a burst of laughter so loud Lauren was sure the walls of the house would shake. Although it was a resounding laugh, it wasn't painful to her ears, it just sent a bubble of happiness all the way through her.

"Which angels have you met, or should I take a guess at a few of them?" he said mischievously.

"You do have a sense of humour, you must be very lonely here with nobody understanding you! Come on, then, guess and see if you're right."

"I may have an unfair advantage over you as I am aware of at least one of the angels you have met," he said seriously. Then a slow smile spread across his handsome face, "But let me have a try, anyway."

He pointed one finger to the ceiling. "I'm guessing, Forcas?"

"Oh, that's too much!" Lauren laughed. "You know I've met him, I said so, didn't I?" she giggled.

"So you did, and I know you met with Ramiel, as it was he who invited me to be here for you when you awoke."

"Did he now? I'm guessing he doesn't trust me to be alone in case I wander away and don't come back."

Elemiah frowned. "I do not think that is his concern in the slightest, I am sure it is more to do with his being worried about you."

"Don't get your panties in a twist, I was just pulling your leg." It was Lauren's turn to laugh out loud. Elemiah's shocked face was a picture. Had she asked him to rob a bank with her, she doubted he would have looked more surprised.

"Rob a bank! Lauren, how could you think that, as to my panties being in a twist," Elemiah looked lecherously, or as lecherously as a blond, six foot tall angel could look, at her, and waggled his eyebrows, "we angels don't wear panties."

Lauren squealed with laughter. "There you go again, surprising me. I thought you angels didn't have a sense of humour," she said, gasping for her breath. "The ones I've met maybe haven't, but you do."

"Then you must have met Ambriel!" he said, and his eyes sparkled with naughty merriment.

"You are too much," she said, smiling up at him. "So what are you the angel of, or are you too scared to tell me?"

Elemiah moved forward and took her hand in his. She gazed up into gentle, emerald green eyes. "I fear not from you, Lauren. I am Elemiah the Angel of Inward Journeys. I watch over and protect those who travel by water. I assist in guiding the mind to comprehend subconscious thought. In many cases, when the mind becomes lost, the subconscious will retain insights that I will open up so that the lost mind can interpret and recover."

"You and Ramiel must have a real blast at times! Do neither of you feel like actually walking into a bar and getting drunk?"

"Why would we wish to do that?"

"You spend your lives walking through people's minds instead of living in the real world."

"What a strange concept," he said, surprised at her comment. "This *is* the real world, the mind is the real world, it has no limitations, no boundaries. It can show us where we will go, and sometimes, just as important, where we have been."

Lauren sighed and looked down at her hands. "You're here to help understand my Mistdreaming, aren't you?" she said unhappily, as she understood Elemiah's role in her life.

"Not I, Lauren, have no fear of that, I am merely here to prevent you, at this time, from Mistdreaming without the assistance of Ramiel." Elemiah stroked her cheek softly. "Do not be afraid of your Mistdreaming, you are an important part of the universe."

"Is it the only reason I am important?"

"Only you can answer that question, Lauren. Were you important before you discovered you could Mistdream?"

Lauren nodded and smiled. "To my mom and dad, my Grandpa Tony, and Grandma MaryPat, I know I am."

"Then you have answered your question. Now, perhaps, the time for such a philosophical discussion is at an end, and you could arise from your bed? Would you care to walk outside? The air is fresh and the suns are warm."

Before Lauren had the chance to answer, Ramiel appeared, his face a mask of worry.

"What is it?' Lauren cried.

Ramiel grasped Elemiah's forearm in greeting. "Are you well, brother?" he asked.

"I find myself happy, yes," Elemiah answered with the time old response.

"And Lauren, did you need to protect her from Mistdreaming?"

Lauren sat up in bed, folded her arms across her chest, and coughed. "Excuse me! Here! In bed. Can hear you!" she exclaimed.

"My apologies, Lauren," Ramiel said. "I wanted to hear from Elemiah to see if you had left."

Lauren was puzzled, how could she have left when she was still in her bed?

"You could have Mistdreamed," said Elemiah.

"Again, with the walking through my mind! Cut it out!"

"I was just assisting you to interpret your subconscious," he said impishly.

"Don't try that on either, it won't work. I have not moved, I'm still in bed, how could I have Mistdreamed?"

"Lauren," Ramiel said cautiously, watching her carefully, "there is much we need to discuss, one is that it would appear you can Mistdream whenever you choose, your body may remain as we see it here, but, in fact, because of your ability to transastralise, you leave what you on the earth's plane would call, a 'soul' in your body's stead. You take your body into Mistdream." Slowly pulling his eyes from Lauren's mystified face, he looked at Elemiah. "Did she transastralise, were you able to prevent it?"

"There was no movement from her body, she stayed in a deep slumber, and," he stopped Ramiel from asking the question, "she did not dream, her subconscious was in total peace, and her sleep was a deep and cleansing one."

Ramiel let out the breath he had not realised he was holding. "Thank the heavens for that. I must speak with her now, Elemiah. I thank you for your help and trust I can call upon you should I require your assistance?"

Elemiah held Ramiel's arm in true camaraderie. "You should never ask that, not after what you did for me."

"Let us not talk of that again, I did nothing others would not have done."

"I shall never forget," Elemiah said. "Should you need me,

you know how to contact me and which channels to go through to find me."

Lauren watched as the angels shared their confidence and wondered what could have happened in the past for Elemiah to honour Ramiel with such devotion. Their conversation hinted that Ramiel had been an aide of some kind to Elemiah.

Looking over his shoulder at Lauren, Elemiah nodded. "You need not concern yourself at this time with our past, I am sure you will learn from Valerie, at some point, what went on." His smile was warm and true as he said, "For now, my princess, I wish you well, that your journeys be safe, that your guide always protects you, and that your future be happy. Until we meet again, sweet Lauren, I bid you farewell." Blowing a kiss at her, she watched as minute sparkles flew through the air as though on a soft breeze, to land gently on her cheek. She touched her face in surprise and looked up to see Elemiah had disappeared and was sad that the quirky, almost magical angel was no longer with her.

"Do not be sad, Lauren," Ramiel said worriedly, "you will meet with Elemiah again, he will never be far from you. I take it you found him to be of help."

"Mmm?" Lauren said dreamily. "Help? No," she continued, "he wasn't of help, not really, he just had a sense of humour. I liked him, he made me laugh, and he understood me being silly."

"Silly? Lauren, you're never silly," Ramiel said, baffled.

"Maybe the wrong word. Anyway, I enjoyed his company." Frowning, she threw an annoyed look at him. "I didn't need him to babysit me, though, you didn't have to do that!"

"Ah, but Lauren, I did, there is much we must discuss, pray get up out of bed, we must hurry. I will be standing by the door. *Blink* and get dressed, we need to go somewhere safe, I must take you to Mistdreaming now."

"What's happened?" she asked tearfully. "Are you going to tell me, please?"

Ramiel tried to say the words, but knew the time was not right. "Get dressed, Lauren, we will sit in the kitchen and have hot chocolate, then we can discuss the matters you must hear before heading to Mistdreaming. No," he raised his hand, "do not ask again, we will discuss this when we are both comfortable. Come, my little princess," he moved to her and caressed her hair, "get ready now."

Ramiel walked to the door and waited as Lauren prepared herself. She "blinked' into a pair of light blue jeans and a comfortable, pink, soft cotton sweater, with medium-length sleeves and a slash neck. "How's that?" she asked as she pulled on her trainers. "I'm ready, is the hot chocolate made?"

"Ready and waiting as we waste time speaking," Ramiel whispered.

"Will we *blink*, or do you want to take more time and walk down the stairs with me?" she asked solemnly.

"I think we should *blink*, our chocolate will be getting cold, and I hate it when the marshmallows melt, because I like the chewy, gooey ones." He smiled, held her hands, and said, "*Blink*, Lauren, and take us to our hot chocolate."

Lauren looked up into his beautiful, sad, blue eyes and knew she was not going to like whatever it was he had to share with her.

"Let's get this over and done with," she said and *blinked* them into the kitchen.

Forcas and Xaphan stood side by side in the centre of the Throne Room in the southernmost point of Hell's fourth realm.

Around their necks they wore iron collars attached to which a thick, heavy-linked chain was pinned into an anchor on the cold stone floor. Their wrists were bound with a cursed rope made of back velvet and tied behind their backs. Their legs, spread eagle, had iron bracelets locked onto their ankles. Chains led from the bracelets into another post on the floor, which prevented either angel from movement.

The decadent room exuded wealth; rich, deep red velvet curtains framed the nine, forty-foot, arched, stained glass windows. Each window displayed one of the nine Demon Kings in varying macabre hellish scenes.

Six massive Aubusson rugs littered across the polished hematite floor. Woven into each rug were the individual marks belonging to the six demon princes.

Nine gigantic, black marble thrones encircled them. Demons were engraved all over the thrones. The armrests on each chair carried the animals the respective kings chose in which to appear, while the headrests bore the symbol of power relevant to that king.

Behind each throne, a naked woman and naked man stood, both wearing neck braces that chained them, enslaving them, to the chair and to the whims of the king to whom it belonged.

The kings' court included twenty-two dukes, ten counts, fifteen marquis, and one knight, but to ensure the court ran smoothly, in all regions of Hades, fourteen Presidents of Hell were in complete control of everything, to ensure the perfect operation was in place for the running of an efficient universe. They had knowledge of every statistic, every torture, and every being that existed in the kingdom. They were able to use their abilities to locate, analyse, prepare, or arrange anything and everything. There was nothing, they believed, could occur in their realm of which they were unaware.

They were only answerable to the Malum Reges.

Forcas was one of the presidents.

Both he and Xaphan stood before three of the ruling Kings of Hell, a Great Prince and one president, who also happened to be a count.

They stood before the Malum Reges.

The Malum Reges are a group of selected demons brought together by the Conjurer, another of the names bestowed upon the fallen angel, also known as Lucifer.

He selected five of his preferred elite nobility to secure the gates to Hell and oversee the Presidents of Hell.

King Baal lounged lazily on his thrown, his dark eyes and hair emphasised his striking good looks when he was in the form of a man. His physique was powerful, although not very tall, preferring to be of lower stature, nearer to the ground as his bestial form was that of a ferocious cat. He held estates to the east and was considered to be the highest king amongst the Malum Reges. Being revered as a Great King, he commanded an almighty, sixty-six legions, but he was known to be a fair king to his legions of demons. However, he suffered no fools and, in battle, was known to have killed his own when they had made blunders.

Teaching the art of invisibility was Baal's forte, and he had appreciated the fallen angel's quickness of mind. Forcas now excelled in the abilities that Baal had taught and had become the master.

King Balam's command of forty legions was legendary. It was said even the angels whispered about his stratagem and the epic battles he had fought and won. He had a warm sense of humour, and it was clearly etched across his handsome face. Choosing the form of man for this trial, his blond hair was tied with a leather thong and hung down the middle of his back. His tall, muscular body was displayed, as he wore only a pair of cotton shorts.

His laughing blue eyes stared at Forcas, and he smiled at him. They had become fast friends after the first Angelic war, they had shared many glorious times, but there was a flicker of doubt in Balam's mind towards Forcas, as he believed the fallen angel was unable to completely cross over into the darkness, choosing to keep the realms of the heavens accessible. It was a place Balam never cared to visit again, two major battles with angels was enough. They remained on friendly terms, and had for centuries, but he had never really trusted him. He watched Forcas carefully and appreciated his amazing abilities and intelligence. The latter, it would appear, had been misplaced, or he would not now be found standing, on trial, in front of the Malum Reges.

King Amdusias regarded Xaphan and frowned. His eyebrows were drawn over green eyes, and he rubbed at the stubble on his chin. He had spoken with the angel not long ago, and he was concerned at the information he may have passed on to the traitor standing before him. He wanted to roar but knew his voice would deafen all who were in the room, and it was essential they were able listen to the bile he was sure would spout forth from them.

Prince Seere watched both Xaphan and Forcas with amusement. He was not a demon of evil, but of good nature. His beauty was on an even par, if not surpassed, the angels. Eyes of sapphire blue, shrouded in thick, black eyelashes, graced the face surrounded by midnight black hair that he softly curled around his features. His six foot four, muscular body was carefully clad in *Armani*, a black T-shirt and black trousers. He was highly regarded, one of the Great Princes, but with the ability to go anywhere in a matter of seconds, his powers were highly sought after.

Although he commanded twenty-six legions, he was uninterested in battle and chose to pursue the fun elements in life. He often appeared in the form of what looked like a winged horse. The origins of his choice of appearance were vague, and Seere was happy to keep it to himself.

Count Glasya-Labolas was a very strange-looking man. He looked like the archetypical villain, with a pointed, sharp face, and thick, arched eyebrows over black eyes. His long nose flared at the nostrils, and his mouth was a thin line. To view, one would immediately sense the evil emanating from him, and he was delighted with that perception. Commanding thirty-six legions of demons, he was known as a brutal, unforgiving leader.

He took pleasure in instructing humans in manslaughter and the art of bloodshed, but surprisingly, he also had the ability to access minds and foresee love. When given the choice between helping to develop love, he often chose to withhold that power, unless it would become beneficial to his cause or give him an advantage in one of his spiteful plans.

He watched Forcas with his malevolent eyes, aware that those present knew of his deep dislike and jealousy of his fellow president. He was more than gratified to be witness to the destruction of his nemesis. A thorn in his side that he would enjoy eliminating, he was pleased to have been the one to ensnare both Forcas and Xaphan when they attempted to enter Hell's gates.

"Wipe the smile from your face, Labolas, this is not a theatrical meet," growled King Baal. "We are here in a court of law, try to remember to hide your pleasure."

"You are a loathsome creature at times, Labolas," sneered King Balam. "We have yet to hear why those accused have deigned to gain entry to our kingdom, and you appear to be reveling in their demise."

"Demise?" asked Prince Seere. "Who said anything about their demise, surely, we have to pass judgement before talk of death?"

"Quite right," King Baal agreed. "What say you, Forcas? Why do you enter Hell's gates with an Angel?"

Forcas looked to his co-accused and shrugged. "Is my crime that of entering Hell's gates, or is it for entering with an angel?" he enquired sarcastically. "As far as I am aware, being one of the fourteen presidents, I am entitled to walk through the realms? Have I misunderstood the rules *you* put in place, King Amdusias?"

King Amdusias passed a cold stare over Xaphan before slowly turning his attention to Forcas. "I am not on trial here, Forcas. It is you who needs to explain your actions to us. *Not* the reverse." Amdusias leaned back in his throne and gripped the arm rests. "Now, if you would be so kind, Forcas, answer Baal's question, or we will pass our judgement upon you *before* listening to a word uttered from your lips. Why do you enter the upper realms of Hell's gates with an angel?"

Xaphan attempted to move forward, but the ankle bracelets gripped harder around him, and sharp needles sprang from within the bracelet, cutting into his skin. Xaphan sucked in his breath as the needles held him in place by tearing through his skin, his blood slowly dripping onto the floor. "Have I the right to speak in this *court?*" he asked.

"You are a *being* of interest to us," replied Balam, "and as such, we will, at one point, wish to hear from you. At the moment, however…" Balam leaned forward and placed his hand on one of his knees. With his other hand, he raised his index and middle finger, making a small, swift, circular motion.

Xaphan attempted to move his lips, and pain spread from his mouth across to his cheeks, shooting to his brain. His head became motionless. Fear etched his handsome face, his terrified eyes seeking Forcas. He opened his mouth, but it froze in a silent scream, just as his head slowly turned to stone.

"Release him, Balam!" shouted Forcas. "This is beneath you, let him be!"

"In a moment, Forcas. For now, we will discuss your indiscretion, without angels' ears hearing our matters, and then our judgement can be pronounced and passed before we decide what to do to your angel friend here."

"I find this distasteful," Prince Seere announced. "Release the angel, Balam, it is not for you to make the decision to quieten him. I, for one, would like to hear what he has to say. You have concluded they are guilty without giving fair trial."

"Well, I believe Balam correct in his course of action," Amdusias quickly stated. "I have no interest in hearing his words. We should eliminate him now without trial. He has no right to be here."

Baal lifted a hand. "We will do no such thing. I do not wish to partake in another thousand year war because we accuse and murder an angel." Seere enthusiastically nodded in agreement.

Baal looked curiously at Balam and Amdusias. "I have no regard for this being's existence." He paused and rubbed his chin, frowning. "But I have to wonder, why the rush?"

"Beg pardon?" asked Count Glasya-Labolas.

Turning his curious eyes upon Labolas, he continued, "Oh, I understand your desire to see the elimination of an angel… any angel; actually, strike that, your desire to see the elimination of any *being* outweighs your regard for justice. What, though, I do not understand, is why the response of Balam and then Amdusias is the same as your evil cravings?"

"What are you trying to insinuate?" Amdusias said angrily.

"It is a simple theory, the need to expel the sin is greater than the need to forgive that same sin. It is a sermon often preached by humans, we here are all aware of their desperate need to be forgiven." Leaning forward, he added,

his lips drawn back in a sneer, "Is it not the very reason for our existence? We live to bring forth their souls to us. Take a look at those we have shackled to our thrones. They are simply existing because we choose to allow their lives to continue on our plane." Baal stood up and walked to the back of his throne. The woman chained to his throne visibly shivered in fear. "I mean, have a look at this one." He stroked the back of his hand gently down the side of her breast. "She is ripe, perfect for usage and, it would appear, more than willing to satisfy." Looking at the girl, he grabbed her by her chin. "Is that not so, my lovely?"

The girl nodded in fear. "Yes, my lord, whatever you command, I am your obedient servant."

Baal laughed out loud. "You see, Balam? She has fear written all over her, yet she stands here allowing my caress," he painfully grabbed her backside, "unaware of what I may have in store for her, but yet she stands here because *she* believes she *deserves* to be here, that her sins have caused her to be sent to this place. Is that not so, child? Tell me, what sins did you commit that could not be forgiven on the earth's plane?"

The woman looked to the others chained to thrones and said, "I killed my husband."

"And did you ask for forgiveness?" asked Baal.

She laughed. "Ask forgiveness because I killed that two-timing rat? Never."

"And you believe this to be your punishment?"

"Of course, I am here because of my sins."

Baal turned, and with a flourish, bowed to the people in the room. "And there, I prove my point."

"What has that got to do with anything?" asked Seere.

"Simply, these *beings* accept their punishment, because of their need to be forgiven for sins…not that we consider using their bodies, as we desire, punishment." He lecherously smiled as he grabbed both of her breasts, twisting and turning them with relish, enjoying the pain he was inflicting upon the woman. "They are in no rush for us to end their sentence. So one has to ask the question again." He stopped his manipulating of her body, and turned to the kings. "Why the rush, Balam? Why the rush, Amdusias? What is it the pair of you know and are hiding from this court?"

Amdusias spluttered outrage. "How dare you accuse me of withholding information! You have no right!"

Baal raised himself to a towering status. "I have *every* right, need I remind you why we are here? This is not a court to fulfil Labolas's desires for blood, it is a court to discern Forcas's objective, we have yet to determine what *sin* he has committed against us, and if there is no sin, then there is no need to forgive, surely? Therefore, there would be no need for punishment."

Balam's face turned a mottled shade of grey. "You accuse us, who stand beside you, of playing false, when he," pointing to Forcas, "stands accused of entering our realm with an angel? How dare you!"

Baal's raucous voice boomed around the room, those chained to the thrones slid to the floor, writhing in pain. "I dare because I have the right! I am the Head of Infernal Powers, I am he, who you are answerable to. You will explain yourselves, and you will explain your need to see a swift execution of your duties!" Waiting for his statement to register, he then roared, "NOW!"

Seere looked at Amdusias and was puzzled, he had known

the King all his life and thought him to be a fair ruler, so his quick decision did give him cause to wonder at the need for such haste in carrying out his demand.

The tension in the room was almost unbearable when Forcas began to speak. "I might be coming to a wrong conclusion myself," he began, "but I believe Xaphan has had a few meetings with King Amdusias." Forcas watched the horror and then fear pass over Amdusias's face, so he quickly continued, "It is the reason I brought Xaphan with me. I am of the opinion that he is wanting to be released from his heavenly shackles completely and make full commitment to this realm." Scowling at the count, he added, "We were on our way to visit with the king when Labolas grabbed us and threw us into The Pit and did not ask us anything before we found ourselves standing before all of you."

"Is this true?" asked Baal to Labolas.

"Well, erm, well," Labolas stammered, "I was not prepared to listen to either as I believed one to be the traitor we have been seeking."

"You didn't think to, perhaps, ask me, maybe even take a guess? Surely, it seems unimaginable, even to you," he sneered, "that we would casually stroll through the gates of Hell, like a couple friends returning from a riotous night out on the tiles?"

It was Balam who spoke first. "Are you truly of this opine, Forcas? Do you believe this is the true desire of Xaphan?"

"He came to me recently, asking if I could set up a meet with one of the kings, and I suggested Amdusias. I have always believed him to be a fair judge." He looked over to Amdusias, who now shrouded his eyes with one of his hands.

"Then you met with an angel without informing the committee?" asked Count Glasya-Labolas.

"I did not feel the need to inform you," he said quickly. "I believed the meeting to be unimportant and wanted to hear what Forcas had to say for himself."

Balam turned his eyes on Forcas. "You attended this meeting as well?"

"He did not," Amdusias spoke before Forcas had the chance to. "It was only the angel Xaphan who showed up at the designated place."

Labolas was outraged. "And you brought him to our realm? You should also be standing before us."

Amdusias changed his appearance from that of a man into his chosen form of the beast king he wore in battle, with claws instead of hands and feet. His head took on the shape of a unicorn; a large, golden horn glimmered on his forehead. The whites of his eyes disappeared, as did the brown irises, and they became totally blood red.

Lowering his head, he pointed the horn towards Labolas and charged at him, stopping within inches of spearing through his chest. Above his furious snorting, he could hear Prince Seere's shouting.

"Stop, Amdusias, STOP!"

Finding some calm, Amdusias's fury slowly dissolved, and he returned to human form, but he remained standing in front of Labolas, glaring angrily into his worried face.

"You will never, and I mean never, assume to be my equal, are we clear on this, Labolas? Because if we are not, I will call the Conjurer and ask him to make a decision on your very existence. Do you understand me?"

"You must have balls the size of the moon to call Amdusias out like that, Labolas, or are you merely stupid?" asked Seere.

"I was not inferring—"

"You *were* inferring," Amdusias spoke over him, "that I was in contravention of our code, and that," he pushed a claw deep into Labolas's chest, "will *never* happen again, do I make myself clear...*Count*?"

"I understand."

"You understand, what?" shouted Amdusias

"I understand, Highness," he replied meekly.

"Shall we return to the matter at hand?" Baal coughed. "That is the subject of President Forcas and his entry into our Realm, with the Angel known as Xaphan, what say you?"

"I believe I may have made an erroneous conclusion to the actions of our President," Balam said frustratedly, "please, continue with the reasons for your actions."

Forcas looked at King Balam. "I will when you release Xaphan, I think he has been imprisoned long enough."

"Do it now!" Baal interjected, giving no chance of refusal.

"Very well," Balam raised the same fingers and reversed the circular motion he had done previously. Xaphan's face began to return to normal, his mouth being the last thing to be freed from its stone prison.

"Are we still to be kept in chains as well?" Forcas asked, watching the colour return to his friend's face. Unspoken words passed between them, and a silent understanding was in place.

"I think we shall keep the bonds in place. Meantime," said Baal, "when we are satisfied that you have not broken any rules, we will then release you and decide upon the measures we will put into place."

"We will hear from you now," King Balam said to Xaphan. "How is it you walk into our Realm with one of our presidents, to what purpose is it you seek here?"

Xaphan shook his head, pleased to be free of the hellish abyss where he had been sent. He focussed on Amdusias but was unable to hear properly, the screams of pain he had witnessed still resounded in his head. "My apologies, sire, can you give me a moment?"

Balam laughed. "I see you were witness to our wonderland?"

Xaphan grimaced, this was a dangerous assignment, one wrong word, and he could find himself back in that black pit, but more worryingly, he might endanger those he was trying to keep safe. Taking a deep breath and closing his eyes for a second, he closed his mind to his surroundings and imagined a different place. One where he could fly freely, unencumbered with the worries of several universes. One where he was only responsible to himself and being alone did not mean loneliness, but meant peace.

"Can you hear me yet?" asked Balam

Xaphan opened his eyes and returned to the present and looked at King Balam. "I'm sorry, Highness, what was the question you asked of me?"

"I simply enquired as to your intentions in this Realm, why you came to be here with President Forcas?"

"I wish to leave the heavens and make full commitment to my brethren on this realm."

"It is as you said," Baal stated.

"Not so fast, Baal," Balam stopped him. "I am unsure if this is the truth, these two…" He waved his hands over Forcas and Xaphan, laughing when Xaphan ducked, trying to avoid any spell Balam might throw his way.

"How do we know this is the truth?"

"We are in Hades, the truth is not really one of our good points, now is it?" asked Seere. "Now if you want torment and anguish, we're on the right track. I think we should take him at his word, I would like to move on from this and begin to trust our President."

"Thank you, Prince Seere," Forcas said, dipping his head in respect.

"I am in agreement," Count Glasya-Labolas said to the surprise of the assembled group.

"You are?" asked Balam.

"Of course, I see no reason to disbelieve them. You were right, Baal, I should have asked questions. What possible good could it have done them strolling through the gates as they did? They came in as though neither had anything to hide. So, yes, I agree with Prince Seere."

Seere slapped Labolas on the back. "Well done, takes a great man to admit he was in the wrong and to then show humility. I am most impressed."

Labolas bowed his head. "I thank you, sire," he said, then turning to Xaphan and Forcas, he said, "My apologies for the mistreatment I imposed upon you."

Baal looked at Labolas in total disbelief. "Well, that means two have chosen to take this response on board. What about you, Balam, and you, Amdusias?"

King Amdusias returned to his throne and gave a cursory glance over Xaphan. "I am unsure. I know of what I learned in the meetings I held with Xaphan, but I will bow to those who believe this to be the truth. However, I will agree in part to take this as truth, but," he stopped, "we must decide, that is, if we agree Xaphan is to cross into our realm, what we will determine is the correct course we wish him to follow."

Forcas lifted an eyebrow. "What do you mean by that?" he asked.

"It would be unwise for Xaphan to be one of our chosen," said Balam. "He can't just join the ranks of demons, there are several options we must consider before allowing his presence to be accepted within our Realm."

"Must I return to the heavens?" asked Xaphan.

"Until we make our decision, I am afraid that will be the case," Amdusias replied.

Xaphan looked totally dejected. "I will anxiously await your judgement, then," he said sadly.

Baal stood up. "And you, Balam, do you agree to take this as truth?"

King Balam hesitated. "I, too, am unsure, but as with Amdusias, will go with the majority. I do not believe either would venture into our realm lightly and be so blatantly obvious. So, yes, I will accept this as truth, and we can decide upon the *right* course of options Xaphan will have to follow."

"Fellow Malum Reges, Xaphan, Forcas, I believe we will adjourn." He walked to the back of his throne and grabbed the shackled woman. "Come, girl, we have business to take care of, I have a need of your body. You," he said to the shackled man, "you will come with us, too, your body is one that can be used as well."

"Now that sounds like the best idea I have heard today," King Amdusias said as he pulled the shackled couple from his own throne. Thrusting himself against the behind of the woman, he said, "This one is a hot little thing. Would you care to join me, Balam?"

The look of distaste that crossed Balam's face could not be missed. When Amdusias growled in anger at his reaction, Balam lifted a hand in apology.

"You misunderstand my intent, Amdusias, the girl would give me no pleasure, I will leave her to your own enjoyment. The man, now there's someone I will take care in pleasuring."

The kings all laughed, excited at the forthcoming events they would be enjoying, when they heard Forcas clearing his throat.

"What is it, Forcas?" asked Baal, his hands flowing freely

over his woman, grabbing her and bruising her as they roamed. "Did you want to join us?"

"That would be difficult, sire, as we are both still chained."

"Ah, of course." Turning to King Balam, he ordered, "Release them, Balam, get them to the Cavernis so that we may retire and go over the…" He bent the girl forwards and entered her. "Ah, that's better, I can think properly now." He began pushing inside her harshly, then withdrew slightly before ramming into her again, hard. "Now that's almost perfect. You," he snapped to the man, "you take her mouth." Baal continued his harsh penetration as the shackled man readied himself.

"What was I saying? Oh, yes, Balam, release them, and we can discuss what to do about Xaphan."

King Balam crossed the room, his face expressionless until he reached Xaphan and Forcas. He unshackled their feet and unlocked the chains from their necks with a sleight of hand. "You are free to go, but we will contact you, Xaphan, shortly."

"Thank you, Highness," Forcas said, respectfully bowing.

Baal moaned in pleasure when the woman's cries of pain echoed around the room. The look of resignation on her face sent shivers of disgust through Forcas. "Shut her up, man," Baal yelled excitedly, to the man.

Xaphan and Forcas began to transastralise, not wanting to see the vile act about to be perpetrated on the woman, but before they did, they witnessed the hatred cast in their direction by King Balam.

Chapter Seventeen

Lauren expected to find herself materialise in her kitchen, instead, she was in the middle of a coffee shop; and not just any coffee shop, it was a Pret a Manger shop. "Slight detour," Ramiel said sheepishly. "I thought it would be better to go out for coffee."

Lauren looked over her shoulder and out the large window behind her, hoping to get her bearings. She recognised the shops on one side, the old building that housed the Clydesdale Bank and knew she was in Hanover Street, Edinburgh. She loved this shop and often came in for a treat.

The food langars, shelved open fridges, to her right, were stacked with sandwiches of all varieties, cakes, yoghurts, and yummy desserts. To her left, leather seats and oak tables were cleaned to a bright shine. The new and modern decorative choice was open red brick walls with posters, in varying sizes, hung, framed in white oak, displaying clever concepts of the food sold in the shop, and covered most of the upper wall. The baskets situated at the front of the counter were heaped full of crisps of different flavours, and the counter was overloaded with an assortment of cookies.

The shop had the most wonderful smell, it hit you like a hot summer's day in Orlando when you left an air conditioned building, and was a mixture of bread baking, together with the wonderful aroma of good coffee brewing.

A man stood behind the counter, tall and blond. He was cleaning the steam arm of the coffee machine. He turned to face Lauren and smiled. "What would you like?" he asked slowly and carefully.

She looked up at Ramiel standing beside her. "Don't tell me," she said, grinning, "another angel?"

"Of a sort, yes," he answered.

"Michael, how would you like to make Lauren a special coffee?"

"Ramiel," he giggled, "what kind of coffee? We have Cappuccino, Latte, Mocha, Filter. We have Skinny Cappuccino, Skinny Latte, Skinny Mocha, and Skinny Filter. We have—"

"Enough, Michael," Ramiel laughed. "What would you care for, Lauren?"

"Actually, Michael," she said softly, "I'd like a skinny hot chocolate, that is, if you make hot chocolate?"

The brightest smile spread across the Barista's face. "We make the best hot chocolate in all the worlds," he said happily. "We make hot chocolate, skinny hot chocolate, hot chocolate with marshmallows, hot chocolate with—"

"Again, Michael!" Ramiel laughed out loud. "Just make a skinny hot chocolate with whipped cream and a beautiful cappuccino for me." Ramiel led Lauren to a seat and waited until she sat before returning to the counter.

"She's very beautiful, Ramiel, is she your girlfriend?" asked Michael.

"No, she's not my girlfriend, my friend."

"Is she an angel like you?"

"And you," Lauren yelled from where she was sitting.

Michael threw his head back and laughed, then he shook his

head from side to side. Closing his eyes, he squeezed his face shut, wrinkling his nose. "She's so silly, Ramiel, I'm not an angel."

"Just make the coffee, Michael," Ramiel said warmly. "I'll let her know all about you when we drink that lovely stuff. Did you know, even angels like coffee, Michael."

"Of course, I know that, Ramiel, you are always in here."

Michael ushered Ramiel away from the counter saying he would bring the coffee and chocolate over when it was made. Ramiel sat opposite Lauren, waiting for the inevitable volley of questions.

"He's not an angel?" she asked.

"No, I suppose you wouldn't think of him in that way."

"How do you think of him, then?"

"We, here, have always recognised him to be an angel."

"But he's not an angel?"

"He is not what humans would conclude to be your idea of what an angel might be, no."

Lauren was perplexed. "But you think of him as an angel?" she said again.

"Him and all those like him," Ramiel stated.

"And he can see me?"

"Yes, it appears he can, in fact, see you, Lauren," Ramiel said softly.

"And he's not an angel?"

"I think I've already answered that question. To you, as a human, he would not be considered to be your idea of an angel, no."

Lauren put her elbows on the table and placed her head in her hands. Lifting an eyebrow in query, she was about to ask another question when Michael placed her hot chocolate on the table beside her arm.

"Be careful and not spill that anywhere, Lauren, you don't

want chocolate on your clothes. Here you are, Ramiel." He handed Ramiel the paper cup, full of the aromatic coffee.

"How can you see me?" Lauren asked Michael.

"Because you're a Mistdreamer," Michael answered in a matter-of-fact voice.

"Well, of course," Lauren laughed. "I should have thought about that," she said sarcastically.

Now it was Michael's turn to be puzzled. "Thought about what, did you not know you were a Mistdreamer?"

"No, ***I*** knew I was a Mistdreamer, I just wondered how *you* knew I was a Mistdreamer," she said.

"Well, that's as easy as pie," Michael said as he showed his brilliant, white teeth in a huge smile, "because I can see you." Then he turned his back to them and walked away, returning to his station behind the counter, leaving Lauren aghast, and Ramiel spluttering coffee all over himself.

Lauren looked with incredulity to Ramiel. "What the …" She began to babble, and she knew she was babbling. "What is going on? I thought only angels and only a few *chosen* angels could see me, and yet, here I am in Pret a Manger, Hanover Street, Edinburgh, and the Barista can not only see me, he knows my name and knows you're an angel! Can you tell me when we left the heavens and returned to earth, or am I back in Mistdreaming?"

Worriedly, she looked around her, then nipped her hand. "I know I'm real, because that hurt, but is this place real?"

Ramiel picked up his coffee and took a sip of the heavenly brew. "Lauren, drink your hot chocolate and take a breath. If there is one thing I really enjoy, it's a good cup of coffee, and Michael, here, makes the best I've tasted. So let's just sit in peace for two minutes." He lifted his hand as she began to protest. "Two minutes, Lauren. Let me drink some of this lovely coffee, then we can talk. Is that okay with you?" Not waiting for an answer, he sipped again, closing his eyes in pleasure at the taste and the wonderful smell floating up to his nostrils.

Lauren sipped her hot chocolate and groaned in satisfaction, the whipped cream was topped with Ghiradelli chocolate powder, and it had melted into the cream. She licked the back of her spoon, closing her eyes with contentment, and when she opened them again it was to see Ramiel smiling at her.

"What," she asked, "have I got cream on my nose or something?"

"Are you enjoying your hot chocolate, Princess?" he asked.

She reddened and nodded. "Why do you ask?"

"Because you're humming and rocking your legs back and forth. I figured you must be in some state of ecstasy to be unaware of what you were doing."

"It's amazing," she said, then she looked down at her hands clasping her cup. "Are you going to tell me how Michael can see me, or should I just let it drop?"

"Of course not," he sighed and placed his cup on the table. "Michael, in his life, was autistic. His brain worked in a different manner to others."

"I know what autism is," she said irritably.

"Then you'll also be aware that autistics live in a world different to yourself?"

"Of course…Wait, are you saying that the world of autism, is in fact, *another world*?" she said, amazed.

"Why is it, humans cannot see beyond their own veil? Why do you always presume you are the only life? And why would Michael's world not be a *real* world, where he can see and do things you cannot?"

"Well, you're opening a big can of worms now, next you'll be telling me people with Alzheimers are in their own world as well."

"And why would they not be? Again, you close your mind to the very facts that are all around you."

Lauren laughed at the possibilities. "How marvelous!" she exclaimed. "But how sad, too."

"How so?" asked Ramiel.

"All the loved ones who care for them, not knowing the truth, that they are safe, alive, and living in another place. They think the ones they love are just shells of their former person, when, they're anything but."

Ramiel waited before responding, wanting to choose his words carefully, so that he did not come across as inconsiderate.

"For those watching, caring, and having to live through the suffering of their loved ones, we angels are aware of the pain they endure. We have teams of angels supporting them, guiding them to the inevitable conclusion. But for the ones with Alzheimer's, they are in the alternate state, we have already led them to a new world. The 'shell' as you so quaintly put it, having been replaced by one of our angels."

"You put an angel inside the body of a person with Alzheimer's?" she asked.

"The time for that person to depart the earth's plane has not been met, so the body must remain. We remove the person from within and take them to a new world. In their place, remains an angel, until the time is right for the body to cease living."

"So, let me get this right, Alzheimer's patients are angels?"

"Yes, eventually, when the illness itself has become too difficult for the body to cope. That is why, when asked questions the patient cannot remember, the angel replacing the human will know nothing of the human's life they are inhabiting, and therefore cannot answer with the right response."

"So why do you not replace those with Autism with angels?"

"You miss the point, Lauren, those with Autism are already

in their own world, why would we replace them?" Ramiel looked at Lauren and could see a multitude of unasked questions, so he continued. "There are many worlds, all of them are not known to man, and if the possibilities within these worlds were available, what do you think man's reaction would be to discovering these places?"

"Well, I would like to believe that man would try and discover how to work with the inhabitants and respect their way of life, but I'm not really sure what they would do."

"Then I think we will leave those thoughts and possibilities to one side, what say you, Lauren?"

Lauren smiled and bobbed her head in assent, then picked up her dreamy, wonderful hot chocolate and drank her fill. When she had finished and placed the empty cup back on the table, Ramiel continued to drink his coffee but watched her over the top of his cup awaiting the appropriate time to raise the subject they had come to discuss. He knew he should no longer procrastinate, but dreaded the reaction to his information. He also knew he must take her back to Mistdreaming, her knowledge was the key to discovering the traitor, and possibly more.

Taking care not to lose any of his beloved coffee, he diligently placed it on the table, but kept hold of it with one hand. Waving to Michael, he asked for another round of drinks and refrained from saying any more until the young man had placed two more steaming hot cups of delicious brew before them.

"Lauren, I must take you back to Mistdreaming. I have to learn what you witnessed on the occasions you entered."

"Are you going to tell me the news you have, or are you going to delay telling me until after I've gone back to Mistdreaming?"

"I think it best we do that, you may not be able to recollect correctly otherwise."

"You're saying whatever has happened is that bad, I may not remember things, is that what you're saying, Ramiel? Is it my mom and dad, has something happened?" she asked, beginning to panic.

Ramiel sighed loudly. "I can see nothing will stop you from learning of the facts of which I am aware, and I promise," he hesitated, "to tell you the minute you return from your Mistdream, can we agree upon that?" he asked.

"And the minute I come back you'll tell me? Do you promise, Ramiel, promise if it's bad or really bad you will tell me the truth?"

"You have my word, Lauren, I will inform you of all that has happened."

"Where do you want to start?" she asked, eager to get on with it.

Ramiel caressed her face, then closed her eyes, and Lauren found herself floating, moving quickly, as colours and light intermingled around her, spinning and turning her until she wanted to pass out. Opening her eyes, she discovered she was no longer in the Pret shop but back in the caves of Hell.

Listening carefully for any recognisable sounds, she held her breath. She didn't hear the torturous noises of her past visit, instead, the sounds emanating were similar to those of feet stomping, perhaps some were marching.

"Where do you find yourself?" asked Ramiel.

"I think I am back in the cavernis, but I am not sure. It's very dark, there's no light at all, and I can hear sounds as though marching is going on."

"Can you move forward, are you scared at all?"

"Actually," Lauren said, "I'm not in the least frightened, it's totally different from the last visit. There's an energy here, an exciting feeling, as though people are readying themselves for a special event."

"Can you see anyone?" Ramiel asked.

"No, I can't see *anything*, but I know there are people or things nearby."

"Lauren, start moving, slowly, and always, tell me what you can see and feel."

Lauren took a step into the darkness, and the purple mist enveloped her, encouraging her to move forward. Holding her hands in front of her to feel the way, she touched something hard and cold. "I think I'm touching a stone wall, I'm going to try and find a way out, there must be a door somewhere." Moving to her right, she laid her hands on the wall, feeling her way around the room until she came to a crevice. Running her hands up and down the crevice, she found a lever, which she pulled, and a concealed door swung open into a large, bright hallway.

"What age are you, Lauren? Look at your hands!"

Lauren looked down at her hands and then her little feet. "I think I must be eleven."

"What makes you so sure about that?" he whispered.

Lauren held back a nervous laugh. "Because I got the shoes I'm wearing on my eleventh birthday."

"Good girl, good girl," Ramiel said. "In that case, remember you are just a little girl and cannot be expected to deal with the dangers you meet. You are only there to look around and take note of what you observe, am I understood?"

She nodded, and in a hushed voice answered, "Yes."

Cautiously, she walked into the hall, taking note of the black and white marble floor tiles laid symmetrically along the long passageway. The walls were red hessian, and as she walked further into the hall, she could see three doors in a row, at the end of the corridor.

As she approached the doors, she asked, "Which door do you want me to go into, or do you want me to stay in the hallway?"

Ramiel's fear for her was growing. "Which one do you 'feel' you would like to enter?" he asked.

She put her hand on the round golden handle of the middle door and turned it to the right. Nothing happened. Turning it to the left, it made a clicking noise. Lauren pushed the heavy door until it opened into a large room.

"What do you see?" Ramiel asked.

"I'm in a huge room, with arched windows and massive chairs, the chairs have animals on the arms."

"Get out of there now, Lauren, you're in the Throne Room, quickly move."

Lauren walked back into the corridor and silently closed the door and stopped breathing, fear turning her blood to ice as she stared into the evil eyes of a demon.

Ramiel, sensing her fear, urged her to move away, but she was frozen, terrified. The beast lifted an arm and moved around her, holding the door to her back, he pushed it open and walked into the Throne Room. Lauren watched as the beast querulously looked around for an invisible force it would never be able to see.

"Move now, Lauren, have you left the room?"

Lauren could only nod, fear having taken a grip of her. "What do you see, is it the same demon, with the green jacket?"

Lauren nodded again, all that was going through her mind was the demon had looked into her eyes, he had seen her.

"Lauren he didn't see you, come, child, move."

Slowly, she took a few steps until she could feel her heart beating normally. When she reached the door, she cautiously placed a hand on the golden handle and pushed it open. The room she walked into was magnificent, a French stone kitchen fireplace was situated in the middle of the wall adjacent to where she stood, it had a raised stone hearth to allow seating in front of the fire. Strewn around the hearth were large cushions and a dark blanket. Two empty crystal wine glasses and a half drunk bottle of Krug Brut Vintage 1988 champagne were placed beside the blanket. Two large, oak, engraved high-backed chairs stood on either side of the fireplace. Lauren described what she saw to Ramiel. "It sounds as though someone was celebrating," he whispered. "What else do you see, look around the room and tell me if you can discern who may be using this room.

Lauren turned from the fireplace and drank in the splendour of the room, the thick carpets, the huge, heavily engraved, oak four poster bed with a red and black damask canopy draped around it, sat opposite the fireplace. The walls were covered with tapestries and works of art. Two portraits were hanging on the wall on either side of the bed. Lauren moved forward to have a closer look but first looked up at the ceiling with its huge, heavy oak beams.

In the centre of the ceiling the initials A and B were painted as intertwining leaves of an ivy. The formation of the ivy then spread and was painted across the beams as though a growing life form.

Lauren moved to have a closer look at the portraits, and was surprised when the blanket on the four poster bed changed position. Carefully, she stepped past the bed and stared at the woman in the painting. In the form of a Van Dyke painting, the background in black, Lauren looked at her Aunty Angela, her hard blue eyes staring back at her from the canvas. She wore a crown of diamonds, the centre of which had a drop of four rubies.

She looked like an evil queen, thought Lauren.

Ramiel whispered to her, making her return to the present.

Again, she walked quietly around the sleeping form on the bed to espy the portrait on the other side. "What do you see?" asked Ramiel.

"It's obviously a king, he's wearing a crown and a massive fur thing around his neck."

"Ermine. Can you describe him?" Ramiel hurriedly said.

"He has blond hair, blue eyes, he's very handsome, actually... " before Lauren had the chance to finish, the door to the room was thrown open, and two children came running in, a little girl who looked to be around the age of six, and a boy who appeared to be ten or eleven. They stopped dead and looked directly into Lauren's eyes.

"Oh, no," she whispered, "two children are here, and they're looking at me."

"They can't see you, just move out of the room, and we will see what is next."

"But we *can* see you," said the little girl. "Can't we, Lucias?"

Lucias began bouncing up and down. "I told Papa she would come back, I told him she wouldn't be able to stay away."

Lauren tried to hush them, but Lucias let out a loud yell, "Mama, Mama wake up, our cousin's here again, wake up, Mama!" he screamed.

The lump on the bed sat up and stared with the same blue eyes of the portrait, directly into Lauren's eyes.

"So it's true, you are here?" she hissed. "Which one are you the daughter of?" Holding her head, Angela began climbing out of the bed.

"I told you, Mama, did I not?" Lucias screamed.

"Hush, Lucias, Mama's not well this day, stop yelling, you have the voice of your father!"

The little boy beamed with delight. "I know I'm just like Papa."

The girl standing beside him nipped him. "You're nothing like Papa, you're too stupid, and he's not even your real papa."

Angela lifted her hand and slapped the girl hard across the face. "You will apologise to your brother, Rachauden. He is the next king, and you should remember that at all times."

Rachauden placed her hand on her face, the red mark raised on her skin, and she looked with venomous eyes at Angela. "My apologies, Mama."

"I do not want an apology, you idiot, your brother is the one you will kneel before and beg forgiveness, not me!"

Rachauden looked at her older brother with barely concealed hatred. "I am sorry, Lucias."

Lucias laughed. "Don't be silly, Rachauden, you were only playing. Come on, let's talk to our cousin."

"Lucias," Angela barked, "you will do no such thing, go and get your father, he needs to be the one to speak with her."

Lucias turned red with fury, he stamped a foot and pushed his mother. "You will not tell me what to do, not you," he declared, "only Papa will tell me, you are just the vessel, nothing else!"

Angela's eyes opened with horror. "Who has been telling you such lies, Lucias? I am your mother, you must do as I say."

Lucias raised his hand and pointed at her; with wild, crazed eyes he watched his mother sit. "I will talk with my cousin, I want to know how Valerie is, I want to hear if she is still going to marry me."

Lauren opened her mouth in shock, not believing what she was hearing, when she heard Ramiel whispering, "*Blink, blink* now, Lauren, and wake up, come back to me, now!"

"She's going to leave," screamed Lucias. "Hold her, do not let her leave, or you will pay the price, Mama!"

Lauren wasted no more time and 'blinked', bringing herself back to Ramiel in Pret a Manger, Edinburgh.

Holding her head, she screamed, "Oh my God, he thinks he's going to marry Valerie, he wants Valerie. Oh, God, what have you done to us?"

Ramiel waved to Michael. "Bring more hot chocolate, there's a good lad," he said quickly.

"I don't want bloody hot chocolate, can you believe what happened? I can't believe you would do that to us? He's crazy, and he thinks he's going to marry Valerie. He was what, eleven? Maybe twelve, and he thinks he's going to marry Valerie!"

"Lauren, go through all the events again, is this the same boy you saw on your first visit to the Cavernis?"

"Yes, he knew me straight away, screaming that I'd "come back" and he "knew" I would." Frightened eyes looked at Ramiel. "He's crazy, Ramiel, he called his mother a 'vessel' said it was his papa that would sort things out, but his sister hates him, and she's only about six years old! How can someone hate at that age?"

"Do you have any names?"

"Didn't you hear them speaking?" Lauren screeched.

"Lauren, I can see and hear nothing. I am only aware of your senses, it was obvious you were terrified, that's why I told you to come back."

"Terrified doesn't begin to describe how I feel." She looked at Michael, who was standing beside her.

"I'm sorry," he said gently, "do you not want your hot chocolate?"

"Yes, yes, of course, I do, thank you so much, Michael."

Michael smiled sadly and touched Lauren's hair. "Beautiful hair," he said, then returned to the counter.

Lauren drank the hot chocolate, wanting somehow to feel she had returned from the place of insanity she had been witness to.

"Names, Lauren?"

"His sister is Rachauden..."

Ramiel felt as though a blow had been delivered to his stomach. "Are you positive that was her name, are you certain it was Rachauden?" he asked worriedly.

"Yes, I'm sure, what's going on, what's so special about the name Rachauden?"

"And you believe she was about six years old? Is that correct? The brother, what would his name be?"

Lauren took another sip of her drink and watched Ramiel's worried eyes over her cup before speaking again. "His name is Lucias, and he thinks he's going to marry Valerie, did you get that part?"

Ramiel scratched his ear nervously, then rubbed his forehead. "This is not good, not good at all. I must speak with Ambriel and find Forcas, we have to get you and the girls to safety as quickly as possible."

"Oh, no you don't, pal." Lauren grabbed his arm. "First, I'm going back to Mistdreaming and find out what the hell is going on. I could hear boots marching."

Ramiel interrupted, "That could simply mean people exercising, you are reading too much into the noises you were hearing."

"And you, who is supposed to be deciphering my Mistdreaming, are not! Either that, or you're simply lying to me!" she exploded.

"I would rather you didn't revisit, it could be even more dangerous."

"Ramiel, I am here, am I not? I have visited, did I not? Therefore, I got out safely?"

"You will be returning as you are now, not as the child you were, you could be ensnared, I don't know how to help you if that happened."

"Oh, I think I know someone who would help me if I was captured, actually, both of them would help. My darling cousins from Hell would kill each other if they thought they would gain something from me," she said disgustedly. "Now, at what point in this conversation do you think you might fulfill your promise and give me the information you have been withholding?"

"Ah, Lauren, I know I promised, but we must go through the Mistdream and work out what it all means."

"I will tell you no more, Ramiel, not one single thing, until you tell me." She huffed, "How can an angel break a promise?"

"We can't, but we can put the promise on hold," he said, trying to inject a little humour.

Lauren stared at him and crossed her arms over her chest. "I'm waiting," she said sadly.

"It's about your parents…

Chapter Eighteen

"That was a close call," Xaphan said when he materialised in the Cavernis. "How did you convince them of my want to join their ranks?"

"I didn't," replied Forcas, "you were the one who did that by reiterating what we had prepared and I'm glad to say it worked, I hate to think what might have happened." As an afterthought, Forcas added, "Balam was in a strange mood, was he not?"

"You would know him better than I, it was Baal that had me transfixed, he's a powerful man, and definitely not an enemy I wish to meet on the battlefield again, to be honest, but if needs must, I will find myself on the opposite side to him."

Forcas began to pace around the cave. "Something was not right," he considered, "we got away too cleanly, too easily."

"Speak for yourself," Xaphan said, looking at his ankles. "I still have the marks of the spikes in my legs, and my face feels as though I have been frozen for decades."

"I apologise for that. I did my best to get you released quickly, but Balam was insistent on keeping you in that abyss. I believe if he had been able, he would have killed us then."

A voice hissed from behind them, "I am in agreement with you there, you may have the right of that," said Prince Seere.

Xaphan pulled the sword from the scabbard by his side, and

Forcas lay a hand on his arm. "Put your sword away," he said quietly, then moved to Seere with a hand held open in greeting. "Thank you, Seere, for your assistance down there, I was just saying to Xaphan, that it was a close call."

"More than you would care to know."

"Are they still partaking in their licentious behaviour?"

"That they are," Seere said with distaste, "and they will be for some hours. Their lust can overwhelm them, and if we are lucky, their brains will not catch up with their dicks for sometime yet!"

Xaphan watched the repartee between the two, shocked at the camaraderie they shared. "What goes on here?" he asked.

"Apologies, Xaphan," said Forcas. "Seere and I have been friends for many moons. He has been most helpful in our search for the traitor."

"Why should I trust this information? You were one of the five willing to have me thrown into the Pits," he growled. "I have no friendship with you, Seere, you could be the traitor, leading us a merry dance that will end in the destruction of the Mistdreamers and perhaps even the heavens?"

Forcas looked at Seere, who gestured with his head. Turning to Xaphan, Forcas asked, "Do you trust me, Xaphan?"

"Of course; you have been instrumental in my search."

"Then trust me in this, Seere is on our side. He is my contact, and I would trust him with my life, he is the one who has been able to arrange all the meetings you have shared with Amdusias. Without Seere, there would have been no meetings."

Xaphan looked at Seere, taking in his dishevelled appearance. "What happened to you? When we left, you were not as this." Xaphan waved his hand in the direction of Seere's clothing. "Did you also partake in the fruits of that poor woman?"

"That I did not," he said unhappily. "Rape is a heinous act, and one I can honestly say, I would never take part. It is only pleasurable to the truly sick of mind, and even then, I have my doubts they enjoy the act. In Baal's case, he enjoys the pain he inflicts more than the act." His thoughts turned to a time in his past, and he smiled. "It just so happens, that I love women and enjoy pleasuring them as much as they give me pleasure. What those animals enjoy doing is hellish." He laughed, cynically, at his sad response.

"What of the man, is he the reason for your appearance?"

"The man, the one I happened upon?" he asked, unsure of the meaning.

"Did you prefer to take the man?"

"Lord, Xaphan, you have a sick and twisted mind. I think you are too near the dark side for me to enjoy your company!" he exclaimed "Of course not, it does not mean the poor fellow is not experiencing the same lewd acts as the woman, for I know he will be, but no, the reason I am in this state, if you must know, is because I had to travel to earth's plane to check on the status of the Mistdreamers."

"What did you learn?" Forcas asked worriedly.

"Lauren remains hidden, I could find her nowhere."

Xaphan looked at Forcas and thought there were still secrets he kept from Seere. Seere did not miss the look and stared at Forcas. "You know where she is?" he asked, outraged.

"I have an idea," Forcas replied sullenly, "and it is better you know not where she is, just to know she is safe. What of the other two, what did you discover?"

"Why I should bother sharing, I do not know." Seere was disgruntled but knew the time for pettiness had to pass. "They are not in a good place just now, with the death of Catherine and the status Callum now finds himself in, both girls are in a very dangerous position. They are open to evil, and it won't be long before one of the demons goes in search of them."

"Who is in the most precarious position, in your opinion?" asked Forcas.

"I would normally say Lauren, but if, as you say, she is safe, then it would have to be Valerie."

"Why say you this?" asked Xaphan.

"It is only now known that there is a master Prince among the Demons who has been covetously watching her for many years."

"What?" shouted Forcas. "When did you learn of this?"

"I have only just learned, Forcas, or I would have shared this information with you. My appearance is because I was nearly caught by him. He came at me with knives as I tried to make the Mistdreamers safe, and I was unprepared for such a ferocious attack."

"Do you have any idea who he is?"

Seere shook his head. "I have had no knowledge of him. It is surprising," he said, pausing, "he must have been shielded by one in an extremely powerful position." Seere frowned. "However, even shielded, there must have been occasion when he was seen by someone. Yet he is a being I and others have never witnessed, despite numerous unsuccessful attempts of late to locate him. And going by the attack on my person, I would say he is a very unstable being."

"Could this be the traitor we have been searching?" asked Xaphan curiously, his distrust of Seere put to one side.

Seere nodded. "It is a strong likelihood that it could be, but until we know who he is, we are still in the dark as to his personage."

Forcas considered this and eventually spoke. "Maybe not," he finally said. "Lauren might have seen him in one of her

Mistdreaming experiences, and Ramiel will soon discover if this is the case."

Seere stared at him in disbelief. "You have known this for how long?"

"For as long as I have known she is with Ramiel," he eventually said.

Forcas reflected upon their conversation. The problem he perceived was what they should do with the knowledge they possessed. Yes, it was possible this unstable 'being' was the traitor, but it was merely conjecture at this point. They had to find a way of drawing the traitor out into the open. That was the stumbling block because the only way he envisaged this occurring was to use one of the Mistdreamers as bait.

If the traitor happened to be the madman Seere described, then the obvious lure would be Valerie. It was speculation, and until they could verify with a certainty who the traitor was, then all the girls, in his opinion, would be targets.

"What are your thoughts, Forcas?" asked Xaphan.

"I am just considering the options we have to find out who this traitor is. One option could be to use the Mistdreamers as bait, and, although distasteful, it may work."

"I think you might find a few angels who would be against that action," Xaphan said curtly. "Myself included."

"I don't think it's a good option, either," Seere said.

Forcas ran his hand through his hair, frustrated. "I was just going through the options, I did not say they were the right choices, or, perhaps, ones we would use." He shook his head, annoyed that either of his friends would believe he would use the girls in such a way, and exasperated at himself for not thinking before he said the first thoughts on his mind.

"What do we know about the traitor? We should go through all the information we have discovered; maybe then we could draw a conclusion, and with that, put a plan of action in place," Seere said, thinking of all the practical solutions to this ongoing problem, one that was affecting his realm as well as many other realms in the universes.

"I have gone through the information many times, and I always end up back with one of the Demon Kings being the traitor," Forcas said as he began to pace once more. "Each conclusion leads me to believe it must be one of them, who else has access to the other realms?" he pondered. "Who would be able to move through realms at the speed it takes to get from here to Tír na nÔg and beyond?"

"A Mistdreamer," Xaphan said.

"We cannot believe it is one of them, why would they now, after all these centuries, suddenly decide to create an imbalance?"

"Furthermore, they don't have the ability or the knowledge to cut through the veil."

"There is that," Forcas admitted. "Then again a Demon King could," he added.

"A Demon King who has the power of invisibility," said Seere.

"Then," said Xaphan, "you must be talking about Baal?"

Forcas nodded. "It makes sense," he said unhappily. "He is a master in teaching invisibility, hell, he taught me everything I know, but I do not believe it suits his purpose to open the veils. He is content in the position of Great King, and this would be removed were he found out to be behind the destruction of the veils."

"Perhaps it isn't a king," said Seere. "Mayhap Count Glasya-Labolas has more to gain from the demise of the veils?" He looked at Forcas. "We know his hatred of you is legendary, he can make man invisible, and in bestial form is a dog with wings. Surely that would give him the ability of swift movement?"

"But what would be his gain in destroying the realms?" asked Xaphan.

"Perhaps it would give him the opportunity to destroy Forcas at the same time?" he questioned.

Forcas thought about this for a while; it was a strong possibility. Did Labolas hate him enough to destroy a universe? "I don't think so," he said aloud.

Xaphan and Seere looked at him and laughed. "You have to say out loud what you're thinking," Seere said, "or we won't know what it is you are not sure about."

"We have a lot to think about," Xaphan began. "The day has been a long one, perhaps we are not in the right frame of mind to be considering these options."

"Then when?" asked Forcas. "We cannot delay much longer, who knows the state the Veil is in now? We must find Kakabel."

Xaphan was puzzled. "You trust him, Forcas? I am surprised, especially after we disarmed him at our last meet."

"We acted rashly," he answered, "and unwisely doubted our own friends. He has always been a friend to me, we should not have taken his sword. My only excuse is that, upon my return from Edinburgh, my mind was fraught with concern about the Chisholms, and I was not thinking properly."

Seere guffawed. "What is going on here, Forcas, what are you not telling me?"

Xaphan chuckled. "I think our fine friend here has become smitten with a certain Mistdreamer."

Seere slapped Xaphan's back, laughing. "You lie, surely? Our mighty President has fallen victim to the deadliest of all pests? The love bug?"

Forcas rolled his eyes in disbelief. They were in the middle of a conspiracy that threatened to end the universe, and his friends were joking about his non-existent love life. He watched as they continued to laugh, and Forcas couldn't help himself when his lips turned up, and he found himself tittering alongside them. The seriousness of the situation and the courtroom debacle had taken an exhausting toll on him, to find a little joy in such a dismal situation lifted his heart.

Kakabel watched with incredulity as the three darkest angels stood giggling. It was an incredible sight, and had he been a writer, he would have loved to wax lyrical about the comedy he saw before him. As it was, he would take a mental picture, store it, and recall the memory when he found himself in a darker and more unpleasant time. *This would be his 'happy' place*, he thought, *because nobody would ever believe him.*

"I have been called for assistance by someone here," he eventually said, not wanting to break the visual spell or the moment.

Xaphan immediately put his hand to his sword and was told by Forcas to resist, as it had been he who had sent out a cerebral message. Kakabel, with arm outstretched, went to Seere and grabbed his arm in warm companionship.

"Are you well, brother?" he asked

Prince Seere's smile spread wide across his handsome face. "I find myself happy, yes."

"Can I ask what caused such merriment that would have the three of you laughing so hard, or is it a jest to be shared privately?"

"No jest," Seere replied, "just having fun at Forcas's expense. That in itself is cause for laughter, would you not agree?"

"Had I the opportunity to make fun of Forcas, then yes, I would find it most amusing."

"I am glad that I can be the subject of such hilarity," Forcas said, still smiling. Then his face sobered. "But we still have business to carry out."

"And this is why you called me?" asked Kakabel. "Please tell me, as I must rush."

"Yet again, you are rushing, what is going on that you never have a moment to talk with your brothers?" asked Xaphan suspiciously.

"And yet again you jump to conclusions before you know the facts," Kakabel answered.

"Enough," shouted Forcas, "do not start your stupid quibbling, we must find out what is happening. Kakabel, what can you tell us about the Veil, is there more news?"

Kakabel tore his accusing eyes from Xaphan and looked to Forcas. "We repaired the original tear in the Veil without too much disruption and, at the time, had been prepared to consider the possibility that it had been a simple mistake." Kakabel held his hand up to stop the onslaught of abuse he expected to come his way from any one of them. "We now know, of course, that it was just the beginning."

"The beginning? Are you saying there have been more tears, that we aren't talking about *one* tear?" asked Forcas.

"There have been seven attacks on the Veil since the original one. Each time we have been able to repair it, but each instance has opened our realm to others."

Xaphan shook his head. "Do you know when the attacks happened, or is there no order to them?"

"Oh, we know there is order, and the attacks are on the increase, and instead of one tear at a time, we are now getting several tears with each attack."

"Is it possible more than one being is attacking the Veil and tearing it? Perhaps an army?"

"If it is just the one doing the damage, then he, or she, is very quick in movement." Kakabel said worriedly, "I know of no being quick enough to cut the Veil six times in one instance, let alone an invisible army."

Forcas was shocked. "Invisible? We are under attack, and we have no idea who our enemy is. The more we try to work out who it might be, the more confusion is thrown into the pot. Were you able to repair the tears?"

"We are working on it at the moment, hence my need for rushing," he glared at Xaphan, "but the Veil between us and Tír na nÔg remains open. The Fae are used to seeing us, but there is an evil penetrating their realm that we assume has been accessed through the tear from this realm."

Seere jumped up. "Tír na nÔg is under threat? What of the dragons, are they safe?"

Kakabel looked at him curiously. "Of that I am unsure, my apologies, sire. I do know, however, that there is a dire situation, but what that may be, I have no idea."

"Which other realms have visibility into our Kingdom because of the attacks on the Veil?" asked Forcas

"Tír na nÔg is the main one, the tear was so wide we have been working on it for most of the week and still have not managed to close the gap. Also, the Realm to the past is wide open, and because so many tears were made at once, we have been unable to completely close this. We have managed to close the earth plane from our sight, and luckily, only a few people were able to see into our realm. Unfortunately, those who viewed us have been unable to understand what it is they witnessed, and their brains have almost closed down. We have sent several angels of recuperation to aid them in recovery, or bring them forth to us," he said sadly.

"Then, what of the other tears?" asked Xaphan.

"The rest were easily closed, but that does not mean we prevented others from sight into our realm."

"You say the attacks are organised" said Seere, "what do you mean by this?"

"They occur at the times when the stars are realigning, once every month."

"If you know this is when the attacks are happening, how have you been unable to prevent the damage to the Veil?" asked Xaphan.

"Have you ever tried to stop an invisible tornado? Because that is what this attack is like – a whirlwind. Only this whirlwind knows our weak points, it hits them first before moving on to what might be the target it is hoping to achieve."

"That target being?" asked Forcas.

"I am presuming, and it is only my own supposition, the one that causes us to focus our attentions on the wrong fissure. If this is the case, then this being is deliberately causing chaos. We rush around trying to close the tears, and, meanwhile, it attacks another area. All of which causes me to doubt what the real target is, and leaves me to question what the traitor is aiming for; and that, my friends, is what most concerns us at the Veil." Kakabel sighed. "Because at the end of the day, we have no idea what the traitor's goal is or it's objective."

"We are back to having to discern who the possible traitor may be and are left with the same possibilities…Fast moving; the art of invisibility; clinical accuracy; battle awareness, and the ability to access other realms."

The four of them said together, "Baal".

"We all agree, the signs are leading us directly to his doorstep, but something has me doubting it is he," said Seere.

"It is too easy," Forcas said, "all the pieces of the puzzle coming together so neatly for us, especially having searched for so long for this traitor, why now, does everything point to Baal? Something is not right."

"You think we are being led down a false trail?" asked Xaphan.

"Something is playing us false, yes," answered Forcas.

"Whatever conclusions you come to," Kakabel said, "hurry

up and find the answer. We will not be able to sustain another attack similar to the one that hit us last week." Kakabel's concern was making him very agitated.

"We have learned one important factor today, however," said Xaphan.

"And what would that be?"

"That whoever, or whatever, this traitor is, it is not interested in destroying angels."

"How do you come to that conclusion?" asked Kakabel, his curiosity piqued.

"How many Guardians, including yourself, guard the Veil?"

Kakabel considered the question and took a mental note. "Including me, there are thirteen of us, why?"

"If this thing can cut through the Veil, when you are all guarding it, then surely it would have the ability to kill you and the Guardians, don't you agree? Yet it leaves you standing, or running around trying to clean up the mess it causes rather than killing you," Xaphan observed.

"Good point, Xaphan. It would make sense, certainly, if the objective is to destroy the Veil, to eliminate those who protect and then save it. That would make its goal a lot easier. Yet the Guardians remain in one piece, while the Veil is slowly being torn to shreds," Forcas announced.

Kakabel bristled. "If you are insinuating it is I who is the traitor..."

"We are not!" said Xaphan, to the surprise of Forcas, "but whoever is behind the attacks, it feels," he stopped speaking and pounded his chest, "well, to me anyway, it feels like a game it is playing, not some master plan to destroy the universe."

"This is a lot to consider," Forcas said, a small smile on his face. "We may have made more progress this night than we thought, but *if* this is the machinations of a naughty child," he hesitated, "when naughty children are caught, do they not tend to become angry when you stop them playing?"

"Children?" yelled Kakabel. "You think the destruction of the Veil is being caused by a child?"

"I am not sure, Kakabel," Forcas said seriously, "but Xaphan is right. Why are you still alive? If it is trying to destroy the Veil, you should, at the very least, have been removed from protecting it, if not that, then you should, by all rights, be dead, to allow the Veil's end. Yet here you stand." He waited for a moment before continuing, several thoughts taking root. "What I am unsure of is whether this is the actions of one or more beings."

"It sounds plausible that it is more than one," said Seere, "but I have doubts that these kind of maneuverings could be instigated by a child."

"I am just surmising," Forcas rubbed his chin, clearly deep in thought, "but to find out more, I must talk with Lauren and Ramiel. Perhaps he will have more insights to her Mistdreaming that will aid us in our quest and we can finally bring an end to this sorry episode."

"What news from Ramiel? Has he taken Lauren to Mistdream yet? What news from the rest of the Infidelibus, have you heard from any of them yet?"

"I will be visiting with Lauren and Ramiel shortly, Kakabel. It is imperative we discover what she has seen, it is the key to the traitor's identity."

"Then let's make haste," Kakabel said. "We have a lot to do, I fear, before this is over and can bring the traitor to account for his actions."

"We must remain together," Forcas said to Seere. "Kakabel, return to the Veil, we will meet you there soon. Xaphan, come with me and Seere."

"I would normally agree with you," Xaphan said, "but think the time is right for me to join Kakabel. You and Seere will manage better without me."

"Do you mean to cast aspersions," asked Kakabel, "or are you willing to help?"

"The time for casting aspersions has to be put aside," Xaphan answered. "I thought I would be of better use helping mend the Veil. Lauren will need Forcas after Ramiel tells her about her parents' circumstance, and I do not feel I would be of any use." He shuffled his feet in embarrassment. "She will be in tears, and I cannot stand to see women cry."

"The mighty warrior is a puppy," Kakabel laughed, then slapping his back, he said, "Come then, Xaphan, we are in need of your assistance. The Veil will close faster if you are with me." He glanced at Forcas. "Are you happy with this decision?" he asked.

"It is good to see us working and trusting each other again. Yes, go with Kakabel, Xaphan. When I have seen Lauren, I will come to the Veil, and we can consider our options."

With a flourish, Forcas spread his wings. "Seere, are you ready?" Seere nodded and let his wings free, fanning the magnificent, black feathers.

Xaphan and Kakabel waited until the other two had transastralised before spreading their own wings. "Come, friend, let us go and hope we can, indeed, close the apertures in the Veil caused by this *child*. We can await news from Forcas while we work," Kakabel said.

Xaphan smiled. "We go into the unknown again, Kakabel, but this time, I feel we are heading in a positive direction."

Kakabel nodded, and together, they raised their heads to the sky, their wings pushed behind them, and in doing so, the heavenly chimes resonated throughout the cave.

Shimmering and twinkling, they transastralised, their radiance remained, shining brilliantly for several minutes after they had left the cave. The darkness cloaked the cave, and the intense silence of evil seeped into the walls.

Chapter Nineteen

"Hush, Lauren, hush my princess." Ramiel held her in his arms, desperately attempting to console the weeping woman, but nothing he said or did was helping. Holding her tightly in his arms, he rocked back and forth, gently massaging her back, crooning softly. "Shhh, my darling girl, shhh, my little love." He prayed for help, his child was weeping, and he felt as though a knife had been stabbed through his heart. He would gladly take her pain himself if it meant her distress was lightened. However, her body trembled with despair.

Lauren felt the warmth surround her as Ramiel kept her secure in his arms, but something had shifted.

"Lauren, you must stop this."

She lifted red, swollen eyes, tears had left small rivers of salt on her face, and she looked up into Cathy's beautiful face. Lauren grabbed her mom tightly. "Mom, Mom, how could you leave me, how could you go?" she wept uncontrollably.

"Lauren, sweetie, come on, you must stop this," Cathy whispered.

"What's the point, you and Dad aren't there anymore, what's the point?" Her breath caught in sobs as she hiccuped tears.

"The point is, Lauren, there are others who need your help,

and for as long as you're holding me, there's danger out there that you have to fix."

"Why should I?" Lauren cried. "They took you from me. They've taken Dad as well, why should I help them?"

"The angels never took me from you," Cathy said, puzzled. "A demon came for me, the angels have always tried to help us. Your dad and I should never have hidden you or your cousins. You three are the way forward, you must fulfil your destiny."

"But I want you back, Mom, I don't think I can stand it if you're not there, the house, it'll be so lonely, how am I going to manage without you and Dad?"

"Well, here's a little secret, Lauren," Cathy whispered, "your dad isn't here, so he must be somewhere? Maybe you should find him, and crying into my shoulder isn't going to help him is it?"

A large tear slipped down Lauren's face, her eyelashes spiked with tears already shed. "I will miss you so much, Mom."

"Don't you worry about your mom, I'll take care of her." Lauren let out another sob as her Grandpa Tony appeared beside her mom. "You've left me, too?" she sniffed.

"I told you that your Grandma MaryPat and I had the most important journey to face. I just had to go first, but I'm waiting for her. I'm watching her, and until she's here with me again, I'll be taking care of your mom." Stroking Lauren's hair, he smiled. "Now, little one, it's time to let your mom go, I promise she'll be safe with me. Go tell your grandma that I love her, that I've always loved her." Lauren looked at her mom, tears filled her eyes, and she sobbed. Then, falling into her mom's arms, she lay on her chest against her heart. Taking her fill of the scent of jasmine, her mom's unique smell, "A mommy smell", Lauren used to say, she lay weeping against her breast. Lauren's face was damp with tears and wet from soaking Cathy's white blouse, before she managed to stop sobbing.

"What's going on here?" Lauren heard Forcas's deep voice as he entered the room, and she looked up to see Ramiel was the one holding her and not her mom.

Lauren could smell jasmine coming from her sweater and breathed in deeply as the scent of her mother filled her nostrils. "She was here." She smiled at Ramiel. "She came to see me, and she was with my Grandpa Tony."

Ramiel glanced at Forcas and lifted a shoulder. "I don't know," he silently mouthed. "Did you Mistdream, Lauren?"

Lauren shook her head. "No, I don't think so. One minute I was being held by you, the next I was in my mom's arms. My Grandpa Tony came as well and told me he would take care of my mom and not to worry. Why would I worry about her now, isn't she safe yet, Ramiel?"

"She's safe, little one, he means that her next adventure won't be spent alone. She'll miss all those known to her on the earth's plane but, now, having passed into another world, things will be quite different for her and your grandpa."

"Lauren," interrupted Forcas, "I have not seen you since the party, do you have time for us to talk?"

"Perhaps now is not the right moment, Forcas," Ramiel interjected a little crossly.

Lauren peeked at Forcas, as she remained holding on to Ramiel, and a sob caught in her throat. "Where have you been?" she asked, her voice a distant echo in her dark tunnel of sorrow. The distress in her voice reached a place deep within Forcas that had, previously, long since hardened, but at the sight of her grief and at the depth of the sadness he heard in her voice, he melted.

Feelings rushed through him, sensations that had been closed off became overpowering; how had this slip of a woman managed to become such an important part of his life? *No*, he thought, *she's not just an important part.* He began to tremble.

Fear was such an unusual sensation for him to experience, and yet he stood before Lauren trembling in her wake as the most powerful of emotions exploded in his heart.

He loved her.

He was in love, and it terrified him. An emotion that should be dead to a fallen angel, now revealed its truth, and he could no more deny this than he could stop the rain from falling or the angels from singing.

He loved Lauren, and he was in Hell as torment raged through him and doubts grasped his heart. It was not possible that she could feel half the emotion that he had growing inside of him…and worried that she would. *What future could they have,* he considered, then pondered the prospect. *Would she want a future with him?*

"Forcas?" Lauren whispered. "Are you still here, where did you go?" She sniffed.

"I am still with you, Princess, my thoughts just led me from what is important."

"Which would be?" Ramiel tried to bring some reason into the room as the heavy weight of Forcas's emotion began to resonate around him.

"Would be?" Forcas's eyes burned with unspoken desire as he gazed at Lauren. "Oh yes," he managed to grind out as he pulled his stare to rest upon Ramiel. "Yes, that would be… That would be," he stuttered, "oh yes, the deciphering of Lauren's Mistdream." He was, at last, back in control, and he spoke intensely. "Have you any news for me and the Infidelibus? Did you discover anything that would help?"

"I think we may have made significant progress, but I am still unsure of who the Demon King may be. What we do know, is that he is the father of Rachauden and an older child, a son, called Lucias."

“We have decided it could be either Baal or Balam.”

“Who is we?” Ramiel asked. “Kakabel or another brother?”

“He is a brother to me, and I have trusted him for many years.”

“That would be me.” Prince Seere walked into the room and waited for the blast of disapproval to hit him, together with the objection to his presence, and was pleasantly surprised to see Ramiel lift an eyebrow.

“I wondered when you would show face. It’s taken you long enough. Are you only now brave enough to enter our realm?” He laughed.

Had Seere been felled by a blow, he would not have been more surprised! “You knew of our partnership? You are not concerned I may be the traitor, or even that I may lead you, Angels, into betrayal?”

“Had that been the case, I think you would, and could have accomplished that many moons ago. You did not, neither did you betray the Mistdreamers, so it was obvious, to me, that you were not the traitor amongst us.”

Forcas let out a belly laugh, relieved to be free of the intense emotion for a few minutes. “Logic, Seere, if nothing else, Angels have logic. Seriously though, you are going to have to develop more yourself if you are to continue helping us in our battle.”

Ramiel’s surprised chortle stirred Lauren as she lay on his chest. His warmth, emanating from deep inside him, had been shielding her from the misery seeping through her body. When she felt the laugh radiate through him, it gently brushed against her cheek like the fluttering of a sparrow’s wings.

“Battle, what battle? Has this something to do with the marching I heard when I was in Mistdreaming?”

“Lauren, I said the marching you heard could have been anything, we must not jump to any conclusions now.”

“Then mayhap we should walk through her dream and work this out together?” Seere asked.

“I’m going back so that I can work it out for myself. I’m not hanging around here while you lot *think* about what I’ve seen, I want to be there physically, and instead of theorizing, witness what’s going on for certain.”

“I’m not sure if that’s a good idea,” Ramiel said.

“I know you’re worrying about me, Ramiel, but you’ll be with me in mist and can tell me to move, but you have to remember these are my past experiences, so I’ve already been there, I’ve already seen what the problem is.”

“And that is what puts you in more danger,” Forcas spoke quietly, “the fact you cannot remember all you have seen, may be the reason for your survival. Mayhap whoever or whatever you have been witness to is aware of your memory lapses,” he looked aggrievedly at Ramiel, who had the good grace to look away, “and therefore has let you continue in your life.”

“Maybe, but surely they would know at one point my memories would come back or that somebody would help me revisit?”

“She has a point, Forcas. That could be why Rachauden was at your party, Lauren, it is possible that your memories were going to return on a certain time or an event would trigger you to recall. Before your Mistdream, did anything occur that was traumatic or different to cause your memory to return?” asked Seere.

Before Lauren had the chance to speak, Forcas stepped forward. “I think Lauren must be exhausted, she has had some dreadful news, maybe we shouldn’t be bothering her with small incidentals like this.”

Lauren blushed and hid her head in Ramiel’s chest. “You see what you’ve done, Seere, she’s upset again, leave her be.”

"My apologies," Prince Seere spoke sincerely. "I had no intention of causing you more grief, I was merely trying to discover if there was a source of power of which you might have been unaware."

"Forcas, I think now would be a good time to take Lauren for some air, what say you? Lauren, do you feel up to walking outside with Forcas? It might help a little. Meanwhile, the Prince and I will go to the Veil, I need to see for myself the extent of damage caused. Seere can remain with Kakabel until the Infidelibus can meet again to discuss our strategy."

Lauren nodded into his chest, not wanting Seere to witness her embarrassment. When she was able to pull herself upright, she stood and walked to Forcas. He held his arms tightly into his body, his mind screaming at him to hold her and keep her safe, to take away her pain. Instead, he gave a cursory wave to Ramiel and Seere, and, opening the door, he walked behind her as they stepped into the warm air.

"Such a lovely day," Lauren said sadly. "Not really like Edinburgh weather, is it?"

"Are we really going to talk about the weather, Lauren? Do you not think we have more important matters to discuss?"

Lauren turned on him. "I think it's an excellent subject at the moment, don't you?"

"Not really, but if you feel it's deserving of discussion then, it's lovely weather and very typical of Edinburgh. That, together with the rain and the wind we'll get later, makes it the perfect day."

Lauren smiled. "Sorry, I shouldn't have grouched at you, I just don't know what to say. I'm exhausted, I'm sad, and I thought, well it doesn't matter what I thought, but," she waited a moment to collect herself, "it's good to see you again."

Forcas's heart overruled his head, he could no longer resist her, and grabbing her gently by the arms, he pulled her into his embrace.

She smelled like wild flowers and sunshine, he thought. "I had to hold you in my arms," he said, stroking her hair as she lay against his shoulder. "You disappeared before we had the opportunity to discuss what was happening between us, and then, well, then the world turned upside down for you. I am so sorry, Lauren, I wish I could take your pain."

Lauren took a deep breath, she didn't want to cry, she had wept for hours and felt there were no more tears left to be shed. Yet here she was standing in Forcas's arms, and her tears were again soaking an Angel's shirt.

Her tears were cathartic, they were cleansing her pain, she knew that, and at some time they would cease, but until then, she would hold on to this man and feel his strength flowing into her that, and, she thought incredulously, *Could it be love she sensed coming from him? Was it possible he felt for her some of what she did him?*

The astonishment at the possibility stopped her tears, she lifted her red, swollen eyes and searched his face for any sign of his feelings.

Forcas watched as she examined his face, her beautiful eyes full of unshed tears, when the sharp pain of realisation hit him hard. He tried to hide the truth from her, but as the agony of his emotions began to overwhelm, he knew she was aware of how he felt. Rather than break the spell with words, he lowered his head and gently, softly covered her lips with his own.

She tasted like a ripe, sweet, Scottish strawberry, and he wanted to devour her.

Tenderly lifting her in his arms, he spread his wings. Lauren whimpered at the loss of connection to his lips. Shivering, she curled her arms around his neck and began to place small kisses along his collarbone. As she progressed towards his ear, the kisses became interspersed with delicate, erotic bites.

Forcas soared through the air, his body brimming with desire as she carried on with her relentless tasting and biting of his neck. He threw his head back when her lips and teeth sucked and licked their way to his Adam's apple before continuing their sensual journey upwardly to his chin.

He caught his breath when he saw the desire shimmering in her eyes and held her closer. Their bodies fused together as one as he flew higher, until, at last, they reached their destination.

Lauren was so absorbed in her tasting and kissing exploration she did not realise she was no longer flying.

"We are here, Lauren," Forcas murmured breathlessly as he retracted his wings.

"Mmm? Here, where?" she sighed.

"We have come to my home," Forcas said proudly. "We are in Lenticularis Tioram, my castle in the clouds." The way he pronounced Tioram sounded more like "Chee-room".

Lauren smiled and gaped at the amazing hexagonal, celestial edifice, built at the top of a mountain of jagged shaped clouds. A pathway of white sand spiralled meanderingly to the silver, arched gates, above which, beautiful crenellations adorned the forty foot high wall, adding the classic castle appearance.

From where they stood, within the castle walls, to one side Lauren could see crow-stepped gables, and to the other side, a prominent square tower rose above the whole castle. A gallery could be seen at the top of the tower with a magnificently constructed overhang enabling one to view the floors below. "Were you expecting an attack of some kind?" she asked, still looking at the building. "The walls are huge."

"They're that high because we have wings," he said rationally.

It was such a simple statement, a practical statement, and said in such a way that made Lauren hesitate for a moment before dissolving into a bag of laughter.

"How stupid of me to not know that, Forcas," she still giggled. "There was me thinking a castle had high walls to keep out enemies, and here you are telling me, they're high, 'cause you all like to spread your wings."

Forcas frowned, he was attempting to make sense of her statement but was having serious difficulty in understanding her meaning. Deciding it would be futile taking a chance in interpreting, he asked if she cared to enter his domain.

"Please, I'd love to see inside, it's amazing," she said honestly.

Forcas lifted her easily into his arms and outstretched his wings, flying carefully so that she could have a good look at his home. She marvelled at the buildings below, she could see stables. *The gables could be a church*, she thought. A beautifully paved courtyard was the central focal point, with buildings leading from it like satellites.

The tower had a slow winding, stone staircase and balustrade, the spindles shaped like urns, leading from the courtyard to the second floor, where an impressive, continuous walkway, with wrought iron balustrade and handle, gave access to the many doors and passages on that level.

Forcas landed outside one of the rooms, a ten-foot oak door, which was carved with cherubim and had large, iron fitments, was closed to them. He pushed it open with his foot to reveal a masculine bedroom, containing a four poster bed with no drapes. A magnificent stone fireplace was on one wall, and a writing desk placed nearby was all the furnishings in the room.

Lauren walked past the bed, suddenly very shy, and opened

the large window, which was on the opposite side to the entrance. It opened onto a small semi-circular balcony overlooking the mountain of clouds.

"Lauren, are you wishing to leave already?"

"Give me a moment, Forcas, it has suddenly become a little too *real* for me."

"As opposed to false, you think that is what I play you? False?" He was horrified.

"What on earth are you talking about?" she asked, surprised.

"You wish for real, which means I give you falsehoods, I can assure you—"

"Shut up, Forcas!" she laughed. "I meant, I just thought all this," she waved around her to the clouds, "has become a little intense, and after the day I've had, intense needs to go back a little." She breathed heavily, hoping he would understand.

"Why do I not ring for some food, Lauren, something that we both may enjoy. Would you like something sweet or savory?"

"Ooh, what a good idea." She clapped her hands. "I think I'm starving, I can't remember when I ate last, but I think it must have been at my party." She stopped suddenly and rubbed her face. "Was that last night? It seems so long ago."

"Last night, perhaps in earth years, but here we work on a different time, days can be years, months can be an eternity."

"What? Are you saying when I go back my family will all be old?"

"No, Lauren, I was simply saying time here is not relevant. Anyway," he said, changing the subject, "what would you care for?"

"How about a vegetable curry on a bed of aromatic rice, with a warm naan bread? Oh, doesn't that sound lovely. What are you going to have?"

Forcas lifted an eyebrow. "Ah, Lauren, I'm going to have a

Scottish strawberry." He smiled as she turned a confused look at him. "You'll know what I mean later," he laughed.

Forcas pulled a cord to the side of the fireplace, and within seconds, a man wearing a kilt entered.

"You rang, m'lord?" he said in a lovely Scottish brogue.

"I did, Angus, my lovely guest wishes a vegetable curry, do we have any of that in the kitchen?"

"I have no doubt Cook has some of that ready, just waiting to be served. Would her ladyship care for naan bread and rice, perhaps some mango chutney?"

Forcas nodded and smiled in acknowledgement.

"It won't take long, m'lord," Angus said and exited the room.

"You have servants?" Lauren said, not knowing whether she should be impressed or offended on their behalf.

"Not servants, no, they live here and help me whenever I return."

"But they serve you, that makes them in servitude."

"Not at all, if you ask Angus, he'll tell you it's me that's beholden to them, and he'd be quite right. This is their home, Lauren. They want to remain here, it has always been familiar to them, and this time, they *choose* to do what is asked of them."

Lauren didn't get the opportunity to respond because Angus returned carrying an enormous silver tray, with one hand, above his shoulder. The tray had several silver dishes, all of which had the most heavenly scents emanating from them.

A young girl followed Angus carrying a table, and behind her, a man, in a different kilted tartan, carried two Chippendale chairs. The girl placed the table in the middle of the room and spread a white tablecloth on top as the young man placed each chair on either side of the table.

Angus lay the tray onto the table and proceeded to set it with silver cutlery and pretty chinaware. Removing the dishes from the tray, he lay them in a single line for ease of service.

"You didn't ask for anything, m'lord, so I thought it best to bring the same fare for you as m'lady requested."

"Very kind, Angus, you shouldn't have bothered Cook for me."

"She was only too delighted to be of some help, and I quote, 'Feeding him up at last.'" With a twinkle in his eye, he produced a china bowl and lifted the lid from it. "I also thought you might like to try a Scottish strawberry, picked this morning in Blairgowrie." His less than innocent smile spread across his face, and dimples appeared in his cheeks. "Unless you would prefer a raspberry."

Forcas watched Lauren and bit his lip hard, holding back the laughter that threatened to explode. "Get out, you daft old man."

"I am that for sure." Turning, he smiled kindly to Lauren. "May you enjoy your food, m'lady, and let me take this opportunity to welcome you to our Castle, it's an honour to meet you at last."

"Erm." Lauren stopped spooning rice onto her plate. "Oh, I'm sorry, I couldn't help myself, it just smells wonderful, what was it you said, Angus?"

Angus smiled again. "Nothing at all, m'lady, just that we're pleased you've come to see us again."

Lauren looked questioningly to Forcas, who shrugged his shoulders. "Don't ask me, I have no idea what he's talking about. I have no doubt all will be revealed at some time." Then he slapped Angus familiarly on the back. "It's good to see you again, old man, and," he pointed to the table, "thank you for this."

"Our pleasure, m'lord, now if you've finished delaying me, I'm sure Cook and others are in need of my direction." He glanced at Lauren. "Will you be requiring breakfast, m'lady?"

Lauren sprayed her rice onto the table, "What?" she chuckled and raised her astonished eyes. "You're a naughty man, Angus."

"That I am, m'lady, that I am. Good night to you both," he said and closed the door as he left the room.

"Well, I never." Lauren piled another spoonful of curry into her mouth. "I see what you mean about him not being a servant." Shaking her head, she bit into the naan bread. "Staying the night, what do I want for breakfast? What a cheek."

"Lauren, would you care to stay for breakfast? Cook's Scottish plateful is renowned everywhere."

Lauren pushed her plate away, suddenly not hungry for food.

Her sensuous eyes raked over Forcas's body. "I think I might like to stay, but you'll need to persuade me. Food isn't really a motivation for me to give up my own bed, to be honest," she purred.

Forcas raised one of her feet and removed her shoe, his thumbs massaged her ankle in firm circles, then he lifted the other foot and did the same, caressing her foot, then stroking it, sending waves of pleasure tingling through her body.

"Please, don't kiss my toes," Lauren whispered. "I'm not very keen on the toe thingy." She closed her eyes for a moment, letting out a soft, contented sigh, only to open them and find herself in Forcas's arms, lying on his bed.

"I hope you're not that fast at everything you do," she said seductively.

Chapter Twenty

Forcas began to shiver, a fierce and powerful emotion poured through his veins as he gazed down at Lauren. The idea of mating with a human had never been an experience he had cared about. Yet she invoked a need so deep within him, he was desperate to share himself with her, to *feel* himself as part of her and she a part of him. He wanted to copulate. *No,* he thought, *he must not think of it in those terms, how had Lauren described it? "Making love" she had said.* Making love to her, an act he had thought to be messy and repulsive, but his body was telling him otherwise.

To have such feelings was dangerous, not just to himself but for Lauren, and until now, he would never have crossed the boundaries written by the Council of Angels. He would not have given his life for any other, and yet, if he continued along this path, that is what would happen.

He could not help himself, he loved her. He wanted her. He wanted a life with her.

A *real* life.

"Lauren, I…"

"Forcas, I…"

Their lips came together as their heads fell against the soft pillows, and their bodies bounced on the comfortable mattress beneath them. Lauren fumbled with his shirt, trying to find buttons, but there were none, so she pulled it from his trousers and lifted it up to his chest. Her hands touched his bare chest, and she sighed at the pleasure she experienced from such a simple gesture. At last, contact with his skin.

Forcas moaned, the shock of her touch searing his skin. He pulled her into his arms and hardened their kiss, their teeth colliding for an instant. His body was aflame, he felt out of control and knew instinctively he had to restrain his desires until he could unleash the power building within him.

Lauren felt him pulling back, knew he was afraid for her, and she was not going to allow it. She ran her fingers through his wonderful hair, luxuriating in the texture, and gently tugged on it before placing her fingers onto his scalp, massaging it in time with their passionate kisses.

Her lower body began grinding against him, gyrating to a sensuous tune, and Forcas was playing the music.

His body reacted to her movements, and desire turned to hunger. He flipped her onto her back and removed her blouse, then with ease unclasped her bra, leaving her small, beautiful breasts exposed. With a quick flourish, he threw his shirt to the floor and wrapped her in his arms, cradling her in his warmth.

His lips found her neck, and he kissed and nibbled his way to her breasts, taking one nipple between his teeth. Gently biting until she whimpered with pleasure. Her fingers grabbed his hair as his hand closed over the other breast, he flicked her nipple until it budded into a hard knot, then proceeded to caress it. He changed breasts with his mouth and took the hardened nipple between his teeth, laving and nibbling until she pulsed with need beneath him.

Forcas had to taste her again, and so his lips returned to hers, their urgency demanding, crushing hers as he ravished her mouth. His tongue found hers, and they touched, tentatively at first, but as their lips ground passionately, their tongues went beyond the first curious touch, as they stroked and promised more.

He became lost in the intensity of their passionate kisses and wanted, no needed, to hold her. His body was screaming for release, and he was scared.

Scared of what was happening. Terrified he would never get enough of her.

Desperation took hold, and he had to hold her, his hand moved lower until, relieved, it covered her breast, and he touched and stroked until she squealed in frustration for more and quickly unzipped his trousers, practically tearing them from his body. Forcas almost passed out with frenetic desire and moved his hand lower, bereft at no longer holding her in his hand until he quickly unfastened her jeans then, pulling them from her, tossed them onto the pile of clothes that now littered the floor.

He could wait no longer, but stopped himself and looked into her eyes. Eyes filled with desire, longing, and something else.

"I love you, Lauren. Let me say this before we make love, so that you are under no illusion that sex is the reason for me voicing these words later. I tell you before this act so that you know they are true. I love you, dear heart."

A tear fell from Lauren's eyes, onto the pillow. She was quaking with desire and knew he was in a state of desperate need.

"I love you, too, Forcas. I love you so much."

Forcas lifted his head in thankful praise, then lowered it and kissed her tenderly.

"I cannot wait any longer, Lauren, this body is quite insistent upon the course of action it must take."

Lauren started to giggle. "Forcas, will you shut up and make love to me, please, before I die of need?"

Surprised, Forcas stared. "You need this, too, it is the same for you, seriously?"

"Forcas, SHUT UP!"

He did.

Their joining could be heard throughout the castle, as Forcas howled in ecstasy, and they both screamed as one in satisfaction.

Two hours later, they lay in each other's arms, Forcas gently stroking Lauren's shoulder as he lay in contemplation.

"I do not believe angels have any idea of how good copulation is, or they would be doing it all the time."

"Lord, will you stop with the 'copulation'! Do you think that's what we just did? We made love, Forcas, not clinical copulation. Love."

He kissed the top of her head. "I know, my princess, it is hard for me to change some of the terminology I have always used, but with you, it is definitely making love."

"It had better be *only* with me!"

He pulled his head from lying next to her so that he could get a better look at her and frowned. "Of course, only with you, why would I want anyone else?"

"Because you enjoyed the 'copulation' so much," she said crossly.

"Lauren, I enjoyed making love with you. I love you and want no other but you, that is why we will be married tomorrow before Ramiel."

"What?!" she screamed.

"Of course," he said matter-of-factly "We love each other and want nobody else, so, of course, we will be married."

Lauren pushed him away from her. "Listen, you angel you, a

girl likes to be *asked* to get married, not told! I haven't said I wanted to get married to anyone, so why would I change my mind?"

"I had not thought of that. I am sorry, Lauren, I did not realise you may not wish to marry me."

"Forcas, don't *tell* me to do something, *ask* me to do it. You never know, you might get a different response."

Forcas sat upright in his bed and turning, knelt to face her. His manhood beginning to grow. He looked down at it, shocked to see it get bigger. "What the devil?" he said. "Why does it keep doing this?"

Lauren spluttered and buried her head in the pillow.

"No, Lauren, seriously, I will get nothing achieved if it keeps doing this, it is most disturbing. I can do nothing to stop it. Whenever I am near you, it just grows!"

Lauren was howling into the pillow, and the more exasperated Forcas became, the more she thought she might pee herself laughing.

"Are you laughing, Lauren? Do you find this situation, *amusing*? It's not, you know. This thing is a living entity, and although connected to me, it has a life of its own that I can't control. I mean, look at it!"

Lauren jumped from the bed and danced around. "Where's the toilet," she squeaked. "I have to go, where is it?"

Forcas pointed at the corner. "A hidden door will take you there. Are you all right?"

"Yes, I'm fine. I'll be back in a moment."

When she returned it was to find Forcas sitting upright, his head leaning against the pillows on the headrest.

She jumped in beside him and snuggled close into his side.

"Wait, Lauren, I must ask you something, it is very important."

"Is it to do with Mistdreaming?" she asked unhappily.

"Mistdreaming? What? No, it is not."

"Okay, fire away," she said and looked up into his handsome face.

"Lauren, I love you, will you do me the honour of becoming my wife, before our friends and family and the Almighty?"

Lauren sucked in her breath, the look of love on his face and the worry she may reject him was too much to bear. The thought she could be the reason he would feel pain grabbed hold of her heart, twisted it, then jumped up and down on it. Her life would never be the same again, she could not live without him, and she loved him, with every fibre of her being, she loved him, and would forever.

"I will, Forcas. I will marry you. I love you, too."

He wrapped his arms around her, pulling her close to his body and his prominent desire. He kissed her with a passion she had never known, feeling the love he had for her as he swept her on his wave of euphoria. The kiss deepened, and she parted her lips, allowing entrance for his tongue to probe sensually. When it found hers, they tussled until Forcas withdrew and moved his mouth to her breast.

Lauren let out a sigh of deep contentment as he nipped and touched and kissed her body until, at last, they came together. As their passions climbed to the stars, Lauren felt as though her body would move into a transastralised form as she panted in ecstasy. She was lost in the incredible love she was sharing with Forcas and, happily satisfied, waited for a second until he shouted out her name in rapturous wonderment.

"Amazing," he said breathlessly. "You," he pulled her close into his side, "are amazing, and I'm fairly sure after that incredible lovemaking, I'm safe now from *it* bouncing back up."

"Forcas, would it be so bad if it 'bounced' back up? Not just now," she quickly added, "I wouldn't be able to cope."

Squeezing her, he kissed her sweet lips. "I don't think it will ever be bad if it bounces back, but tonight you must get some sleep, we have a busy day ahead of us tomorrow."

Lauren snuggled closer, the warmth from his body hitting her like a blanket, and exhaustion slowly crept into her as she closed her eyes.

When she eventually drifted into sleep, the events of the day, together with the sorrow in losing her parents, floated away like bubbles on a gentle breeze. As colours surrounded her, she felt the pull of Mistdream move her to another realm and happily allowed the transastralising to take place.

She delighted in the warm satisfaction her body was enjoying, and thoughts of her cousins came to mind. She called silently to them, needing their counsel, their friendship, and to let them know she was well and happy.

"So are you going to open your eyes, or do you intend just standing their like a tube?" Valerie's seductive voice whispered.

"Maybe when you open those beautiful eyes we'll be able to see what a *dirty stop out all night* you are?" Mairi giggled.

Lauren screamed and threw her arms around her cousins, revelling in the sight of them. They looked amazing, Mairi had a glow about her she had not seen before, and her Mistdreaming blue encircled her body like a protective barrier. Valerie's Mistdreaming red flowed around her like a huge, silk pashmena, as though caressing and loving her.

"Do you want to tell us where we are and how we got here?" Valerie asked curiously.

Lauren took a glance around her, surprised to see lush green fields, purple mountains, and beautiful fir trees all around them.

"If I didn't know any better, I'd say we were in the Highlands, but look at that sun." She laughed. "It must be Spain."

"Nah, I think you were right the first time, it looks like the Highlands. It's so beautiful there, I'd love to get the chance to go there again," said Mairi.

They stilled as something swished passed them, touching their hair, lifting their colours. Their Mistdreaming colours reacted and shifted to the touch, forming a barrier between them and whatever was attempting to approach them.

"You are inn Tír na nÔg," a voice sang hypnotically. "You are in the land of the Fae, welcome back Mistdreamers, we have missed you."

They watched as the air shimmered before them and a shape appeared, changing into a tall, noble woman dressed in silks of bright, swirling colours. She was stunning, with long, flowing blonde hair reaching down to her waist. Her face was almost too beautiful to gaze upon, with bow-shaped lips, high cheekbones, a small nose, and eyes that changed from silver to blue, then back to silver.

A crown held her hair from her face, the diamonds hanging around her forehead highlighting the translucency of her skin.

"We've been here before?" asked Valerie.

She nodded.

"Hell, I wish I could remember this," Mairi said. "Tír na nÔg, the land of the Fae. I used to love them when I was a kid."

"You used to love my husband, King Finvarra, Mairi, and you always teased him; he has missed seeing you."

"Well, trust you," Valerie said to Mairi, "to turn the head of a king, and a married one at that," she laughed.

"Why are we here?" asked Lauren.

"You wished privacy to speak with your sisters. For a time, this was the only place you three were safe from the outside world, but we now find ourselves with a threat of our own."

"Are you Queen Oonagh?" Lauren asked.

The queen smiled indulgently at her and again nodded. "You are beginning to remember, are you, Lauren? You will have to remember everything if you are to help save many."

Valerie shook her head in dismay. "That's a helluva lot to put on one person's shoulders, what if she can't remember?"

The queen shot a querulous look at Valerie. "All of you must remember, not just Lauren, but for now, she is the protagonist that will instigate the procedures to ensure all the safety of the realms."

"Would you believe it?" said Mairi. "Something good after the shit day we've had."

The queen laughed, throwing her head back as she did. "You have always brought joy to our realm, but now I fear you may be the cause of some evil that is with us. I am sorry, but I must go; make your meeting short and return to your worlds." And with that curt message, she disappeared.

"Well, I never," Valerie crowed. "Who'd have thunk, us with fairies, next we'll be told there're dragons, too. Talk about far-fetched. Anyway, let's get this on the road, Lauren. I want to wake up from this dream, what's up?"

"Are you all right?" Mairi asked, ignoring Valerie's cynicism.

"I'm more than all right." She smiled happily. "I'm in love, and he's in love with me."

"We are talking an angel here, aren't we?" asked Valerie. Lauren bobbed her head in assent. "But he's an angel, Lauren."

"He's asked me to marry him, and I've said yes, and we're getting married tomorrow. That is, if the Council of Angels agrees to let him marry a human."

"What happens if they turn him down?" asked Mairi worriedly.

"Then we'll figure something out. For the time being, we love each other and want to be together."

"Well, that's just great." Valerie kissed Lauren's cheek. "I'm really happy for you, but it still doesn't answer why we're in the land of nod with you. How come we Mistdreamed over here?"

"I think it's because I needed to talk with you, and when I started to Mistdream, I began searching for you."

"We can do that when we Mistdream, call for other people to join us?" asked Mairi.

"I'm not sure," Lauren said honestly. "I just know I needed to see you both, needed to tell you I'm happy and not to worry about me and…."

"Yes?" they both said together.

"Would you come to my wedding and be my bridesmaids?"

The three girls jumped up and down, cuddling each other. "Of course, we will," Valerie said, "but," she paused, "have you heard about your mom and dad yet?"

Lauren's grief flared up, and tears sprang into her eyes, her lip quivered, and she looked up at the sky. "I know my mom's dead, yes, and that my dad is in some kind of limbo. Nobody knows where he is, the angels have searched for him, and they can't find him."

"I'm so sorry, Lauren," Mairi comforted her. "We had no idea your mom had been taken, I…" she sniffed, "I walked into the restrooms and found your mom."

"I thought it was an angel that found her," Lauren said.

"It was Appoloin who found her and the murderer, but I was in one of the stalls. I wish I could have helped her, I'm so sorry."

"We've been through this before," Valerie hushed her. "If she'd known you were there, chances are, she would have killed you as well."

Valerie, always the practical one, asked Lauren if she had

any information to share that might help them work out what was to be done. Lauren explained her dreams had been assessed, but no one was certain who the traitor was or where he or she was hiding.

"So we're still at square one?" asked Mairi. "We're still in danger, aren't we?"

"I think so, yes, but the angels are coming up with a plan to save us, and once I can definitely pinpoint who the traitor is, or at least guide them in the right direction, then we will be a lot safer."

"I wish we could help you," Mairi said.

"Maybe we can." Valerie had a brilliant idea. "What if we arrange your wedding, you say it's tomorrow, not much time, but time enough for us to get something sorted, a dress, a cake. What do you think?"

Lauren hummed and hawed. "The details of the wedding haven't been settled yet, I'm not sure if it's going to be held in Mistdreaming or on the earth's plane. I won't know until tomorrow. If it's in Mistdreaming, you will have to come here to me."

"Valerie," Mairi laughed, "she's with a bunch of angels, they can do magic, can't they? I'm sure they can make a dress and a cake for her, all we have to make sure is that we attend, is that right, Lauren?"

"Please," Lauren said gratefully. "Please, be there."

The wind changed, and their colours began to swirl around them. "It's time to go. We love you, Lauren, we'll be there."

Lauren opened her eyes and smiled as Forcas pulled her into his arms.

"Good morrow to you, my love. Did you Mistdream somewhere interesting?"

"I went to Tír na Nog and met the Fae queen."

"I'm impressed. Did she tell you anything of interest?"

"She said her realm has an evil presence and thinks it's because we Mistdreamers have been there; me, Valerie, and Mairi. And they say they're coming to our wedding," she said happily.

"Wedding, oh, yes, wonderful," he said as he nibbled his way down her body. "You don't mind if we wait for a few moments? There's something I've been wanting to taste."

"Good Lord, Forcas, what is it they say, "Give a man a strawberry and he'll eat the whole punnet"?" Lauren squealed and squirmed as Forcas began working his way through the whole punnet!

"What did you say?" Ramiel asked angrily.

"We wish to have your permission to marry. We are in love, Ramiel, and want to start a life together."

"I can't believe you're saying this, no, I can't believe I'm hearing this!" Ramiel exploded.

"What is your problem?" Lauren asked. "Why do you not want us to be together?"

"Could the simple fact that Forcas is a fallen angel perhaps be the reason for my strong disbelief and incredulity at your audacity in approaching me with this request!?" he yelled.

"Well, if you're going to be like that, I'm leaving." Lauren turned in a huff.

"Just a minute, missy!" Ramiel yelled "You're not going anywhere, not until this is cleared. Have you forgotten you are in the middle of a dangerous mission, one that must be sorted out or you and your cousins, your family and all the realms may end?"

"No, I haven't forgotten, nor have I forgotten *you* taking my memories from me or my mother dying at the hands of some evil witch. So, no, in your face, Ramiel, I haven't forgotten. Here's something for you, have you found my father yet?" she screamed.

"We still search for Callum, he appears to be Mistdreaming, but we have yet to locate him."

Lauren held back the tears that threatened. "Let me marry him, Ramiel. I love him. I will go on all the Mistdreaming missions you ask, but let us be together."

"You are wasting your breath, dear heart," Forcas said miserably. "He will never give his permission." Turning a sneered look at Ramiel, he asked, "Will you, Father?"

Lauren looked puzzled. "He's your father, Forcas?"

Not giving him the opportunity to respond, Ramiel quickly said, "I am the father to many, and you are wrong, Forcas. I will take this matter to the Council of Angels and ask for their advice. When they have made their decision, we can go ahead with plans if they allow the marriage to proceed."

"We're getting married today," Forcas said stubbornly.

Ramiel was aghast. "Today? The Council will not agree to anything today, you will have to wait until they have met."

"And if she is carrying my child?"

Ramiel was livid, he could barely conceal his fury. "She could be pregnant? How could you, Forcas? How could you mate with a human, you know it is against the Council's orders."

"Well, you are in no doubt as to my regard for the Council and their decisions. So far, I am in breach of many of their rules, this one being the most important and one that has more significance to me and my future. A future I do not have any longer in this realm, as you know."

"You jump the gun, Forcas. It has not been determined

whether your action will cause that outcome. Let me go and talk with Ambriel, he will have news of their decision, and I will broach the other matter."

"And what other matter would that be?" Ambriel spoke as he walked into the room, gesturing an acknowledgement to both Lauren and Forcas.

"I want to marry Forcas," Lauren spoke up.

"Well, we have a bit of a problem with that," Ambriel pondered.

"She also may be carrying my child," Forcas added.

'Mmm, what a pickle. What do you think, Ramiel? Are these people in love? Would the almighty ruler be happy to bless their union, what say you?"

"I say the Council must give permission before they take this rash step."

"Rash?" shouted Forcas. "It is hardly rash. I love her, and I want a life with her, and she loves me, Ramiel."

Ambriel waited for the tension in the air to settle before speaking again. "I can understand why Ramiel is slightly perturbed." He lifted his hand, stopping anyone from speaking. "Angels and humans are rarely allowed to become one. However, we are speaking about a family of Mistdreamers who have interacted and helped angels for centuries, and, I believe, in this instance, the Council will give agreement to their marriage."

Lauren let out a sigh and kissed Forcas. He smiled lovingly at her and pulled her tightly into his arms. "Thank you, Ambriel," he whispered.

"However," Ambriel continued, ignoring Forcas, "as a member of the Council, I have to inform you of our decision upon hearing of your last infringement. It is an act that cannot go unpunished, and one for which you must be disciplined, Forcas."

Lauren looked at Forcas and lifted her shoulders, shaking her head in query.

"He breathed life, his life source, into that of a human, Lauren, and we cannot allow this, so a decision has been agreed."

"And what would that be?" Forcas asked, dreading the answer.

"We are afraid we must remove you from angelic status, and you are to reinstate yourself to the earth's plane, where you will live the life of a mortal."

"And that's his punishment?" Lauren asked, surprised.

Forcas could barely move, dread now replaced with fear. "A human, I am to lose my wings after all this time?"

"You will retain the marks of angelic status until you redeem yourself. If you are able to accomplish this as a mortal, then we may consider restoring some of your gifts. If you decide upon crossing into Hell's gate and become fully demonic, I am afraid you will find yourself at a loss on that as well. We have spoken with the Council of Demon Kings, and they are happy for you to become mortal." He stopped and smiled. "I believe they think if you are human they have more chance of claiming your soul than if you are half angel. Personally, I think they have their work cut out for them, given your new status."

"What new status would that be?"

"We are going to place you in a position of trust on earth's plane. You will oversee the safekeeping of fallen angels and guide them in the right direction. If you can fulfil this obligation, we may visit your angel status in the future, and of course, as a married man with a good woman to guide you on your correct path, how could you go wrong?"

"I am to do this with none of my powers?" he asked anxiously.

"Oh, I am certain the Council have agreed to let you retain some of your gifts, but you will have to learn yourself which ones are still with you."

Lauren heard music drifting outside and looked out the window. "There's so many people out there." She laughed. "I can see my mom and my grandpa," she squealed. "There's Michael from Pret a Manger, Valerie, and Mairi; they're all here."

Ambriel took her hand in his. "They have come to celebrate your wedding, but first, we must give a gift to you, to start you on your new life." Ambriel handed Forcas a legal document, and he opened it, astonished at what he read.

"Well," Lauren said impatiently.

"It's a house, Lauren, for us. Well, not so much a house, but a castle in Scotland." Then with concern, he said, "It's not in Edinburgh, can you give up that city and come live with me in a new place?"

"Don't be ridiculous, Forcas, of course. Tell me where it is, though!"

"It's Castle Tioram near Loch Moidart and the Shiel Estuary, the west coast of Scotland."

Lauren drew her eyebrows together and looked at Ramiel. "How is it I know of this place?" she asked.

Ramiel shook his head and smiled sadly. "It's the traditional seat of Clan MacDonald of Clan Ranald. Your Park ancestors were a sept to his clan." He took Forcas's hand, putting aside his objections, and shook it. "I wish you well. Please, take care of her, she is very special to me." Then, smiling, he added, "You've got your work cut out for you with that castle, it was burned down in 1715. It's just a shell, but good luck with the improvements, you may just find yourself in a bit of a legal battle with the Scottish authorities if you try and change it around too much."

Lauren touched Ramiel's arm. "I need a moment with you, Ramiel. Do you mind?"

"Of course, what is the problem?"

"It's not really a problem, it's a wish. Can you grant wishes?"

"We're not the Fae," he laughed, "but I'm sure I can come up with something. What is it you wish for, Princess?"

"I'd like you to give me away, and…"

Ramiel was taken aback by the request, his heart double flipping at the thought of handing his daughter into the care of Forcas, although he had put his objections to one side, he was was still seething.

"And? What else is it you are wishing for, how can I help?"

"I don't have a wedding dress, I'd like to have a proper wedding dress. I know it sounds very 'girly', but I want to get married in a proper dress, not my jeans and tee."

Ramiel touched her shoulder. "I think we have already arranged the dress." He took her hand and led her from the room. Opening the door to her bedroom, the first item she saw was a dress hanging from the wardrobe door. "Your cousins are, how can I say it? Very gifted in 'arranging', they tell me. If you would like to prepare yourself, I'm sure they will join you in a moment." He smiled tenderly at her. "We will await your presence downstairs."

Ambriel called for Ramiel's return and asked him to gather the Infidelibus. "We must talk immediately," he stressed.

"Appoloin waits here already, he refuses to leave Mairi's side. Kakabel cannot come, there are too many breaches in the Veil, and Seere is aiding him. Sammael and Adramelechk are searching for more information about the child Lauren saw in Mistdream. I have news for them, and they will return shortly."

"And Xaphan, where is he?"

Ramiel shook his head. "I am unsure, I know he is on a

dangerous mission that he and Forcas have been working on. They believed it safer not to include everyone in their plans until we were sure of the traitor."

"That makes sense, we have heard there is a demon army on the march, we need the Mistdreamers to confirm this."

"Today? How can you ask that of them on Lauren's wedding day? Come to think of it, how can you allow Lauren to marry?"

Ambriel laughed. "Stop acting like a father and go check on Lauren, she must be nearly ready to see her anxious bridegroom. Just look at him as he stands their nervously awaiting her return. He loves her, Ramiel, take faith from that. We can discuss the Mistdreamers after the ceremony." As he moved away, a slight breeze drifted past him. "What was that?" he asked. "Did you feel a change in the room?"

"Yes, we have been experiencing this for some time. It is the spy, the traitor, and he can cross between both realms."

"I think I hear Lauren calling you, go to her. Let her and Forcas have their special day, we will resolve this later. Ah," he said, looking around, "I see Xaphan has arrived with the rest of the Infidelibus, Paschar and Omniel, too. I must speak with the archangel before the wedding."

The members of the Infidelibus stood with Forcas, laughing and teasing him about his forthcoming nuptials. All of them were dressed in the MacDonald tartan.

Omniel's presence exuded power; a tall angel, taller than Forcas, he kept his mighty wings spread as he scanned the room. His short, dark, curly hair framed a beautiful face of angular proportions. Bright blue eyes feathered with black eyelashes could see through to the soul. He commanded respect.

Paschar stood with him, pointing to and naming those who stood outside the house.

Lauren lifted the white silk dress from its hanger and held it to her chest; her mom's wedding dress.

"Well, did we do good?" Valerie asked.

Tears ran down Lauren's face, too choked to answer yes.

"Come on, lady, let's get you ready, there's a bunch of people waiting to see a Mistdreamer and an angel get married."

"Not just that, did you see how nervous Forcas is? Can you believe it, an angel being nervous, it's almost as though he is human!"

Lauren left the girls and luxuriated in a hot shower while they dressed. When she returned, it was to see them waiting in their bridesmaid's outfits. She nearly cried at how beautiful they looked. Their midnight blue, long, velvet, sleeveless dresses had royal blue silk sashes tied around their waists. They had tied their hair up in ponytails, held together with gypsophila and forget-me-not flowers.

They pulled Lauren's dress over her head and fastened the tiny buttons from her waist to her neck. The long, 'A-line', round-necked, sleeveless dress, had embroidered flowers rising from the hem to halfway up her thigh, the stamen of the embroidered flowers was a tiny seed pearl. It was pinched in at the waist, and her cousins had never seen her look more radiant.

"Final touches, cuz," said Valerie as she swept Lauren's hair into a ponytail matching her own, adding a clasp of gypsophila and yellow roses.

"Take these." Mairi handed her a small posy of wild flowers tied together with a yellow satin ribbon.

"It's time to do the needful, let's go girls." Valerie tried not to cry but couldn't stop a tear falling.

"Don't cry, Valerie," Lauren soothed. "I'm just getting married."

"I know," she sobbed, "but I just get the feeling we won't be together for too much longer."

"Enough. It's her wedding day, stop your tears, and let's get down to that handsome, nervous angel, who can't wait to get married to you, or is it something else he cant wait to do?"

Lauren blushed from the soles of her feet to the roots of her hair and brushed passed them. "Yes, let's go," she said emotionally and smiled into the beautiful blue eyes of Ramiel, dressed in the Park tartan, who had waited patiently outside the room for her.

"You look beautiful, Lauren. Your mother will be so proud to see you wear this dress. Come, Princess, let's go."

Omniel waited in full view, his wings, rigidly facing backwards, were raised high above his shoulders. Paschar, the Angel of Vision and protector of the Veil and heavens, stood to his right and held a large book, opened, for Omniel to read. Ambriel, the Angel of Oneness and the angel responsible in unifying all living beings with angels, stood to his left, holding a magnificent claymore, the handle heavily bejeweled with amethysts.

Lauren walked behind her cousins, and Ramiel placed her hand through his arm, squeezing her hand in comfort. When they entered the room, she was taken aback to see the archangel and the two senior angels standing with him. But when Johan Pachabel began playing his Canon and Gigue, she thought she was going to cry until she saw Forcas and his Infidelibus brothers standing beside him, all in full MacDonald regalia. Ramiel squeezed her hand again and began walking with her towards the Archangel. Valerie and Mairi stood on the opposite side to the Infidelibus. Ramiel placed her hand into Forcas's hand and stepped back; a feeling of overwhelming sadness, tinged with a veil of joy, encompassed him, and he found the emotion very strange, indeed.

When they said their commitments to each other and

Omniel announced them to be husband and wife, Ambriel lifted the sword above their heads. Omniel declared, "That he, this angel brother of ours, and she, our sister Mistdreamer, are brought together in love. May they be forever one in a marriage of love, friendship, and understanding. Let nothing cut this bond, and may the sword of Damocles protect you both." Turning, he then announced, "Please, welcome Mr. and Mrs. Forcas MacDonald to the universes." As he finished speaking, a cheer could be heard echoing across the heavens.

When everything was over and a few people remained, Lauren looked around the room, then stared at the white gold wedding band she now wore. Tears came suddenly as her thoughts returned to the events of the day. Forcas moved quickly to her side. "Is all well with you, my love?"

"All is well, Forcas. I am just happy, so very happy."

Chapter Twenty-One

Jocelyn Park rubbed her wrists, the manacles she had worn for years had been removed, but the marks would be embedded in her skin forever, and for that, she would be eternally grateful. A sad smile adorned her once beautiful face, now marked with scars from the constant beatings she had received.

The beatings had ended when she betrayed her fellow Mistdreamers, and unable to endure any more of the torture, had passed on information that should only be known in the Park clan. Her punishment for that betrayal was all around her.

She gazed at the room that was her prison, as sumptuous as any palace, but her prison, nonetheless. Walls painted in a beautiful Prussian blue, with spirals in gold leaf, adorned the elaborate cornices and central ceiling rose.

Huge scatter cushions were strewn carelessly across the White Carrera marble floor and were used for both a bed and seating. Beautiful Bedouin designs were embroidered into the cushions in red and navy, exotic patterns woven like mystical spells.

There were no windows as the vista beyond her room was that of black, coal-like walls that winked red beneath the heat they expelled. There was nothing in the room that Jocelyn could use as a weapon or as a tool to bring about her demise. It had been very carefully designed, and she smiled again, allowing herself to sleep. To go to a place where she was happy.

Jocelyn had a plan.

"You can smile, Mother?" the gentle voice of her daughter whispered behind her.

"You can walk in my room whenever you choose, Angela, it does not mean you have the right to walk into my dreams."

"You have no dreams belonging to you," she snarled. "You sold them to us, or have you forgotten?"

"Sold them? Sold them? Do you mean when I was bound and beaten, then raped by your demons until I could take no more pain. Is that what you mean?"

"Raped?" asked Angela. "You lie! You were a willing participant on many occasions."

"On one occasion, I gave in to lust, hoping the coupling would not be harsh or painful and that a modicum of warmth could be shared with me. Sadly, I chose the wrong person to believe in."

"And which demon would that be?" Angela said, her voice full of contempt.

"Why, daughter dear, that would be your husband. Balam." Jocelyn watched the horrified look cross her daughter's stunning face and laughed out loud. "You didn't think he kept his insatiable hunger just for you, did you?"

Pain and doubt rose in Angela's mind, the thought her husband had betrayed her with her own mother was too much to contemplate. She was aware he satisfied his incredible lust, at times, with lower demons, but was it possible he had used her mother in such a way?

Jocelyn rose and stroked her daughter's face. "Oh, you poor girl, you did think that? How awful to find out your life was nothing but a dream."

"You lie," she eventually said and pushed her mother away, then laughed. "For a moment, you had me wondering if it was possible, but I know it to be the imaginations of a desperate woman."

"What would I be so desperate about, Angela, to claim that your husband used my body, repeatedly?"

Angela slapped her mother across the face. "Retract that, Mother, it is a lie, and you know it is. Balam has his *needs,* most of which I am more than happy to oblige," she shuddered, "but there are those I will not share, and I am only too pleased when he goes elsewhere but," she stopped her mother from speaking, "he would not go to you for that kind of relief!'

"Angela, Angela," Jocelyn cooed. "Take a look around this room, I have no fetters, no whips, or masks. On occasion, I have the company of a young woman, and she is very happy to oblige in the games Balam sets forth."

Could it be possible, Angela thought, *did Balam really play with her mother?* The items she had spoken about were those she refused to have in their bedroom. She refused to share her bed with him and another, but was aware this was one of his desires. Had he broken his word and used her mother so?

"My only regret with him is the child," Jocelyn continued.

"The child, what child, what are you talking about, Mother?"

"Oh, my poor darling, your husband appears to have kept so much from you. Maybe it was to cause you no pain. If that was the case, then he is truly able to love."

Jocelyn turned from her daughter, the repugnant thought difficult to hide from her face.

"To use your daughter in such a way, was beyond reproach. I would have thought, even in Hell, the sanctity of a father and daughter's bond should not have been used thus."

"Rachauden? You speak of Rachauden, what did he do to her?"

"Enough, Angela, let us not talk any more of this, it is too painful for both of us, I see. Let us have a pleasant visit, even though you are uninvited. I have not seen you in, how many years, is it, ten, twelve?" She frowned at Angela. "Nonetheless, you are here, why do you not conjure up some of that Earl Grey tea, and you can tell me of what happens on the outside world. Have you news of the Mistdreamers?"

"Always with the Mistdreamers, Mother, why do you forever wish to hear about them? They certainly don't want to know about you. Your name is spat upon in the Park clan, for they are aware it was you who betrayed them." Angela cruelly threw the words at her and smiled, conscious she had hit a painful mark, but Jocelyn remained calm. If her plan was to be executed effectively, it required her to accept the words dispassionately.

Jocelyn sighed in resignation. "You have a point, child, but I grew up as a Park, in their clan. Because you captured and held me here against my will for more years than I can remember, does not sever the emotional or familial ties to them. That is the simple reason for my asking."

Angela's was incensed. "It was always them, Mother, wasn't it? You never had time for me. Maybe if you had shared the identity of my father, I could have stayed with him. Maybe," she growled, "he would have cared more for me than the clan you were always so keen on helping."

"Oh, I doubt that," Jocelyn sneered, "your father's only thought was for himself, you were an inconvenience, and one he was not interested in. He wanted me to get rid of you and did all in his power to make sure I miscarried."

Angela was shocked, her mother had never shared anything about her father before. She was always told the clan was her family and had grown to hate their interference in her life. "Rubbish, you lie about him just as you lie about Balam. You're very good at that, when did you learn to become such a skilled liar?"

"When I was with your father," Jocelyn taunted.

Angela rushed at her mother, grabbing around her throat. "You cannot help yourself, can you? It's almost second nature to you to spout forth this crap, isn't it? My father was a good, hardworking, honest man, and you betrayed him, used him up, and when you'd had enough, walked away!"

"Your father was a drunk, wife-beating piece of scum, who slept with anything and everything, and when he was done catting around thought he could climb into my bed, and if I wasn't willing, he decided to climb into yours, and that's when I left him, to protect you."

Angela let her hands drop, shocked at what her mother was saying. Then, her shock turned to doubt. Could it be possible after all these years, her mother told the truth?

"Yes, go on, Angela, think about what I've said, then think about what your husband might be doing, or has done to your own daughter. Did you know what he was doing? Did you not care? Did you let him because it meant you didn't have to endure his sick, lustful appetite?"

Angela's mind was in turmoil, her mother always managed to do this to her, that was why she stayed away. After every visit with her, she would return to Balam and tell him their conversation, and he would calm and reassure her, promising it was fiction.

But she was sure there might be some truth in her mother's words this time, something rang true. Her daughter had always wanted her husband, she knew that, so Angela had done her best to keep them apart. Why, she had even introduced Rachauden to that wretch Labolas, allowing her to join his little rebellion.

"I will find Rachauden and get the truth from her, she cannot lie to me."

"She's too afraid to tell you the truth, don't you believe it." Jocelyn thought quickly, if Angela left then her plan might fail.

Angela laughed. "She's always been afraid of me, but I can tell when the truth spills from her mouth." She turned snakelike eyes at her mother. "Unlike you, who have always managed to avoid my spell."

"Why don't you wait, Angela? Have some tea, Balam is due soon, and you can work out if I am being dishonest? If he doesn't appear, then I've lied, but if he turns up for his usual *meeting* then you can work it out for yourself."

"It proves nothing, Mother—" Before she could finish, Balam walked into the room.

"Okay, Jocelyn, are you ready? We have to be quick." Stopping short, he spied Angela. "Oh, Angela, what brings you here to visit with your mother?"

"She's my mother, Balam, how could you?" she screamed and ran towards him, nails extended. She clawed at his face and neck in a frenzied attack that caught Balam off-guard. As she continued to attack him, Jocelyn slipped from the room unseen.

"Are you crazy, woman?" Balam said, pulling Angela from him. "What the hell is wrong with you?"

"You've been having sex with my mother, and your own daughter, and you ask what's wrong with me?" she screeched.

"What? What are you talking about? Jocelyn, tell her," Balam looked to where Jocelyn was last standing, "tell her, Jocelyn…"

Angela saw the horror on his face. "What's wrong, don't like getting caught with your lover?" she said spitefully.

"She's not my lover, you fool, she's not here! Where the hell is she?"

Angela scanned the room briefly. "She's gone."

“I can see that. What did she say to you this time? You’re an idiot, Angela!”

Angela puffed out her lower lip. “Don’t call me that. She said you were lovers, and that you did those awful things with her that I won’t let you do to me. And she said you and Rachauden were lovers.”

“I am a Demon King, Angela, I have told you this a million times. I have lustful desires, I enjoy these activities, but not with you, and certainly not with your mother or my goddam daughter! Now, excuse me while I go in search of your mother. Get yourself together and go and apologise to our daughter.”

“There’s no need to do that,” Lucias said as he entered the room.

“Why would that be, Son?” asked Balam.

“Because she’s dead. The angels that meet in the Cavernis killed her.”

“Good,” Angela said nastily. Balam slapped her across the face.

“You are not a mother, you are nothing,” he spat at her and grabbed her by the hair and, watching her fall to the floor, he dragged her. “You are happy our daughter is dead, you *delight* in her loss?” he roared, causing the lights to flicker.

Lucias sneered, watching his mother’s distress brought little comfort at losing his sister, but at least it gave him some delight to see her pain at the hands of his father.

Balam held Angela as she sprawled across the floor and spoke with his son. “How is it you know this, Lucias?”

“I was witness to the angels’ last meeting, and Appoloin announced he had killed her. I want retribution, Father. I want him dead. He was with Mairi when he killed my sister. I want her dead, too.”

“Steady, Son, steady. We must handle this carefully, we do

not want another war, but you are right, we must get justice for her murder. Has your contact aided you in cutting through the Veil?"

"He has made it possible for me to gain entry, yes, but he refuses to assist. I have accomplished much without his help. I can access the Veil by myself. He is more of a hindrance now, and we need to decide what should be done of him."

"Then get rid of him, if he is no longer required, he is just excess. What of Labolas? Does he know of Rachauden's death?"

"I have not informed him of it, as her leader, he should have been more aware. For a rebel leader, he's a bit ignorant, is he not? Why did you put him in command? Surely, his hatred of Seere is not enough for him to lead us into battle?"

"Labolas is the best person to do the job ahead, his hatred will keep him alive when we cross into the other realms."

"What of her?" He pointed to his mother. "What will you do about that?"

"She will be punished in the appropriate fashion, but first, we must seek out her mother before she causes more damage."

"There is no need to search, I know where she has gone and will track her down and, as you say, punish her in the appropriate fashion."

Lucias left his father and went in search of Labolas. The Count was a stickler for training and would be found at the battlements putting his men through their manoeuvres, no doubt using new souls as target practice before finally skewering them with his sword.

Sure enough, Labolas was exercising his legions of demons, preparing for battle. "Are you well?" Lucias asked.

"As well as can be expected. My men grow weary of waiting, is there news of the Mistdreamers?"

"Do you think your demons are ready to take on the might of an angel army, are they prepared for what may come?"

Labolas was disgusted at the question, this little upstart thought he was in charge because he was Balam's son, but he was also the whore Angela's son, and he thought there was too much mortal in the boy.

"Well? Have you an answer for me?" asked Lucias.

"They are well-prepared and ready now, if need be."

"Then let us move, we start for the Veil immediately, and you had better be right, Labolas. I will have many hours of pleasure torturing you, if you fail me this eve."

"Does your father know you are taking us into battle?"

Lucias laughed. "Don't be ridiculous, he's too busy with the whore to care about our rights of rule." Looking with anticipated excitement, Lucias held Labolas's eyes for a few moments. "Prepare to make yourself and your demons hidden, we fight for the worlds we will rule. Let us go, Labolas, we fight together."

"Kakabel, Kakabel," Jocelyn whispered, as she entered Mistdreaming. "Kakabel, where are you?"

"I am here at the Veil, what is happening, Jocelyn? Where have you been for these past years? We have searched for you."

Jocelyn entered the Valley of the Veils, it had been many years since she had entered this hallowed place and immediately felt at peace. She stood in the centre of Glencoe, surrounded by the seven mountains that guarded the Veil. The only means of entrance allowed to her and other Mistdreamers was that of the devil's staircase. A stark, poignant moor with mountains capped in dark grey stone fingers, that beckoned many, promising an easy ascent, luring them to an untimely end.

But Jocelyn loved it here, whether it was because of her sept's allegiance to the MacDonalds and their gruesome history in the Glen, she was unsure. All she knew was, it was where she felt most at home.

Her green mist colour warmed around her, clinging as a baby would to a departing mother. "I am here, Kakabel. I was taken by King Balam and have been held for," she thought for a moment, "I do not know how many years."

"It is good to see you, sister, let us care now for you and return you to your proper strength and health."

"There is no time, Kakabel, they are coming."

"Who is coming?"

"The Demon army is coming to the Veil, they are going to break through and enter the other realms so they may rule them."

"They have no idea how to break through, have no fear, little sister."

Jocelyn, ashamed, turned from him. "They know, because I told them how to enter. Please, forgive me, get my clan to forgive me, I could not take the cruelty any longer. I promise you, I never stopped trying to escape to inform you and my family what I had done, what I had become."

Kakabel raised his head and opened his wings, released his sword from its scabbard and sang in words not known to man, calling for his brother angels, informing them of the betrayal committed against them.

The sky lit up with angels answering his call, and they descended with wings spread wide; a cacophonous ringing, resounded throughout the Glen as they spoke all at once to Kakabel.

"We have been betrayed, and the Veil has been breached. An army is advancing from Hell and will attempt to enter the realms of the universe. We must be prepared for battle."

"Who is the traitor?" asked Ramiel.

Jocelyn stood straight, prepared for her punishment. "I am," she said evenly.

A hundred angels of war, in full army regalia, complete with sword, helmet, battle axe, and shield, turned angry eyes upon her. The Infidelibus, Ambriel, Paschar, and Omniel did not.

Archangel Omniel lifted both arms. "Enough!" he said with raised voice.

"How say you, Mistdreamer Jocelyn? You have deceived and betrayed the angels you swore to help and protect, on a whim?" he asked gently.

Jocelyn was horrified. "It was no whim!" she yelled. "I was tortured and raped by demons until I could take no more. To my eternal shame, I will regret not being strong enough to withstand any more pain, but I had reached my limit, I had suffered their abuse for years." She fell to her knees weeping. "I used to pray somebody would find me, I hoped there would be a hero to rescue me," she held her breath trying to regain some composure, "but the longer I was kept manacled and beaten, the longer I knew no one was going to come. I was desperate, in agony; I could no longer think straight."

Omniel reached out to take Jocelyn's hand. "You are no traitor. Come, Mistdreamer, let me take you to a place where you will recover."

She was almost on her feet when a pain struck her in the centre of her spine. Throwing her head back, she opened her mouth to cry out, when suddenly, her eyes flew wide open in terror, and a deep red line was drawn across her throat. The last breath expelled from her body, she crumpled to the feet of Omniel.

"Who dares commit this treachery here, in our holy Veil? Show yourself, betrayer of Angel," he boomed. "Who shields himself behind a mask of cowardly invisibility? Show yourself, I say." He raised his sword toward the sky, and a bright blue light shot from the blade. The mountains moved closer into a circle, surrounding the angel army, and the sky turned black. The blue light soared into the sky and illuminated a clear dome, then it split into thousands of light shards that fell as arrows into the throng of angels. Each light arrow disintegrated into dazzling tiny stars when contact was made.

Some arrows remained steadfast above the ground and did not break up. The angel nearest to these arrows slashed his sword below the light, and in every instance, the air flickered and a demon fell to the ground, decapitated.

Archangel Omniel called the angels to arms, and the army broke into five cohorts of twenty angels. The first cohort centred in the middle of the glen, with the remaining four in a cross formation within the circle of the mountains.

The centre cohort readied bows and arrows and pointed them to the dome. The cohorts in the cross formation prepared for battle as the angels to the centre of each cohort used their shields to form a protective covering around the whole group. The Angels on the outer edges raised their swords.

As if one well-oiled mechanism, the four cohorts began stabbing, pacing each thrust to a tempo of four beats. On the sixteenth beat, the cohort turned clockwise ninety degrees, and the thrusting continued to the same tempo until the cohort had turned a full 360 degrees.

Meanwhile, the central cohort let fly their arrows. The black sky came awash with magical light as a tidal wave of arrows exploded into a dazzling sea of glittering stars before falling like drops of bright, silver rain, exposing the demons.

Screaming rent the air, and the smell of putrid, burning flesh rose from the ground as the demons fell to their death.

Blood and guts poured over the heather, a sight seen many times in its history. Demons sliced with machetes and stabbed with swords, hitting some, and killing a few angels as they tried to plough through the carefully, strategically prepared army.

Count Glasya-Labolas watched in horror as his legions suffered multiple death blows and knew they were losing, had no chance of winning. He called them to retreat. Lucias hid under a dead demon, safe from being found by the rampaging angels, when he caught sight of Kakabel.

Kakabel fought back to back with Sammael, they kept their feet wide and legs apart, moving in a hypnotic dance of perfect symmetry. Their swords looked as though they were extensions of themselves as they parried and thrust, keeping their balance with ease, their flourishing attacks finding the mark on every occasion. As Kakabel knelt, then slashed his sword in a swift, agile motion, Sammael would thrust at chest level. Perfect partners in movement.

Four demons fell to the ground, and they turned to face another rush of demons. Lucias swept the area for signs of Labolas and eventually caught sight of him making his way to the Devil's staircase, many of his demons following. *So he called retreat*, thought Lucias, *funny how the signal did not reach my ears.* Lucias crawled from one dead demon to the next, hiding himself until he was at the edge of the Veil.

"You will help me escape this place," he said softly, holding a knife into the angel's back, a knife dipped in evil waters then spelled by one of the many witches he held prisoner. "Or prepare to watch the Mistdreamers die."

"Why should I care about the Mistdreamers?" asked Paschar. "They mean nothing to me."

"Ah, but they do, Paschar, they mean everything to you and

your friend Ambriel, do they not? What about Ramiel? Xaphan, will I tell you of all the Infidelibus?"

"They are Ambriel and Omniel's pet projects, not mine. My job was to protect the Veil."

"A fine job you've done, haven't you? What good was it having a lock when you can't find the key?"

"You had no right to take her or to abuse her in such a way, she was an innocent," Paschar said, horrified.

"But we kept her safe from those wanting to enter the realms, did we not, we made sure no other could get through?"

"By harming her? Why, what was the point?"

"To break her, to find out all she knew, and it was fun watching. Now, Paschar, move, get me out of here."

"You said there would be no war, and look what you have done, look at those lying dead here, demon and angel fallen. It was supposed to be a simple case of gaining access to the other universes. Why did you do this?"

"I had no choice," Lucias replied sullenly, "the Mistdreamers were about to inform the Infidelibus of me."

Kakabel finished off the last demon, and he and Sammael held each other, glad the fight was over, and laughed, clapping each other's backs in camaraderie. He watched as his teacher and fellow guardian of the Veil, Paschar, his body stiff and in obvious pain, turned his back and moved to leave the battlefield. A figure followed him, and Kakabel strained to get a better sight of who it was. His movements were familiar, the way he ducked and dived, he was watchful and alert, taking great care to not be seen.

Kakabel continued to watch. "Do you see Paschar?" he asked Sammael. "Who is following him?"

"Looks like Xaphan to me."

"That's who it is!" He slapped his thigh. "I knew I recognised his movements, but why is he watching Paschar, what is going on here?"

"There's only one way to find out," Sammael said tiredly. "Let's go and ask him."

"I think not, he is on a mission we have not been party to, I just wonder why it is Paschar he is choosing to protect."

"Let us follow, cautiously, and see what is going on. We can leave Adramelechk and Ramiel with Omniel. I do fear this was one time we could have used Forcas and Appoloin's assistance. We did overcome, though, did we not?"

"A useless waste of life, if you ask me, and for what reason? Do we yet know what the purpose of all this carnage was about?"

"I have a feeling Xaphan is about to find out. Come, let us follow and give our protection to him. He is as vulnerable as the rest of us, despite his arrogance to the contrary."

They followed, careful not to be seen, hiding amongst the ranks of the dead, their speed of movement bringing them near to Xaphan in seconds. When Paschar reached the Devil's staircase, Balam was waiting; his anger could not be contained as he looked around the devastation on the Glen.

"I might have guessed it was him," whispered Kakabel

"Let us hear what he has to say to Paschar," Sammael hushed.

"What are you doing, what has happened, I told you not to go to war," he bellowed.

"Who are you trying to fool, Balam? You were behind this from the start, look at my fellow angels, you were supposed to take the Realms with ease, not kill. I would never have helped had I thought you would do this."

"Do not dare to speak to me, Angel," he roared. "You have caused this with your betrayal."

"I simply assisted you to get access to realms, not to carry out an act of war on the heavens."

Balam raised his hand and prepared to throw a bolt of magic into Paschar, but never got the opportunity. Kakabel threw his sword, and it pierced Balam's heart, the angelic blade sending white lightning bolts throughout his body. Rivers of light ran through Balam's veins, his eyes opened wide in horror as light exploded behind his pupils. His body began to jerk, then, picking up speed, shook uncontrollably, the light reaching his fingers and toes, constantly vibrating until it imploded with a loud bang and disappeared into nothingness.

Kakabel watched with disbelief as the Demon King vanished; a whisper in the air alerted him that trouble was nearby. A vibration beside him caused him to look around, and then he fell in agony at Sammael's feet. His life source pouring from his mouth.

Sammael fell to the ground and pulled his friend into his arms, then yelled for assistance. Paschar moved away, hidden from view with Lucias's aid as Omniel appeared beside Kakabel.

"He dies," Sammael cried, "can you do nothing to help him, Omniel?"

"I cannot, apologies."

"Then what was the point, tell me what was the point of it all, why did we aid the Mistdreamers? Help him, Omniel, please, he is a good Angel. Help him," he begged.

"There is something I can do, but you may not like it."

"Do anything, save him, Omniel."

"I cannot save him in his angelic state, whatever was forced into his body is killing the angel from the inside. I can, however, give him mortal status."

"Mortal?" Sammael was horrified, then quickly decided, "Give him life, let him live as a mortal, he deserves to live."

Omniel pulled the essence from Kakabel and watched as the angel's life ended. His hands expelled a light and, placing them on Kakabel's head, he whispered words calmly, soothingly, and waited as the light entered his body.

"He lives?" asked Sammael.

"Wait, Angel," Omniel insisted

Kakabel's body slowly changed from a solid form to an outline. Omniel cast his hands across the outline then, moving them in circles, began chanting in a melodious rhythm. The outline shimmered until Omniel stopped his incantations, and it evaporated.

"He lives," said Omniel.

Chapter Twenty-Two

Lauren gazed up at the magnificent castle; unlike Lenticularis Tioram, this castle was built directly on top of a rock at the highest point of Eileen Tioram. The misshapen pentagonal curtain wall, with an arched barrel-vaulted entrance, was more part of the rock than that of the castle. She gazed at the forty-foot, cornered walls, built directly into the rock, without foundations and, not for the first time, wondered if they were mad at trying to restore it to its formal glory.

The castle was built on the rocky summit of a tidal island with a nearby sheltered beach that would make an ideal defensive site. The stone tower house, built against the east part of the curtain wall, was a central focal point within the castle grounds. Other buildings, or part of them, could be seen from outside the walls.

As she and Forcas neared the islet, walking along the sandbar to the east of the castle, they rambled along a series of paths, overgrown with bracken, heather, and many bramble bushes. They studied the area and the position of the castle as it overlooked Eilean Shona and the Sheil estuary, the perfect location to be sheltered from prying eyes.

“Ramiel wasn’t kidding when he said there was a lot of work to be done,” Lauren said as they entered the castle walls. “It is just a shell. I don’t know where to start, do you?”

"We have already started, Lauren. The authorities have given permission for us to restore it, and that's a good beginning. We have workers arriving on the morrow to begin excavation. There is not much you can do to help us then, but you could go over the plans again and ensure we have the right of it."

Lauren shivered, and Forcas wrapped his arms around her. "Let us return to John and Emma's Bed and Breakfast and get some warmth into us."

"Is it just warmth you're after?" she laughed.

They had arrived at the Emma's a week previous, having visited her home in Edinburgh to see the remains of her father, still lost in Mistdreaming, his *frame* as still as the dead in his comatose state. She had been sad to leave the city she knew as home but was excited at the next step of her life, if not a little wary at what she faced. When they had arrived to find the castle just as Ramiel had explained it would be, she had arranged temporary accommodation in the small town of Moidart and was looking around for an apartment until enough renovation could be done to enable them to move into the castle.

They needed everything, from bricks to latrines, a roof to a floor. The castle had been burned down in the Jacobite uprising of 1715 to prevent it from falling into enemy hands. Since then, it had fallen into a state of terrible disrepair. Although a very daunting challenge, could it be any worse than facing Hell's gate and an army of demons? She thought not and laughed at her stupidity. It was the practical side of her nature that took over and began making plans.

"Come on, then, let's get back to the B and B, I think this Highland air has tired me out, either that, or you not letting me get any sleep has exhausted me!"

Forcas wiggled his eyebrows. "I didn't hear you complaining, Mrs. MacDonald. I did hear you moaning, though!"

She hit his arm. "You are a monster, you don't need to remind me," she laughed, embarrassed at the memory of her lusty shouts of passion.

As they approached the Bed and Breakfast, Forcas stopped her. "Be careful, something is amiss here," he whispered.

"You be careful, and remember you are not an angel before you go charging in and doing anything daft!"

They entered the house cautiously, prepared for anything, but were astounded to find Kakabel waiting for them, hands on his lap, sitting in the large, dark hallway.

"What the hell?" laughed Forcas. "How come you are here?"

"I am trying to recall, but I am having problems in remembering. Are you well, brother?" Then turning to Lauren, "Little sister? You both look well, marriage seems to suit you both."

"We find ourselves happy, yes," Lauren said and launched herself into Kakabel's arms.

"It's so good to see you," she said, wrapping her arms around his thick neck. "Are you well, brother?" she asked.

"I find myself happy, yes," he replied and smiled at Forcas's jealous reaction to his wife being held in his arms.

"I think your husband may call me out if you do not untangle yourself from my person, Lauren."

"Oh, don't be daft, he's just pretending," she laughed.

Kakabel raised his eyebrows and glanced at Forcas, his frown and the shake of his head said it all. "I think you are too newly married to understand him, but given time, you will realise he has a powerful jealous nature. Why, look at him scowling at us, are you jealous of your brother, Forcas?"

Realizing he was being teased, and amazingly, enjoying it, Forcas plucked his wife from Kakabel's arms. "As you say, we are newly wed and had intended to *rest* this afternoon."

"So that is what they call it here, rest? I must remember that."

Lauren turned scarlet. "Stop talking about me as though I'm not standing in the middle of you two giants. There will be no *rest* this afternoon, I want to hear all that has been happening from Kakabel."

"Lauren," Forcas whined, "we need our rest, and we have only been gone from their plane for a week."

"A week here could be ten years there," she reminded him.

"She has a point there, Forcas. I did, however, wish to speak with both of you."

"Then come into John and Emma's lounge, it would be better talking in comfort than sitting in the hallway. There are other guests in this Bed and Breakfast, and I would not wish them to overhear our conversation."

Lauren led them into the bright, comfortable room, plopping herself down in one of the large settees. Emma had kindly left a fire burning, so the room was cozy. "Would you care for something to drink?" she asked. "Tea, maybe?"

"I am not sure, do you think I would?" Kakabel asked.

"I'll ring for a tray and get us something to eat at the same time, you look as though you could power through a stack of sandwiches, both of you."

After Emma served them a tray of tea, sandwiches, cake, and biscuits, which Forcas and Kakabel devoured, they settled down.

"What is it you wish us to help you with?" asked Forcas.

"I need to know why I am here and what happened," he said sadly. "The last thing I remember was being on the battlefield with Sammael; after that, I have no memory."

"Battlefield, what battle has occurred in my absence?" asked Forcas.

Lauren didn't wait for an answer. "I take it you want me to Mistdream and find out what is going on?"

"It will not happen, you will not go to a battlefield, Lauren, it is not the place for you to visit, it would be too dangerous."

"Forcas, before you start laying down the law, let us remember this marriage is a partnership, not a dictatorship, and if I can be of help by Mistdreaming, then I will do my job."

"But Forcas is right, it could be very dangerous."

"Then I won't go alone, I'll take Mairi and Valerie with me. It would probably be better if they came, three of us will see more than just one. What do you think, Forcas?"

"I think you should not go, you should stay and rest with me, that's what I think."

"Come on, let's get this thing on the road, the sooner I've Mistdreamed, the sooner we can get back to resting." She laughed. "Come with us, Kakabel, up to our room, it's best you're there when I cross into Mistdream. I will have a better connection to your last vantage point if you are there."

Emma was waiting in the hall as they came from the lounge. "Ah wasnae lissin in, ah promise yi," she said with fear.

"What was it you think you heard, Emma?" asked Lauren.

"You're one oh the fae aren't yi, lass?"

Lauren smiled kindly. "Is that what's worrying you, Emma? Because if it is, I can assure you, I'm not one of them." *I may know the queen of the Fae*, she thought to herself, *but I'm not one of them.*

"No, ah wasnae worryin' about tha' ah've kent they're around fir sae loang it hasnae boathirt me. Ah wiz jist hopin' tae meet one thur kind afare ah deed."

"I'm sure you will," she laughed. "With faith like that, I've no doubt they'll visit with you." Lauren touched her arm, and a spark of heat shot through her. "Do you mind, Emma, if my husband and I take our friend to our room? We have a lot of catching up to do, and we don't want to disturb the rest of your guests."

“Ah’ve nae bother about tha’ at all, the bonnie man’s got his ane room here, thaw? Yi can all dae whit yer wan’in’. Ah’ve goat ma cleanin’ tae dae afore the dinner. Ah’ll be seein’ you lay’urr.” She bustled away, back to the kitchen.

Forcas and Kakabel watched her hurry away. “What did she say, Lauren? Was she talking in the Gaelic, ‘cause I’ve learned that language, and I’m fairly sure she’s mistaken with her words.”

“Come on, you two,” she sighed. “She was just talking in old Scots, let’s get this over and done with,” she said as she opened the door into their room.

The light shone brightly through the large windows, so Lauren pulled shut the curtains and turned on one of the side lamps beside the king size bed and lay down. Forcas and Kakabel sat in the small settee at the foot of the bed and waited.

“Stop watching me,” Lauren spat, “or I’ll never be able to Mistdream. Forcas,” she asked, “could you sit with me until I cross?”

Forcas was by her side before she closed her eyes, holding her hand and praying she would not be able to leave, when her body stilled. He knew what was about to happen and watched his beloved wife transastralise, leaving him bereft without her presence.

“I thought she left her body behind, she takes it with her?”

Forcas continued to look at the space Lauren had occupied. “She only leaves her frame behind when she returns to Mistdream, her whole self goes when she transastralises.”

“Do we know where she is, or if she’s safe?”

Forcas stared at Kakabel. “We do not, she could be in the worst place, and we would have no idea, we have to hope she connects with her mist before going on this mission, and hope she takes Valerie and Mairi with her.” He stroked the bed cover she had lain upon.

“Mairi,” whispered Lauren.

Mairi’s eyes shot open. “What the…how did you get into my bedroom?”

“I’m here Mistdreaming, and I need you to transastralise and come with me. We have to go for Valerie first, though.”

“I’m not sure I can, especially with that moron Appoloin sitting outside the door, it was difficult enough leaving my frame and meeting you in Tír na Nog. He went ballistic when he found out.”

Lauren lowered her voice. “Is he still with you? Good Lord, we have to hurry, there’s been a battle, we have Kakabel in human form staying with us up north, and we have to find out why. Now, listen carefully.”

Lauren explained the mechanics of transastralising and hoped Mairi would be able to manage the change.

“We better hurry, he’s about to come in,” Mairi said, panicking.

“Okay, try to complete the transition, and we will pass to Valerie.”

With great concentration, and Lauren holding her hand, both girls transastralised to Valerie’s bedroom.

“Valerie,” they both whispered, “wake up.”

Valerie opened her eyes to see two blurry objects and grabbed her glasses from the unit beside her bed. When, eventually, the girls came into focus, she let out a squeal. “What are you two up to?” Lauren explained what they had to do and then added it would probably be a *little* dangerous as they would be going to a battlefield.

Valerie laughed. “Hell, if going to a battlefield is a little dangerous in your eyes, I’d hate to see what a *lot* dangerous is. I’ve got to let that Seere fellow know where we’re going, I’m not going to risk him getting nuts on me again.”

"You have Prince Seere outside your bedroom?" asked Lauren, "What is happening? She's got Appoloin outside of her room!"

"I'm telling you, Lauren, they're really nuttier than fruitcakes. Give me a moment."

"We don't have time, really we have to go now, can you transastralise?"

"I've done it a couple of times, but I'm not too good at it."

"Okay, take our hands, the three of us must envision Glencoe in our minds, then both of you have to find your mist colour and allow it to take you there. Can you manage?"

"Together, I think we could manage anything, let's try," said Valerie.

The three girls closed their eyes and did as Lauren had suggested, colours swirled around them, pulling and pushing, twisting and turning, faster and faster. Valerie opened her eyes, just before she transastralised, to see Seere enter her room, and he did not look happy at all. She stuck her tongue out at him, threw her head back laughing, and they all exploded into a million stars.

"Goddam it," Seere shouted.

Without any warning, he heard Appoloin's voice roaring from behind. "Where is Valerie?" he asked.

"The little twit has just transastralised with her two cousins, one of which you were supposed to be watching."

"You weren't doing such a good job yourself. Where did they go to?"

"No idea, but I know a man who does. Let's go see Forcas." They lifted their wings and opened the ceiling to the sky and shot upwards.

The three Mistdreamers landed on the battlefield and looked around them at the horror. No words of description could ever detail the carnage found on ground covered by blood, guts, and mutilated bodies. They scanned the area for angels they would recognise and saw Kakabel, he was with the angel known as Sammael, and they were both following Paschar.

"Do you see that little weasel?" Lauren asked. "The one with Paschar, that's our cousin Lucias."

"Where does he fit in the family?" asked Valerie.

"He's An…" she looked at Mairi, "this is going to be hard to tell, and I'm sorry I can't do it any gentler, but he's your brother, Mairi. Your mom is with a Demon King, and they have two children, one is Rachauden, the other Lucias."

"Rachauden is my sister?" she screamed.

"Shh, hush, Mairi, I'm sorry but, yes, she's your sister, you know of her?"

"She killed, oh this is awful," she wept, "she killed Aunty Cathy, your mom."

Lauren felt as though her legs were taken from under her, a little piece of information Ramiel had forgotten to let her know, he'd just told her that Cathy had been murdered.

"Let's go say "hi" to our cousin," said Valerie, "he looks a right wee snake!"

"Oh, look, he's got a knife in Paschar's back," said Mairi. "Should we try and stop him?" Her mist clamored around her. "Okay, okay, it was just a suggestion," she hissed.

"Why don't we go a little nearer and get a better vantage point."

As they walked closer, a demon walked in front of them. Mairi and Valerie held their breath, but Lauren kept walking. "He can't see you, come on."

Valerie looked to Mairi and mouthed, "He can't see us!"

"And neither can the angel," she said as the demon was stabbed through the chest and fell to the ground. They climbed over him and walked quickly until they were in a better line of vision to see what was unfolding with Paschar.

Suddenly, another demon appeared. "He's the one that's with Aunty Angela," Lauren declared. "I recognise the tattoos on his fingers, do you see them?"

Mairi nodded, her insides churning, all the agonies of being an abandoned child zooming around her head. The mist encompassed her, cradled and protected her, soothing her hurt.

They watched the whole scene unfold before them. Balam's execution, Kakabel's death, and they witnessed Paschar and Lucias leaving. The angels were so busy with Kakabel, they had not seen the traitors open a doorway and Xaphan follow them through it.

"We need to follow them," Lauren said, a little frightened at the prospect.

The three Mistdreamers took the dangerous step of pursuing Lucias and entered the split in the Veil. Darkness immediately closed in on them, but their mists pulled them forward. They blindly felt their way until they reached a wall. Stumbling along with nervous hands, Lauren found a lever that opened a hidden door onto a passageway, lined with torchlights.

"I think we're in the Cavernis," Lauren whispered.

"That you are, cousin, I've been waiting such a long time for the pleasure. Let me welcome you to my home and introduce you to some friends. Unfortunately, I cannot introduce you to my father or my sister as you," he pointed to Mairi, "murdered them. No matter, I will have fun exacting my revenge on your sweet body, just as I did on your mother and your grandmother's."

Valerie couldn't help it, her mouth had always gotten her into trouble throughout her life, and she'd uttered "Ewwwww" before she could stop herself.

Mairi and Lauren began to giggle, it was a nervous reaction, but then, the whole situation was ridiculous, and the trio started to laugh.

"You laugh at me?" screamed Lucias. "I, who have always loved you?" he said to Valerie.

"Eh? Loved me? Who are you? I've never met you, how can you possibly love me?"

"I have watched you always, I love you," he said, stroking her neck.

"I'd get your paws off me, you dirty little pervert."

Fury erupted in Lucias's chest. "I think not, you are mine, and," he smiled as he took one of his talons and ripped her blouse open, "you will obey me forever."

"Where's Paschar?" asked Lauren.

"So you know now of his betrayal, not that we could have done anything without the help of your grandmother, Mairi. You really have been unlucky with the maternal side of the family."

"And you've been lucky with the father side, I take it?" Lauren goaded.

He punched her stomach. "That should kill the runt growing inside you," he sneered, "my father was a great man, and you will pay for his murder." Turning, he called for Labolas. Lauren could not straighten, the pain shooting through her body. "We need to get out of here fast, think home, girls, now."

Just as they were beginning to dissolve, a woman came screaming toward them, eyes bright with madness, hair tethered to her face. She ran at them with nails ready to scratch when Lauren shouted, "NOW".

Lucias turned to his mother and pulled her away, then, grabbing Lauren's jeans, he tugged and ripped at her legs. Lauren kicked with all her strength, but he remained holding her. She twisted and shook until her jeans became free of her and she was able to complete the transastralisation. Dissolving, she watched as Lucias screamed "NO," desperately seeking to gain purchase on her before she left. Lauren smiled at him, and that was the last thing he saw of her before she vanished.

Labolas entered and separated him from his mother. "Be sensible, Lucias, we will find the Mistdreamers. We will not stop until we find them and punish them. Get hold of yourself, and let us plan their demise. The angels will know of you now and will recognise the danger their Mistdreamers now find themselves in and so, will secret them somewhere. We will find them, sire. Wherever they are."

"So long as you leave that bitch Valerie for me, you can take care of the others. I want her."

"As you wish, sire, let us retire and decide where to go from here."

"If you get the bitch Valerie then I get the bitch Mairi. I will have her, she killed my husband."

"Such motherly devotion. You can have her. Come, Labolas, what is your plan?"

Xaphan hid in the shadows, listening to them discuss how they would ensnare and kill the Mistdreamers on their return to the Veil. He crept in the darkness, searching for the opening to return him to his own realm and go in search of Ramiel.

"He loves me?" screamed Valerie as she hit her bedroom floor. "He's an idiot!"

"He may be an idiot, but he knows who you are, Valerie," Seere said as he entered her bedroom.

"What? No, 'welcome back', Seere?"

"You were foolish to leave without me, but now you are back we must contact the Infidelibus."

"Are you okay for us to leave you?" asked Lauren. "I know a

certain husband and ex-angel who want to know about our Mistdreaming."

"I'm fine, Seere *the wonderful* is here," she said contemptuously. "I'm sure the world will right itself."

Seere shook his head. "You have no idea of the danger you are in, do you? Any of you?"

"I think," said Mairi, her first words since seeing her mother, "we are only too aware of the danger. If it's fine with all of you, I'm heading home. I have an angel to pacify, and he's going to be mighty mad with me."

"Your angel is here," said Appoloin. "Come, Mairi, let me take you home." He lifted her in his arms, and she lay an exhausted head on his shoulders. "Just this time, Appoloin, next time, I use the transastral thingy."

Lauren looked worriedly at Valerie. "Are you sure you will be okay?"

"Will you please go! I'm fine, really, Seere will make sure I live, won't you? Anyway, I've got papers to mark for work tomorrow."

"You're not going in to school, are you?"

"Got to pay the mortgage, you'll be there, won't you, Seere?"

"Until the Infidelibus tells us you are safe, I will be with you, Valerie, yes."

Lauren kissed her cousin's cheek. "See you later," she said and burst into a million stars.

"That is so cool," said Valerie and fell asleep. Seere stroked her face, then pulled the covers over her.

Lauren opened her eyes to see Forcas worrying. "What happened, are you well?"

"Let me rest a moment, and I'll tell you all, but first, kiss me, Forcas."

Lowering his head, he covered her mouth, ignoring Kakabel as he left them to their privacy.

Xaphan called to Ramiel and the members of the Infidelibus. "We have lost two of our brothers to the mortal plane," he muttered, "and at a time when we need them the most."

"What have you discovered?" Ramiel asked.

"I would like to hear this, also." Omniel walked into the room with Ambriel. "You have lost two, and now you have gained two in their stead. Those on the earth's plane will be of service and great help to us in the future. Utilise them properly. Now, Xaphan, what have you discovered about the traitor, Paschar?"

Xaphan went into detail about what he had overheard and how he believed Angela and Lucias to be bordering on psychosis.

"Labolas is not, he is using them for his own gain, but they are too caught up in their own madness; they cannot see past their own aims. It makes them even more dangerous. We must move the Mistdreamers quickly. Valerie and Mairi are their main targets, so I suggest we return them to the Veil and find a safe realm for them."

"What of Lauren and Forcas, they have Kakabel with them now as well, do they not?" asked Ramiel.

"They do," said Omniel. "His presence will be of the utmost importance in the year ahead. They have made their castle a safe haven already by housing him."

Ramiel sniggered. "Housing, have you seen their derelict castle?"

Omniel smiled and nodded his head. "They have another home until the castle is complete. They will be needing a few more rooms, though, I believe." He laughed. "The Fae have spelled the castle cornerstones, they will be hidden from the likes of those Xaphan speaks of."

"Some of the tears to the Veil have not been closed, we could use them for the Mistdreamers safety."

"Good idea, have you chosen a realm for them?" asked Omniel.

"I think we will wait their arrival before making that choice final, we have been spied upon before, and I do not trust the air in the Valley, not with so many slain demons' blood still running through the heather."

"We must act quickly," said Xaphan, "they are already preparing to return and intend to bring the Mistdreamers with them. Thanks to Paschar, they can slip into the earth's plane without our knowing. We should prepare the girls and their guardians, they need to have final moments with their families."

"We want you to visit our new apartment," Lauren spoke on the phone to Mairi. "Bring your dad, I've already spoken to Valerie, so everything's sorted. We've not got much space, so Emma's preparing rooms for you all in her Bed and Breakfast. See you tonight, Valerie's heading up straight after school, why don't you come up now, Mairi?"

"I would, but I've got a matinee first. Whenever that's done, I'll head up. I'll see you tonight?"

Lauren put the phone down and sobbed. Forcas held her in his arms. "Don't cry, my love, it's for the best. A party is a good way for everyone to see each other again."

"Can you remember the last party we were at? It didn't end so well, did it?"

"I don't know about you, but I met the girl of my dreams at that party."

"I'm going to have to say "goodbye" to them," she cried. "I can't bear the thought of not seeing them again."

"You can visit them in Mistdream, so long as you are careful and leave no trail of mist behind."

Kakabel came into the large sitting room. "Dear heavens, could you two stop holding each other and touching each other for just a few minutes? It's really horrible."

"Jealous?" asked Forcas as he nipped Lauren's backside.

"Everything is sorted, Seere and Appoloin are here already. They're hanging fairy lights in the courtyard of the castle. Emma's done a real treat with the tables, they're all set with cloths and candles; place looks magical."

Lauren busied herself for the rest of the day. It was difficult, as she was feeling unwell, made worse with the knowledge of what was going to happen later. She folded napkins, helped Emma finish trays of food, and covered them with streams of cling film.

Forcas had bought a jeep and ferried the food in stages up to the castle. Lauren laid everything out as Emma had shown her, and it was soon time to ready herself. She showered and pulled on a tight-fitting, red silk, Chinese dress. *It's a bit tight*, she thought, *must be all Emma's cooking.* Then she looked at her stomach. *Surely not*. Smiling, she lay a hand across her tummy. *Was it possible, already*?

"Are you ready?" asked Forcas and stopped, she always took his breath away. "You are the most beautiful woman in the worlds. Let us go and meet your family, it's time."

They welcomed Valerie, and she scowled as she spied Seere standing beside the buffet table. Alexander hugged Lauren and shook Forcas's hand, welcoming him into the family. Graeme waved to Seere and headed straight for the food, having kissed Lauren and clapped Forcas on the back. Mairi arrived a few minutes later with Appoloin.

"Look who came for me, we flew up, if you catch my drift," she said and winked at Lauren. "This place is amazing. Are you going to start reconstruction soon, it could use a roof, a floor, pipes….Going too far am I?" she laughed.

"It burned down in 1715, it can withstand a few more years like this," Lauren laughed.

They were talking, drinking, eating, and enjoying each others' company when Omniel appeared, with Ramiel and Ambriel.

"Mistdreamers, thank you for inviting us into your home, this is a very important night."

The air became ominously silent apart from Lauren's soft sniffing. Forcas held her in his arms.

"We come to bless the home of our Caretaker Forcas and his beautiful wife, Lauren. Their safety has been ingrained into the very ground you stand upon by the Fae, our brothers." He waited a moment. "But we ask you to understand what is about to happen." Alexander and Graeme looked at each other and stepped forward. "Wait," said Omniel, "what we are about to do, is to ensure the very lives of your daughters, it is them, and only them, we wish to make safe. I ask you all here to bid farewell to Mairi and Valerie."

"I'm not going anywhere," said Mairi. "I've just opened in a new play!"

"And I'm going nowhere either. My kids are expecting me in tomorrow, I've just got a new apartment!"

Omniel motioned to Seere and Appoloin, who took hold of their charges. Alexander and Graeme reached out to grab them, but they disappeared.

"Where are they?" growled Alexander. "Bring her back now."

"Did you know they were going to do this?" Graeme asked Lauren.

Omniel held their forearms. "Do not blame Lauren, she has met with the evil that threatens your daughters. They are in serious danger until we can dispense with that evil."

"Where are they?" Alexander roared again.

"Listen to Omniel," Ambriel cut in. "He's telling you the truth, Mairi and Valerie are being hunted by an evil that will not stop until they have killed your daughters. We have removed the girls, and they will be in a safe place soon."

"What of Lauren, how is she safe here? Why could they not have remained here?"

"This castle can only protect the chieftain of the clan and his wife. The wards were set by the Fae; there are limits to the protection they could put in place."

"I'm so sorry, Uncle Graeme, Uncle Alex. I wanted them here with me, but it wasn't possible."

Alexander dropped to the ground and held his head in his hands, Graeme likewise. "They'll be safe, Graeme," Alexander said.

"You can see it? Really?"

"I can, and they'll find Callum, they'll bring him home to us."

Lauren collapsed in a heap of tears, and Forcas lifted her in his arms as she sobbed into his chest.

"We must go now. We promise, your daughters will be guarded and protected." Omniel, Ambriel, and Ramiel opened their wings and flew like rockets into the sky.

"Graeme, Alexander, Kakabel, come with us, we will find some warmth at Emma and John's. Let us talk of the time when your girls will return, and we will be a whole family again."

Alexander helped Graeme to stand, grief and shock leaving him numb, and they headed toward the entrance of the castle. A subtle shift occurred in the air, a ripple of perfume floated around them. Lights danced, merrily bouncing all around them. A shower of stars fell to the ground and spread out like an ocean wave and crashed against the walls. The magical wave flowed all the way to the top of the castle.

They all stood transfixed as, little by little, the castle changed. The tower windows were reinstated, slated roofs covered the buildings, shoddy brickwork was renewed, the courtyard paved over, stairs leading to the tower grew one by one. A continuous walkway appeared above them, encircling the interior walls. They watched, mesmerized, mouths agape, as, little by little, the castle repaired itself. They eventually stood in a completely renovated, modernized castle, complete with drapes hanging from windows, horses in the stable, and geese running around outside the kitchen buildings.

Lauren smiled up at Forcas. "Well, I guess we know where one of them went!"

With Thanks To

I could not have completed this book without the help and encouragement from so many people but my thanks especially go to:

My husband and best friend Paul, I love you.

My boys Paul-Mark, Michael and Christopher and my daughter-in-heart, Hayley for putting up with the "author" mum.

Valerie Bocker, Lesley Knox, my "reading" ladies.

Mary-Pat and the late Tony Forrest, thank you for sharing Biloxi with us.

Pret a Manger your coffee is good enough for angels.

Castle Tioram and it's owners it is a truly magical place.

Emma and John MacDonald, Mingarry.

My editor Melissa Gray thanks for bringing it all together.

Troubadour Publishing and JeremyThompson for taking a chance on me.

Marius Iwicki, Zsuzsanna Markos and Kuba Ralowski talented, beautiful people.

Mike Wells and Diana Gabaldon thank you for the encouragement.

The many twitter and Facebook friends who have urged me on to the finishing line.

Lightning Source UK Ltd.
Milton Keynes UK
UKOW03f1004271213

223638UK00001B/5/P

9 781783 062614